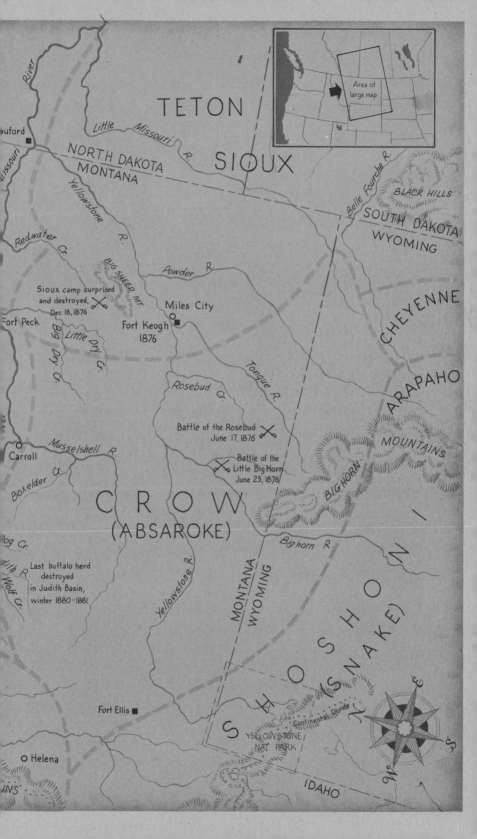

Walks
Far
Woman

THE DIAL PRESS NEW YORK 1976

WALKS FAR WOMAN

by
Colin
Stuart

Acknowledgement

My thanks go to a number of friends and family who have been
helpful (or patient) while this book was being written, but I wish
to record my special gratitude for Diane Raintree's insights and
invaluable suggestions.

Manufactured in the United States of America

First printing 1976

LC Number: 76-40694
ISBN: 0-8037-9365-0

To Our
Indian Great-Grandmothers

Contents

part one

part two

part three

Author's Note

This is a work of fiction. Its principal characters are the product of the author's imagination, except that Walks Far Away Woman is a composite drawn in part from his boyhood memories of stories told by two elderly Montana Indian women.

The author is conscious of his failure to consistently render into written English, either literally or in flavor, the spoken English of such women. They tended to introduce the word order and processes of a wholly unrelated language, while at the same time omitting certain sounds common to English words and including other sounds known only to their native tongue. The reader here who will imagine an elderly, illiterate woman who grew up in a Central Asian nomadic tribe before learning a kind of French or English will appreciate the problem.

All named Indian chiefs and Métis leaders (except Left Hand Bull), all named army officers (except Major Hatton), all named scouts and traders (except Jack Sinclair and Fergus Bushytail), and all named law-enforcement officials in either the United States or Canada are actual historical figures. For some of these, certain incidents have been invented here, but with every effort to follow the facts available concerning their actions and personality traits.

Montana and Dakota Territories. It may surprise some readers that in 1874, when this story opens, the eastern two thirds of Montana and the western one third of what is now North and South Dakota still remained almost solely to Indian occupation—but such is the fact. Forts within that area were trading posts rather than military garrisons until after the defeat of General Custer in 1876.

Much of this story is set among the *Teton Sioux*. A brief note on this people appears in brackets in chapter 7 on page 70. The author apologizes to those Dakota (Santee), Nakota (Yankton), and Lakota (Teton) who resent being called Sioux (derivative from an Ojibwa word) for using the popular term here. Also, he apologizes to the scholarly for his use of the word *Sioux*, rather than the technically correct *Siouxan* in reference to the Sioux language.

Black*foot versus* Black*feet*. These people, when speaking their own language, call themselves *Siksika*, which is a singular collective noun. To the author, general adherence to that form in English appears to be least awkward. Therefore, in this book the plural of *Blackfoot* will be *Blackfoot*. However, the tribal council for the portion of the tribe occupying a reservation in the United States (part of the people live on reserves in Canada) has prescribed the form *Blackfeet*. Confusingly, an entirely unrelated people, one of the subtribes of the Teton Sioux, are also known as Blackfoot or Blackfeet Sioux.

PART ONE

Summer and Fall 1874
and
A Few Days in
the Summer of 1946

Chapter One

WALKS FAR AWAY WOMAN

(Territory of Montana, Late July 1874)

Walks Far Away Woman ran from the camp, her moccasined feet covering ground faster than they ever had before. She knew she could not outrun men chasing her on horses. But she ran on, as though she could last forever. The Rockies, which she knew as the Backbone of the World, were barely beyond her sight to westward; the International Boundary, being surveyed in this portion only that summer, lay but a hard day's ride to northward.

She was a rather tall, long-legged young Pikûni Blackfoot girl, born near the Marias River eighteen winters past, in the Moon When the Jackrabbit Whistles at Night, of a captive Teton Sioux mother and a Blackfoot father. Her arrival in a lodge counting three wives and several children caused so little excitement that she was never formally named, but simply called the Baby. When she was a toddler and needed a name, they called her Walks Far Away, from her habit of excessive wandering. Unlike Blackfoot men, who might change their names several times during a lifetime, Walks Far would keep the same name always, merely adding the ending -aki, for "woman," when she married. She had early revealed the high, narrow-nosed good looks and glowing skin for which many girls of the Blackfoot tribe are noted.

Grown now and married, Walks Far was sometimes spoken of as a manly-hearted woman. This was not to call her femininity into question, but to express admiration and wonder that any such clearly feminine person could do manly things so well, though often, too, there were tones to suggest that all women's activity, by the nature of things, should be limited to women's traditional work.

Only this morning Walks Far had been sitting peacefully outside the lodge with her much older half sister. Both were grateful for a little rest in the swift-warming sun before taking up their work again. Their shared husband, Finds the Enemy, snored deeper into his afterbreakfast nap inside the lodge. It was but one more quite ordinary morning in their extended visit to this camp of another band of their tribe. She had dreamed no dream, had seen no sign to warn her that a person would have to run for her life that day.

All three in the lodge had risen at dawn, and at the moment Sun edged above the eastern rim of the world, the older sister, as first wife or sits-beside-him wife, ceremoniously carried Finds

3

the Enemy's sacred medicine bundle outside to be hung from its tripod of red willow sticks. While their husband sang a Sun song that belonged with the sacred bundle, the two wives said separate prayers to Sun. With that finished, they all went off to the men's and women's sections of the creek for an icy bath. Then, while the older sister returned to prepare the breakfast of singed jerky, boiled buffalo meat, and Juneberries, and to do the camp chores, Walks Far went with Finds the Enemy to water their horses and turn them onto fresh grass.

Among the horses was a fine one that Walks Far had herself taken from the enemy. The past summer she had gone out with a war party their husband had led southwestward over the Backbone of the World into the country of the Snakes. There, exactly as her dream had foretold—a dream their husband had come to believe that he had dreamed—she crept into the Snake camp and stole the fine horse. She called that horse Puhpokan —"dream"—and she had won races and many robes with him, not only against other women but against men. Perhaps she could find a race this afternoon, after her work was done.

Now the roots had been brought out, after the morning dew was gone, and had been spread upon the ground to dry in the sun. Much meat had been hung again to the wind on the drying rack of poles, and Walks Far and her sister paused to sun themselves a little before beginning a back-breaking day of scraping hair from the hides pegged out upon the bare ground. They each kept one eye open, guarding against the camp dogs and also against small boys who practiced a warrior's stealth by sneaking up to steal meat from the drying rack.

Walks Far thought nothing of it on hearing her sister say she had dreamed once more of that bitterly cold morning three winters past when soldiers had attacked their smallpox-ridden camp on the Marias without warning, killing about 170 of the people. Walks Far had been too young to marry then. She had escaped the smallpox and the massacre and survived the freezing march to find friends after the soldiers burned the lodges and drove the horses away. As a memento of that march she showed in her right cheek a small pit that was a frostbite dimple. It made her look only merrier, though. None of her sister's and Finds the Enemy's children had survived, yet life was good again. For a considerable time following that massacre on the Marias, Walks Far had lived with her sister and Finds the Enemy. Not until about a year and a half had passed did she truly become the second wife, or takes-care-of-him wife.

Finds the Enemy was almost invariably a successful hunter. His medicine stayed strong as he stole more horses. He went near the agency only for the annual distribution of treaty goods; and, because many of the items were actually useless to Indians, he wisely traded them back to white men instead of merely throwing them away. He refused white-man's water, the *napi-okee*, that the white sneaking-drink-givers traded the people and that made them go crazy, give up their winter's meat, kill one another. Finds the Enemy departed whenever the whiskey traders came to a camp. He traded only for useful things, like iron blades for the antler-hafted hide scrapers or beautiful warm, light blankets that could be had for only a few dressed, heavy buffalo robes. He had even traded for a short but wonderful many-shoots gun that could fire seven times before he needed to put more shiny cartridges in through the butt. Also, he had got a hundred of those cartridges. Walks Far and her sister had counted them, laughing at the thought of eating the hundred buffalo and elk, the deer and antelope and mountain sheep that they would bring. Only the other day, on the way to this camp, Walks Far had taken this new gun on a small detour to bring in fresh deer liver for supper.

So their lodge was a prosperous one, happy except for its present childlessness. Walks Far sometimes found herself wishing, however, that their husband could be a younger man: Finds the Enemy counted forty-four winters.

There was a white trader in this camp. He had smiled at her last night and again this morning while watering the horses, and she had smiled back. His lodge and wagon stood near, just across a tiny gully. Finds the Enemy was friendly with him because he was not a sneaking-drink-giver. His name was Jack Sinclair, which was not only meaningless but contained at least three sounds that were both absurd and difficult for a Blackfoot to pronounce. Anyway, the people called him "Blackfoot Man"— Siksikakwan—because some of them said that his mother had been a Pikuni. Still, he looked like a white man, not hulking and bulky as most, but trim, almost handsome for a white man. Other white men all seemed to look too much alike, so that it was hard to tell them apart or say which appeared ugliest.

Jack Sinclair's wife had a beautiful baby with hair the color of a sorrel horse, as well as two other children more than old enough to ride ponies. She spoke outlandish Pikuni mixed with Cree and with funny sounds that Finds the Enemy said was Frenchman—the earliest kind of white man. She ruined her stews by putting *salt* in them!—which only a white person would do. So, she must be as much white as Cree. Walks Far delighted to lick at salt, but she didn't want a good stew or any other cooking ruined with it.

Jack Sinclair had many wonderful things, among them one that Finds the Enemy now wanted badly for hunting and war —an indescribable strong-medicine thing of black leather and shiny metal. If a person looked through it the right way, distant objects got much closer and bigger! And what was just as funny, looking through it the other way made objects grow smaller! Jack Sinclair's wife said that the Creator must have been looking through it the get-small way when he made *some* men—a particular part of men, of too many men. That woman said such funny things!—things made all the funnier by her accent.

Walks Far thought how pleasant it would be to have a white husband and be rich as that woman, yet it would be embarrassing, too: Jack Sinclair traded for everything needed, *often including meat!* Half the time he just sat around in the shade of his wagon, fixing things. The men said he was a better hunter than almost anyone, whenever he was not too lazy. Yes, it would be terribly embarrassing to have a lazy man like that. Other women would snicker.

The sun was warm on Walks Far's hair now, as she prepared herself to work on the pegged-out hides. She stood up in a new pair of plain, strong moccasins with rawhide soles cut from the well-smoked top of an old buffalo-skin lodge cover. These hard-soled moccasins were just coming into style among the Blackfoot, and Walks Far wondered why no one had thought of making them that way before. She slipped from her shoulders the loose dress that was her single garment in summer, let it fall around the belt at her waist, then found a scraper. Her sister also bared herself to the waist, rose with a sigh, and picked up another of the sharp, hoelike scrapers.

But there was a distraction. Something was beginning that would alter Walks Far's whole life, alter it much quicker than she might have boiled a little water over a hot fire. Two Crazy Dogs or dog soldiers—the society of rising young warriors who enforced the regulations of the camp—came riding along the lines of lodges, coming close. People shouted at them in broad camp humor, and one of them responded with delightfully fresh wit.

They rode naked except for their blue trade-cloth breech-

clouts and beaded moccasins. Each had an otter-skin bow case
and quiver slung across his back, a trade gun across his thighs.
Both their faces were painted with red ochre set off by bars and
dots of white, and their blue-black, otter-tied braids were oiled
to a shine. The white-tipped tail feathers of a four-year-old eagle
slanted from the back of each shining head. Decorated riding
quirts with clublike handles of heavy elk antler hung from their
wrists, a long eagle feather among the greased lashes. Their
ponies too were adorned with eagle feathers, feathers which
fluttered and twirled from manes, forelocks, and long tails on
their streamers of red and blue cloth. Both these ponies were
pintos and were made more colorful by red-ochre or white-clay
handprints applied to contrasting areas on rump and shoulders.

All this was a common enough sight, and it exemplified a
proud people—alive, wild, untamed, and free, in the best country that Napi had created.

Walks Far felt a special thrill. She was looking at the handsomest man, absolutely, that her eyes had ever beheld. He
whirled his pony to answer someone's sally, his haughty, almost
cruel face easing into laughter at his own words. Every long
muscle of his lean body rippled, then held, sharply outlined
beneath his skin, skin marred only on the chest by honorable
scars from the sun dance.

His impact grew on her. Disloyal thoughts swept her into her
most frequent fantasy: to be the wife of a young man like that!
to keep a fine lodge for him, to ride out behind him on visits,
a mountain-lion skin across his saddle, a lynx skin across hers,
and with a baby in a beautifully beaded cradle board slung at
her left knee . . . and, yes, the nights in the lodge, nights when
she would rub both their bodies with the wild mint that made
anticipation all the more tingly, that heated even the skin for
love.

His eyes found her and lingered, appraised her in leisurely
arrogance. Walks Far could not help meeting his eyes. He
wheeled his pony into a kind of dance that brought it closer
than was proper. And for her particular benefit he made the
pony rear a little, caused it to leap a pace before bringing it to
a sliding stop. That stop ended halfway into the patch of ground
where the roots lay spread for drying, and it threw dirt over
them all!

Walks Far was disgusted, but her sister was instantly raging
as only a good Indian woman can: "I'll teach you some manners,

7

you pretty boy," she screamed, snatching eagle feathers from the pony's mane with one hand and swinging the scraper at the pony's head with the other.

He lashed at her with his quirt, shouting, "Stop that, you crazy woman," and backed and whirled the pony so sharply that it struck the lodge cover and knocked both Walks Far and her sister into a tumbling tangle upon the ground.

Finds the Enemy was already outside, his angry eyes taking in most of what had happened in a single sweep. Apparently he recognized the second dog soldier: "Are you the son of Cree Moccasins?" he asked scathingly. "Cree Moccasins was a man! Does his son have nothing else to do but ride around dressed up fancy as a Crow and play at being a dog soldier, riding over women's things and knocking down peaceful lodges! I can see that even that gun you are carrying is only a boy's plaything, too broken to shoot."

"Be careful what you say to me, *old man*. I will ride over you." And he was already doing just that while still speaking and while Walks Far's sister, up again, ran screaming at the handsome man's pony, her sharp scraper swinging.

Finds the Enemy rose unsteadily. He had somehow got hold of the broken gun before he went down. In the voice of a person whose wind had been knocked out of him he managed to command, "Bring me my many-shoots gun." Then he attacked, swinging the dog soldier's broken gun like a club.

Walks Far scrambled inside the lodge. As she ducked out through the doorway again, carrying the many-shoots gun, a bowstring twanged. Finds the Enemy's knees buckled because of an arrow through his belly. The screaming sister was covered with blood spurting from a deep cut her scraper had sliced across the pony's neck and shoulder. The handsome man, showing a bleeding gash in his thigh, swung the heavy elk-antler handle of his quirt down on the sister's head with all the strength in his arm.

Walks Far distinctly heard the skull crack. Calmly, with a peculiar clarity of mind and with a strange feeling as though she were only some chance spectator to this scene and to her own actions, she instantly sighted the gun at the handsome face. A bowstring twanged again, and she felt the little breeze the arrow made as it passed between her bare arm and breast. She fired. A pure lead bullet large as the first joint of her thumb jolted that whole handsome head up and back, abruptly haloing it in a pinkish mist as the entire body lifted a little before tumbling from the far side of the pony.

She swung the gun to the man who had killed her husband, and as he desperately fitted a third arrow to his bow, she shot him off his pony and saw it bolt into the gathering people. A large man leaped straight at her, twisting the gun from her hands so violently that he stumbled and fell.

Walks Far, still in her strange clarity, could already see what would happen next. More dog soldiers would come. One would shoot her through the belly too, and then they would knock down the lodge and give the things to poor people. She had no influential friends or relatives here.

She turned and ran behind the lodge, behind other lodges, then broke into the camp circle to head for the creek and the horses on the flats beyond. But instantly she recognized the futility of any attempt to cross the aroused camp. She could not possibly reach the creek, much less the horses. So, snaking and weaving among shouting people, she doubled back between the lodges and ran for the low ridge behind. That too seemed hopeless, but she had never yet let hopelessness defeat her.

Chapter Two
THE FINE KNIFE

(Last Day of the July Moon, 1874)

Walks Far Away Woman neared the ridge top, with pursuing horsemen strung out so close behind that she saw their lashing quirts from the corner of her eye. The face of the ridge seemed steeper than she remembered. She felt sick from running, and the throbbing in her temples was blinding. She knew she would find no cover on the ridge, only a few thorny buffalo-berry bushes, a stunted juniper here and there or an aspen or two; but most of these were on the slope facing her pursuers.

She topped the ridge—actually only the rim of a mile-wide but shallow valley—and knew she was out of sight for a moment. She saw no cover that would not invite immediate search: Far out on the nearly level prairie a twisting line of wolf willows marked a small creek; a couple of tiny coulees leading toward it offered sparse cover. That creek was much too far, and the tiny coulees would only be attractions to pursuers' eyes. But there were patternless small swales in the prairie, some holding little patches of buckbrush not much higher than the dry buffalo grass. She angled off for one of the smaller of these and crawled in. She felt no concern about her tracks, for the grass was already crisscrossed with those of people and horses.

She found herself eye to eye with a half-grown rabbit. Instantly her hand closed around its neck, choking it to death before its scampering away attracted attention. Her legs felt as though she were still running, her chest was heaving in agony. Her throbbing head seemed to burst as she vomited up all her breakfast.

There was a kind of hiatus from which she emerged to renewed awareness of something that, strangely, had almost ceased to concern her, for the moment at least. Men were on the ridge, noisy riders spreading along it in either direction. Jack Sinclair, in his white man's hat, had that looks-far thing at his eyes. Shortly, she saw him point to the northeast in a chopping Pikuni gesture, then quickly lead off that way, with the other men spreading out in a sweeping line. One of the early pursuers turned back from the opposite direction and passed so near her patch of buckbrush that she feared he could smell her, or that his pony would spook.

Then she was alone, but the flies came, interested in her and her vomit, as well as in the eyes of the dead rabbit. Sun rose high, seeming to stay straight overhead to punish her. She, who was no stranger to thirst, had never been so thirsty. She prayed to Sun, offered him bargains until she felt faint.

A coyote loped toward her despite the noonday heat. He crouched down less than a lodgepole length away, with a friendly, teasing grin on the broad face he rested on his forepaws. He called her by name, and she knew that Sun had heard her. "Walks Far Away Woman," Coyote said, "I know all about you and I have something to tell you. I think maybe you will get out of this, if you are careful. You will live to have a lodge of your own. But I would not go back to your own band. For something will very likely happen to you on the way."

"I think so too," Walks Far agreed.

"I think you should go east nine days' fast walking from here," Coyote went on. "You must get south of the Big River [the Missouri] and east across the Musselshell. After a while you will come to the head of Redwater Creek on the north side of Big Sheep Mountain. Your Sioux mother's people are on their way north, gathering wild plums and currants and getting ready for fall buffalo hunting on that creek."

Walks Far did not see Coyote leave. After that there was nothing but the hot sun and the flies, the stupor of waiting, and the thirst. Toward midafternoon, she was roused by riders returning from the northeast. She saw that one pair, Jack Sinclair and a tall important Pikuni she knew as Big Lake, would pass only a little farther off than where the coyote had stopped. But, as they drew close, their gaze was toward the ridge, and Jack Sinclair was talking, making gestures in that direction.

Walks Far saw him hold his horse back ever so little and stealthily drop two objects to the ground. Big Lake checked his pony instantly and held his head in an alert attitude of listening.

"Siksikakwan, I think I heard some little noise."

Jack Sinclair kept riding on. "You heard my belly telling me how hungry it is."

Big Lake rode up beside him again. "Your belly speaks no louder than mine," he said, and laughed.

Walks Far watched the late northern sun slide down at last over the western edge of a world already grown chill, one where nights often were as cold as the days were hot. Sun's wife, Moon, came up at the full, so bright that shadows were cast. It was the beginning of the Moon of the Home Days [August]. Walks Far waited no longer. She went directly to the place where Jack Sinclair had dropped something, located a two-fist-size bladder of pemmican such as the Pikuni often carried at belt or saddle for emergency rations, and a good heavy knife!

Walks Far returned to the buckbrush and, sweeping up the rabbit, headed for the creek to eastward. There, among the willows, she drank carefully, washed herself, and examined the knife. It was a fine knife, the finest she had ever seen. The blade was longer than her foot, the ornate guard and pommel of a shiny white metal. She saw that the handle, faced with a fine kind of bone, was carved to show the leaves and bloom of an unfamiliar plant. Someone had marred the pommel by boring a hole through it.

Walks Far used the knife to cut a thong for that hole from her dress and to hang the knife from her wrist. She tied the little bag of pemmican to her belt, then skinned and gutted the rabbit, eating liver, kidneys, and heart. After drinking again and making sure to leave no sign, she stepped carefully onto the grassy east bank of the creek and was off across the moonlit prairie in a woman's fast trot, knife in one hand, skinned rabbit in the other. Redwater Creek, where she had never been, lay more than a quarter of a moon away in a country generally empty except for war parties.

[Yet in her old age she was destined to ride over somewhat the same direction and distance in a good secondhand Buick sedan, which took only half a day. She was warmed in the crowded car by the wine and beer passed around by the much younger Indians, who ribbed each other and sang over the car's blaring radio. Her own white-enameled tall chamber pot rested on the carpet at her still-moccasined feet. If need be, she would order a stop and sit comfortably on that chamber pot on the highway's shoulder. And, if a grinning white face went past in a slowed, horn-blowing car, she might be inspired to show a little of what she had learned over the years in her changing world by mixing Blackfoot, or Sioux, or Cree, with English in happily goddamning those *napikwan,* those *wasichu,* those *wapiskias* homemade bastards and all their works to their own Christian hell.]

Chapter Three

KIPITAKI

(A Summer Morning in 1946)

It was a sunny Montana morning in haymaking time just after the end of World War II in a one-business-street town lying well north of the Missouri River and far westward on the state's high prairies. Two blocks of paved street ran due north, from the empty highway, the railroad, and a tributary to the Missouri.

At the winter-cracked curb in front of Dahl's Hardware, Farm Implements, and Building Materials an ancient Indian woman waited, sitting high on the passenger side of a parked Dodge touring car that had already become a topless, rusted relic long before its home conversion to a pickup truck.

The old woman was not impressed by the town, though a little more than fifty summers ago, when gangs of those blond whites called Swedes came laying the Great Northern tracks across the prairie, she had found a kind of magic in the town's almost overnight growth here on its wide flat beside a small but good creek. Long before that, when she had been but a girl, her people often pitched their lodges here in the spring in order to put their horses on the good, early grass. She had learned to swim in the creek. It had run clearer then, with cottonwoods growing along it.

The town had been bigger in the beginning and for some

years afterward. Many more stores, saloons, and other buildings housing more or less mysterious white enterprises had stood on this main street where vacant lots were now grown with the pale green of mustard weed and the darker green of Russian thistles. Both had come with the white man, and they had come to stay. For years there had been board sidewalks up both sides of the street—such a waste of wood! White cowpunchers who had spent all their money would crawl under those sidewalks to sleep off a drunk out of the wind. The old woman knew the whites had even stolen and put into their own words an old Blackfoot joke about the wind: "Don't let it bother you. None of it ever stops; it all goes right on through!"

Now, except for the addition of garages, gas stations, a motel, and of course the movie theatre (which since the coming of the talkies would no longer admit illiterate Indians at children's prices), not much was left of the town. Even the fine bank building of mellowed red brick now housed a beer joint and pool hall. Upstairs, a veterinary doctor lived and had his office. He had been known to pull human teeth out of sympathy, and to treat bad accident cases in emergencies. Of the few whites the old woman had truly liked, she liked this one especially. He had saved Buffalo Spirit.

A little while ago she had done her shopping in McMurtrey's, the only other remaining large store. It sold nearly everything that Dahl's did not. There, after deliberation and without a sound of either her English or coyote French, the old woman's hands had indicated in quick, graceful signs that she would take three yards of the fine red paisley and four spools of thread, including one of a new kind. The very young white salesgirl had convincingly demonstrated its surprising strength while saying over and over, "Nylon. New nylon. I like 'im; you like 'im. Strong for moccasin. You *like* 'im."

The old woman moved to the bead counter. She ignored the tiny seed beads and the middle-sized pony beads to purchase, at length, just four of the large chief beads, each of them a pale blue. Then, at the other end of the store, the old woman regarded the bananas with even greater deliberation, but the clerk there was knowing enough to be not at all surprised by her abrupt sign that she would take the two ripest of the fragrant, terribly expensive fresh peaches. Walks Far knew that at this early season they came all the way from Mexico, which she thought of as the country of the *Espaiyu*—"the Spanish."

As the old woman left McMurtrey's, she saw standing on its

slight rise a little way beyond the northern end of the street the relatively modern brick and glass high school. It was by far the largest structure in a county as large as some states. That school —rather its green lawn and sprinkler system—did impress her. She thought the flag, flying from its white pole against the high, midcontinent blue of the sky was very pretty, prettier than that other one across the Line in Canada. Soldiers carrying either of those flags had shot at her, had cost her friends and loved ones. Still, both flags were pretty. Once, for a period of several years she had done them in myriads of tiny glass beads on gauntleted buckskin gloves she made. McMurtrey's had bought the gloves, paying her as much as two dollars a pair (fifty cents for plain moccasins), to send them on to another store at Glacier Park. She climbed into the pickup and waited, not minding the morning sun. She could wait forever. Only very rarely had either waiting or action ever taxed her.

The old woman's wrinkled face was the color of bacon rind and she was shrunken like weathered rawhide. The only remarkable thing about her, to the eyes of passing white people at least, was the string of wooden spools she wore as a necklace. Her own people, however, recognized this as a way of showing how much sewing she had done last winter making things for the poor. Ninety years of prairie sun and wind, of smokey lodge fires and wood stoves had not much dimmed the brightness of her quick, knowing eyes. She still managed to hear anything she wanted to hear, as now with the two young men talking just ahead.

For Grandson, barely twenty-one and her youngest, had finished buying the mowing-machine parts and now lounged against the right front fender with a town Indian, Enos Weasel Head. Both eyed the empty, polished black Ford convertible parked next in front, with its top down. The two were working up a bet about a girl everyone, including the old woman, knew would have to be the owner of that car.

"That girl *will* speak to me when she comes out," Grandson insisted.

"She won't know you from a big pile of horse manure, which I'm beginnin' to think you're full of," Enos taunted.

"Remember," Grandson said, "remember about the basketball, how when we was in high school it was her, practically all by herself made the school board let us Indians play on the regular team!"

"So what? That don't mean a goddam thing—so long as they got theirselves a winnin' team! And now, she's been away to college."

"She used to sit right ahead of me in classes at high school and we used to talk about the lessons."

"Only because you made goddam sure you sat right behind her."

"Okay! But I'll bet you two beers she speaks to me."

Enos looked more scornful than ever. "If that skinny *napik-wam* bitch can even see you now—see you from nothin'—if she don't lose you like a fart in a whirlwind, I'll buy *you* six beers! You ain't in the USO club now, dancin' with some white babe that thinks it's patriotic and romantic both, dancin' with a soldier and an Indian at the same time. You're home, boy! Don't you know that yet?"

The old woman knew something about that girl's family that people seemed to have forgotten. She was tempted to tell the two boys about it, but decided against it.

So, all three Indians at the pickup began to wait, and the old woman's waiting held a timeless quality that young Indians would never quite understand. A passerby might have thought her senile or asleep, but her mind was clearly remembering that other sunny summer day long ago—1874 by the white man's calendar—a big Pikuni Blackfoot camp not too far from this place, the handsomest man she had ever seen . . . his head suddenly shot half away. She remembered the agony of running until she knew she could run no more, yet she had kept on running.

The old woman was so lost in recall that the first she knew of the girl's coming from Dahl's Hardware was a pleasant voice: "Why, Dewey Elk Hollering! And Enos. How long have you been back, Dewey?" The girl tossed a couple of packages onto the seat of her car.

"Oh, two-three weeks now." Grandson stood up, straight and tall, and tilted his wide new hat low over his eyes as he smiled.

"What a way to have to see Europe—all that terrible destruction," the girl said.

The old woman saw a very good-looking girl in a pale blue summer dress that set off the deep tan on her face, bare arms, and legs. The girl was healthy looking too, with a notable grace and strength about her. She had long legs and was slender, but was not really skinny at all. The old woman sought no clue from the girl's dark hair, but narrowly appraised the dark eyes, the modeling of the cheekbones.

"I was in the army in the Pacific—the Philippines, Okinawa. That's why I got back so late," Grandson was saying.

Enos spoke. "He got himself a whole chestful of medals."

The girl looked up at Grandson and said, very soberly, "I'm sure he would, if anyone would."

"Oh, I got only one that really 'mounts to anything," Grandson said, and the old woman could see a kind of sudden courage growing in him. He put fingers to the girl's elbow and did something that astonished Enos Weasel Head. "I want you to meet my gran'mother. Mrs. Elk Hollering, this is Janet Sinclair."

"How nice to meet you, Mrs. Elk Hollering."

The old woman's expression scarcely changed, but her eyes might have smiled, and she did raise a hand in graceful sign of acknowledgment. Then she too did something that astonished Enos. "My real name is Walks Far Away Woman," she said, in passable English syllables.

"That," Janet Sinclair said, "is a lovely name I would envy."

Grandson interrupted as though from a sudden idea, rather than from quickly gathered courage. "Say!" he told Janet. "There's going to be a kind of picnic dinner and dance out at our place Saturday night. A big party, people coming from Havre and Great Falls. I'd like to bring you."

"Why, I'd love to," Janet said, and Enos saw no sign of hesitation.

Enos could hardly believe any of what he was hearing. He felt inspired to assure Janet, "You won't haveta eat dog. Us Blackfoot don't eat dog—not like them Sioux."

Janet gave him a kind of thoughtful look, then turned back to Dewey, "What time will I see you?"

"Oh, I'll come around 'bout four o'clock."

Shortly after, Enos Weasel Head watched the old Dodge and the black convertible drive off, headed their separate ways into the prairie. He needed a beer, and he had the goddamnedest story to tell. He would wander over to the pool hall and try to promote a little drink. He probably wouldn't tell the story there, though, not just now—at least not until he had time to digest it, embellishing and arranging it properly in his mind over the drink. What he had seen and heard was just like the people said: All those Elk Hollerings were kind of screwball anyhow, real *auwahtsahps*. That Dewey had more guts than a slaughterhouse: real nervy. No wonder he'd won all those war honors, those *namachkani*, on Okinawa: Sometimes he was crazier than a goddamn loon—maybe because of that crazy old loon he had for a grandmother.

Enos knew something about her that he'd never quite dared rib Dewey about. Enos's own grandfather had told him how that old woman—they called her Kipitaki for "Honored Old Woman," these days—had once run away to the Sioux. And what was worse, it was said that for a time she had been the wife of a black horse soldier, by God, practically here in her own country. And there was something else: Dewey always claiming to be an actual full-blood, and the whole family going by an Indian name, though it was well known that Dewey's grandfather had been some kind of Cree mixed-blood named McKay.

About eight miles out on their way home Dewey brought the grinding pickup to the top of the only significant rise on the way. There the old woman signaled a stop just as he had half expected she would when he first smelled the peaches. Wordlessly she gave him one now but got out with the other to walk off a way toward an isolated, very large boulder. It was notably unlike any other large rock or smaller stone in this part of the country, and Dewey had heard it explained as a glacier-borne erratic.

Dewey knew that two or three years before the war some of the whites had talked of having the boulder moved, if possible, to serve as a tourist attraction beside the main highway at the edge of town. But at the first word of such talk the veterinary doctor had driven out with a bottle of good whiskey to see old Mike Quirk, who owned that gravelly piece of prairie. The upshot was that old Mike had parted with one acre extending from the country road to include the boulder, and despite the mellowing effect of the whiskey, or perhaps because of it, he asked and got the outrageous price of eighty dollars for his bill of sale. The veterinarian divided the acre into five hundred tiny parcels, all properly described. These he deeded separately and according to law to puzzled recipients in Boston, New Orleans, and San Diego, while saving the largest parcel, the one around the boulder itself, for the old woman. Legal fees and related costs amounted to far more than the veterinarian had paid for the acre, and he was forced to ask Bob Sinclair for an advance against future professional services. Also, he stayed sober until the whole matter was squared away.

Even from where Dewey sat in the pickup, eating his peach and watching a hunting red-tailed hawk, that boulder did strongly resemble a buffalo lying at rest among a few bushes of prairie rose—so much so that Dewey, though he pretended not to admit it, felt a certain discomfort about the whole matter, and about going any nearer.

The old woman felt no discomfort at all, but only gratitude for the serenity of this holy place—that, along with a kind of mystery and awe at the unintelligible but very powerful designs pecked or scored into the buffalo-spirit boulder by the Old Long-Ago People, or perhaps even by those tricksters, the Little People. She seated herself on the warm ground between two thin clumps of the prairie-rose bushes and faced Sun across the back of Buffalo Spirit while she ate her peach, saving the last good mouthful for pressing, along with the peach stone, into Mother Earth. From where she sat, with the road behind her, the wide prairie land revealed no sign of white man's works.

Raising her face briefly to Sun so that he would see her clearly, she then bowed her head and in her mind shaped a prayer, which today included something she had never thought of before. The intensity of the prayer grew inside her until she felt she might burst with it. Abruptly, with her body rocking, she again lifted her face, and in high-pitched singing sounds having no precise meaning even to herself she sent a signal of her prayer to Sun. She had been sending him a great variety of prayers using those same singing syllables ever since she had arranged the sounds in a moment of ecstasy early one morning more than seventy summers ago.

As she finished each of the necessary four parts to the song, she tossed one of the new blue chief beads toward Buffalo Spirit, and with the last she stood up with an alacrity surprising for a person of her years. Grandson would be impatient to get the mowing machine fixed. But before rejoining him she produced a tiny packet of tobacco wrapped in a swatch of red flannel and tied it to one of the prairie-rose bushes as an offering to Sun. Many similar packets weathered on the bushes; Buffalo Spirit was surrounded by a greater number of glistening beads than a person would wish to count, and among them a variety of feathers had been thrust into the ground by their quills. For this was a well-known sacred place to which older people still came, some from very far away.

Back in the moving pickup, the old woman remained silent for about five miles more, then spoke to Dewey in Blackfoot. "There is a fine knife that belongs to me. Jack Sinclair gave that knife to me a long time ago. He was that girl's grandfather."

"I would like to see that knife," Dewey said, also in the old language.

"It is put away, but I will find it."

They rode another couple of miles in silence, and again it was the old woman who spoke: "I can see that girl really likes you. I think you should marry her."

"For Christsake!" Dewey exclaimed in English. "Are you crazy! What the hell are you talking about!"

"Something I have learned a lot about," she said, still in Blackfoot. "And I have something else besides a knife that you have never seen. It is a ring for you to give that girl when you ask her to marry you, and it is a ring she will like, though you will have to make it fit her. There is a diamond larger than I have ever seen a white woman wear. Also, there are six green stones made to look like three-leaf clovers. That ring is worth more than a thousand dollars."

"Old Grandmother," Dewey told her in Blackfoot, "you have been listening to your dreaming ear. Where did you get a ring like that, and where have you been keeping it?"

"It is in the little bag I wear around my neck right now, and I got it on the Greasy Grass, that creek south of Elk River, the Yellowstone, when Sitting Bull and Gall, Two Moon and Crazy Horse killed all the soldiers. I was also with your grandfather in a big fight with soldiers in Saskatchewan, after the starving winters began."

"You mean you were at the Custer fight? You couldn't have been there—just Sioux and Cheyenne were there with a few Arapaho. The Blackfoot wouldn't go along with Sitting Bull."

"This person was there," the old woman said. "She was there, and she has the ring to show you when we get home."

"How come you never told me about it?"

"There are many things I have never told anyone. But I will tell them now, to you and that girl, if you would like to listen."

Janet Sinclair, alone in her open convertible, was covering the few miles home to the only "modern" ranch house in the county, the only house of any kind sending a daughter to a private school. She was just back from her second year at Macalester College in St. Paul. Her foot kept the accelerator pedal well down, though she was actually holding the car at something less than her usual driving speed.

She was feeling sort of surprised at herself: She had readily accepted a date with Dewey Elk Hollering—an Indian. Of course, Dewey was actually some kind of breed, a mixed-blood, but she knew that he almost belligerently identified with the full-bloods. Janet admitted to herself that she had felt half fearful of the risk she took in speaking to him this morning. Other white girls speaking to an Indian former classmate had been surprised and hurt to find themselves magnificently highhatted by receiving no word in return, nothing more than a brief stare from sardonic dark eyes.

She laughed aloud at the thought of what some of her friends might think of her date with Dewey—probably that it was all too typical of her, funnier than her wishing to major in geology or the fact that she was devoted to playing her bagpipes. How could they know of the excitement she was feeling about this tall, slender boy she used to watch on the basketball floor, all lithe grace that could flash into such incredible speed and power? And Dewey was bright, too. She had been grateful for his patience and helpfulness as her lab partner in biology. But she couldn't recall ever having exchanged a word with him anywhere except at the high school, not until this morning. Also, he had always been especially attentive to that Marie Nequette, who was at least half Cree or Blackfoot. As far as Janet could see, Marie Nequette didn't excel at much of anything except in art class. The trouble was, Marie was possibly the only girl in school who might have been called truly beautiful. She didn't seem to be withdrawn either, as so many Indians and mixed-bloods appeared to be. Janet wondered what had happened to her by now.

Janet was thoroughly aware that her grandfather, Jack Sinclair, had surely been a mixed-blood of rather vague antecedents, but one who had the happy knack of accumulating money and land—the more so after his Cree wife died and he married Janet's grandmother, Jeanie Cameron, who came from Missouri in the early 1880s to teach the first school on the ranch. So, Janet told herself, at least one sixteenth of the blood in her own veins was almost certainly Indian, even if neither she nor even her father showed much sign of it. Janet and her family, like some of the other families dating from early times in Montana, took their dwindling Indian heritage for granted, as something quaint and half forgotten. While Janet knew that her father held much more sympathy and tolerance for Indians than some of his neighbors did, she also knew he would have been astonished to find anyone viewing him as something other than a white man.

Janet secretly treasured her Indian ancestry on one point. She deeply loved this high prairie country in which she felt it her good fortune to have been born, and in loving the land, she would ignore her heavily Scottish heritage to think only of those other ancestors who had come down the old north trail in the great arc from the Bering Sea eons ago. Janet held a vivid mental image of these people moving into the empty land: lean-bodied men and women, scantily dressed in skins and leading pack-laden dogs as they strode southward through a sea of grass.

She had received some of this imagery from her father, a man whom some people thought a little peculiar for a rancher. As she grew older, she often gave the picture certain illogical details. In her imagination those migrating people marched southward under the brightest of summer stars. At their head strode an incredibly handsome young man who looked golden as though the night were day, and he swung Janet's hand in his as they marched along together, side by side. Her father would have pointed out that this was most un-Indian.

Now her father was waiting as she drove into the barnyard and on around the corrals to stop at the small pumphouse and hand him the package of gaskets and bolts from the seat beside her. His hat and face were grease smudged. He asked her to wait; then he and one of the hands working over the dismantled pump tried the gaskets before he came back to the car for the ride up to the house.

"Took you longer 'n usual," he said.

"I was remembering what you said about not driving too fast."

"Anything going on in town?"

"Well, you remember Dewey Elk Hollering—the basketball team? He's home from the army. I heard how he was wounded on Okinawa and was in a hospital in Colorado for a long time. They say he's all right now, and that he won just scads of decorations."

"Forgot to tell you when you came home. He's been back

quite a while. Ran into him one morning awhile ago, just after daylight, clear over by Packsaddle Butte. Happened to see this old car there, like somebody had tried to hide it in the brush. I was just kind of sneaking up to have a look see, and when I was almost to the car, all of a sudden that kid came lopin' down off the butte out of the junipers. We kind of surprised each other. He had an old blanket under his arm and an army canteen in his hand, and he wasn't wearing a damn thing except moccasins and a breechclout!—just like some old-time Blackfoot on the prowl, and he had a kind of smeary circle of red paint on his face.

"Well, we both said 'Howdy,' and he looked kind of embarrassed. He grabbed a pair of jeans and a shirt out of the car and put them on, at the same time asking me to stick around until he found out whether he could get that old clunk started. We ended up having quite a talk. He seemed awful glad he'd run into me. Asked about you, too, wonderin' if you'd be home this summer. He's filled out to be a kinda good-lookin' kid. Wish he'd been one of those the army taught how to fly. I been thinkin' we oughta get some kind of a little airplane for here on the place. Come in real handy."

Janet took a deep breath. "I've got a date with him for Saturday night, a kind of dance or picnic or something out at their place, from four o'clock on."

She didn't look at her father, but she heard him say, "Well, if you're going to some whoop-up like that, you wanta make sure you got something in your stomach. You absolutely can't tell when they might happen to decide it's time to eat. Maybe the minute you get there, but maybe not till midnight. And you be damn careful young lady!—if that kid's as crazy as his father was at his age! And you better fix it to have him let you do the drivin'. Though, I gotta admit those young-buck Blackfoot are just about the safest drivers there are: always real careful to stay exactly in the middle of the road!"

Chapter Four

A BLACKFOOT BOY
AND FIFTY CENTS

(A Summer Evening in 1946)

On Saturday afternoon, fresh from her shower and dressed for the unusually warm weather, Janet waited in her room. She hoped Dewey wouldn't come whirling around to the backyard and sit there blowing the horn, expecting her to grab up sweater and purse to come running out. . . . A full forty-five minutes passed, and they brought a growing irritation as she more than once peered down the drive and along the empty road as far as she could see. She wandered into the living room, picked up a magazine, and became conscious of muffled male voices from the kitchen.

Janet marched in there. Her father and Dewey, their hats on the backs of their heads, sat at the kitchen table, each with a hand hooked around a stubby of beer. It looked as though they had been there for a couple of hours, and their laughter over what had to be a man's joke suddenly stilled. Dewey sprang to his feet with a guilty look. He was dressed much like any young Montana ranch hand, in freshly washed blue jeans and a chambray work shirt. The simple outfit emphasized the contrast between his broad shoulders and lean hips. His opened shirt collar was turned up jauntily at the back. Inside it, snug around his strong brown neck, Janet saw a splendid choker of polished old tubular bones, elk teeth, knucklebones from a bear's paw, and large, colorful antique-looking glass beads. She hoped he had put it on because it was so handsome, not in any attempt to be defiantly Indian.

"You about ready?" he said. "I got here a little early. Hope you don't mind ridin' in a jeep. I got one down at Great Falls on a war-surplus sale to veterans."

Then, as though Janet would find the matter of intense interest, he added, "I'm riggin' a posthole digger from the power takeoff. Your dad and I have been figuring it out."

"If I'd only known," Janet said. "Perhaps I'd have been able to contribute something in this last hour."

She found that first jeep ride exciting. Dewey took her back around the barn and corrals for seven cross-country miles of prairie, bouncing over gopher and badger holes, whipping at high speed through patches of buckbrush, grinding in four-wheel drive up and down the banks of small coulees. At the first fence, Janet drove through, while Dewey held the barbed wire and pole gate open, then gladly kept the wheel at his urging. A coyote appeared from nowhere. Janet pressed the accelerator to the floorboards in a wild, brief chase, while Dewey whooped and yipped in a way that made her spine tingle and set her yelling too. The coyote ran safely up among the capping rocks of a small pinnacle to turn and look back, grinning at Janet and Dewey exactly as though grateful for having been included in their fun.

They drove on over somewhat smoother land. Dewey relaxed into a kind of angular sprawl on his side of the jeep, and Janet felt him gazing at her with something like the coyote's pleased grin. She said, "What else have you been doing—besides fixing up this jeep?"

"Hayin' a little, and getting ready to hay. And I just finished up puttin' in a water system I talked my dad into paying half of—runnin' water and a sink in the kitchen, and a part of the back porch closed in for a toilet. Remember my old gran'-mother that was with me the other day? Well, she doesn't get excited about much, but she sure was excited to see that water piped in. When I told her it would be finished next mornin', she couldn't sleep a wink that night. And when she saw that water start comin' out of the faucet, she began to sing one of her old-time songs, just like one of my sisters or girl cousins was

26

havin' a baby or something. For two-three days she'd keep turnin' that water on, just standin' there watching it like she couldn't believe it.

"Say! You ever hear about the Indian that was an electrician's mate in the navy, how he came home and put electric lights in the council-house latrine, becomin' the first Indian ever to wire a-head for a reservation?"

Janet groaned and gave Dewey a sad smile while shaking her head wordlessly.

Dewey pretended to be abashed. "My old gran'mother, she does say that my jokes are worse than some damn Sioux. Now I'm afraid to tell you the one about the Indian who joined a yacht club because he wanted to be a red son in the sail set."

"I don't know about the Sioux," Janet said, "but I think you're worse than my father. My father says you've got just about the best land and water of any small ranch in the country. Are you going to help work your place?"

"I do wanta stay here, but I've been thinkin' for a long time how I'd like to be a veterinary doctor. Go to college on this GI Bill. Some of the old people, they think I oughta be a lawyer, or a teacher and coach, but I'd just like to be a veterinary doctor."

"There ought to be plenty of practice for you right here in the county. My father's always cussing and complaining about that old drunk in town."

"It was him that gave me the idea," Dewey said. "Him that first started talkin' to me about it. I guess he always was my best grown-up friend. My people all like him. You'll probably see him at the party."

"If I do see him, I'll be doubly reminded not to talk too much."

Dewey ignored that to tell her, "My people, they like your dad, too. Especially for things like buyin' Marie the dress."

"When—how was that?"

"You don't know anything about it? Well, when Marie was gettin' ready to start high school, she and the women worked all year makin' beaded moccasins and stuff to buy her some shoes and stockin's and a real dress. When they all went to town to buy 'em, they had to take their wagon because their car wasn't runnin'. Marie wore her new dress and shoes right out of the store, but when she started climbin' a wheel back into the wagon, wearin' those shoes she wasn't used to, she slipped and

27

got axle grease smeared all over her new dress. It was ruined, and Marie couldn't help from cryin'.

"Your dad happened to come along, and he says, 'What's that pretty girl cryin' about?' Then, when he found out, he says, 'By God, there's more dresses in that store!' and he bought her a real good one."

This was all new to Janet, but she now realized that the story had its sequel on a fine day in what must have been the following spring. Her mother had still been alive then, and they were all eating lunch in the sunny dining room when the sound of the kitchen door opening was followed by what seemed the cautious steps of someone walking barefoot over the linoleum. Her mother had looked apprehensive and her father was shoving his chair back from the table when a big Indian man walked in and said, "Howdy, Bob. For you." He threw a beautifully beaded martingale with matching bridle and stirrup covers into her father's lap, then hurried out.

Her father had looked both pleased and rueful as he exclaimed, "Goddamnit, I should have known better."

"Bob, whatever is going on?" her mother wanted to know.

"Nothing—nothing much except that I've probably adopted us another family from here on out."

Those presents, which her father clearly prized, were worth considerably more than the cost of a girl's dress.

She felt Dewey's admiring gaze; he seemed to be hoping she would say something more. After a little he spoke, his voice softer and lower, perhaps an insinuating voice. "Janet, you've got beautiful hands." But instantly he made her feel a sudden sharp disappointment by adding, "And that ain't all!" Janet was somewhat conditioned to interpret this as a reference to her rather prominent breasts, and she felt a deep relief emerging when she gathered a different meaning as Dewey went on, "You can really use 'em, too. You shift gears easier and quicker'n I do. Back there, chasing that coyote, you herded this here jeep around like a veteran. But don't let my gran'mother know we tried to run down any coyote. She's funny about coyotes. She goes out and talks with them, just like two people talking. Sometimes I don't believe it, but if you could see her, you'd almost believe it too. She says her father's oldest wife, a Flathead woman, taught her how."

"I thought she was magnificent. I would like to have talked to her more."

"She said the same thing about you. She says she knew your gran'father way back in the buffalo days. She says she'd like to show you some things he gave her back then, and that he wanted her to run away with him once, but she already had a good husband and a baby. She says your gran'father helped her get rid of some horses she and my gran'father stole after the country was already 'bout full of *napikwan*—I mean whites."

"Dewey, I'd love to hear those stories. I've always wanted to know more about Grandfather Sinclair, especially since I've been away to school—history courses and things. Do you think she'd really open up and talk to me?"

"You'd have to come listen to her two or three nights a week all summer to sort out what you wanta hear. Why, I been listening to her stories for years, but I just learned the other day how she lay in the brush beside my gran'father while they both fired at Canadian soldiers and the Mounted Police at a place named Cut Knife Hill in Saskatchewan; how, before that, she was with her Sioux husband on the Little Bighorn. You know, the day the Sioux and Cheyennes gave Custer an arrow shirt. . . ."

"Dewey, I can come just any time she's in the mood."

"Well, I think maybe I can work it, if I go about it right. But I warn you, you'll have to drink her tea. She makes it in a skillet on top of the stove, with the tea and brown sugar just thrown into the water and all brought to a boil. Like as not, she'll add butter and whiskey. You listen to her and you learn almost more'n you wanta know. Like the other old people who can't read and write, she *remembers*. She remembers *everything*."

They drove on in silence under the still hot sun. Dewey opened the last gate, and they turned upon a rutted public road that seemed to run from one nowhere into another. When Dewey spoke, his mind was still on his grandmother.

"She's all excited," he said, "and already in the mood for tellin' stories. You remember Marie Nequette? Well, Marie's been makin' sketches of her for three days, getting all set to paint her picture." Janet felt a little miffed.

"Will Marie be at the party?"

"Sure. That's how come she decided to hurry home and surprise us—all the way from Los Angeles, ridin' with the Bear Childs and helpin' drive. They came straight through without stoppin' once, except to feed the kids, or when they had blowouts from not bein' able to get any new tires. Got here three days ago."

"Whose kids?" Janet asked.

"The Bear Child's. They seem to have five or six, all ages, besides the baby. You know Mattie, she's about the same age as Marie. Marie was workin' for a year in a defense plant, takin' art classes at night. She's so good at it," Dewey announced proudly, "that they gave her a scholarship for goin' full time all next year, without havin' to work, if she decides to go back and take it."

Out of a short silence Dewey spoke in a drowsy voice, "Now we're on the road, I think I'll get me a little shut-eye. I haven't had much sleep since the Bear Childs came." And with that, he closed his eyes and slumped at once into apparent oblivion.

As the road dropped off the high prairie into a fairly wide coulee, Janet saw Dewey's home, with the barn, the feed racks, and the corrals ranged above a good creek, along which cotton-woods and chokecherries grew. The site differed little from that of her own home, but the man-made structures here, though built for identical purposes, looked wholly basic and modest. A low frame house, which apparently had been painted once, half hid a very old but sound log cabin to which it was attached. There were no walks and no shrubbery, but Janet was surprised indeed to see a fine garden. The barn and the corrals offered an impression of casual, rickety construction, yet they also looked functionally sound. Janet saw every building showing rough repairs where her father would have made neat replacements.

Actually, Janet told herself, the place looked hardly different from that of some white small rancher, yet there was something indefinable that would have told her at once that this one was Indian. Perhaps it was only that the man-made ugliness appeared to blend better into its setting. Despite this, Janet could not avoid seeing the rusting, long-stripped hulks of old cars standing around in plain sight, especially the two abandoned just where she followed the road across the unbridged creek. This, while not exclusively Indian, was yet typical. It was an Indian way the Elk Hollerings had of suggesting their worth and affluence in having owned so many.

The Elk Hollerings, in some ways at least, were a world removed from dwellers under Hill 57, the Indian slum at Great Falls, and from many of the reservation Indians she had seen, those who merely existed, lost in hopelessness, poverty, ignorance, and degradation, the large families jammed together in one-room cabins, the necks of undernourished children swollen wider than their heads from scrofula and its ulcerating, horribly scarring sores. Still, they could count themselves lucky if they escaped the trachoma that could make their dark eyes blind.

Dewey came wide awake as the jeep forded the creek. "Drive up to the house," he said. Cars, some of them rather new and others looking only a little better than the abandoned hulks, were parked along the creek near two tree-screened canvas lodges. Others laid quiet siege to the house. Among the Montana license plates Janet saw all the Pacific Coast states and North Dakota represented, also the province of Alberta. Deep quiet reigned, and almost no one was in sight except for a horde of momentarily staring small children and two slightly older boys in faded pink shirts who hurried toward the barn. Indians appeared never to go anywhere without their children. At least half of the children carried bottles of pop. On the shaded side of the house four or five matronly women with heavy braids sat on the ground and watched another who worked over a rough table. The working woman swung a heavy length of peeled green sapling with all her strength to beat a huge mass of very thick dough. It appeared that all the women were taking turns at this clubbing.

Janet wondered if Dewey had brought her too early. As she parked the jeep and stepped to the ground, she said to him, "You never did tell me the reason for the party."

"Oh, no reason much. You might say the family sorta feels like we've been honored with good luck and stuff. Old Gran'mother and my father, they decided to kill a coupla steers. Word got around, like it usually does."

"When does it begin?" Janet asked. She nearly turned her ankle on one of the empty beer cans, and almost tripped over an old deer's skull with sharp antlers that could have punctured her rib cage had she fallen. The skull and two or three tin cans were attached by a length of small rope to a panting dog that had taken refuge under a car.

"Oh, it's been going on for four, five days now," Dewey said. "Some of the people came early and had to leave early—like my older sister, who is married to a Yakima. Some of the others had to get back to Wolf Point and places. Let's go see Old Gran'-mother now, before something happens. She's probably still tryin' to teach some of my cousins how to play poker and black-jack better."

Janet followed Dewey past the well and its old hand pump and the watering trough, then past the bent-willow framework of a sweat lodge and on toward a patch of buckbrush and chokecherry. A small bower had been cleared all around two close-growing chokecherries, and in their shade on a low kitchen stool sat the old woman. A loose pile of dollar bills was at her feet, and she was dealing cards, flipping them out expertly to four young men, one of whom sat cross-legged while the other three lay propped on their elbows. Each simple movement of her hands spelled an exquisite lesson of quick, definite grace and seemed, like her eyes, to belie the age-shrunken body and the wrinkled face. She had on fresh, plain moccasins of smoke-tanned buckskin, the uppers showing snug lacing about trim ankles before they disappeared under a long-skirted dress of heaviest blue-black serge. That sleeved dress, which Janet saw to be cut like a slimmed version of what was called a squaw dress, should have been stifling on this sultry day. Yet the old woman looked cool as a mannequin in an air-conditioned dress shop in Great Falls. A long, simple necklace of beautifully graduated white dentalium shells arranged in clusters of threes and alternating with large, old dark blue glass trade beads, and a narrow binding of bright red, white, and blue yarn for each of her long gray braids constituted Walks Far's sole effort at Indian adornment.

Her eyes brightened on seeing Janet. She smiled and raised her hand. Graceful fingers shaped in the air what could be only a happy, welcoming sign, then she said, "Glad you come. Got something belong Jack Sinclair long tam ago. We talk pretty soon. You see."

"I'd really like that," Janet told her.

One of the young men on the ground grinned up and said, "Hi, Omaca—. Good to see you."

"Hi, Danny," Janet said, and she too groped for a name. "How's—ah, your sister—Aileen?"

"Fine. She's around somewheres. A wonder you didn't see her."

Danny was dressed from head to toe like a railroad brakeman —striped overalls, striped jumper, striped cap, and all, with a red handkerchief around his neck. Janet always found it hard to think of Danny's being a breed, even though the Indian blood showed strong as the Irish in his clownish face.

The other young man, the handsomest Indian she had ever

seen, and apparently something of a dandy, fascinated and irritated Janet. She felt his eyes appraising her body slowly from
behind the large, gold-rimmed dark glasses beneath his wide-
brimmed, high-crowned black hat. He alone of the young men
wore moccasins, and they were beautifully beaded in a
predominantly white geometric design. Above his black trousers he had on a drab Canadian-army battle jacket with three
bright ribbons over the left breast pocket. A purple silk scarf
was closely knotted at the side of his neck within the opened
collar. His hair had grown just long enough for short braids.
Janet learned that his name was Adam Many Horses.

He had hands graceful as the old woman's, and he strongly
resembled Dewey, except for more finely chiseled features that
gave him a somewhat feminine face and made him look deli-
cately cruel. He lost his bet and stood up, saying something to
Dewey in Blackfoot that plainly referred to Janet. Again she
heard the word *omacanuks*—all of it this time. Danny McGaffigan and the others laughed delightedly, and Dewey quickly
told Handsome Boy in English, "You're nuts. Of course not!"

Handsome Boy smiled and spoke with what may have been
perfect English diction, "Well, then, laddie, you would not
mind a-tall if an ordinary person should choose to use it." He
turned and swung off toward the house like a marching British
soldier.

Danny McGaffigan scrambled to his feet, declaring, "I'm
gonna follow that Indian. I gotta *ta kipskas* just as bad as him.
That new, blue toilet that cost Dewey fourteen dollars extra
ain't too good for Danny, neither."

It amused Janet to see Dewey still embarrassed and furious
as the remaining pair of young men began questioning him
about his jeep. Janet knelt and said to Walks Far, "Will you deal
me a hand?" Her father had told her more than once that she
was very good at blackjack, but while Dewey and the two others
headed back toward the jeep in sudden argument, the old
woman gave her a swift six-dollar lesson to the contrary, then
ended the game by saying, "Come, we find something Hi'm
show you. Next tam you come, Hi'm tell long-ago story 'bout
Jack Sinclair in gone tams. We make plenty tea. You come?
Dewey not bring you ever'tam, you come anyhow?"

"Dewey said you had a story I'd like."

"Dewey good kid," Walks Far said with a kind of confidential
chuckle. "He get mad easy, but he good kid—maybe he bes'

gran'son I got. Adam Many Horses, he good gran'son too. He make Dewey mad 'bout blue toilet. He say Dewey fix that toilet 'cause you come. Dewey not lak Danny and Adam call you name all Indian kids give you in school."

"They did! What name?"

"Don' tell Dewey. He get mad with me. All Indian kids call you Omacanuks—'Fifty Cents.' You rich! Ever'day you 'ave fifty cents for lunch!"

Janet felt a confused astonishment and was trying to decide whether or not to laugh about it as the old woman led off in a surprisingly fast, shuffling trot down the path through the buck-brush toward the well, only pausing to add, "Marie Nequette, she mad at Dewey. *Ah-i!* Marie plenty mad."

"Marie! What did he do to her?"

"Bring two Jap scalp from Okinawa."

"What!"

"Ah-i! When Dewey go away, Marie say get plenty scalp. Dewey not forget. Two-three days ago Marie come home. Dewey give her present—two scalp in candy box. Marie open box, then she cuss him. She throw box in stove, then cuss him some more. She stay plenty mad."

"Well, I should think so," Janet said.

As she and the old woman joined Dewey and the two young men who were intently examining the jeep, half a dozen other young people, Marie Nequette and Enos Weasel Head among them, appeared in a group from around the barn and began shouting for Dewey.

"Goddam," Janet heard Dewey say under his breath.

Marie called a greeting, "Hi, Janet. Our big, brave Dewey wants to show us he can still ride a horse." Marie was prettier, more poised and confident than ever, and her clothes were striking too. Despite the heat, she was wearing a dark blue velvet Navaho blouse with a turquoise-set silver concha belt around her hips. She was loaded tastefully with silver and turquoise necklaces and bracelets. But her skirt of pale blue linen was modish as anything Janet owned. She was also wearing high-topped, hard-soled Navaho moccasins, with silver conchas up the sides.

"This is no time to ride that horse," Dewey said.

They hooted at Dewey, challenging him, taunting him in two languages. Marie was worst of all. She razzed him scathingly, with a viciousness to be dared only by a girl, and then only by one for whom he must feel great familiarity and fondness. She held a silver half-dollar out to him and said, "I'll give you fifty cents. You used to want to do anything for fifty cents!" And Janet, already furious, saw half the growing crowd suddenly doubled up in laughter. Dewey shook his head slowly, sadly, then said, "All right. Let's get it over with."

A clearly excited Walks Far hurried Janet along, with Marie, Mattie Bear Child, and Aileen McGaffigan joining them at the corrals. Marie was quite friendly, and seemingly sincere. As they climbed the corral together and stood holding on to the top rail, Marie said, "Wouldn't it be something if Dewey can ride him?"

Janet had never seen a meaner or more reptilian-looking little horse than the wiry broomtail two riders brought in crowded between them. They got Dewey securely mounted from off the corral gate, then wheeled into the clear. That mean-eyed little horse squealed and made for the middle of the corral in a series of stiff-legged, twisting jumps that jolted Dewey but did not lose him. Then, as though feeling properly at center stage, that little horse put on an enraged show. He seemed to go spiraling straight up from bunched feet and to buck twice before hitting the ground. He came down only to reach for the sky again, and that time he left Dewey sprawled strangely on thin air while he shot from under and went on jumping and bucking more wildly than before.

Dewey struck the ground on one shoulder, went into a lax roll, and lay facedown, utterly still for a moment. But he rose quickly to his feet, grinning as he picked up his hat and dusted the clay and trampled dry manure of the corral from his clothing. His face was dirty too, and a sleeve of his shirt had ripped raggedly away from the shoulder seam. Again Janet heard Dewey razzed, as mercilessly as before, but the crowd escorted him to the shady side of the barn for wild toasting with cans of foaming warm beer.

Janet realized that old Walks Far had disappeared. Before long she had had a couple of beers and began to feel comfortable and enjoy herself more. It struck her that even though she had never been to a party where she felt so conspicuous, she had also hardly ever been to one where she found herself so taken for granted, and that was flattering. By the time she drained her second can of warm beer, she told herself that she liked Marie Nequette very much. Clearly Marie and Dewey were suited to each other. That was apparent, as was the close, easy bond between them. They would make a handsome couple.

"Come on," Dewey was urging her, "C'mon up to the house and see my folks while I find a clean shirt."

Women still sat on the ground at the side of the house, gossiping while one of them continued to whale away with the peeled club at the mass of dough. Janet met Dewey's mother, a stocky, pleasant-faced woman with flour whitening her braids. She, the beater of the moment, paused to smile and say, "Glad you hadda come. You hungry? We eat good pretty soon, dough beat already after. You get a chance eat Red Rivers's *gollette?* He's made good for eat with meat."

Dewey led on across the back porch, where Janet saw the new convenience, agleam in its robin's-egg blue, beyond a half-open, homemade door in a cubicle of bright new lumber. She found herself in an unexpectedly spare kitchen, its walls never finished. A group of men with their hats on sat around a kitchen table exactly as her father preferred to sit with his cronies. But here, instead of shot glasses and a bottle she saw only a small board decorated with old brass tacks, upon which one of the men was cutting a strange piece of tobacco. Dewey gestured toward the powerful-looking man doing the cutting and said, "That's my dad." Stripping off his shirt and the handsome choker, he began to wash up at a cheap, new kitchen sink beneath the single tap. His father smiled and said, "Howdy, I see you before, those sometimes with Bob Sinclair."

Another voice said, "Howdy, Miss Sinclair."

It was Dr. Timmons, the alcoholic veterinary doctor she had disparaged while driving out. He was the only other white person she had seen. The men ignored her as she waited while Dewey washed noisily.

Janet saw, beyond the men at the table, a huge, ornately nickled old cooking range with integral warming oven above it and water reservoir at the side. Hot coals from the stove had burned several holes through the large scrap of floral-patterned, worn linoleum on the floor before it. The stove was now cold, and nothing in the kitchen suggested a meal in preparation. There were a couple of shelves in the room, but boxes nailed between the bare studding held most of the utensils and dishes. Old sheepskin coats, mackinaws, and denim jumpers hung on nails driven beside the doorway, and there were a couple of rifles on nails above.

"Come on," Dewey said, and Janet found herself in a much more finished and cluttered room. From the dingy, old-fashioned wallpaper a thousand gold cornucopias spilled lush bunches of grapes. On a toy-strewn, deep-blue rug stood a lavender davenport, its deeply carved mohair upholstery badly worn. Competing for attention was an enormous pot-bellied heating stove, riotous with nickled curlicues and many small, mica-paned windows in its door.

Janet saw a fine cabinet radio laden with dust and a functional shortwave set. She could smell the acid in the batteries on the floor. Cotton quilts, blankets, and sleeping bags were stacked, not too neatly, under and upon all the furniture. There was a faint Indian smell of smoked buckskin, though Janet could see nothing to cause it.

"Things are kinda torn up for the party," Dewey said. "Wanta look at the family album?" He gestured toward a surprising number of studio-type photographs on the wall beside the dead stove, then disappeared into another cluttered room. Janet made her way to the pictures; many were old and most of them appeared to be wedding pictures of young Indian couples sitting in stiff solemnity, uncomfortable but proud in starchy clothing they had probably never worn again. Janet found, under two braids of human hair tacked to the wall, a picture of Dewey in uniform, and either the uniform or the photographer's lighting made him look much more typically Indian than he looked to her. It occurred to her that, actually, Dewey would never look very much out of place among either whites or Indians.

He rejoined her, now wearing a soft, expensive shirt cut like the shirts rodeo riders wear. His initials were embroidered in blue silk on the left breast pocket. "These braids," Janet said. "Whose are they?"

"Mine, cut off when I started high school," he laughed. "That was the last time I really cried. They told me I could. Everyone else was."

"I'd have cried too," Janet told him. She became dimly aware of a screaming woman somewhere outside, and of a man's loud, drunken voice.

Abruptly the shrieking was muffled in a prolonged and not easily identifiable grating of metal from outside, with many shouting voices now added. "Goddam," Dewey said. He sprang to a window and, after the merest glance, went rushing out through the kitchen yelling something in Blackfoot to the men getting up from the table.

Janet followed, found herself in a small crowd that materialized as though from every shady place to gather around a topless Model A pickup entangled in a barbed wire fence and tilted half on its side. Dewey had grabbed wire cutters from somewhere and was already in the car, working desperately with them to free the strangling, bulging-eyed, purple-tongued driver from a barbed snarl binding his bloody neck down to the steering wheel. Dewey gave careful, calm orders to the men to hold the pickup tilted precisely as it was. Danny and Enos worked with him at the wire, and they got the driver safely cut free.

Dr. Timmons made a quick examination and announced with relief, "He's drunker than anything else. He'll be all right, soon's he sleeps it off." So, women washed and bandaged the lacerations and laid the lucky drunk beside his disentangled pickup. It looked little the worse except for a flat front tire. His wife sat down on the ground, drew his head into her lap, dug into her handbag, and began to comb his hair.

Aileen McGaffigan told Janet, "That Dave Two Stabs, he got so drunk Cecile wouldn't let him have any more. Then he got mad and started for town to find a drink by himself—when he couldn't even find the road outa here!"

Janet said, "When do you think we'll eat? All this beer on empty stomachs!"

"Oh, not for a while yet. People have been eating all day. Say! You hungry? We got a turkey in the car that hasn't been touched."

The turkey proved to be a small one in a covered chipped-enamel roasting pan on the floor of a hot, old sedan. As Aileen twisted off the two drumsticks, Janet was relieved to see that the bird had been baked without stuffing. She closed her mind to all thought of food poisoning and, like Aileen, gnawed gratefully at the tough, overcooked, dry flesh.

"We need a beer to get this down with," Aileen said. "In Blackfoot we call turkeys and chickens, all luncheon meat, and anything else like that 'useless food.' Only fresh meat from something like a cow or the buffalo we used to have is 'real food.' *Ai-ee!* You hear that thunder?" And Aileen lapsed into the English of an unschooled Blackfoot girl, "You think it's gonna had rain so we're hadda dancing in the barn?"

"It's stifling enough for something to happen," Janet said. "Anyhow, I just have to have a drink of water." She and Aileen walked back toward the kitchen door.

Incredibly, a woman was still beating the dough with the club. Aileen rolled her big almond eyes and said in her husky Indian voice, "I just love *gollette;* it's worth waiting for, even without jelly on it."

"Just what is it?"

"Bread, real thin, like a pancake. Flour, salt, and lots of marrow grease mixed into a thick dough. The longer and harder you beat it, the better."

"This batch ought to be delicious," Janet said, feeling a reservation about the marrow grease as she asked, "What else will there be?"

"Meat!" Eileen said ecstatically. "Meat they're roasting down by the crick. Haven't you been smelling it all evening?"

Janet was glad to be able to say no. The fragrance would have been unendurable. Surely the meal would be served before dark. Her wristwatch showed a quarter till nine, and the sun would be down before an hour was past.

She and Aileen finished their drumsticks over good cold water in the now empty kitchen. Mattie Bear Child and Adam Many Horses came in and went directly to the shortwave radio in the living room. Janet and Aileen joined them. Adam found the news on a Calgary station, but it failed to give the score he sought for some minor Canadian baseball game. The music that followed proved a disappointment to him too. He took a mouth organ from his pocket, eyeing Janet as he held it up to say, "A Yank invention—your Benjamin Franklin, no less." He played several bars expertly, then began to sing soldier doggerel to the same simple tune, in an exaggerated Cockney voice:

"Prang the bloody fortress,
Prang it good and strong,
We have to prang the fortress
For the Hudsons are all gone."

"That's an air-force song, isn't it?" Janet said uncertainly. "Were you in the Canadian Air Force?"

"I was definitely on the ground, in the artillery." Adam switched to a pleasing slow pathos on the mouth organ and sang a familiar song—

"We are the D-Day dodgers, in sunny Italee,
Happy on the *vino*, merely on a spree.
We landed in Salerno, the Jerries gave us tea. . . ."

He was well along with a fine rendition of "Lili Marlene," when other young men and girls came in. Janet wondered where Dewey could be and noted that Marie was also missing. The singing went on, mostly of ballads. Some of them proved to be the most bawdy, to say the least, that Janet had ever listened to.

A woman came from the now sweltering kitchen with a swift announcement in Blackfoot. Aileen signaled Janet, and they hurried outside with the others. A small, intently gazing crowd stood silent in a dusk that was not merely of twilight, their eyes fixed on the old woman who sat alone on the bare earth, halfway toward the barn. Other people stood watching from there. She was chanting in a high voice, pausing to draw smoke from a small, black stone pipe with a very short wooden stem. She blew each puff carefully toward a black, lightning-laced thunderstorm sweeping in close from the direction of Packsaddle Butte. The rolling black cloud was still well beyond the farther rim of the coulee, perhaps half a mile away, but Janet heard, or imagined she heard, the distant roar of the wind and the ruinous hail.

Marie appeared suddenly, rushing out with a wide, tambourinelike drum and padded drumstick and sat a little to the left behind the old woman. Marie drummed as she added her voice in what sounded like any high-pitched Indian singing, and the old woman raised some small object in her palm and held it toward the low sun obscured behind the onrushing storm.

Large, scattered drops of rain began to fall, and people took shelter on the porch or backed up against the house under the overhang of the roof. The old woman and Marie went on singing. The huge, black squall stopped at the brink of the coulee, abruptly appeared to lose force, to flounder there before it turned away, dwindling as it drifted off along the rim of the high, open prairie. A man's awed voice broke the silence, "She don't let that hail hurt nobody's hay!"

Janet, only half out of the scattering rain, was arrested in a sort of daze that mingled what she had seen with disbelief. The rain ceased abruptly, and Marie and the old woman stopped singing. Marie ran for the barn. Her hair looked wet. The shoulders of her velvet blouse were darkened, and white-clay mud stuck to her linen skirt. The old woman strolled nonchalantly toward the house and approached Janet with a smile. A shiver gathered at the back of Janet's neck and flickered down between her shoulder blades as she saw there was not a drop of water on either the gray braids or the serge dress. "H'im glad storm come," the old woman said. "Now you not laugh at some story Hi'm gon tell you."

"Why, certainly not," Janet said. "I never would have."

"Marie sing ver' good," the old woman said thoughtfully. "But she get wet. She's gon hear some story Hi'm tell you and Dewey. She's pretty lak me those tams in story. You lak Marie? She's lak you."

"Of course," Janet said. "Anyone would like Marie." And Janet found herself adding, "She and Dewey will make a wonderful pair."

The old woman showed a kind of horror, without the least change of expression.

"They cousin both way!" she said. "Cousin—double cousin!"

Janet hoped her own expression did not reveal the pleasant shock she was feeling. "Why, I never guessed that," she said. "But they even look a little alike."

"They born same day. Born my birthday. Last rib day in"— and here she found the English sounds in *February* nearly impossible—"last day in Pwep-u-eddy Moon. You plenty hungry? Marie and you hadda feast with old woman pretty soon."

Dewey joined Janet, and from then on she became far less a spectator, much more a happy participant. She danced by yellow lamplight to the radio in the living room and by dimmer, lantern light to Adam's piano accordion in the barn. She learned to beat Marie's drum and accepted a third beer. Chill moved in behind the thunderstorm, and Janet, feeling relief that the old woman's power did not include temperature control, guessed that the thermometer must have dropped thirty degrees in the past hour. In contrast to that, she was enjoying a relaxed human warmth she could not remember having felt at any other party. Janet, like all the other girls identified with a particular escort, followed what she understood to be a custom modernized from the old times and wore Dewey's hat, even while dancing with someone else.

Between dances in the barn loft, she heard the girls talking about how a certain Charlene TomSharpe had just suffered a couple of broken ribs from being kicked by one of the horses stabled below—and not because Charlene had had too much beer. A girl Janet had not seen before explained: "That Charlene, I already knewed about her. She's wanta be warm alone quick with some boy, for sneaking place on hay under manger where nobody seen in front them horses. They don't thought that team are maybe kicking sonsabitchers!" Janet understood the situation.

At one point a conversation turned on wonderment that white people could drink cow's milk when even a milk shake made so many Indians get sick and throw up. Janet announced that she too was unable to tolerate milk. When Dewey explained to everyone that a great many Indians and Negroes, as well as most Orientals and a few whites, lacked a necessary enzyme to deal with milk, Janet said, "Why, I must be more Indian than I knew. My grandfather was supposed to be almost half."

She was hoping her words had sounded neither boastful nor like an attempt to be ingratiating, when an older, solid-looking man, who apparently had heard only a little of what she had said, spoke from the background: "You ain't the only one! Just look around, young lady. And like I told the town council over our way, human nature being what it is and Saturday nights and such being what they are, you only need to wait about fifty more years and you probably won't have any of your 'Indian problem' left." The man finished with a sardonic laugh, then walked away into the darkness.

Marie and Adam Many Horses were indignant. They would never concede that real Indians and Indian attitudes might be diluted by admixture with white blood. That man, admittedly, was becoming very influential and important, but he was a disappointment, to say the least.

Later, in a quiet moment, Janet saw the old woman again and said, "You were going to show me something of my grandfather's."

"Too many people now. Show you and Dewey after sometam. Now you dance. Don' you lak dance with Dewey?"

"Oh, yes! I do. He's one man who really likes to dance." The old woman laughed as though she had heard something quite funny and very pleasing.

Still later, as Janet ate beside the old woman among the other women and heard bursts of laughter from the already well-fed men on the porch, Adam came to stand, with unexpected diffidence, in the doorway. Clearly he had been sent to repeat a joke, one that may have been either better or worse than Dewey's jokes.

He stood straight, his right hand upraised and the palm forward, looking for all the world like an Indian in stoic caricature of himself as he asked, "What does this sign mean?"

The women hesitated, but a voice or two answered doubtfully and warily to say, "Peace?"

"And this?" Adam asked, lowering the hand to hold it touching his ribs in front of his left elbow.

If any woman or girl guessed the answer, none risked it. *"A little piece on the side!"* Adam told them solemnly, then fled from the burst of screaming giggles. Janet was surprised to find herself happily and rather loudly retelling the joke as she explained it carefully to a puzzled woman whose mind, or English, or both, appeared to be hopelessly literal.

She ate more than she ever had at a Thanksgiving dinner, though, of course, she had consumed nothing in the past twelve hours except three beers and a scrawny turkey leg. Now she was served berry soup with a very lean steak, filet cut from grass-fed beef but garnished with generous strips of sizzling fat. She found the steak awkwardly larger than her plate, but folded it upon itself and ate it all, not to mention the fresh Oregon cherries, the canned peaches and pears that came with the steak, and the various kinds of cake that followed. The crisp hot bread, the thin *gollette,* proved an indescribable treat with or without jelly, so tasty and rich with marrow fat that it might have been buttered. Janet saw women adding Karo syrup to a kind of potato pattie, to their canned fruit, and even to the stickily frosted cakes and the already sweetened strong coffee and tea.

All food was thoughtfully made available to Janet, but with no attempt whatever at urging some particular dish or a second helping upon her. The women appeared to assume that any person would possess individual tastes and would naturally choose what to eat and how much of it. Janet had never, as a guest, felt so relaxed at a meal—or such easy rapport with a group.

Once when Janet said, "Thank you," a woman who suddenly revealed English as precise as Adam's spoke to her in an aside. "In Blackfoot, we have no real term for 'thank you,' though we may say *sokahpi!*—'good.' We don't have a word for good-bye, either." Janet was so astonished that she answered, "Thank you," and they both giggled.

The old woman openly admired her appetite, then surprised Janet by saying, "Sometam when garden up, Hi'm gon make you good black-man supper. Indian people, white people, not cook good lak black people."

Janet supposed the party would soon draw to a close. The crowd did thin somewhat, and all beds were covered with sleeping children, but the younger adults recovered sufficiently from their huge meal to jam themselves into the living room for more talk and story telling, more singing, and more dancing to music from the shortwave radio. After an hour or so Janet had a beer or two with Dewey. They sat close now, pressed together by the crowd, and Janet, knowing she must get home before daylight, listened to Marie's drumming and thought the remaining time was growing all too short.

A middle-aged man came in briefly and declared that a drum should be beaten inside a house only for a ceremony and then never by a woman. Marie quickly lit a ceremonial pipe and easily persuaded the man to sing and smoke up a good store of proper grace for holding the curse away from her continued drumming.

Dewey disdained Janet's tailor-made cigarettes and tried to teach her how to roll "real smokes" from a Bull Durham sack such as the other girls handled so deftly in providing for themselves and the man whose hat they wore. She learned to say *ikkamonenapi* for a roll-your-own cigarette and *moneyimahn* for a tailor-made, but her pronunciation of *ahboatskinahpstahkkan* for the "cow tobacco," or Bull Durham, set Dewey shouting with laughter, exactly as though he'd heard a kind of hilarious pun, and she suspected that perhaps he had.

Marie began still another song, in Blackfoot, beating out each refrain on her drum before she sang the words. The song sounded sad, but with the sadness burlesqued and teasing. Though people appeared to find Marie's words amusing, they avoided each other's eyes and granted her complete silence. But Enos and Danny whispered together and eyed Dewey challengingly. Janet clearly distinguished the name Omacanuks in each refrain and guessed Dewey to be the object of teasing about herself.

As Marie completed the next refrain, Janet called out quickly, "What does that song say?"

Enos and Danny both tried to answer, but Dewey was quicker. He spoke more loudly than would have been necessary and in the firm, definite voice of a man who warns against any contradiction. "Oh, that's just an old song. It's hard to say in English, but it's about some Blackfoot boy thinkin'—thinkin' he can't live without fifty cents."

Some of the group giggled at that, others laughed aloud, but no one offered a different interpretation. Janet rose quickly to her feet, and as she stumbled across Dewey's feet into the cleared space, he asked her a stupid question, "Where ya goin'?"

She made the most of it, and with no effort to keep her voice especially low, she answered him. "Don't you think Fifty Cents has to visit the blue room, too!"

When she came back through the kitchen, he was waiting for her in the open doorway to the living room and he was smiling happily. He put a finger under her chin and tilted her face up. "Okay!" he told her, and then with his face bent still closer, he smiled into her eyes and added softly, "Hi! Hi there, Omaca-nuks."

"Hi there, Elk Hollering," she said in much the same low voice.

On Tuesday, Janet was back for the first of those many visits in which she heard the old woman tell stories. On afternoons she was alone with the old woman, usually under the choke-cherries in the patch of buckbrush; in the evenings she and Dewey listened together in the old woman's room, the parti-tioned-off kitchen end of the old cabin. It was cool in there then, with a pleasant smell of sweet grass and dried roots, of mint and rose hips and buckskin. The place looked largely empty except for numerous small bundles hanging all around, and the low, homemade bed and an ancient homemade stove, rather like a Franklin stove. Still, the room contained an amazing number of things, and the old woman's quick hands could make those things appear as though by a kind of magic. Except when Walks Far was brewing a pan of the syrupy tannic acid she called tea, the stove would be opened to show but a tiniest flicker of fire. Janet was cautioned not to look too much or too long at this, especially in the darkness, for anyone who sat in the dark and gazed at a fire while thinking or talking of the past surely risked going blind.

As the old woman told what she remembered, Janet kept rather disorganized notes, which ultimately strained a large loose-leaf college notebook, and she expanded her diary as well. [This book is the result of an ordering and free development of those materials by one who became a kind of cousin of Janet's.] The old woman told first about the day she had to run. The day was seventy-two summers past, and those times were gone forever. But as she pointed out, the place from which she ran was still there, in her words less than two looks east from Packsaddle Butte.

Chapter Five

UNDER-WATER PEOPLE AND A SUN-STONE

(Early August 1874)

At the first dawn of her flight Walks Far Away Woman stopped at a place of water and berries, eating two handfuls of the berries and what was left of the rabbit. With her knife she cut a digging stick for gathering roots in the dusk before going on. That done, she went upstream to sleep for the day and had the luck to kill a fool hen, a kind of prairie chicken, with her digging stick.

She settled down in a hiding place safely away from the water and sheltered from wind and too much sun. Her stomach felt reasonably full. But she hungered for real meat—*iksisakuyi*—for only the meat from a ruminating animal was generally fit for humans. Egg-laying creatures especially were to be avoided whenever possible. She looked into the bladder of pemmican Jack Sinclair had dropped for her. It was the best kind—*mukah-kin*—with chokecherries mixed into the pounded dry buffalo meat, the suet, and the marrow fat. She ate just one pinch, but a big pinch, then slept until dusk.

Shortly after midnight she had to deal with a fear that she had never had to face all alone, and this time her feeling included a dread of the supernatural. She came to the Missouri, the

Omach-k'tai or "Big River." Though she liked to swim, and swam well, she felt a Pikuni's apprehensiveness about large streams and lakes, finding them sober, threatening, and mysterious. She had never swum after dark, and the prospect filled her with such terror that she tried not to think about it, or of the under-water people who waited under the dark surface to pull even the strongest swimmer down.

She was near the point where the Teton and Marias join the Missouri. Fort Benton, where the *napikwan* brought his terrifying and monstrous fireboats, lay upstream. There was a regular crossing here, sometimes used by her people when they went south of the river to hunt. Walks Far had, in fact, crossed here before, but in broad daylight with a large band of people helping to frighten away the bad spirits by making a kind of shouting happy holiday out of the necessity of crossing and with the very young and the very old safe on rafts of lodgepoles or in willow-framed bullboats covered with green buffalo hide. The big crowd of swimming ponies, dogs, and people had splashed the mystery out of the river then.

Now, she had to search alone in darkness along the fearsome stream to seek a dry dead bush that would float high and not turn in the water. From the debris on a small bar she snatched the first bleached, brittle bush she thought might serve, but tested it carefully at the stream's edge. It did not roll over easily, even when she tried to make it turn. So, closing her mind to what her preparations were for and stripping off all that she owned, except the tiny beaded bag at her throat containing a piece of her own umbilical cord (which at five or six years of age most people put away), she tied her braids up in a knot behind her head. Then, lashing everything securely atop the bush, she fastened one end of her belt to the bush and clasped the other end in her teeth.

Trembling from far more than the chill water, she waded into the Missouri, floating the bush ahead. Abruptly, and almost to her relief, she was forced to swim. She swam easily and strongly, carefully maintaining a calculated calm, yet the fear did not leave her. . . . She found herself more than halfway across, and in quieter water.

Sheer terror took her. An under-water person nuzzled at her leg, slid clamily along her left side. She distinctly saw a huge gulping mouth and one horrible eye break water! Having no knowledge of the huge Missouri River catfish, she needed all her will power to keep from abandoning the bush in terrified floundering. She tried to swim on the very top of the water, with only the tips of her fingers and toes. When she waded out upon the south bank at last, she was perhaps more shaken even than she had been when she escaped the camp, and one of her feelings was of having just completed the most courageous act of her life.

Daylight saw her well south of the Missouri, still heading generally southeast. She would have to risk some traveling in daytime now. Rough country lay in her way, with creeks to be crossed. She held them in her mind's eye—Arrow Creek, Wolf Creek and its big brother, then Dog Creek. From Dog Creek she needed to strike the headwaters of Boxelder Creek and follow that downstream to the Musselshell. Coyote had failed to mention all the creeks.

By the late nightfall she was on Arrow Creek, having covered, on disintegrating rawhide-soled moccasins a distance that would have made a tiring day's ride on her beloved Snake horse. Full dark had already fallen by the time she washed, ate her supper, and went off a way to find a place for safe sleeping.

She curled herself beneath a big-trunked, low tree growing where she thought no person in his right mind would come to look. She felt near exhaustion, but true sleep would not come to bring her real rest, even though she had carefully placated the tree spirit with a low-voiced song. Ghosts, bad spirits, owls all came and bothered her in hazy, frightening dreams. She got up once and scouted the site carefully. The moonlit world proved silent and empty as when Napi first made it from a ball of mud Muskrat had brought up out of the water between his forepaws.

She slipped back under her tree, but the bad spirits hovered round till dawn. She finally slept soundly until Sun wakened her with his warmth. She looked overhead for the first time—and was up and running in one terrified, supple motion. That tree held a dead person, and she had been sleeping directly beneath him. But she stopped, went back nervously, and feeling only a little less fear than she had felt at the Big River, she forced herself to climb the tree.

The body lay bound in a good buffalo robe upon a platform of lashed sticks and poles. Walks Far summoned her courage and unwound a middle-aged man who had been dressed in very fine things for burial. He had dried in this climate, not gone soupy. She judged him to be of the Guts People—the Aht-tsi-sinawa, as the Blackfoot called their neighbors and frequent allies the Gros Ventre, and she saw that he had not been dead very long.

He had a bow, a clumsy thing, hastily and even crudely fashioned of green wood, very likely by a relative who had kept his gun. But Walks Far had not been thinking of a bow. The trade pipe she saw on a thong around the man's neck, the long antelope-skin tobacco pouch with its fine beading and quillwork tucked under his belt, these were raising her excitement. And she found exactly what she was looking for! A smaller pouch along with the tobacco pouch—his strike-a-light of flint and steel!

She well knew that robbing a dead person not only invited all kinds of misfortune but that the dead person's spirit might actually follow and try to reclaim his property! But just as birds and eggs might be eaten when real meat was not to be had, so did necessity take some of the curse from robbing the dead. Moreover, Walks Far was of a most practical people who had long ago worked out proper ceremonies with incantations or prayers to cover nearly every disturbing situation. So, she looked further. To take much would hardly expose her to greater danger than taking only a little.

She considered the beautiful spirit moccasins, which were beaded over their entire surface, even on the soles, like babies' moccasins, such moccasin soles as important men exposed while sitting in ceremonial lodges as well as when laid out for burial. Walks Far judged that they would not be much too large. She untied and took these moccasins along with his tobacco pouch, the strike-a-light, and a piece of vermilion from his paint bag. Nor could she resist that robe. The buffalo from which it came had been skinned by a cut along the backbone and removal of the uppermost side; then the heavy animal had been rolled over and the other side taken. When the halves had been dressed, they were sewn together with a broad strip of quilled red flannel over the seam.

Walks Far, coveting the red flannel and half the robe, ripped off the flannel and cut the seam of the robe before neatly winding up the dead man. She took half the binding cord, too. Going off a little way with her loot, she sat down. First she made the things into a bundle to sling over her shoulder, then she chanted earnest appeasement to all the spirits around that place.

That night she dined on the roasted flesh of prairie dogs so easily snared at their holes with a string trimmed from her dress. They were very good eating, with the hot fat dripping down her fingers from their tiny ribs—almost as good as real meat. When she went off and found a separate place to sleep, she had a buffalo robe to keep out the chill, the wind, and the dew. Also, her knife was in a sheath quickly made from a small part of that robe and worn inside her belt.

Aside from the dead man the only sign of humans she had seen thus far was an empty white man's road she had crossed warily a way south of the Big River. She knew that road to be made by white man's wagons in summers when the river ran so low that the fireboats could get no nearer Fort Benton than the mouth of the Musselshell.

In all her traveling as far as the Musselshell, Walks Far still saw no living person, but she constantly saw whitetail and black-tail deer, distant mountain sheep, a lone bull elk, many antelope, and countless buffalo with accompanying bands of gray wolves. Many hawks and a few golden eagles soared above her. She cared to see no person, and she hoped to be seen by none until she came to the Sioux camp on the Redwater. Still, she would have liked to come upon someone with a horse to be stolen. On her sixth night she crossed the Musselshell well south, near the mouth of Boxelder Creek, and told herself it was only a nothing after the Big River.

She was now well into country where she had never been, but she knew that she had to go straight east, passing the head of Big Dry Creek and going on to the head of Little Dry Creek. Big Sheep Mountain should be three nights' fast going from the Musselshell. She held this geography in her head, not from Coyote's instructions but knowing it from the accounts of hunting bands, of many war parties returned safely from raiding the Sioux and the Crows.

Walks Far's travels, and an end to Walks Far herself, almost came on the east bank of the Musselshell. In seeking a secure sleeping place after her night crossing, and after an early breakfast of roast porcupine killed with a club the evening before, she came upon an abandoned war lodge. The growing dawn showed this crude fort and shelter, a cone of logs and poles erected by some war party, to be well hidden. Walks Far saw that it also commanded a good view both up- and downriver and of all eastern approaches. Someone had torn the tunnellike entrance away. There was even a little pile of firewood, with a long-cold fireplace at the inner end of a small half-burned log pushed through the widened doorway.

She would take a chance, roast more of the porcupine, have a real bath, wash her hair and rebraid it! Soon she had a fire started at the end of the log and the last of the porcupine meat speared on sticks for roasting. As she had often done in better days, she fashioned a comb for her hair from the porcupine's tail. While sitting there in the lodge undoing her braids, she noted absently that many birds were calling from the surrounding undergrowth. Then, as she looked casually out through the doorway while shaking down her hair, she was all at once chilled by a new, abrupt terror: There was a false tone in some of those bird calls; a crouching man's upper arm was clearly visible behind a bush not four long lodgepoles from the door!

But she had not come this far to be raped or scalped, or very likely both. She grasped at her one chance. Perhaps those men had surrounded her without ever seeing her well.

With her heart pounding against her ribs as though they might burst, she untied her belt and dropped it so that her dress would flap loosely. And with one hand throwing ashes onto her head and all over her hair, the other hand was busy smearing charcoal onto her face and throat. She seized the burning long log from the fire, and making a crazy old woman's high screeching, rushed with the smoking big stick straight at the man behind the bush.

He shot to his feet, a look of amazement on his face as he skipped backward a couple of steps. Then, with a strange cry, he turned and ran. Walks Far saw another man and she made for him. He backed away nimbly, but was already breaking into laughter as he turned and ran. She in turn got a surprise. That second man was almost black all over and his calves were large as the calves of mountain-living Kutenai! She nearly forgot to keep screeching, but two more men came laughing and stumbling from the undergrowth beyond the lodge, circled her in wary stride, and ran off after the first man, whooping derision at him.

Walks Far watched them assemble with their war bundles on the riverbank a short way downstream, a war party of young men scarcely beyond boyhood. The black one grabbed a huge stick, gave a kind of high shriek, and Walks Far saw him reenact her attack, sending the remaining two young men into spasms of laughter.

Abandoning her roasting porcupine, she snatched up her other things and fled from that place to an utterly inconspicuous one well up a dry coulee. All that long thirsty and hungry day she looked very much indeed like an old hag, so crazy that she had been abandoned by her people.

She thought those young men must be Crows. They wore their hair in the Crow style and two of them had the faces of almost feminine delicacy sometimes seen among the Crows. Also, she had heard that a black white man had become a Crow chief. These young men were almost certainly on their way to steal horses from either the Assiniboins or her own people. But who were her people now? Anyhow, she had very likely caused one of those young men to be called a new name, one that he did not feel bucked up about.

While the hot sun slowly crossed the sky, Walks Far grew thirstier and hungrier. A thick patch of prickly pear covered the ground almost within reach of the hiding place she dared not leave for a moment. From the prickly pear she might squeeze out drips of a thick sticky juice to allay her thirst. They were also passable eating, though anyone taking even just a little of the juice or raw flesh risked an unforgettable case of diarrhea. Yet in knowing this, Walks Far spent that day with the temptation of the prickly pears barely overweighed by her fear that the war party had decided to search her out. She saw a rattlesnake and horned toads, neither of which were good omens.

For the next three nights she drove herself at a harder pace in almost treeless country. The going was easier here, but water was far apart and some of that water undrinkably alkaline. She came to Redwater Creek and Big Sheep Mountain on the third night. The Big Dipper—the "seven brothers"—showed that some of the night remained. She bathed thoroughly, purified her body by brushing it with sage, painted a sun circle on her face with the dead man's vermilion, and in sheer vanity painted the parting in her hair. She dressed but ate nothing, and, cacheing everything except the tobacco pouch and long strip of red flannel, she searched for a high place. A huge flat rock beside a stunted buffalo-berry bush satisfied her. She tied the tobacco pouch and red flannel to the bush as offerings to Sun, then sat upon the rock facing the east and waited, head bowed.

A glow came. For an instant the bottom edge of the eastern sky was rimmed with a streak of fire that grew humped at midpoint. Rays of brightness shot from that point, like the spreading feathers of a war bonnet filling the east and reaching to the top of the sky. Sun came up, and when his whole disk showed, Walks Far looked him full in the face, her voice abruptly lifted in a chant of gratitude. She repeated the chant four times, and with each repetition felt surer that Sun heard her as he had never heard her before. She bowed her head humbly.

After a while she was amazed to see something beneath her eyes that had not been there when she came. The rock now showed a neat, wind-sculptured pothole large enough to have held both her feet comfortably, though it was nearly filled with yellowish sand. Atop the sand, precisely at its center, lay a stone the size of a big musket ball and as perfectly round. At first sight Walks Far supposed that it was indeed a musket ball, and when she picked it up, it proved to be nearly as heavy. Yet it was unmistakably a kind of dense stone with a somewhat glazed appearance that caused it to glint a little. [Janet Sinclair saw this object and could not decide whether or not it was of meteoric origin. She noted that Walks Far still regarded that long ago find as the transcendent moment of her life, and that Dewey Elk Hollering did not like examining it.]

Very slowly it dawned on Walks Far just what it was she held. Sun had heard her, had given her a sign—more than any mere sign. She trembled. Her heart pounded so hard she felt faint, so shaken that she could not have spoken her own name. Sun had given *her* a special token, a Sun-stone, made perfectly round by being close to Sun on this high rock for so long that it had gathered to itself the shape of Sun—with the power of Sun!

In her shock of wonder and humility Walks Far collapsed into a kind of faint, from which the heat of the fully risen Sun aroused her at last. Nothing like this had ever happened to any person she could remember, and she knew that nothing quite like it could ever happen to her again. She discovered that Sun had given her a song to go with the power of the stone. She sang that song in ecstasy, then composed and sang a song of her own.

She untied the small bag from around her neck. Reverently she put the stone in with the piece of her umbilical cord, double-knotted the bag around her neck again, and went off downhill for her bundle. Still dazed by her wonder and still singing her songs, she trotted off in broad daylight down the east side of the Redwater. Nevertheless, she went cautiously, taking full advantage of all the cover that offered. Almost at once, Coyote came quartering up out of the sun. He sat down in the buffalo grass and, showing his teasing, knowing grin, he said to her, "Well, Walks Far Away Woman, I see you found Big Sheep Mountain all right."

Chapter Six

CAPTIVE

(Around August 6, 1874)

Well before noon, as Walks Far moved north down Redwater Creek, she saw signs of many people in this part of the country. Pony tracks were everywhere, and twice she crossed the double skid marks left by travois. Once, far off, she saw what looked like a hunting party of seven riders, five men accompanied by pack-horses with two women to do the butchering. Walks Far hid herself and watched them out of sight, then moved on more cautiously. Her life would not be truly safe until she managed to reveal herself within the camp.

She came to a chokecherry patch and for a moment thought women were in there, but it proved to be only a bear hoping the chokecherries were ripe. She saw two more riders, a pair of boys skylarking on their ponies, and then, on the creek bank, the tracks where an uncountable number of ponies had watered. Turning from the creek but paralleling it, she went swiftly on, but more cautiously, and was soon lying on her belly amid clumps of prairie rosebushes on top of a long, rounded ridge. Before her, beyond a coulee running into the Redwater and at a distance that made voices too faint to hear, a sizable camp stood on a flat near a grove of ash trees. [This was in the vicinity of today's town of Brockway, Montana.]

Her mother had been right about one thing: Sioux tipis looked more handsome than Blackfoot lodges, the arrangement of the poles being less bunched at the top and the cut of the smoke ears longer and more graceful. Walks Far thought of how little she knew of Sioux speech—most of that about woman's concerns—though of course she could rely on the common sign language. Now that she had followed Coyote's advice and was here, she felt apprehensive about entering the camp. . . . She remembered a winter night when she was twelve and Crees had fired into the Blackfoot camp. The men had chased those Crees and killed them all, except for one woman her father had seized alive. Her father brought that woman back at the end of his lariat, stumbling amid the severed arms and legs and feet dragging at the ends of other men's lariats. Her mother had tried her best to stab that woman. . . . Finding aunts or uncles or cousins in this particular band was too much to expect.

Perhaps she should just hide until well into the night? She could steal a horse, take a gun, and ride all the way to the South Guts People—the Arapaho—where young Blackfoot had been known to go for a year or two. She rejected the thought, and hoped that no Pikuni war party had stolen horses from this camp recently. . . .

She felt a sharp prod in the ribs, and half rose to flee, but instantly stopped when she found herself staring up into the muzzle of a long, glinting gun barrel with a grinning old man's face behind it. The gun barrel motioned her to stand up. She realized the old man had not been ten steps away among the rosebushes the whole time. He was probably the oldest man she had ever seen, an amazing assembly of wrinkled skin; thin, long bones; and big joints. His gun was a flintlock of an ancient-looking style she had never seen. Though he clearly was not decrepit, she thought it would be no trick at all to wrest the gun from him and flee, if she could just catch him off guard.

His grin widened for a moment at her surprise, then he spoke, with unintelligible sounds croaking from toothless old gums. Walks Far felt foolish at having let herself be caught by one of the aged warriors who traditionally outposted a camp in good weather; and gathering her elementary Sioux and simultaneously conveying the message by signs, she told him she was a Pikuni who had left her own camp nine suns ago to come to this camp to find relatives of her Sioux mother.

But when she made the sign for Pikuni, rotating her closed right fist against her lower right cheek, the old man crackled in sheer delight and gave her shoulder a smart rap with his gun barrel. "Pikuni! Pikuni!" he cried, pronouncing it more like "Pekony." She knew by his sharp little blow that he had half seriously counted coup on an enemy.

The old man motioned with his gun barrel that she should walk ahead of him toward the camp, then tilted back his head and let out an old man's horrible yell. Almost at once she saw horsemen coming out at a hard lope, a small crowd of men and boys on ponies.

The old man marched her straight on, and the crowd of riders, except for three good-looking, mature men, veered to either side and wheeled to follow at a respectful distance. The three men turned to ride close. They looked to be important men; and Walks Far saw that one of them wore his hair shaved high on each side, leaving only a bristly roach running back from his brow to a braided scalp lock. She thought the style very odd indeed, but knew it to be a part of his personal medicine.

"*Hau*, Grandfather," the man with the roached hair called, "I see you have caught a fine woman." Though he appeared to hold the old man in deepest respect, there was also a kind of amused tolerance.

The old man made no response, and the question had been spoken as though no answer were expected. Walks Far, realizing now that the old man was nearly deaf, found the roached younger man addressing her directly by both voice and sign, "Who are you? Where do you come from?"

"I am Walks Far Away Woman, a Pikuni woman. I have traveled nine suns from a big Pikuni camp northwest beyond the Big River, and I came here because I killed the Pikuni men who killed my husband, and because my mother was Teton Sioux. She was White Earth Woman, wife of Freezes to Iron, who was killed by Pikunis." Walks Far thought it just as well not to mention that the men *she* had killed were dog soldiers.

"*Hau!*" the three men exclaimed. They conferred earnestly, but with a certain amusement, and again the roached man addressed her. His question was unexpected, for it concerned a famous Pikuni warrior of legendary exploits, of strong medicine, great skill and daring.

"Does Mad Wolf still have his scalp?"

"Yes, I think so," Walks Far told him, and the statement appeared to provide grim satisfaction to all three men. They turned their ponies away, the roached one saying again, "Well, Grandfather, you have caught a fine woman. But she needs meat on her bones."

Walks Far not only felt ridiculous at being marched along by this ancient, knobby-kneed caricature of a warrior, but fearful too. She realized she might become the drudge of this old man and some crone of a wife, having to live with them in a poor, tiny tipi behind the main line and having to eat meat saved for the poor, the sick, and the helpless. If that were to be her lot, she would certainly run away.

She gained a growing escort now. For, as they neared the tipis, the pony-riding boys were joined by fleet children and the camp dogs. Still, the crowd stayed smaller than she would have expected. The dogs recognized her as a stranger, forcing the old man to hop creakily about in clubbing them away. He seemed bent on parading her the whole length of the rather straggling semicircle of tipis and so close to them that she was almost among the tumbling, naked toddlers and their puppies.

This camp of buffalo-hunting Sioux, except for certain decorations on the tipis, looked little different from the camp of buffalo-hunting Blackfoot she had fled. The smells were the same—smoky, leathery, meaty smells. And the flies. She saw rich tipis and poor tipis, large and small, with neither great wealth nor large size bearing much relationship to neatness and good housekeeping. Except for a grandmother or two, few women and no marriageable girls were about. Nor were there many men. Walks Far felt both relief and disappointment that her entry created so little stir.

She saw that most of the adult people were gathered well out from the center of the camp under the shade of two big ash trees, watching some kind of ceremony or contest, and a feast was being prepared. Girls, one after another, advanced before the crowd, stooped, and thrust one hand into a hole in the ground, at the same time biting on a knife picked up in the other hand. Walks Far knew enough about the Sioux to realize what was going on. The eternal gossip of a camp had come to accusation. Those girls were being required to declare their virginity by taking a strong-medicine oath that would bring fearful lifelong consequences to all liars. Almost no girl ever showed the courage or stupidity to lie, because any man who knew her to be swearing falsely could walk up and disgrace her forever by throwing dirt in her face, though he too must swear to the truth of the accusation by thrusting his hand into the hole and biting an arrow.

Walks Far knew also that married women who spread vicious tales or those who were suspected of adultery could be subjected to a very similar test. Any such woman who refused to bite the knife would very likely be plastered with filth or driven from the camp, or both. Also, an adulterous woman, just as among the Pikuni, might have her nose sliced off by her husband or by her own humiliated brothers.

She was very near the eastern wing of the camp now, and the old man prodded her through the open doorway of a fine tipi. She turned to the left side as a woman should do, falling to the ground in the near universal posture of a sitting Indian woman, her weight on her left hip, feet back and on the right and, because there was a man in the tipi, with her eyes downcast.

The ground in the rear of the tipi was carpeted with buffalo robes. More buffalo robes made pallet beds; and on one of these pallets at the center rear, with the tipi cover rolled up behind for air and light, a vigorous man sat whittling. He was propped against a willow-wand backrest, and Walks Far saw that his right leg stretched out stiffly before him in a rawhide splint. Three or four freshly whittled small wooden buffalo lay about him, but at the moment he was carving a bowl from an ash burl and appeared to find nothing at all extraordinary in having a strange woman thrust into his tipi. After a moment his knife stilled.

"Hau, Grandfather," he said to the grinning old man, who now squatted to the right of the doorway, leaning on his upright gun.

That was all the cue Grandfather needed to burst forth into an extremely wordy if quite factual account of his morning's adventure. Only at the end did he reveal that this was a "Pekony" woman who had run away from her people.

The whittler set his knife to the burl, grinned arrogantly, and began to whittle again, saying, "Pekonies piss inside their women." He laughed aloud. "Well, Grandfather, you have caught a fine Pekony woman. What are you going to do with her?"

"Keep her," Grandfather said happily.

"That is just what I would do, but I would get more meat on her ribs. What are you going to call her?"

"Pekony Woman."

Walks Far boldly spoke, clearly and firmly, without being spoken to, and outrageously violated another custom by looking each of those Sioux men squarely in the eye as she said, "I am Walks Far Away Woman; that is my name."

"*Hau!*" they exclaimed together, averting their eyes in a kind of shame for her.

She felt increasing exhaustion. She had no clear idea yet as to what her future might be, but, feeling thirsty and hungry, she found herself growing angry about something. "I am going to get some water," she announced, standing up and going to the skin water bag hanging from a forked post within the doorway to the right. There was also a battered tin cup. She took it and drank her fill.

"Bring me some of that water," the whittler said. She did so, and he told her kindly, "The women will come pretty soon."

That was the moment Walks Far dreaded most.

The whittler suddenly spoke to Grandfather and made a sign she did not catch. Grandfather rose at once and went out. She heard his cracked old voice receding as he called repeatedly for someone, and after a little he came back with two sixteen-year-old boys. Gently, the boys stood the whittler upon his one good leg, got their shoulders under his arms, and walked him outside.

Grandfather squatted again and regarded her with childlike happiness.

She pointed after the whittler and asked in signs, "Are you his grandfather?"

"No."

"His wife's grandfather?"

"No. I am everybody's grandfather."

"Is he a chief?"

"No, but he is an important man and his wife is the head chief's sister."

"What is the matter with his leg?"

"His ankle was twisted. He stepped in a hole while running."

"What is he called?"

"Scalps Them."

"How many wives does he have?"

Grandfather held up a little finger. "She is called Red Hoop Woman."

"Do they have children?"

Grandfather raised the little finger again and made the sign for girl.

"Do you live in this tipi?"

"No."

"Am I going to live in this tipi?"

"No. You are going with me." He showed utter happiness about that.

Walks Far heard women's voices approaching and put her hand close to her knife. A tall, stern-faced woman with a thick, rounded body above her high waist entered as though she owned the place. It had to be Red Hoop Woman. A half dozen determined-looking matrons followed her. Like Walks Far's Sioux mother, these women had a blue dot tattooed on their foreheads. Each had on rather large, stiff leggins reaching from ankle to knee, giving them, in Walks Far's eyes, a very clumsy and outlandish appearance. Her own mother had adopted the bare-legged Blackfoot way.

Red Hoop Woman screamed after the hastily departing grandfather, "Come back here, you old fool!" then forgot him instantly as she spoke in belligerent tones to Walks Far, "Has anyone hurt you?"

"No," Walks Far said, swept by an intense feeling of relief at the woman's concern.

"They say you are a Pekony woman whose mother was a Teton Sioux," Red Hoop Woman declared, "and that you have been a whole moon coming alone to this place."

Allowing no time for an answer, Red Hoop Woman hurried on. "But we will put some meat on your ribs, and maybe we can help you find some relatives this winter. There is plenty to be done before then."

Walks Far, in a daze of good feeling, found herself eating from a wooden bowl of prairie turnips cooked with fat, from another bowl of gooseberry mush, and, with these, all the real meat she could hold. A huge, still sizzling slab of broiled, fat buffalo ribs appeared before her on a piece of rawhide, and draped heavily across those ribs lay a streaming sausagelike special treat. It was a buffalo cow's fat small intestine, cleaned and stuffed with choicest tenderloin, tied at the ends to retain the juices, then boiled. [The Teton Sioux and Blackfoot names for this truly gourmet dish have identical meanings—crow guts.] Walks Far drew her knife and fell to eating.

Of course, Walks Far told Red Hoop Woman much of her story. When she told of putting the four young Crows to flight, reenacting some of the parts, it could have been just about the funniest thing the women had ever heard. Her revelation that Sun had given her a Sun-stone (was it only this morning?) appeared to be the most awesome thing they had ever heard. They were clearly awed to be in her presence. They kept pressing her for details about one thing and another until she grew so drowsy that had she been at home in her own lodge, she would have declared storytelling time at an end by one of the traditional remarks such as, "Now the dogs are fed and they are scratching their full bellies."

Red Hoop Woman changed the subject at last by saying thoughtfully, "You can make Grandfather's moccasins for him. Like a child, he loses a moccasin somewhere and does not even know it. You can be a great help to us with Grandfather. You can make sure he does not go somewhere without eating any breakfast."

"Where does Grandfather sleep?" Walks Far asked.

"In the small tipi, with my daughter."

One of the women giggled. "That old cousin of a crazy white man will try to crawl in the bed robes with you."

Walks Far laughed and pointed to her belt, saying, "I have a big knife for taking care of any little thing," and was delighted to hear that she must have made the funniest remark ever. This encouraged her to tell a story that Jack Sinclair's wife told so well. The story proved so successful that it was probable that most of the women were hearing it for the first time. Walks Far remembered her mother saying that a good storyteller was as welcome among the Sioux as among the Blackfoot:

It seemed that a Cree boy and a Cree girl were much attracted to each other, but the girl's mother and grandmother watched her closely. The only time she and the boy could exchange a word was when she went for water. They just couldn't stand this, so they made a plan, and in the darkest part of that night the boy slipped under the lodge cover beside the girl's bed. But as he crawled on in under the dew wall, the girl's mother was up very early and lighting the fire into a big blaze! That boy knew he had better say something, and what he said was this: "Has anyone seen my horse in here?"

Chapter Seven
GRANDFATHER'S PEOPLE

(Toward September 1874)

Foremost among matters Walks Far found amusing in her new
life among the Sioux was their attitude toward sex. They
seemed to find it an even more awesome, more terrifying mystery than did the Blackfoot, but the men's advances were no less
insistent.

Unmarried Sioux girls were more carefully watched and
chaperoned than Blackfoot girls. Walks Far was all the more
amused to discover something that her own Sioux mother had
never required. Red Hoop Woman's pretty young daughter,
Fire Wing, was forced to wear an uncomfortable rawhide chas-
tity belt much of the time. Also, some mothers tied their
daughter's legs together at night.

At that age Walks Far had been presented a heavy-handled
quirt of elk antler, exactly like the one used by the handsome
dog soldier to crush her sister's skull. The hope had been that
Walks Far would defend her virginity with the quirt when she
went for wood or water, or to bathe. Walks Far had used her
quirt once, feeling regretful about bloodying the boy's nose so
badly.

During all her life with Red Hoop Woman and Scalps Them,

Walks Far was neither wife nor daughter, and not exactly a sister, though the kindly pair often called her that. Yet, so far as woman's work was concerned, she could have been all of these. Never had she worked harder; rarely had she known anyone who appeared to enjoy work as much as Red Hoop Woman.

Her special charge of looking after Grandfather proved less burdensome than exasperating. In some ways he was like a precocious, irresponsible child, sly and devious, but her exasperation gave way to increasing fondness for the old relic of a warrior. Often he would sit and regard her happily for long periods of time, would even stroke her hair, which was nearly unthinkable for a man to do with other people around.

Once, as she and Red Hoop Woman cut fresh meat to begin the process of making jerky, Walks Far asked, "Is Grandfather your grandfather or great-grandfather?"

"He is my great-great-great-grandfather," Red Hoop Woman said.

Walks Far pondered that; it seemed impossible. "Just how old is he?" she asked.

Red Hoop Woman straightened from her work and answered by signs, stretching them out dramatically—*128 winters!*

Walks Far, from utter disbelief, said nothing. She knew no one lived *that* long.

But by questioning Grandfather as he watched her at work or on the days when he carried his ancient flintlock to guard Fire Wing and herself as they took a dog travois for picking chokecherries or currants, she learned that he could offer a kind of account in support of his claim to such age. In the first place, he had been born when not all the Teton Sioux, moving west under pressure of eastern tribes sooner armed by the white man's guns, had yet crossed the Big Muddy River (as the Sioux called the Missouri). In fact, he had been born only four winters after a party of Brulé, their thighs badly sunburnt from the unaccustomed riding, brought the first horses known to any Sioux subtribe—horses traded or stolen from a southwestern tribe that had built a stock stolen from the Spanish whites in earlier years. Winter counts showed those first Brulé horses to have been acquired 132 years past [in 1742].

Thirty-three summers later, when Grandfather was twenty-nine, he had been with the first party of Sioux to venture westward as far as the Black Hills, which they came much later to call their "meat pack." He had counted forty-six winters when he helped defeat the Rees, thus enabling the Tetons to feel relatively secure west of the Missouri, had been an old man of seventy-seven and had not participated directly in the fighting by which the invading Sioux finally drove the Crows out of the Black Hills.

Walks Far decided to double-check Grandfather's claim. From a freshly killed buffalo she took out the *tampco*, a small section of especially delicious meat embedded in the huge strip of sinew running from shoulder to rump. She carried it to the tipi of old Father of a Mudfish, medicine man of great power, renowned elk dreamer and buffalo dreamer. He had his name, and perhaps his profession, because a wife, who died in the process, had delivered him a stillborn child that looked to the midwives frighteningly like a mudfish.

Father of a Mudfish welcomed the gift. He struck Walks Far as being a brightly intense, shrewd, and solemnly dignified old man, yet one who greatly enjoyed talk, especially if it provided him an opportunity to be slyly whimsical. When Walks Far managed to express diffident curiosity about Grandfather's age, old Father of a Mudfish answered her with a question of his own, and after that he hardly gave her a chance to speak again.

"What person," he asked, "is old enough to doubt the truthfulness of a good man who says he can count 128 winters? You are a lucky young woman to have been captured by Grandfather and taken to Red Hoop Woman's and Scalps Them's tipi. That was the first good thing from your Sun-stone, which I have heard all about. Sun will often show you when to act quickly. There is no need saying that you too will live to be old. But you ought to have a husband and babies! I do not know what is the matter with the young men these days, letting such a hardworking, pretty girl go uncourted. If I had such a pretty young wife, I wouldn't be able to keep from sleeping with her every night. But, as you know, if I were to do that, I could no longer be a medicine man—not until four days after sleeping with a woman—and you would make that impossible!"

Old Father of a Mudfish appeared to admit her to some inner circle because of her Sun-stone, and was suddenly reminded of something: "You have not seen a certain handsome young warrior named Horses Ghost. He has gone away with some other people for a while, but in his vision quest, Horses Ghost was given a pretty but not too uncommon kind of Sun-stone. It is not round, but has many flat sides. A tiny fragment of Sun glints from inside that stone, which is harder than new ice and much easier to see through." [Janet Sinclair was intrigued to discover that throughout World War II, Dewey Elk Hollering had worn just such a quartz crystal containing a fleck of gold in a tiny bag around his neck, and that he still wore it.]

Immediately following this talk Walks Far became conscious that she was being watched, by—of all things!—a much too elegant and willowy young man. His long braids were beautifully done, he had painted his cheeks with vermilion, precisely as a girl would paint them. His fingers and his ears were loaded with trade-silver rings, and he wore a woman's dress. He was a *winkte*. He lived a little apart in a tipi of his own, and he may have adopted his way of life less from homosexual inclination than from a boyhood frailty or sensitivity that made him unable to compete successfully with other boys in the harsh training of a warrior people. *Winktes* were tolerated, derided, yet feared, too, because they were believed to be persons who possessed mysterious powers. There was even a small mystery in the fact that they, though by no means exactly women, excelled at tanning skins and produced the finest quillwork and beadwork.

The *winkte's* gaze frightened Walks Far, but she felt reluctant to mention the matter to anyone, even when, after a few days, she caught him slyly arranging two small twigs in the form of a cross upon one of her footprints. She rushed at him, but had the good sense at the last moment not to strike him with the wet stinking hide she happened to have in hand. Still, she told him in the strongest Sioux she knew, plus stronger Blackfoot, what she would do if he cast any of his spells on her: "I will make you even less of a man than you are."

He backed away, the twigs in hand, as he gave her a bold and beautiful smile that was also frightening. Walks Far likewise backed away, still railing at him as she angrily swished the wet hide over the ground and erased her tracks from the dust. "If I find you following me again," she warned him, pausing to touch the knife at her belt, "somebody is going to come after you without waiting for a dark night to sneak into your tipi. Somebody who knows how real stallions are gelded."

Then, on an evening when she had been so put out with Grandfather as to scold him more than she had ever dared to do before, he went out into the dusk, wearing for once what appeared to be a chastened look. But in a short while he came back carrying an ordinary, unpainted "Indian suitcase" or parfleche. He took his usual place, watching her with the familiar childlike happiness. After some time he spoke:

"I have found an old parfleche, but inside it is a very useful bag of the kind made to hold all the best things there are. I give them both to you."

Walks Far took the parfleche and untied it, unfolded the envelopelike flaps. Her heart skipped! She gave a small, almost wounded cry—that dress! finer than any but the richest of women might expect to own in a lifetime. Beautifully made of superbly tanned antelope skin, it was a trifle more formfitting than a Blackfoot dress. The heavy fringes from the underside of the sleeves hung all the way down to the squared hem, which was finished with short fringing. Just above the hem, a hand-wide band of quillwork matched the coloring of the other, wider quillwork band running across the shoulders and down the three-quarter-length sleeves. Equally fine stiff cylindrical leggins such as Sioux women wore were included, along with exquisite moccasins—and now she knew! That *winkte* had only been measuring her footprint! He had spent days carefully cutting all those fringes, dyeing all those quills, softening them in his mouth, then flattening each one by drawing it out between his teeth just before he applied it.

There was more to *winkte*-made dresses than their mere beauty and their indication of wealth. They clothed their owners in a vague magic that was a kind of good medicine. Walks Far felt uncommonly humbled by the gift.

"Why do you give me this dress, Grandfather?"

"Because you are maybe prettier than my first-time wife, and because you are much easier to get along with. Your mind does not often get beyond itself."

That was a Sioux way of saying that she seldom grew angry —and Grandfather went on, "But what is this crazy talk about a dress? I said I was giving you a bag of the kind that holds all the good things there are. That is just what I have done."

Even allowing for irony in the part about her mind not getting beyond itself, no man had ever said such generous and gallant things to Walks Far. She wondered if she'd ever find a man who would. She wondered, too, how Grandfather could possibly have paid or traded for that dress. Aside from his flintlock, powder horn, and bullet bag, he owned absolutely nothing except a change of breechclouts, the bedraggled eagle feather in his hair, the knife and drinking horn at his belt, and the pair of ordinary, plain moccasins she had made for him. Later, however, she would see that Grandfather had the power of getting whatever he might want from people, merely by the asking.

Receiving that gift from Grandfather seemed to establish Walks Far as a thoroughly accepted member of the family, however ambiguous her precise position in it. Previously, they had treated her very well, but had provided only those things necessary to make her comfortable and presentable and to make her work effective. But now she became the beneficiary of what seemed an almost competitive giving, though of course none of the items approached the dress in richness and splendor. She did not neglect to beg another delicious *tampco* from Red Hoop Woman and send it to the *winkte*.

So, Walks Far suddenly felt that she was accepted, was a part of a Sioux family, a family without beginning and without end, wherein even the parents of son-in-law or daughter-in-law were as closely included as were cousins, endless kinds of cousins, each distinguished by different terms and forms of address, as were all sorts of other relatives. Members of the preceding generation, even though they might be younger in years, should be spoken to in respectful terms. Walks Far dwelt in constant apprehension about using the wrong form. Though Blackfoot family organization and customs were rather similar, with many of the same general rules, rules strictly forbidding any communication between mother-in-law and son-in-law and even circumscribing communication between mother-in-law and daughter-in-law, Walks Far found it a strain to behave properly with "relatives" she had not grown up knowing, particularly when the family system provided no end of complexities, nor of these relatives. Moreover, an oddity of the Sioux tongue added to her strain, for the usual mode of speaking required a person to indicate approval, disapproval, or indifference to actions mentioned; and this fact could create hazards for a person not yet sure of the proper forms.

These Sioux! Sometimes they amused her. Though they were ready as Blackfoot to encourage and reward individual worth, Walks Far soon learned from Red Hoop Woman that great value was placed upon the fact of birth into an important family, so much so that, as Red Hoop Woman believed, even Red Cloud, great Oglala chief and warrior-statesman though he might be, would never quite "belong." "And that Oglala fighting chief named Crazy Horse," Red Hoop Woman confided, "comes from a family I never thought amounted to much."

Walks Far could hardly have misunderstood the warning Red Hoop Woman delivered the second day they spent working together. "I believe I am lucky to have you in my tipi and helping me," Red Hoop Woman said. "And you are lucky to have fallen in with one of the very best and most important families of Hunkpapa Sioux."—Walks Far was more grateful than impressed about that—"You should always remember," Red Hoop Woman went on, "that no woman of this family has ever given cause for so much as one whisper of gossip about her virtue. I myself might slice off the nose of any woman who brought dishonor to my family and my tipi! Women of this *tiyospe* will always live in the old Lakota way, just as the men of this *tiyospe* will never allow the white man, the *wasichu*, to drive us onto one of his reservations."

Walks Far knew that *tiyospe* meant the band, in this case made up largely of two huge interrelated families, and that in some ways it was more important than family because its members worked first for the good of the band and secondarily for themselves. It was the unit that made the often harsh life possible. The band made its living and traveled together, hunted together, and worked together. Much as among the Pikuni Blackfoot, when Walks Far began to think of home here among the Teton Sioux, she might think not of Red Hoop Woman's tipi but of the band with its "circle" of welcoming tipis. [Walks Far explained to Janet that a number of the *tiyospes*, or "bands," made up a subtribe (Walks Far's new people were of the Hunkpapa subtribe), and they and six other subtribes constituted the Teton Sioux or Lakota division. These Tetons alone were more numerous than all three Blackfoot divisions together and the Sioux numbers were increased still further by the Santee (or Dakota) and the Yankton (or Nakota) divisions.]

Walks Far soon learned that just as nothing of much importance happened without Red Hoop Woman's sanction, Red Hoop Woman missed hardly any little thing that went on. Scalps Them, with his ankle nearly mended, unexpectedly relapsed into invalidlike behavior, constantly demanding that Walks Far bring him water, help adjust his willow-wand backrest, or massage his leg. He seemed to smoke more, too, and

70

constantly called her from work to bring a glowing coal from the fire to light his pipe. He would then speak gratefully to his "sister," stretching out the conversation while looking at her in such a way as to suggest that his thoughts were not brotherly at all.

Walks Far received another message from Red Hoop Woman. This message, as was often the case, began obliquely, yet it led to something clear and definite. Red Hoop Woman delivered it while the women of the family had their supper, after the men were fed. She began in a conversational, almost gossipy style and as though prompted by some rambling thought about Buffalo Berry Woman, wife of Scalps Them's foolhardy younger brother.

"I have always liked Buffalo Berry Woman very much," Red Hoop Woman said, "but I certainly hope that our crazy brother doesn't get himself killed. For much as I like Buffalo Berry Woman, I don't want Scalps Them to take her for second wife, as our Sioux way requires—unless, that is, someone else wanted her and she was willing.

"My father had my mother and her sister. We were happy in our tipi," Red Hoop Woman mused on, "but for at least so long as I am able to do a woman's work—and I can go on doing the work of two women for a long time yet—I will *never* have another wife in *my* tipi. . . ."

Walks Far got the message, feeling that Scalps Them would, without a doubt, receive much the same. At any rate, she had no desire to be anyone's number-two wife again. Though, in a way, she had loved Finds the Enemy, she was determined that her next husband would be of her own generation—a young man.

Red Hoop Woman was going on in a kind of digression about the white people: "I have heard that even their great chiefs get along with one wife only. That is something to be said for the whites. But I am glad I was not born a white woman. Very far away to the southeast I once saw some white women—poor, bony, pale creatures who clearly do not get enough meat to eat. Most of them seem to have too many babies, too, which, as I have heard, they almost drown in cold water when they name them. And they have to live in those gloomy houses, maybe no worse than Mandan houses, but *isolated* and *lonely!* Just imagine no other people, having only a man to talk to for days on end. . . ."

71

Suddenly Walks Far realized that Red Hoop Woman had returned to simpler matters, to the immediate future. "Fall hunting is almost upon us," Red Hoop Woman said. "There will be no end of work, no rest until Cold Maker comes from the north and freezes the buffalo hides too hard for dressing. Then, before the White Wolf—the blizzards of real winter—comes howling down over this open prairie land of bitter alkali water, we will move south to a fine sheltered camp on the Tongue River at least, though I prefer the Black Hills. Game is always plentiful there in winter. The valleys give shelter to people and horses. Grazing is good, the creeks run clear, their waters sweet, and there is all the firewood anyone could possibly use.

"Many bands will be camped there, in other valleys less than a short day's ride apart. Ah! the visiting, the winter games, and the dancing—plenty of young men eyeing the likely girls and thinking of taking a wife in the spring. Of course, though, there never are enough young men." [Walks Far explained to Janet that constant warfare among the plains tribes caused adult females to outnumber adult males. Blackfoot and Crow women were said to have outnumbered their men by a ratio of about five to three. The difference was possibly a little less among the Teton Sioux.]

"I will certainly see to it," Red Hoop Woman declared, "that our Walks Far is not overlooked by anyone who is worthy. Next spring will see you well married, with a tipi of your own, if I know anything about it. Meanwhile, we should all keep our minds on just one thing—getting ready for winter. Why, when I think of all the winter's food supply, all the buffalo robes to be dressed for Scalps Them's trading, I get worried that too few days are left. Scalps Them will soon be hunting again. Sometimes I see that he forgets to limp for us. He is always a sharp trader, but generous with the things he gets. You will have your share. I will see to that, too."

All this made Walks Far smile inside herself. If Red Hoop Woman only knew! Walks Far had quickly concluded entirely on her own that in any circumstances Scalps Them was hardly the man for her. True, he was not too old. He would be vigorous for a long time yet, was obviously able in more than the expected ways, and if a strong man with a face and teeth that made him look remarkably like a grinning, good-humored horse could be handsome, then Scalps Them was handsome. Obviously he was a seasoned warrior and a fine example of the four virtues—bravery, fortitude, generosity, and wisdom—with loyalty overlying them all. He would expect the same from a wife, plus truthfulness and childbearing, and that was only as it should be.

What woman could ask for more? But Scalps Them had proved to be one of those admirable people who are also utter bores—a compulsive talker! If ever he ran down it was only to plan just how to set the stage for another of his eternal puns, the rather elementary play on words that the Sioux, these Sioux especially, appeared to regard as the highest form of humor. Scalps Them never failed to explain his puns carefully, making sure that Walks Far would understand. And such boasting! not only by Scalps Them, but by the other men as well. Walks Far had never heard the like. Though the Blackfoot likewise were a self-confident and arrogant people, who called themselves the "Real People" and often referred to other tribes as the "No-Goods," their individual boasting tended to be more a kind of calculated understatement. [Dewey Elk Hollering and Walks Far were at pains to have Janet Sinclair understand, however, that no "real Indian" would ever allow himself to create the impression that he felt superior to his fellows. Janet was left somewhat confused.]

Walks Far had more than once hardly been able to resist asking Scalps Them if he feared that a period of silence or humility would make him look stupid. She did dare deride him about his count of coups or war honors. "Among the Pikuni," she told him, "only two warriors can count coup in killing a single enemy. Why do the men here allow four coups to be counted in such a case? The enemy must be pretty dead by that time!" She hurried on boldly, "Though the Pikuni take plenty of scalps, they don't make such a big thing of them." And she added a Blackfoot saying, the truth of which she had confirmed in her own experience: "It is harder to steal a good horse than it is to shoot a strong enemy."

Scalps Them was visibly irritated with her. "Yes," he said, "I have also heard that the Pekonies have so little of speech or ideas beyond a few old sayings that nearly all of their talk has to be by signs, which makes them unable to say anything new or important in the dark."

But just now, Walks Far knew she must answer Red Hoop Woman, and of course she would begin with a similar appearance of indirectness. She would tell her a Blackfoot story, one that didn't amount to much as stories went, but it had a whimsical Blackfoot touch and helped form a background for Walks Far's own feeling of being in no great hurry to marry, even had she seen a desirable young bachelor in camp. Soon she was telling Red Hoop Woman:

"Long ago, so long ago that nobody's grandmother remembers, perhaps even before the first Blackfoot people came down the Old North Trail, Blackfoot men and women lived apart, at opposite ends of the same camp. For the women this was a pretty good arrangement, except that the men's part of the camp was always so slovenly and dirty as to be a disgrace. Also, the men were so helpless and so demanding of all kinds of attention, that the women got worn out from having to go back and forth day and night, especially when the men imagined they were sick. Finally the women decided they would have to take the men into their own fine lodges if they wanted any rest and peace. But ever since that happened, with men underfoot all the time, Blackfoot women have been wondering about the wisdom of these long-ago-people grandmothers."

While Red Hoop Woman chuckled over the story, Walks Far added a statement that was not entirely a white lie: "I am looking forward to those winter camps. I am looking for a man who is young enough that I can bring him up the way I want him. A dream has told me I must do that."

Chapter Eight
VISITORS AND STRONG MEDICINE

(September 1874)

There came a morning strangely still and heavily sultry for high northern prairies. The people went about subdued, as quiet in the full day as in the stillness of an evening. Walks Far, too, felt a trifle subdued as she almost lazily scraped the hair from a hide. She let herself think of her sister and their husband a little, but she did not actually dwell on something that was past and ended forever. She lived in the present to a degree that not even her own grandchildren would ever be able to understand. And because she had not been able to mourn her sister and husband properly, she hardly mourned at all.

No doubt she would meet them someday in the Sand Hills up by the Red Deer and South Saskatchewan rivers, the land where Blackfoot dead went to live a shadow life, hunting shadow buffalo, and knowing neither joy nor sorrow. [Walks Far told Janet Sinclair that among the old Blackfoot people she had never heard of a "happy hunting ground."] Here and now was the real life, the only good life. So! Thinking as a Blackfoot, she would hang on to it, make the most of it, stretch it out. "May you live to be old," one Blackfoot would say to another.

Still, Walks Far felt something like guilt. She realized that nearly as much as she missed her husband and and her sister, she missed the fine Snake horse she had left behind. And there was another and quite unexpected thing she missed—the mountains. Although she had never spent a night in the mountains, except when on her horse-stealing raid, the close-set, jagged peaks had so often been there on her western horizon, shining with snow through most of the year. At night, if she were close enough, she could see their sharp black silhouette held raggedly against the stars.

But this Redwater country! Walks Far thought, as she worked. Though as fine for antelope and buffalo as any country Napi had ever created, he must have made it when he was absent-minded about people. In late summer they found the water not of the best, and wood was always scarce. The land itself was all too much the same. Like Red Hoop Woman, Walks Far already felt a little tired of it. . . .

She saw four strangers come riding into camp—two white men and two male Indians whom Red Hoop Woman said looked like Yanktons. Left Hand Bull greeted them, saying to the older white man, "I am glad to welcome you again to my tipi, my friend and brother." The white man answered in almost fluent Sioux, but with a Yankton accent, saying, "I have wanted all summer to visit my good friend and brother, Left Hand Bull." The four pipe carriers and other important men of the camp assembled with the strangers in Left Hand Bull's tipi. Scalps Them hurried in with hardly a limp. The white man made large gifts of tobacco, both the flat kind and the twisted kind, and added small coils of narrow bright ribbon for the important men's wives. All smoked a pipe passed round, and there was much dignified talk, the sharing of news. Soon Left Hand Bull ordered the feast for which he had signaled his wife when the strangers approached. Walks Far, as a girl pretty enough for showing off to strangers, helped serve it.

She came last to the very young white man. He held his knife ready and smiled up at her while sawing off a liberal helping from the hump ribs she bore in skewered on a strong stick. She saw then that he was clearly a mixed-blood like Jack Sinclair, and not much more than a boy. He looked almost too young, she thought later, as she stood outside and listened to the men talk following their heavy meal. The older white man spoke, leading up diffidently to a great hope he held: "My brother, Left Hand Bull, should honor us with a visit to Fort Peck when the fall hunt is over. Bring all the people and let them see the many fine trade things that come so easily and cheaply on the fireboats. Fort Peck, luckily, is not far away for you. I can give much more for good fall robes there, or for good jerky and pemmican, than almost anyone else in this whole country. [Janet Sinclair was somewhat amazed to discover, from examining one of Jack Sinclair's surviving account books, that the trade of a buffalo-hunting Blackfoot family, which included two or three adult males and their several wives, could be worth fifteen hundred dollars a year to the trader.] I want all my Sioux brothers, especially my brother Left Hand Bull and his people to know this."

Walks Far saw the young man come alone from the tipi and go to his fine mare. He spoke to the mare fondly, called her the Blackfoot term for "Sweetie," and continued in fluent Blackfoot soft talk!

Walks Far felt a swift rising warmth, almost a shiver of pleasure.

"Are you Pikuni?" she asked. "Are you mixed?"

The young man smiled. "Yes, I am half. I am the son of Medicine Snake Woman, a Kainah [Blood], and of Alexander Culbertson, one of the first long-knife white traders to come to the Real People. I am Joe Culbertson. Who are you; what are you doing here?"

Walks Far gave him only a brief account. She wanted to hear him talk.

"Do you want to go back?" he asked. "Come with me to Fort Peck. If you wish, I will send a medicine paper to Jack Sinclair to ask if he thinks you should come back."

"No," she said, with a sudden conviction that surprised her a little. "I do not want to go back. I will not go back for a long time."

"I will see you again," he said, with a smile. Taking something from his saddlebag, he hurried back inside the tipi.

Gunshots sounded distantly, muffled in the oppressive air. To the southwest, on the crest of the same low swell of ground from which Walks Far had first viewed the camp, a rider waved a robe, then guided his horse into swift tight circling. A returning war party signaling success! More horses appeared on the ridge, scores of captured horses, and eight more riders. All the riders, two older men, five young men and two boys, had stopped earlier to fix their hair, blacken their faces and paint their bodies for a triumphant entry. They all sang their war songs as they drove their captured horses toward the camp and waved painted sticks from which streamed the scalp locks of enemy slain.

Walks Far had seen similar successful returns of Blackfoot war parties, of young men bringing a wealth of horses along with proof of the bravery necessary for gaining admission or advancement in the warrior secret societies, and of earning gifts needed for acquiring a wife. The older members of the war party were maintaining or adding to their status in the tribe.

There would be general feasting now, and a scalp dance. Walks Far could wear her new dress. A camp that only this morning had contained hardly one eligible young man now seemed to be filling with them. And, in addition to the scalp dance, there would be night dances!

The returning raiders drew close, driving the captive horses at charging speed just beyond the "circle" of tipis and raising a heavy cloud of dust. One young man led what looked like a superb buffalo horse. It equaled in value perhaps fifteen or more of some of the other horses. The herd was turned away in the cloud of dust and brought round again more slowly. Mounted men and boys hurried from the camp to take the herd in charge. The raiders rode closer. They shouted their names, announcing their deeds while riding twice along the row of tipis. The young man who had led the buffalo horse cried out:

"I am One Horn. I killed two enemies. I took their horses. At night I led a buffalo runner from a big camp of the Crows and visiting Nez Perce. I did all this without my *kola.*"

One Horn was in ecstasy! His eyes looked crazed, and Walks Far saw a white foam of saliva giving odd prominence to the wide mouth in his blackened face. She knew the word *kola* could mean far more than "friend." As One Horn had just used it, it meant "a life-long, sworn partner in war, in hunting, and in all else."

The raiders dismounted at the meeting lodge, where the visitors from Fort Peck stood half forgotten. Relatives and friends ran to hug them. Others ran to kill young dogs and puppies for the pot, and one shouting woman was seeking to borrow jerked buffalo tongues for a feast in honor of her son. One of the pipe carriers offered a pipe to the four directions, to the mother earth, and to the all-enclosing sky, then pointed it to each member of the war party, including the boys.

"Tell us the truth, Feather Earrings," Left Hand Bull said to the leader, then warned, "You are talking through the pipe, my brother."

Feather Earrings, a small, wiry, mature man, recounted the story clearly and simply, saving details and embellishment for later tellings, and related precisely what each member of the party had accomplished. There had been nothing really exceptional about the venture except in the measure of its success. "It took us a long time to find a Crow camp," he said, "but then we found one, not only Crows but Slit Noses from beyond the mountains—a very large camp—and the Crows and Slit Noses were dancing together. They had only two guards for all their horses. We killed them with knives, and they did not cry out. We slashed their throats in the Sioux way so that those who lost their horses would know who had taken them.

"We saw no one chasing us," Feather Earrings went on. "But only the second day after stealing the horses we ran right into another war party of five on foot. We think they were Flatheads, or maybe Pend d'Oreille. They were resting and smoking just over the top of a little hill and not watching out. We shot three of them right there and rode the other two down when they tried to run. As you see, all of us have returned." Here Feather Earrings allowed himself a shadow of a smile, "But as you can also see, Little Hand now has a big hand and a sore hand from being shot through the left hand!"

The party had counted a total of twenty-four coups on enemies killed. Feather Earrings was able to say, by consulting a small bundle of tiny sticks taken from a wrapping at his belt, just who had earned precisely what coup, including those earned by taking horses. As he finished, he asked, "Have I told the truth?"

Each member of the war party said separately and clearly, "You have told the truth."

The pipe carriers spoke. "You have done good deeds," they said, and Left Hand Bull repeated their words.

Walks Far saw the raiders relax, now that the formalities were over. They threw their scalp sticks to one or another of their sisters or female cousins who crowded around, and they received new moccasins in return. Feasting and dancing could begin almost immediately, to go on all night, possibly through four nights. The raiders might give away horses and themselves receive many valuable presents. Parents would give away all kinds of things, including horses, in honor of their successful sons.

But Walks Far and all the people had been growing increasingly aware that the celebration would be interrupted. For, in the short space since the war party's heralding gunshot sounded, the sunlight had turned a sickly yellow, and a huge black cloud, the blackest Walks Far could remember, had followed the war party in from the south. That cloud swiftly darkened all the sky, blacking out the sun and bringing the mutter and crash of thunder. At best a thunderstorm with only hail, at worst a prairie cloudburst was on the way.

People shouted and ran every which way. Women screamed orders at their men, who hastily pounded more stakes around the circumference or at the center anchor pins of the tipis, then closed them against a wind certain to come. Walks Far heard a whispering rustle from distant, untrampled grass; and on someone's tipi a loose smoke ear snapped like a rifle shot.

She looked to discover what kind of medicine old Father of a Mudfish would make, only to see him wildly busy like any ordinary person in the process of trying to get his tipi secured. Walks Far rushed toward the center of the camp, taking out her Sun-stone as she ran. She raised it in the direction of Sun and began to pray, chanting the prayer in a high-singing voice and falling entirely into Blackfoot.

A wall of dust, a roaring, incredible wind struck her, tore her breath away, and knocked her down, left her half dazed and cowering. A dog, curled up like a ball, rolled toward her. Suddenly he stopped rolling, found his feet, and ran away yipping in terror. But she could *hear* that dog! The wind was already past, already dying. Lightning flashed and shook the earth, but instantly she was on her feet, her voice lifting again to a high chant in Blackfoot. Hailstones large as wild plums pelted her, bruised her. She prayed to the Thunderbird, as well as to Sun; she implored the Thunderbird to rope the hail and rain, to use his lariat and drag the storm away. The huge hailstones stopped falling before the ground was even covered and big raindrops fell, just barely enough to settle the dust.

Miraculously, Sun burnt a hole through the black cloud and sent down a wide shaft of washed light shining over the whole camp, while all around, a stormy darkness remained and the hail, then the rain, pounded the rest of the prairie in such a cloudburst that the water could not readily drain away.

Old Father of a Mudfish came to help her now, singing and beating a drum. Some other people were singing or smoking pipes and blowing puffs to the sky spirits as they joined in chanting prayers. Suddenly Walks Far heard shouted Blackfoot: *"Akatsis, akatsis!*—the rain roper! You have brought him here." Joe Culbertson then called out to all the people in his strangely pronounced Sioux: "Look! The Pekony woman has brought the rainbow—two of them!"

She turned and saw the two beautiful arches with wonder, though without surprise. She also saw that half or more of the tipis were blown down, their covers and furnishings strewn out by the wind. To the north, and within easy sight both east and west, the sky still held black while the rain poured down. But in the camp area, nothing was more than a trifle damp, and the afternoon air held the quality of any pleasant summer evening. Her Sun-stone glinted its great power from her palm. Old Father of a Mudfish, beating his drum and still singing, danced a shuffling circle four times around her. She quickly put the powerful object away.

Still feeling the daze of her own power, she was aware that Joe Culbertson had come close and was speaking to her.

"I think they will give you a fine present," he said, then added the strangest, most absurd statement she had ever heard spoken in good Blackfoot, "If they do not give you a present, *I am going to put a bug in somebody's ear.*"

She looked at him closely. He appeared to be serious, entirely in earnest, so that she wondered if he were a little crazy.

The blown-down tipis were up again within less than the space of time required to light-butcher a buffalo, and the camp returned to normal, except for the excitement in the air. Also, the coulees ran bank-full of foaming yellow water, adding to the flooding torrent already pouring down Redwater Creek. The white men, with their curiously hurried comings and goings, would have to stay the night, whatever they had intended.

Chapter Nine

GIFTS AND SCALP DANCING

(September 1874 continued)

One Horn had given his scalp stick to Suzy, his only unmarried cousin, and Suzy invited Walks Far to a night dance, a rather formal social affair for young people to be held within a few days, after the dance-until-morning dancing, or scalp dance, was over. [Walks Far assured Janet Sinclair that these scalps were not "bloody things" at all, for as One Horn and the others rode home singing their victory songs, they had rubbed grease and vermilion into the flesh, crudely tanning it and reddening much of the hair as well as the flesh. If not too hard-pressed by pursuers, warriors might even stretch the scalps within little wooden hoops. Walks Far also explained that scalps were ordinarily thrown away following the scalp dance, though a man might ornament his clothing or his bridle with them.] Suzy let Walks Far hold the scalp stick with its two small disks of human flesh and the long locks of hair. To Suzy and to Walks Far these scalps were far more than victory trophies. For, though they came from the dead, they symbolized life; and the human spirit, as everyone knew, was especially related to a person's hair. Moreover, the fact that these particular scalps came from vigorous men was not without a kind of vague sexual connotation.

This was explicit in the genitals that Little Hand had brought back from the man who had wounded him.

Walks Far liked Suzy, with her odd and meaningless name, and the pair of them often worked and skylarked together. Suzy was full of fun. She alone among the girls and young women in camp—despite feet large as a man's—gave Walks Far real competition in a foot race. Suzy counted about sixteen winters. She was what white people would have called "adopted," though the Sioux hardly thought of her in that way. Except for her big feet, with hands to match, she was a tall, slender, rather pretty girl. Her hair was straight, almost as dark as Indians' hair, though finer. She had eyes blacker than Indian eyes, for they lacked the common brown flecks in the pupils, and also the encircling ring. Sun and wind had burned her skin darker than that of some of the people, but where the sun did not reach, she was shockingly white.

Red Hoop Woman had been able to tell Walks Far only a little about Suzy, only that about twelve or thirteen summers past, to the east of here, the people had encountered a travel-worn, hungry band of Santee Sioux, almost all of them on foot. The Santees said they had fought a big war with the whites—the *wasichu*—in Mini-so-ta. The whites had won the war.

The people fed the Santees, then gave them food and horses, and when the Santees moved on, they could give nothing in return except Suzy and her twin sister, Lizzy. That was all, except that Lizzy had died after a little while, which, as Red Hoop Woman believed, was almost to be expected of one child in any set of twins.

Suzy remembered two words of white-man speech, "no-no" and "hot-hot." Now, her cousin had won great honors, had made their family considerably richer in horses and, in fact, had given Suzy a horse of her own, as well as the scalp stick.

Walks Far was in her tipi, blackening her face and putting on her new dress and moccasins in preparation for the scalp dance when she heard a small buzz of voices from outside, the sound of a picket pin being driven, then Left Hand Bull's voice clearly announcing, "I give this horse; I give it to Walks Far Away Pekony Woman who has a Sun-stone."

He was gone by the time Walks Far got outside. Though she felt excited and grateful on seeing a fine, strong, gentle horse that was not too old, she also saw it to be one which would win no races. She well knew that with such a good horse and her beautiful dress, she was already far richer than some of the women in camp. She had had no expectation of receiving a horse, but having been given one, she could not quite still her regret that it was only a squaw pony. Left Hand Bull's wife told her the horse was called Badger, for a reason she did not know.

She left Badger picketed for all the women to admire or envy, and leaving off the ugly leggins, she hurried toward the dancing. Suzy, with eyes kindled by excitement as she held the scalp stick high, made room for her to join the other girls in their shuffling dance, moving sidewise round and round a circle to the powerful rhythm of rattles and a drum, and to the rhythm of the girls' own singing. That rhythm would have been hardly different in any other Plains Indian camp, and the girls sang it with one clear voice or another rising to lead:

"Hi-ya—ah-he—hi-ya—ah-he—*hah!*
Eh-he—oh-he—ya-ya—eh-he—o-*he!*
Ya-ya—hi-ya—hai—*hai!*
Yi-ya—hi-ya—hi-ya—*hah!*"

In the center of the circle, around the fire and the four beaters at the drum, the men who had counted coups sang their own songs, occasionally breaking into leaping or heads-up stooping, their sinuous bodies gleaming with sweat, as they stamped and whirled to the rhythm of the drum and the girls' singing. The stars came out, and the dancing went on and on, with the leaping, nearly naked bodies of the young warriors looking wilder and more lithe as the firelight brightened. Girls with scalp sticks generously gave all their friends an opportunity to carry them for a little while.

It was a fluid affair in which dancers and onlookers alike might turn for a time to the giving of presents, drift away to rest awhile, or eat at some tipi offering a feast. It was in such a pause that One Horn came up, and without ever looking at Walks Far, asked Suzy, "Who is this pretty stranger in the fine dress whom I saw carrying my scalp stick?" He was paint-smeared and sweating, but handsomer than at first sight. Walks Far could smell him, but found the smell not unpleasant.

Suzy explained Walks Far as though she were not there, and One Horn said, "You can tell her she can kick my moccasin if she wishes." By this he conveyed his willingness to have Walks Far choose him as partner at some social dance. He went back to the men, but she caught him looking at her more than once that night.

During another lull in the dancing Joe Culbertson came up smiling to Walks Far and Suzy. He produced a dirty white stick, about finger length, with red and green stripes spiraling around the white, then broke it into three pieces.

"Here is something you will like," he said in Sioux, and putting one piece in his mouth, he added, "But it is not to be swallowed."

The two girls soon agreed that it tasted even better than white man's sugar and it lasted longer.

Joe smiled at Suzy and said, "I think you are the kind of person who would look to white people like one of their pretty girls. You do not look just like a Sioux to me."

Suzy giggled at him, and he tried talking with her in a strange language filled with those difficult sounds so often included in white mens' names until Suzy laughed aloud. "You are making crazy talk. I am Lakota—Sioux."

Joe did not press the matter, but he had a teasing comment in Blackfoot for Walks Far, "I think that someone is no longer a Pikuni. I can see that she has already become a cut-throat Sioux, even though she prays in the language of the Real People!"

Walks Far borrowed Suzy's words, saying, "I am Lakota."

"Of course," he said. "And you have a Lakota horse! Also a Lakota dress, a beautiful dress, but without any elk teeth on it, as a beautiful Blackfoot dress would have."

"I am more than satisfied," she said.

"I can see you are." And I can see you are not thinking that five of those scalps could be Pikuni."

She could only repeat to him what she had just said: "I am Lakota."

"A cut-throat Sioux, with Jack Sinclair's knife," he went on. "I knew that knife when you brought me meat in the lodge. There is only one knife like it. I was glad to hear how you got it."

Walks Far felt a little irritated with him. Something about his smiling eyes made her uncomfortable, even in the semidarkness. They were honest eyes, but they missed nothing. She sensed him to be a truly clever person and one who revealed that cleverness in his own good time. Moreover, his hair was cut disgustingly short, much shorter than Jack Sinclair's.

But he had a present just for her, a small package wrapped in oily yellow paper, which was one of the first pieces of paper she had ever touched.

"It is an Arkansas stone for that fine knife," he said. "It sharpens much better and more easily than does a stone from the creek. That 'printing' on the 'paper' says that you must put water on the stone when you are sharpening, and afterward you must wash the stone well."

Walks Far unwrapped the small package carefully, feeling half fearful of the powerful white man's medicine that could turn words and thoughts and messages into those little squiggles, then hold them there like ghosts before bringing them to life again. The tannish-colored stone was as wide as her three smallest fingers and twice as long. It showed an utter perfection of flatness and squareness—a powerful thing! She rewrapped it carefully in its paper. Sometime afterward, she made a buckskin case to help preserve those mysterious little black markings on the paper for the strong medicine they lent the stone.

Later that night as Walks Far rested again from the dancing, she was relieved to see Grandfather. He had gone off somewhere without breakfast and she had not seen him all day. Now he and the older white man were the focus of intent listeners. Grandfather had given the white man a beautifully quilled pair of saddlebags of the kind called "for putting every possible thing in," and was saying:

"I give this to my white brother, my generous young grandson. I give it because my young white brother and grandson is generous to my people, who all call you their brother. Yes, thank you for this tobacco—such a fine big twist of the best tobacco there is. I will keep it to smoke at a time for remembering my brother, my generous friend. But have you no tobacco that is already cut? I would like to smoke a little of that already cut tobacco with my brother, right now.

"*Hau.* Thank you, my friend and brother. Have you a block of those little sticks that make fire? That is good! I may keep them! Thank you, my generous brother. Because they are but little things, perhaps you can spare another block of them? All my sons and grandsons, all my friends and brothers will thank you. Now they can shoot antelope with their trade guns. They can make caps for the guns from these fire sticks. We starve for antelope. Some of the children and old people with bad stomachs need to eat lean antelope meat."

Walks Far began to be puzzled as to where Grandfather could be leading. The men brought in plenty of antelope meat, which was so lean as to be tasty only when drenched in melted buffalo fat.

Grandfather was still talking. "My people are poor in guns. As you see, I have only this very old flintlock, and though some of the younger men have trade guns that shoot with caps, they have no caps. The fire end of these little sticks will work. It takes a great many. Thank you, my brother.

"I am the Grandfather of all Tetons who hunt between the Big Muddy River and the Yellowstone. I will tell them all how generous you are. By the way, friend, the strings for my hair are poor things. They are dirty. I need a little piece of that pretty ribbon such as you gave for the women. You will see to it? I know you will not forget; nor will I forget to tell all my people to trade at Fort Peck, and nowhere else. All trails will lead to Fort Peck."

Walks Far did not doubt that the white men knew, just as well as she and the other onlookers, that Grandfather had not yet revealed just what he really wanted. She thought that Grandfather was laying it on too thick, however hypnotic his effect on people often appeared.

Now Grandfather returned to the matter of the band's poverty in guns, and Walks Far heard him truly outdoing himself this time. She hurried on to the dancing, but on returning to the tipi at dawn, she saw the glint of yellow metal from the frame of a new Winchester that hung, along with a heavy bag of cartridges, from a tipi pole over Grandfather's pallet bed. In the days to follow there was much speculation in camp about who would be given that gun, but for all anyone could tell, Grandfather had completely forgotten it.

Walks Far had danced all night, but the morning brought work for the women, while the men slept. Scalps Them and Red Hoop Woman would give a feast that night, and Walks Far helped prepare puppies for a feast dish that she did not yet exactly relish, however tender and delicate the white flesh might be.

Water in the coulees ran sufficiently low now that the white men and the two Yanktons decided to travel on. As they rode by, Joe Culbertson laughed and called to Walks Far, "I too have learned to like eating dog. Maybe we are both coyotes." The word he used for coyote, *kis-ee-noh-o*, could be taken literally as "small wolf." It could also be taken as "trickster" or "wanderer," or to suggest that a person was neither this nor that, neither dog nor wolf—a kind of bastard.

Chapter Ten

CRAZY ONE

(Late September 1874)

To Walks Far and to the people, a camp move in summer weather usually held much of the quality of a holiday. Thus, when the camp shifted northward a short day's march down Redwater Creek following the scalp dancing, the holiday spirit definitely lingered.

Walks Far proudly rode a fine new saddle on her newest horse, this one a powerful, skittish, light-colored buckskin with long brown mane and tail. A rich brown stripe ran the length of his backbone and a series of horizontal brown bars showed high on each foreleg. Suzy and Fire Wing rode beside her, Suzy on the horse One Horn had given her and Fire Wing on a pony of her own. Walks Far had earned the new buckskin, and without any obvious help from her Sun-stone. This was a second horse that had belonged to Left Hand Bull.

Riding Badger to water on the day following the cloudburst, she found herself near Left Hand Bull and other people with their horses at the creek bank. Left Hand Bull was giving thoughtful, possibly distasteful, eye to the handsome buckskin, perhaps the best-looking of his many horses. Walks Far simply

ached to own such a truly fine horse once more. Boldy, bra-
zenly, in reckless disregard of convention, she rode a little
closer to Left Hand Bull and called out to him in this public
place, before listeners, as freely as a man might have done:

"That is a very fine horse. He looks like he should have been
trained as a buffalo runner."

Left Hand Bull gave no sign he had heard. Then he decided
to answer, though of course he spoke as if addressing the wind
rather than Walks Far.

"Someone could be right about that," he said glumly. "I was
going to train him, but he is already a five-year-old, too old to
start training for a buffalo runner. And nobody can ride that
horse. He is good for nothing but to win bets from crazy young
men who think they can ride anything."

Walks Far was surprised and disappointed. Then her heart
gave a leap of sudden excitement. She tried to speak casually,
translating the Blackfoot version of a bit of wisdom embedded
in a saying common to all horsemen, a saying that among white
cowpunchers would go: "There's never a man that can't be
throwed, There's never a horse that can't be rode." And Walks
Far went on to say, "If you will catch that horse for me and let
me keep him until four days from today, I will ride him. I will
bet you my horse."

Left Hand Bull did not smile, but there was a kind of smiling
condescension in his voice as he gazed across Redwater Creek
and announced, so that all could hear: "Walks Far Away Pekony
Woman with a Sun-stone, if you can ride that horse for as long
as it takes two dogs to sniff each other at just one end, I will give
you that horse."

The listening men laughed loudly, which inspired Left Hand
Bull to add, "I will also give you a fine saddle. But if you are
going to ride that horse, you must begin by catching him yourself. That horse killed a Cheyenne who tried to steal him."

Then as if the whole matter had been meaningless, or too
trivial for another word, he called to his two young boys, and
they started turning his horses away.

One of Walks Far's young male "cousins" was near, mounted
on his pony, and like an adult buffalo hunter, he had a long
rawhide rope coming back from the pony's halter to end in a
coil tucked under his belt. Walks Far, with her knife already
out, kneed Badger close to him, saying, "Cousin, I will pay you
for this rope." She snatched the coil from under the amazed

boy's belt and cut it, leaving him barely a lead rope's length as she wheeled Badger about and raced in among Left Hand Bull's horses. She fashioned a lariat loop as she went, and got the buckskin roped from less than a horse's length away, with no difficulty at all. How that animal bucked and kicked among the others at the sudden indignity! And, as he screamed in wild-eyed rage, Walks Far suddenly felt small qualms. But she got him free of the herd just as Left Hand Bull raced up shouting his fury.

"You crazy woman. You will kill yourself! If that crazy horse had kicked my bay buffalo runner in the head and broken his jaw, as he almost did, I would have killed you!"

Walks Far could not hang her head; she was too busy. But she said apologetically, if firmly, "I have to know this buckskin's name."

"I call him Crazy One, but he is so crazy that he does not know his name or anything else. You make a pair, you crazy woman. You will see how crazy you are, in four days. *You* go away from here, *now!*"

The young cousin came galloping up with another rope from somewhere. He tried to help Walks Far, but he was a boy of but twelve or thirteen years and obviously frightened by the buck-skin. Yet, together, they managed to get the horse picketed a little distance behind the tipi. By the time Walks Far managed to snub a halfhitch in the picket rope around the big buckskin's nose so that the pain of his fighting the rope would reconcile him to haltered quiet, she had concluded that the name Crazy One was apt.

She abandoned the final nights of scalp dancing and all else to devote herself solely to preliminaries for breaking Crazy One. Red Hoop Woman proved sympathetic, if highly dubious. So, Walks Far stayed with Crazy One almost constantly, sleeping only in short snatches, going again and again to talk sooth-ingly to him. She spoke his name over and over, her hand gently jerking at his picket rope all the while. Except for the name, all other talk was in Blackfoot, for she felt that tongue to be beyond doubt more persuasive with horses than any other, just as Black-foot, next to Cree, was said to be the most effective language a lovesick suitor might use in courting.

Her dead husband, Finds the Enemy, had been a renowned horsebreaker as a young man. When he had been still younger, he had gone with a party of adventuring Blackfoot so far to the

south as to reach the country of those white men called *Espaiyu*
—Spanish." There he had seen and been much impressed by
the infinitely patient slowness and obvious effectiveness of the
way in which the *Espaiyu* prepared the best of their horses for
the final breaking. Finds the Enemy had combined the *Espaiyu*
way with the Blackfoot way.

Walks Far kept Crazy One half starved for both forage and
water, and it was she alone who led him to the creek, who
allowed him to drink just a little and who fed him just a little,
making sure he heard her voice all the while. He soon accepted
the lead rope, but it was a long time before he allowed her to
creep along the rope to his nose, though toward the very last
he accepted a dried cake of sweet berries from her hand. She
pressed her breast to his nose to make sure he knew the smell
of her, borrowed a clean old dress to wear, and finally succeeded in passing her own working dress over his nose, along
his neck and shoulders—yet any effort to condition his back to
the slightest weight only threw him into his rage. He simply
would not tolerate so much as an empty rawhide saddlebag or
even a scrap of robe.

She also tried to get Crazy One accustomed to the young
cousin's voice and smell, and to the crowding closeness of the
boy's pony. That boy had become devoted to her project,
though other boys came and shouted at him teasingly, "Little
Dog, are you going to learn how to ride in a woman's dress? Are
we going to see a girl's pretty little *shan* between your thighs
while you are flying up in the sky?"

Walks Far felt grateful to Little Dog; she would have further
need of him. But for breaking such a horse as Crazy One she
would also need a skillful, fearless rider—a strong man on a
good horse of his own. One Horn rode almost as well as any man
she had seen, and because he had condescended to suggest that
he would not be adverse to having her "kick his moccasin," she
sent Suzy to him the first day with a carefully worded message.

Suzy returned with a discouraging report. Grandfather, who
had made himself an interested spectator to Walks Far's strange
preparations, was there to hear what One Horn had to say.
According to Suzy, One Horn could be extremely funny, and
was the greatest of humorists when he wanted to be. He had
laughed and scoffed as only an able and utterly confident man
who also believed himself to be a humorist could ever do, and
he added, "Not even I have been able to ride that horse. True,

the comes-from-afar woman with a Pekony Sun-stone has indeed stopped the cloudburst, but no one, though nearly every man tries, has ever found medicine with power over a crazy horse like that one. If by chance this woman has discovered such medicine, I will give her my five best horses for it—after I see it work! I have other things to do than make a fool of myself by helping some plainly crazy woman make a spectacle of herself. I will not even bother to watch, unless I run out of things to laugh about."

Suzy thought that Never Talks, her brother, a rather sad-faced boy somewhat older than herself, might help Walks Far. Suzy believed him to be more mature and able than people gave him credit for, though Walks Far might have to promise to give him Badger if she won. The brother could not resist a gamble. Suzy would talk to him.

Walks Far, discouraged but persistent, went on trying her gentling tactics on Crazy One. But only shortly after One Horn's refusal, she was astonished to see him coming up, marching almost like a sullen captive ahead of Grandfather, whose absence she had not even noticed. They stopped, One Horn looking intently at Crazy One and Grandfather giving Walks Far the happiest of his neat-gummed smiles. One Horn could not wholly suppress all the sullen anger in his voice as he spoke, but his words were almost casual, wholly generous, and polite. "Grandfather has said that you would like me to help you win a small bet with Left Hand Bull. I tell you the truth when I say that I would like to see Left Hand Bull lose a bet."

Walks Far guessed every word of this to be quite true, but she also guessed that among the reasons for One Horn's carefully suppressed anger was the fact that, by helping her, he could hardly bet against her. But he continued to speak, turning from her and addressing only Grandfather: "I know exactly what she wants; it will not be necessary for her to show me. Little Dog can bring her the horse I will ride. The woman is welcome to use that horse in all the Pekony medicine making she wants to try. I will come back on the third day, trying to look and smell like a Pekony, if that is what she wants. On the fourth morning, when she gets herself trampled and drowned, it will not be because I have not done my best. Grandfather, you have heard me say this."

He turned his lean back and strode away, a fine example of a tall young Plains Indian warrior. Two white-tipped tail feathers from a four-year-old eagle stood upright behind his head. There was a scar from the sun-dance sacrifice just beneath each of his shoulder blades. Snug around his arms, above a neat pattern of small scars on the biceps, he wore narrow bands from the leg of a deer, with the hair and the two dewclaws left on. A breechclout of blue cloth edged with red flannel flapped disdainfully between his narrow hips, which tapered into the leanest of long legs, slightly bowed.

Walks Far regretted that One Horn would now be furious with her. He was the only man in the camp who could quicken her pulse in the slightest.

She went back to work with Crazy One and became aware that a competent-looking, near middle-aged man whom she knew only by a name—Runs Stooped Over—had joined Grandfather and Suzy to watch. After a while Grandfather called her close and said, "Runs Stooped Over rides as well as One Horn, and he has broken many horses, beginning long before One Horn got his second teeth. He has gained much wisdom about horses. He says he and his relatives would be tickled to see Left Hand Bull lose a bet with a woman, that it is already very funny that Left Hand Bull has made a loud bet with a woman.

"He says that, as everyone knows, most horses can be broken in a day, though a few horses take two days. But he has neither seen nor heard of a horse taking more than a reminder on a third day—that is, if several good horsebreakers have worked on him without giving up. Runs Stooped Over also says that although he doesn't think strange ways of doing things, even Pekony ways, are always crazy, he does think the only way you can be pretty sure of winning within three more days is for him to go get his relatives right now, and start helping you break that horse in the Sioux way."

Walks Far had seen that way, as it was applied to a mean and difficult horse. With two lariats choking the horse's wind, it was allowed to fight the ropes for a while. Then, after one of the ropes was made to entangle the horse's feet, it was tripped to the ground with a quick, hard jerk. One man sat on the horse's head while other men hobbled the forelegs and tied them to one hind leg. Some man, not necessarily the eventual rider, settled himself in something like a rider's position, and the man who had been sitting on the horse's head jumped clear. The horse sprang up, but its hobbles threw it again.

This was repeated until the horse stayed down from utter

exhaustion, whereupon the passing of hands and a robe and the tapping of fists or a quirt handle over the horse's body preceded a folded heavy robe thrown over his back. When the hobbled horse found strength to rise again, he threw off the robe but was instantly tripped by the hobbles. Eventually, exhausted, the horse tolerated the robe, or was simply unable to throw it off. At that point the rider bridled the horse, and while the other men again patted and tapped the horse's body, he mounted. The hobbles were cautiously loosed. The rider, if he stayed on, as was quite possible by this time, walked and trotted the horse and, as the animal recovered, ran him hard, but with care not to wind-break him.

Some horses needed breaking all over again on the second day. Walks Far felt no qualms about the essential brutality of all this, and she might have welcomed the offer by Runs Stooped Over had he appeared before Grandfather brought One Horn. But she politely declined, and Grandfather seemed to approve. She was determined now to ride Crazy One in her own way. ["Hi'm give people good show. Hi'm get that One Horn plenty wet, plenty muddy same tam Hi'm win fine horse," she told Janet and Dewey.]

By noon of the third day Crazy One was accepting her and tolerating her touch on his neck, shoulders, and withers without having been thrown and snubbed. He also accepted a folded robe slid back to his withers so long as her hand was there. But when she backed away, he instantly bucked off the robe. One Horn was as good as his promise. He came and said no word to Walks Far, but he worked long and patiently with her and Little Dog and with Crazy One, letting Crazy One know his voice, his smell, and at last his touch. In the late afternoon, following a prompting from Walks Far conveyed through Grandfather, One Horn and Little Dog each mounted his own horse. With Crazy One crowded close between, they led him across Redwater Creek through the deepest pool they could find, a pool having a muddy bottom and water up to the horses' shoulders. Later, sometime before sunset, they repeated this, and Walks Far was happy to see that on neither occasion was Crazy One much more difficult than any ordinary unbroken horse.

As they all rode back, a remarkable thing happened at the very edge of camp. Crouched there, with the horde of wild camp dogs strangely oblivious, a grinning old coyote that looked oddly familiar to Walks Far almost barred their way, yet neither One Horn nor Little Dog saw him. Walks Far glanced back over her shoulder toward the low sun. That sun seemed to speak to her through her quickening pulse, and she was half surprised to hear her own voice call out clearly, "I am going to ride this horse right now."

People in the nearer tipis heard. They shouted to others. Half the camp abandoned suppers and all came running, calling out last-moment bets.

Little Dog shouted like a warrior eager to charge. "Let's go! —*Hoka hey!*" One Horn spoke directly to Walks Far for the first time, his voice almost pleasant, perhaps a little excited, as he said, "We must make sure Left Hand Bull is here to see this."

Left Hand Bull did not keep them waiting. In full view of all the people One Horn helped Walks Far mount astride behind him. Then, with Little Dog on the left, with One Horn holding a good grip on Crazy One's halter rope close to the lower jaw from the right, and with the remainder of the rope coiled on his arm, they all rode into the muddy creek. Walks Far talked softly to Crazy One all the while.

In shoulder-deep water Walks Far put her hand on Crazy One's neck and cautiously shifted from One Horn's horse to Crazy One's back. Before One Horn could pass her all the rope, and before Crazy One felt all her weight, he jumped and bucked. But of course in plunging his head down to buck, he got his nose under water. He raised his head in a snorting, screaming rage, made a powerful lunge through the roiling water, and tried to buck again, only to soak his head a second time. He'd had enough of that. He lunged wildly, giving Walks Far a busy time in staying on. ["But Hi'm hear people on bank count loud."] A chanted unison: "TEN . . . ELEVEN . . . TWELVE . . . THIRTEEN . . ." Red Hoop Woman's unmistakable voice was already rising triumphantly, shouting to her brother: "Left Hand Bull, two dogs have had plenty of time to sniff each other at *both* ends!"

Later, Walks Far heard how Left Hand Bull had raised an acknowledging hand while giving a generous smile before hurrying back to his supper. Her horse was won! But not yet truly broken. Though Crazy One's humping and frenzied lunging in the muddy water tired him quickly, he bucked again the moment Walks Far rode him out into water sufficiently shallow that he could get his head down. Not until she tried him in shallow water for the third time did a trembling Crazy One tolerate her upon his back.

She rode him then, rode him hard but carefully, resting him

and trying out all his paces between the harder runs. One Horn had simply disappeared, but the boy, Little Dog, followed until she sent him away with words of gratitude, adding, "As soon as possible, I will let you ride this horse the length of the camp for all the boys and everyone else to see."

She wished to be alone for thrilling to the power and beauty between her knees. This horse was one from the most beautiful tribe of animals Napi ever created. She raced the long shadow she and Crazy One now threw across the prairie in the sunset. She composed a new riding song, and in singing it to the evening air, she had never felt more alive and wild and free. But proud and thrilled by now as she might be at owning Crazy One, Walks Far was much too wise to develop exquisite love for any horse. A good rider and a spirited horse might achieve a mutual fondness, but it would be only from having established a kind of truce, one in which respectful enemies yet know better than to wholly trust each other. [However, Walks Far spent more time, and seemed to enjoy the recollection more, telling Janet and Dewey about this horse than about any other event or character in all her long story. "Nobodies of Hunkpapa seen Indian woman 'ave better horse, those gone tams," the aged Walks Far declared in enduring satisfaction and pride.]

Exactly as she had judged they would do, Crazy One's powerfully muscled hindquarters and short, strong back gave him great propulsive power, so that he broke quickly into full speed, yet the lightness and handiness of his forequarters enabled him to swerve nimbly, to make sharp turns and check quickly like the best of swift buffalo runners. Added to this, his good feet, and legs with fair length of limb, promised a racing speed perhaps equal to that of her lost Snake horse. Yet that exciting possibility made Walks Far feel a trifle disloyal and guilty, the more so because she found that Crazy One carried his head in a more desirable way. Her Snake horse always kept his head beautifully but irritatingly high, while Crazy One ran with his head low, exactly as a good hunting horse or war horse should.

She rode on into the cooling prairie, alone and careless of any lurking war parties. In deepening dusk she returned to the creek, dismounted, and splashed water on Crazy One before rubbing him down with handfuls of grass and turning him loose but hobbled into the camp herd.

She would probably need to mount him in the creek again tomorrow, but Little Dog alone should be enough help then.

Now, with rope coiled on her arm, she hurried into camp, running in the fast flat-footed trot of any moccasined young woman. She was tired and mud-splashed, hungry too, but a very proud young woman of some wealth.

Red Hoop Woman, with a crowd of women and girls still excited and gleeful over her triumph, welcomed her home. "Someone who has hardly eaten for four days has a feast waiting for her," Red Hoop Woman called out. "The women are rich from winnings, though old Father of a Mudfish is richest of all, for he bet everything on you."

The famished Walks Far felt at first as though she could consume the whole feast by herself. For a while she enjoyed the women's talk and jokes at the expense of men in general, as well as of One Horn and Left Hand Bull. "One Horn was so wet and sulky," Suzy's mother said, "that my husband was almost afraid to compliment him on now knowing as much about fish and frogs as about horses and women!"

Buffalo Berry Woman giggled in relating: "Runs Stooped Over pretended to feel sorry for Left Hand Bull. He brought in an old, broken-down, stringhalted mare, found a broken saddle to put on it, and sent one of his youngest nephews to picket that poor old piece of wolf bait in front of Left Hand Bull's tipi!"

Walks Far found all this and much more amusing and highly gratifying at first, but after a while she unexpectedly felt irked. Clearly, the women were finding her triumph so very funny, precisely because, in any large sense, they thoroughly accepted the limitations imposed by the woman's role. To Walks Far the triumph lay almost entirely in the fact of having Crazy One for her own. She had never really doubted she could ride him, given the proper chance, and when she had known for sure, after seeing Coyote, that she would do it, she had lost the excitement of gambling, for she risked nothing. Though she felt good remembering Coyote, she also felt frustrated and lonely, particularly so after Feather Earrings's wife laughingly told her, "Now One Horn and other young men will not know just what to make of you."

Later that night, with Grandfather snoring away in the darkness, Walks Far in her own bed formed a kind of vague resolution to behave more properly in the future. Still, she would not have passed up such an opportunity as riding Crazy One had offered for anything. She felt sleepless, stimulated as though from dancing with some very exciting man she had chosen, and before she was able to sink suddenly into mindless peace and sleep, she had solaced herself with a bit of Blackfoot woman's wisdom: "It is easier to find a good man than a good horse; no horse ever chased a woman."

Chapter Eleven

THE SMALL-BUILT ONES

(End of September 1874)

So it happened that when the camp prepared to move on a crisp bright morning with a hint of fall already in the air, Walks Far was the owner of two good horses, yet there were people in the band who owned only a single poor travois horse, and at least one family owned no horse at all. Walks Far herself would own less material wealth before that day was over.

The planned move had been announced the day before by a singing herald, and during the evening the women had done much packing in readiness. Thus, when Left Hand Bull's tipi cover was loosened in signal, all the tipis came down, travois and horses were packed, and the band got on the move in less time than it would take to burn dry firewood down to a small bed of coals. Scouts led the way, police societies guarded the flanks and rear. No one was permitted to hurry ahead or linger behind or go off on his own to hunt. People traveled more or less in the order, starting from the east, in which their tipis had been pitched. Many of the people—more people than among the Blackfoot, Walks Far thought—traveled afoot, including quite a number who owned horses.

Definitely separated at the rear, but well ahead of the rear guard, marched a party of girls over whom old Father of a Mudfish had performed a very necessary ceremony, and for a highly practical reason. For, if normal camp procedures with respect to these girls had been followed, the band could never have moved. The girls were menstruating. [Janet Sinclair noted that Walks Far absently let this detail slip, and that for all the old woman's utter frankness of thought and language about other things, including sex in general, she absolutely refused any further comment on this matter.]

Just before the tipis came down that morning, Walks Far, whose admiration for the Winchester hanging over Grandfather's bed had developed into covetousness (though without any real expectation that he would give it to her), suggested to Grandfather that he might wish her to carry it and the bag of ammunition on her horse. She saw Grandfather's face take on an expression as though he had completely forgotten the gun, and her hopes rose, particularly when his face abruptly brightened at her to say, "I knew that I intended to make a present to someone! Perhaps I am no longer calm in my mind."

That last statement was a way of wondering if he might be growing senile. She assured him he was not, and he smiled at her happily and gratefully, then asked her to bring the gun and cartridges to him. When she put them in his hands, he announced, "This gun is for Bobtailed Horse. He is a good young man who has a good young wife, but they have had much bad luck and are now very poor. Perhaps I should find him a good buffalo runner also."

Walks Far, as she watched Grandfather turn away, somehow couldn't help feeling poorer by one fine repeating rifle and a wealth of cartridges. Grandfather had almost led her on, or, possibly, he had been testing her in some way behind that childish grin. She forgot about the whole matter as she harnessed a travois to Badger, the horse Left Hand Bull had presented her the day of the cloudburst. Then, abruptly, Grandfather was back, and if such an ageless man can be said to look less than half his winters, that was the way Grandfather now looked. He spoke to her urgently, with authority, with an oddly gripping and hypnotic quality in his voice. "I want you to give me that horse. No, leave the travois hitched. I must give them both to someone. Come with me."

Walks Far said, "I will give you this horse," and she followed him as though dazed, leading the horse and travois and wondering why he was taking her horse rather than one of Scalps Them's many horses. Grandfather struck off for the opposite end of the camp where one poor, small tipi, alone of all the camp, still stood. A very old woman, one grown too aged and frail for walking, sat on her pallet in the tipi, with food laid out all around her. Grandfather addressed a near middle-aged man, who held two loaded travois dogs on leashes and was shouldering a pack.

"*Hau,* Takes a Cheyenne Lance, why are you leaving your mother here?"

"She has said that we must do this. As you know well, it is our Sioux way." The man paused, then spoke strongly, "We have no relatives; I will beg no man for a horse when I have nothing."

"I am your grandfather. I give you this horse and travois. This woman will help you take down your tipi and pack your mother on the travois," Grandfather said, and turned away.

Walks Far and Takes a Cheyenne Lance worked swiftly, silently, and there were tears in his eyes and in the eyes of the old woman. Only as Walks Far started to leave did anyone speak. "I know you," Takes a Cheyenne Lance said. "And I know that you have not had this horse very long. I will remember." Then he added, "People say you are a medicine woman, and also a person who always sees happy, and because of that happy things happen when you are around."

Walks Far, in hastening back to help Red Hoop Woman, realized that her good feeling came from the fact that it was *her* horse that had been given away, rather than one belonging to Scalps Them.

In the new camp that evening, after the men had been fed and the women had eaten, and as bedtime approached, Walks Far took small pieces of vining juniper she had rooted up from the ground while on the way. She now built a tiny bright fire in the tipi she shared with Grandfather and Fire Wing. Lighting a twist of fragrant sweet grass, she chanted and smoked out any bad spirits who might have been enclosed while setting up the tipi, then chanted thanksgiving, and followed it all with a singing prayer. Though she chanted and sang very softly, Grandfather surprised her somewhat by adding a high-pitched monotone from where he sat on his pallet bed.

She could not help thinking what a curious and remarkable old man Grandfather was—despite his questionable claim to being 128 years old! Walks Far knew now that in the band was another very old man named Makes As Brothers. He looked as old as Grandfather, but claimed no more than 103 winters. While she was still thinking of this, Grandfather spoke, exactly as though she had been carelessly speaking her thoughts aloud.

"That old Makes As Brothers is growing senile," Grandfather declared, and Walks Far felt a kind of shiver as he went on, "He tells people he can count one hundred and three winters. But I know that he is no older than the youngest son of my own grandson's second wife. Those two boys went with a war party when they were both twelve years old. He is eighty-seven, no more. It must be that he is no longer calm in his mind, to forget that I am still here to remember."

Grandfather finished with such a laugh that Walks Far felt compelled to look at him, and what she saw then gave her bigger shivers. Grandfather's eyes were not human eyes; they caught the firelight and reflected it from glowing depths, just as did an animal's eyes! And not only that—Coyote sat there grinning at her! Walks Far clapped her hand over her mouth and averted the eyes she quickly closed. She was filled with a kind of deep awe from having been granted a brief glimpse into profound mystery. By the time she dared look again, Grandfather had taken off his moccasins and was grinning at her in the familiar fond way. His shoulders shook in an old man's silent laughter as he scratched himself before curling to sleep in his buffalo robe. [Janet Sinclair later wrote in her journal, "She related all this to Dewey and me just as anyone might relate a memorable but not particularly extraordinary experience. Dewey seemed to be made a little uncomfortable by it. I suppose he feared I might be scoffing secretly."]

The band moved to the new camp not only because grass for the ponies had been grazed away around the old camp but especially because scouts had located a more favorable position for intensive, organized fall buffalo hunting for the winter's meat supply. In the last of this Yellow Leaves Moon and on through the following Falling Leaves Moon, the buffalo would be at their fattest and best, and because of their fat, they would be somewhat slower running. Later, in the next moon, the Hairless Calves Moon, or Frost Moon, some people would seek hides for tipi covers, though Walks Far believed those taken in midsummer, when the hair was short and the hides were thus more easily prepared, served just as well. Late in that same moon hunting primarily for robes might begin; but the best robes were not taken until the Sore Eyes Moon, which followed. Then the hair was most silken, fluffy, and thick.

To Walks Far and to the people, not all the buffalo, even those of the same age or sex, looked alike. At hardly more than a glance she could differentiate their age with at least ten names, seven of these applying to animals of four years or less. She could give another seven names to the typical variants among buffalo as distinguished by coloration and build, and also by apparently inherited traits, such as hair length, shape of horns, or size of head.

She had only to look at rendered buffalo fat to know the approximate age of the animal from which it had come. She knew that all the kinds of buffalo were good for something and she knew what each of them was best for. For good eating her first choice was a four-year-old cow taken in the fall, though bulls of the same age or younger, taken in midsummer, were almost as good. In Sioux, she called either of these a "small-built one" or a "four-tooth." Either cows or bulls of that age were the ones most sought by robe hunters in winter, when the hair looked like fine fur.

Walks Far's buffalo lore was endless. She knew it was the cows that decided when and where the herd should move. She knew that unlike other animals, and particularly white man's cattle, buffalo often turned head rather than tail to a blizzard; that their blowing in crossing a river created an unforgettable sound, which carried for an astonishing distance. But of all the curious things she knew about the big animals, it was oddest that old bulls mated only with young cows, and young bulls only with old cows!

Now she faced the meat-making season, and nothing about it was new to Walks Far. For many days past, the men had been finishing arrows, trying their short hunting bows or making new ones, testing and retraining their prized buffalo-running horses. Those who preferred a saddle in the hunt made repairs and adjustments. Every butcher knife in camp, whether man's or woman's, was sharpened, as were the axes. Women built meat-drying racks from such poor poles as the Redwater country afforded. No old clothing was thrown away, for the time ahead would be bloody and greasy.

Individual or small-party hunting from the new camp was forbidden under severe penalty. A violator might have his tipi and weapons destroyed by one of the police societies, and a flagrant offender might be banished from the band or even get an arrow in the belly.

Walks Far and most of the other women and girls, as well as the boys, followed the hunters when they left camp on the second morning after the camp move; indeed, only the old and sick remained behind with the three warriors designated as camp guards and armed with half of the repeating rifles in the band. For, though Crow, Assiniboin, and other enemies should be doing their own hunting, one could never be sure. Moreover, a band of Assiniboins had once regarded this Redwater country as their own hunting ground and resented the Teton intrusion.

Of course, many muzzle-loaders and a few single-shot breechloaders were owned by the people, but the muzzle-loaders were extremely difficult to reload and cap on a fast-running horse. The single-shot breechloaders were also awkward to load, slower than bow and arrow, which, moreover, somewhat equalized the hunters' chances in a group hunt such as this. And, as Walks Far well knew, the bows and arrows were preferable on other scores. Arrows did not have to be procured from traders; and, with the owner's mark on each arrow, terribly bitter arguments about just who—or whose husband—had felled a particular buffalo were prevented. Those who owned the repeating rifles could use them later, especially in the winter hunting for robes. Meanwhile, these weapons were retained for defense.

The party of hunters and women moved quietly eastward in cover afforded by a coulee that kept them hidden and downwind, southward from the herd. They approached as close as possible, taking advantage of a small tributary coulee and a swell of land. Walks Far saw a scout materialize from the buffalo grass to signal a stop and silence: The buffalo herd grazed only a short way beyond the crest of the swell. A good horse could outrun the clumsy-looking but longer winded animals for only a space.

The hunters quietly dismounted from their ordinary riding horses to mount their led buffalo runners. They tucked the coiled end of a long halter rope under their belts to assure a chance of catching their horse again if they should be thrown during the chase. The hunt leader lined them up, left-handed bowmen and the two or three who chose to hunt with lances took their places on the left. Here was where a courageous, well-trained buffalo horse could count—an agile, sure-footed, long-winded mount able to keep speed over a long, hard run, alertly avoiding holes and uneven ground as well as the slashing horns of an enraged or wounded buffalo.

At a signal from the leader, Suzy's father, the whole line of mounted hunters rode silently over the crest, trotting their horses until the buffalo became alarmed and the herd sped off in the opposite direction. Walks Far and the other women heard the whoops marking that moment, then the excited yipping of the suddenly racing riders. Now the women rushed over the crest to watch. They saw a kind of dangerous race in which it was every hunter for himself, with every hunter doing his best to make the first kill and to kill more than anyone else. Every man expected to kill at least two buffalo in a single such run, but if he killed more than five with bow and arrow, it might be viewed a remarkable feat.

Back in the Blackfoot country Walks Far had seen men die in hunts just like this, her older half brother tossed and gored, then trampled under the hooves of the herd, until little was found for the family to bury and to mourn. She had seen Finds the Enemy's horse gored, its belly ripped open so that it screamed and swung sharply aside, tripping and going down in the tangle of its own spilled-out entrails. Finds the Enemy, by luck and fast footwork, avoided the horns and the sharp hooves as the onrushing herd cut that horse to pieces. Now, a silently watching Red Hoop Woman and Walks Far knew that Scalps Them, with his bad ankle, would have no chance at all should his horse go down. They knew that such hunting was only for courageous men and horses; and though men might will themselves to courage, as nearly all of them did, only a very few horses could be trained to lose their fear of running in close beside the buffalo and those murderously hooking horns.

Scalps Them, Left Hand Bull, One Horn, Feather Earrings, Runs Stooped Over, and other men whom Walks Far recognized were now up with the fleeing buffalo. As usual, the cows took the lead, closely followed by the bulls and with the calves increasingly falling behind. Walks Far remembered an enduring argument among both Blackfoot and Sioux—whether the cows could actually outrun the bulls or whether the bulls held position behind the cows in an effort to protect them. Walks Far believed the latter, for only very rarely did any cow clearly outdistance the bulls. Each of the hunters, with an arrow already fitted to his short bow, raced ahead through the growing cloud of dust, bypassing the bulls to get at the choice cows. At a dead run, parallel with the selected cow and often riding so close that he could almost kick it, the hunter loosed his arrow. He aimed less often for the heart than for a point just forward of the hip bone. He hoped for a clean penetration, for hitting a rib meant only an enraged buffalo. The bowstring's twang gave the trained buffalo horse the signal to swerve a little, then run in close again to afford the rider a second shot, for more than one arrow was usually needed to bring down a buffalo.

For the watching women the dust and increasing distance soon made it nearly impossible to note the kills made by their men. Then, after a while, Walks Far saw that the run was over, that the riders, now outdistanced, were walking their mounts back to the women. A man named Hole in the Sky had taken a bad fall and his horse was limping, but that had been the only accident. Dead buffalo cows and a few choice bulls made dark lumps, strung over the prairie. But killing still went on, as boys mounted on colts or slow ponies emulated father or uncle or older brother by shooting the calves fallen behind. But the men soon ordered this stopped in any area near the butchering. Wives—number-one wives—met their husbands, and each took her husband's heaving buffalo horse, first to walk it, then splash water over it and rub it down. The butchering began, and this was a hard task, at which men and women worked swiftly together, usually in silence uncommon with Indian women.

Still, a now blood-spattered Suzy soon ran over and demonstrated her aptitude for gathering the news. "One Horn did his best to make the first kill," Suzy said, "but that strange ugly little man, Feather Earrings, beat him to it. And not only that," Suzy went on, "Feather Earrings and Runs Stooped Over had tied in killing the most—six cows each—to One Horn's five. Runs Stooped Over might even have killed seven!—if his exhausted horse had not stumbled." Then Suzy added proudly, "My father got the three choicest cows taken by anyone."

"Of course," Walks Far told herself. She had already learned that both Suzy's father and mother appeared to be driven by an obsession over excellence and quality. Suzy's mother may have worked no harder than Red Hoop Woman did, but she never rested. Aloud Walks Far said, "Scalps Them and Left Hand Bull both did very well; they killed four fine cows each."

Walks Far felt a secret pleasure that One Horn must face the fact that the camp contained hunters more able than he, yet she regretted having put him in such a position during the breaking of Crazy One that he could hardly be expected to court her. He would become a more able man, and he was handsome enough to do, besides being almost the only man she could regard as available. She wished she were butchering beside a husband of her own who had killed these buffalo and that they were taking this meat back to the fine, well-kept tipi they shared. That would go a long way toward easing the work required to skin and "heavy-butcher" a four-year-old buffalo cow down to the bones, under a hot sun on the open prairie. [Walks Far disillusioned Janet Sinclair about Indians' utilization of every part of a buffalo. They could and often did make use of nearly every part of the animal, but about fat times Walks Far said, "H'im seen Indians kill pipty, maybe hunnah jus' for tongue"—possibly for the tenderloin and *tampco* as well, and if it happened to be choice, the hide also.]

Butchering Scalps Them's kills was only the beginning of the work. Walks Far and Red Hoop Woman had to take all that meat back to camp on packhorse or travois, and they personally usually carried home the choicer portions of the entrails. In camp all that meat needed to be sliced for jerky, then dried with great care to keep it from spoiling in the process. Jerky that was to be made into pemmican would need to be cooked, then dried again and pounded into powder with a stone maul, after which it had to be mixed with dried pounded chokecherries and melted marrow fat. The result, which would keep for a year, was then stored in sacks fashioned from skins peeled in the spring from unborn buffalo calves. The meat that Red Hoop Woman wanted merely dried had to be carefully packed in the envelopelike rawhide parfleches, with each layer separated by uncooked strips of suet and dried wild mint along with dried berries gathered earlier and still being gathered by the girls and the *winkte*.

Much of this required a great deal of cooking in a country where wood was scarce, as Red Hoop Woman regularly complained. Smouldering buffalo chips and the vining juniper that burned almost in a flash, after having been laboriously uprooted by Walks Far, Red Hoop Woman, and Fire Wing from its ground mat and dragged in on a dog travois, constituted about all the fuel available. In addition to helping with the butchering, the meat curing, the meat drying, the berry picking, the pemmican pounding, and fuel gathering, Walks Far helped prepare the meals. And the Sioux tended to eat three times daily, whereas Blackfoot usually ate but twice. She also had to chase dogs, magpies, and sneaky small boys from the drying meat and berries, help water the horses, and keep an eye on Grandfather. She was gorged on meat, but she felt as lean as when Grandfather had marched her into camp. Yet much of this work had a way of becoming almost fun under the curiously successful merging of communal and individual effort that eased Indian women's days.

But those hides! Always, eternally, there were hides Walks Far had to dress, not only the buffalo, but the antelope, deer, and elk. Each one required periods of backbreaking labor spread over about ten days. There was always the soaking stink of it, the pegging out to dry, followed by the laborious, stooped-over work of careful defleshing and, except in the case of winter robes, the dehairing. If a softened hide were wanted, the process continued through endless pounding and twisting, then the breaming, with the two women sawing the hide seemingly forever across a log or a rawhide rope. And when the hides were thus made soft enough, some would be wanted browned by smoking, or whitened by careful hand rubbing with the proper clay.

In considerable degree this made up the story of a woman's life, with the work only peaking somewhat in the fall. This, Walks Far was well aware, helped explain some of the holiday spirit arising from either short or long camp moves—the vacation from those hides! Walks Far had enjoyed but two vacations from such work since she was about fifteen. Accompanying her husband's war party into the Snake country accounted for a long one of nearly two moons, her nine-day flight from the Pikuni camp for another.

However, Walks Far always found the first organized, successful fall hunts exciting and pleasant times. People seemed to be at their finest and happiest. In a day or two more, a special hunt for the sole benefit of the aged, the unfortunate, and the poor would be held, and traditionally, the first kill of the first day was reserved especially for them and so designated by tieing a knot in the tassel of its tail. Thus, they too were now enabled to enjoy an impromptu midday feast out on the open prairie, for a freshly killed buffalo cow afforded the most tasty of raw morsels, more than anyone could eat.

Walks Far vied with Suzy in slurping down long, thin strips cut from a liver, and Fire Wing, her eyes ecstatic, gulped from a drinking horn filled with still warm blood. Walks Far sliced off a section of the soft nose gristle, which went so well with liver, or with the brains that Red Hoop Woman and Scalps Them scooped from the chopped-open skull. A little way beyond, Suzy's parents lunched on kidneys. Still further away, a relaxed One Horn contentedly sucked marrow from a broken leg bone.

A laughing man presented Grandfather with the testicles of a young bull mistaken for a cow in the dusty excitement of the run. Grandfather ate them gratefully but, no doubt, with more hope than real faith in their regenerative power. Old Father of a Mudfish came and asked for the scrotum. He wanted to dry it and fashion it into the shell for a ceremonial rattle. The *winkte* came by, and even he wore a slovenly old dress today. He sought gall bladders from which to make yellow paint, and Walks Far was happy to give him one, promising him as many more as he could use. Scalps Them hurried away, but came back shortly, his unceasing talk filled with complaint: Someone else had gotten the bull's phallus—the *che*—and if he, Scalps Them, expert bow maker that he was, could be expected to keep on making bows for half this band, then all those thoughtless and miserably ungrateful people should be able to remember that good bows required plenty of good glue! How did anyone think that he could ever keep truly good glue on hand without a *che* to boil down now and then!

Suzy hurried back to help her family, and Walks Far, under Grandfather's happy gaze, again fell busily to her butchering in the hope of shutting out Scalps Them's tiresome monologue. A question she had wanted to ask Grandfather for some time came to mind.

"Grandfather, why are Suzy's parents so sad, and why do they work harder than anybody else?"

"Because their favorite son was killed by the Crows last summer. That young man was born with all the Sioux virtues and was handsomer than Horses Ghost—perhaps handsomer even than I was at that age."

"Where *is* this Horses Ghost? I would very much like to see him!"

Grandfather stared at her swift, bloody knife as though something about it puzzled him, then rudely turned his back in abrupt impatience and went wandering away.

Chapter Twelve
INDIAN SUMMER
(October 1874)

For the most part, days in the Redwater country remained warm, but nights grew swiftly chill, with frost stiffening the buffalo grass at dawn. Wedges of geese winged southward, their honking cries loud in the dark sky as Walks Far dozed off to sleep in her warm bed robes in the small tipi behind Red Hoop Woman's. Buffalo berries, edible only after the first frost, made bright abundance among the thorns on their strange, blue-dusted bushes with the silver leaves. The people felt well fed and contented. Having already made nearly enough meat for winter, they no longer ran the buffalo in organized hunts, but once again let individuals take the fat cows when and where they chose.

Very late one night during this period Walks Far wakened in terror. She was conscious of a chill draft from a slit in the tipi cover and dew wall and of a whispering man, his palm pressing hard over her mouth! "Be quiet, Pekony Woman," the whisper said. "Get Grandfather's gun for me quickly. An enemy is trying to steal my buffalo runner."

Walks Far recognized Feather Earrings, that homely but oddly attractive little man who counted more coups than any other man in the band. She knew that he, as did many of the men, kept his prized buffalo runner picketed in front of his tipi at night and, for further security, often ran a long halter rope in under the tipi cover and kept it tied to his wrist as he slept.

Swiftly she got the gun and gave it to him with a whisper of her own, "Remember the double set triggers and to shake the powder loose and level in the pan." She thought he flashed her a disdainful grin as he went creeping away around toward the front row of tipis, where his own stood second on the right. Impulsively, but with a stealth as great as his, Walks Far followed and was crouched almost beside him as he prepared to fire from near the front of the adjacent front-row tipi, that of Suzy's mother.

The enemy already had the horse cut free. Its rope was coiled on his arm, but he still squatted there on his heels to do something at the picket pin. Walks Far could see that he wore a white man's coat. Feather Earrings fired, then instantly charged through the enveloping smoke, leaving Walks Far burned by sparks from the pan and blinded by the huge muzzle flash. But she did see the enemy lying prostrate as Feather Earrings clubbed him once, then began quieting the rearing horse. Walks Far saw that the enemy had waited to tie a worn moccasin and a new one to the picket pin in taunting sign that he had walked a long way here but would ride home.

The camp was a sudden uproar of screaming and shouting, with armed men bursting, still half asleep, from their tipis. But then, while Feather Earrings was still talking soothingly and patting his horse, the downed enemy rose swiftly to his feet and dashed between the tipis into the darkness. Men pursued on foot and on horseback, some riding far out and not giving up until well past daylight. None of those men discovered a trace or sign of a war party or of the man who fled. They should have looked much closer around camp. That enemy had made his last run. It was but a short one. An old woman, the first to go that morning to the patch of brush and its convenient ash log private to the women and girls, found him still conscious, but helpless. The women gathered and finished him, not too quickly, and not before the old woman had taken his coat. They then dragged the body far enough away that it could be left to the dogs and coyotes.

There was very nearly another death that morning, for Walks Far was caught off guard. Feather Earrings's wife, bloody knife in hand, suddenly rushed at her screaming, "Now I know the secret medicine making that keeps my husband out all night!"

But Red Hoop Woman tripped her headlong into the dust, then stood in front of her and shouted, "White Calf Woman, you don't know what you are talking about."

Yet Walks Far, her own knife ready now, had a sickening feeling that Red Hoop Woman appeared to be a little uncertain herself—*the slit tipi! Grandfather's gun instead of Feather Earrings's own! The powder burns on her face!*

Suzy was yelling at White Calf Woman too. "It is somebody else that maybe you should stab . . . somebody—"

"Stop!" Suzy's mother said in her sharpest voice. "I know a girl who is maybe going to get herself stabbed for just gossiping!"

Old Father of a Mudfish walked up wearing his greatest air of dignity and mystery. "You are a bunch of crazy women," he said. "Feather Earrings and I were making medicine together all night. He is learning four times four new songs. Do you wish *me* to bite the arrow!"

"No," Suzy said. "You are telling the truth. I heard One Horn grumbling to his mother all night about that singing—didn't he, Auntie?"

"He was worse than the singing," One Horn's mother said. "He has always been a strange son who does not enjoy music very much."

Walks Far felt that no part of Red Hoop Woman's glare was now directed at her. White Calf Woman's fury had dwindled somewhat and she appeared to feel uncertain, though she did get in an ambiguous final word. "I think my husband makes more medicine than you can remember," she told old Father of a Mudfish, and with that she ran to her tipi and angrily threw every single personal possession of Feather Earrings's out the door. She had divorced him.

He came riding back after a while and pretended to notice nothing strange. He surprised and delighted one of Runs Stooped Over's young sons by asking him to take care of his horse, then went and sat in the shade with a group of the men, talking and joking with them for the whole day. Not until sunset and the evening chill did he go to gather up his scattered things from the ground. As he turned away, his arms full, White Calf Woman appeared in the tipi door to ask as though from casual curiosity, "Where are you going with all that?"

Feather Earrings answered easily. "I am going to live for a while with One Horn and his mother."

White Calf Woman let him go for a moment before she called out and went to join him. The two of them stood there talking for quite a while. No one could hear what either of them said, but White Calf Woman suddenly laughed as though at a big joke and started back to her tipi. Feather Earrings let *her* go about halfway before calling out. Again they talked quietly, and the end of it was that she took the things from his arms and followed him home and inside. They closed the door at once, and if they had any supper, it was a cold one.

As Red Hoop Woman and Walks Far had a fine late supper together, Red Hoop Woman said apologetically, "Sister and good friend, I am ashamed to say that for just a little while this morning I was not sure what to think about you." Then, as the conversation went on, she astonished Walks Far with a near-whispered confession. "I will also tell my good friend this: I, myself, might think about Feather Earrings were I not a virtuous woman. Just the sound of that man's voice sometimes gives me funny feelings."

Walks Far had to fight back laughter. The thought of that wiry little Feather Earrings being overwhelmed by an ardent Red Hoop Woman evoked mental imagery too hilarious for words.

On the whole, the camp life went on pleasantly that fall. Of evenings a wastefully large fire, built to light gatherings of people for drumming and dancing, might send golden sparks toward the stars, nowhere more plentiful and bright than in that country on a brisk fall night. Grandfather rushed the winter season somewhat, at least in the eyes of other men, by proudly wearing a capote Walks Far made in the Blackfoot style from an old gray army blanket Red Hoop Woman had. His skinny old frame looked odd indeed in that bulky three-quarter-length coat with the attached hood and with mittens dangling on thongs from the sleeves. Young men would laugh, call him "Pekony Woman's Husband," and say, "That is not the way she should keep a man warm."

Walks Far had done other sewing for Grandfather and herself in preparation for the real cold of winter—heavy moccasins cut large enough to allow a layer of buffalo-hair insulation between them and the feet, knee-high leggins of buffalo skin with the hair left on, and, for Grandfather to wear with a buffalo robe, a fluffy-haired buffalo-skin hood having mittens fashioned from the same skin and attached by heavy strings. She made for herself a hood with mittens. It was identical to Grandfather's except for the vanity of wolf skin instead of buffalo. Also for herself, she made women's winter panties, one pair from the soft skin of an unborn buffalo calf and another from antelope skin.

Fourteen-year-old Fire Wing got into trouble with her strait-laced mother, Red Hoop Woman. Early on a pleasant evening while the light was still good, Fire Wing and other hectic-eyed girls of approximately the same age had roamed the camp capturing small boys, the biggest small boys their own numbers could overwhelm and toss in a blanket. The tossing invariably so loosened the boy's breechclout that it abruptly failed of its function, whereupon the girls ran away screaming, their worst fears realized again! It appeared that Fire Wing had been the ringleader.

A shocked Red Hoop Woman, nearly speechless from shame and embarrassment, could only say, "That any daughter of mine would forget herself and act like that—!"

"All the girls were doing it," Fire Wing said defiantly. "It was just like last fall. And all the other grown-ups just laughed and pointed to where the boys were trying to hide."

Grandfather added, "Girls have been doing that every fall since I can remember."

"But can't you just imagine," Red Hoop Woman asked him, "what *my* mother and grandmother would have said if *I* had ever behaved like that!"

Grandfather grinned steadily at her until she suddenly blushed deeply and covered not only her mouth but her eyes with her hands.

Two or three days later a pair of young men on night duty guarding the horse herd reported seeing two men skulking away on foot into the sunrise. To the young men, they looked like Pekonies, and they had stopped to make a feeble attempt at setting the prairie afire. The older men decided that skulkers who let themselves be seen so easily, against a rising sun at that, were nothing to worry about. Scalps Them said, "Not even the Pekonies are that crazy."

Late the following afternoon on the prairie Runs Stooped Over, since nicknamed Scalps a Pekony Dog, was peacefully butchering a buffalo beside his wife when who should ride up but One Horn, his single-shot carbine across his thighs. As the two men began to talk about nothing much, One Horn suddenly peered into the low sun, his hand shading his eyes. "Enemies!" he shouted. "Pekonies!"

It was true! Three men in those wolf-skin caps some Pekonies wore even in the summer came charging from a coulee. One Horn, without dismounting, raised his gun. Squinting directly into the sun, he swiftly got off a magnificent shot that sent one of the charging riders sliding slowly from his horse. The other two riders swung wide, each firing one harmless shot while the wounded man crawled painfully into cover under a cutbank filled with buckbrush. Then, as One Horn got off a shot that missed, both the mounted enemies suddenly fled through more buckbrush, while One Horn and Runs Stooped Over taunted them and saw them simply abandon their wounded man to race on across a coulee, fleeing like dogs, especially when they saw help coming to One Horn and Runs Stooped Over. Runs Stooped Over was already on his horse, racing One Horn to count first coup on the wounded man under the cutbank. He won by a horse's length, dismounting on the run and rushing to stab the wounded man with his spear-tipped bow. At the second stab he faltered and gaped. He was stabbing a dead dog that wore a wolfskin and buffalo-horned fur cap and had a pair of old leggins and moccasins stuffed with grass attached to its hindquarters! A grinning One Horn welcomed the earnest-faced men arriving to help, and a grinning boy rose from the buckbrush a little way off down the coulee. Runs Stooped Over grinned too and pretended there were no hard feelings. He joked about it and clasped hands with One Horn.

But the elders could not forgive One Horn for crying enemy when there was no enemy. People hearing the shots and the yelling had been badly frightened. Men rode hard to the rescue, one of them seriously laming a good horse. Walks Far herself had helped herd all the free horses into camp at a run, getting dirt over everything. Some women and the young children were terrified, babies cried, and dogs pulled down much drying meat from racks abruptly left unguarded.

The four shirt wearers, sage advisors, met in council with Left Hand Bull, who soon called One Horn before them and sternly announced the punishment decided upon: "You are forbidden to ride a horse until you have shown that you can behave responsibly. You will not walk anywhere out of plain sight from camp. From sunrise until darkness you will keep watch, seeing that no little child strays too far away, and you will help the women guard the meat racks. Meanwhile, here is a Winchester and eight cartridges, which you must carry at all times in order that we may all feel safe. This you must do for four days. Any cartridges wasted will add a day. Do you understand this?"

"I hear you, so of course I understand," One Horn said, not sounding truly chastened.

Walks Far heard Left Hand Bull and Scalps Them talking about all this as one brother-in-law to another. Left Hand Bull snickered a little and said, "I wish I had been there to see Runs Stooped Over's face." But he went on wearily, "That crazy young man One Horn! Why did he not choose someone besides Runs Stooped Over! someone who is not ambitious to gather a following and break away, or even become chief here."

"Yes," Scalps Them agreed, and was then caused to wonder in turn, "Why could One Horn not see that he may have angered forever someone who could be dangerous to have for a personal enemy?"

Left Hand Bull had no answer to that, but he said cheerfully, "Well, we can at least be glad that his friend Horses Ghost is not here. It could have been worse."

"Maybe yes, maybe no," Scalps Them said. "I sometimes think Horses Ghost may be the smarter of those two."

That name again, Walks Far thought. Red Hoop Woman told her the whole of it—Whirling Medicine Cloud Sacred Horses Ghost! "He is," Red Hoop Woman said, "an almost too handsome young show-off, though he is as able as One Horn. His family is of the oldest and best, but unlike One Horn, this Horses Ghost is always painted and dressed like a dandy.

"About two summers ago, when Horses Ghost was still hardly more than a boy, there was much talk about Feather Earrings's pretty young wife trying to persuade Horses Ghost to steal her. That may be why Feather Earrings went to join Sitting Bull's band for a year. If so, it didn't do him any good, because while with Sitting Bull, a Yankton, who also came visiting, stole that wife! She is said to be living with him around Fort Peck, right now."

Chapter Thirteen

Visitors! Three mounted men bringing two good pack mules came riding toward camp. Walks Far knew they called themselves Métis—"mixed"—and that they were a blend of French and Cree. Yet they looked different from most half-breeds, more like a "new people," which was another way they had of describing themselves. Very often both of their parents and grandparents had also been Métis.

Red Hoop Woman spat as the riders approached. Obviously, Red Hoop Woman did not like the Métis. Once, far to the east of here, Sioux had been defeated in a big fight with them, but Red Hoop Woman had more than that against the Métis.

Walks Far knew they were not a trouble-seeking people, though they would fight either white men or Indians as need be. Her dead Blackfoot husband, Finds the Enemy, had explained to her that the Métis lived a little in both worlds. Even those among them who farmed on the North Saskatchewan River and elsewhere might roam the whole of the northern prairies in huge parties, as perhaps the most persistent of buffalo hunters.

Walks Far now saw these three as strangely drab-looking men

in black cloth, though they wore bright sashes. They were dressed in ugly, loose-fitting black wool trousers that were stuffed inside knee-high moccasins finished in bright bands at the tops. Also, all wore little round black hats neither so tall nor so wide as the hat most white men wore.

Red Hoop Woman was saying, "These Métis are less to be trusted than are the whites when it comes to trading. White traders usually have prices that are about the same for all people, especially those traders at Fort Peck. Most white traders, at least the ones who live in their forts, usually keep their word. Unless the white chiefs have somebody watching too closely, those traders are glad to sell powder and ball or cartridges to bands like this and Sitting Bull's band. We are going to live in our old Sioux way, and *never* go onto a reservation! This country belongs to us. The *wasichu* will never take it.

"Walks Far, you should just hear Scalps Them and Left Hand Bull tell what Sitting Bull, and Gall too, think of those Métis! In the fall three years ago not even the trader at Fort Peck dared sell ammunition to any of us Hunkpapas who will not go to the reservation. So Sitting Bull went to Grandmother's Land—Canada—to see the Métis. They promised him they would meet him and all his people on Frenchman's Creek at the end of two moons, when snow was on the ground for their sleds, and bring plenty of ammunition to trade.

"Those Métis came, all right, but they had no ammunition in their sleds, only firewater. All the people, even little children big enough to hold a cup, got drunk. People began to fight each other, husbands and wives, and many who had been friends. A few were killed, and some of Sitting Bull's people tried to kill him. Giggling men and women slashed tipis or knocked them over in the snow. And they shot into the horse herd, laughing just to see somebody's horse go down.

"When the firewater ran out," Red Hoop Woman went on," the Métis were gone. They took all the meat and good robes the people had traded just to get drunk! The people wouldn't look at one another. They were so ashamed that they broke up and sneaked away by families. Most of them have joined together again, but two of those families are still here with us."

Walks Far had seen the same or worse in the Blackfoot country, though there the sneaking-drink-givers had always been white men who came with wagons and built a small, strong fort.

Today's visitors were formally welcomed with a kind of wary

politeness. Left Hand Bull and the shirt wearers smoked with them. The Métis leader, a stocky, powerful man hiding an Indian's face behind a white man's full beard that made his black eyes look strangely piercing, revealed at last that he had not come to trade—not now. "We have brought only a few poor presents and some unhappy news."

The accent given by the Métis leader to his barely adequate Sioux words and the sound of the other Métis talking to each other in their own language as they opened their packs of presents reminded Walks Far of the way Jack Sinclair's wife spoke. It was pleasantly musical, except for odd sounds made in the nose. The leader especially reminded Walks Far of a lost snow goose honking from a slough on a dark, foggy night.

The Métis's presents were plentiful but lacking in much excitement and variety. There was a great deal of the very strong tobacco that the Blackfoot called "real tobacco" and enough small Jew's harps for every woman and child. When the honking-voiced leader delivered his message, his piercing eyes grew peculiarly expressive, now sad and now angry. "I am most sorry," he declared, "to be riding around to bring bad news, but I feel I owe it to my Sioux brothers. We have learned from some of our Métis people who are able to read the medicine talk the whites put on the papers they send around just what the whites south of the Medicine Line are doing, or plan to do. So, I must tell you how the paper talk says that all white men have been warned to trade nothing with Indians who refuse to go to the agencies, give their names, and begin farming!

"Also, my brothers, you should know that the papers tell how Longhair Custer—the same who was on the Yellowstone last summer marking out an iron road for the firewagons until you drove him away—has taken many long-knife [U.S.] soldiers and diggers for gold to your Black Hills. They are there right now, there where the white man has promised the Sioux by treaty never to go!

"When we Métis learned these things, we were made sad, then we were made angry. We believe that both our Sioux brothers and ourselves ought to be allowed to live in our own way. We have decided to do as much as we can for our Sioux brothers.

"Accordingly, at the end of the Frost in the Tipi Moon we shall bring sleds filled with powder and ball, and as many cartridges as we can get for Henry and Winchester rifles, and for the Sharps and Spencer carbines, to Frenchman's Creek. We will bring no firewater. You have our word. Sans Arc and Blackfoot Sioux we have already visited have promised to come. Tell all Sioux people except those tame Yanktons at Fort Peck. The place of meeting will be where the Medicine Line, which the whites have marked only this summer by piles of stones, crosses Frenchman's Creek. In this way, if soldiers from the south or the new police from the north should happen to come to one side of that line, we can take our sleds to the other side and laugh while we trade."

Left Hand Bull made a carefully worded promise. "We will send someone to see you at Frenchman's Creek at the end of the Moon of Frost in the Tipis."

"That someone," Red Hoop Woman declared to Walks Far, "will not be Scalps Them. He has already promised me to spend the winter in the Black Hills. And we will just see for ourselves what the white men are doing there."

Scalps Them disappeared the night following the departure of the three Métis with their pack mules. He admired mules, and Walks Far was not surprised to hear him talk repeatedly with Left Hand Bull about what fine animals those two mules of the Métis were. "I would certainly enjoy stealing those mules," Scalps Them declared.

"It would be better," Left Hand Bull said, "if you would only help Runs Stooped Over steal those mules. That would be good for him and for us. He is an ambitious and discontented man."

Scalps Them had hardly gone to sleep that night before a dream wakened him, and of course it involved Runs Stooped Over, to whom he wanted to go at once and relate the dream. Red Hoop Woman made a flow of objections, pointing out to Scalps Them, "You made yourself a reputation as a warrior and stealer of horses a long time ago. At your age you should let young men steal horses, while you advance in your secret societies. The same goes for Runs Stooped Over. You two should grow up and let ambitious young men who need coups and wealth for a wife steal those mules."

Scalps Them said, "Woman, if you do not understand why I must do what my dream has told me to do, then I am not going to tell you." He went directly to Runs Stooped Over's tipi, wakened him, and said, "Runs Stooped Over, I have had a powerful dream, which told me that I must help you steal those mules from the Métis. We must start tonight. You must bring two boys from among your relatives."

Runs Stooped Over accepted the idea at once, pausing only to quiet his wives' objections by saying, "Though I do not care too much for mules, they, like horses, do not talk nonsense to a man. I will enjoy a few days of peace and quiet."

The pair rode off in the middle of the night, taking along two boys, who felt much honored, even though they would have to do all errands and the cooking. No effort would be made to steal those mules for several nights, of course—not until the Métis would feel no reason for especially suspecting Left Hand Bull's band. However, it was good to be scouting the country now and then.

Meanwhile, Red Hoop Woman and Walks Far went on with the meat and hides, and nothing much happened until One Horn put his name in everyone's mouth again. The restriction on his freedom had been as brief as it had been severe, but he smarted. For, on the second day of his restored liberty he did what none of the people could remember a Hunkpapa ever doing, though—and this coincidence in itself was very uncommon—a namesake of One Horn's among the Yanktons had been famous for the swift and dangerous feat. One Horn went out and ran a fine fat buffalo cow on foot. He kept up with it long enough to sink two arrows and kill it! What was more, after resting well, he repeated the feat, running another cow even farther and using but one arrow!

Men talked of nothing else. One Horn flaunted his pride by fixing the tails of those two buffalo as ornaments on his mother's tipi. Suzy reported him to be thinking about a giveaway feast, and of changing his name to Kills Them on Foot.

Walks Far found that Grandfather alone refused to be overwhelmingly impressed, though he did admit that killing buffalo that way was something of a feat, particularly for these young men nowadays who had to have a horse just to go piss. But anyone who owned a memory as long as his memory could recall the days before there were hardly any horses. Such a person would know that it had been by no means unheard of to kill buffalo on foot in the long-ago time.

This monologue suggested to Walks Far a possibility that she was on the point of mentioning to Grandfather. But abruptly, she thought better of it, only to see him grinning at her in that way that always made her shiver between the shoulder blades because of a feeling he had read her mind.

She did hope One Horn would take that new name quickly. If her plan worked out, he would be all the more chagrined. She would run hard each day, get Suzy to run with her. . . .

Scalps Them and Runs Stooped Over came back safely with the mules, and, true to their word given to Left Hand Bull, they brought no Métis scalps. "It had been great fun—just like old times," Scalps Them reported when Left Hand Bull came privately into the tipi, but I wish my dream had not required Runs Stooped Over to keep both mules."

Walks Far hardly listened. No detail was too small for Scalps Them, and almost every one of those details made for a separate, usually dull, adventure. To Scalps Them's surprise, which he explained at length, the Métis unexpectedly turned east along the south side of the Big Muddy River, and opposite the mouth of Big Muddy Creek had camped for two days, doing nothing except for shooting a white-tailed deer. Then three tipis of Crees crossed the river and joined them. Together they killed two buffalo, and all feasted themselves into a stupor, along with their glutted dogs. So, early in the night, instead of waiting till late, Scalps Them and Runs Stooped Over crept in, cut the mule's hobbles in the darkness, and took off their bells. Scalps Them described every cautious step of the approach and of the cutting. He told how he had stayed there, cleverly and carefully tinkling the bells until Runs Stooped Over had time to get the mules back where the boys waited with the horses.

As he did that, Scalps Them had an inspiration that could have come to only such a bright man as he. Still tinkling the bells, he walked slowly to the river and tied them to a willow branch, which he bent and caused to skip with the current. Those bells went on tinkling perfectly. He regretted having to leave them behind, one bell in particular; it had the most pleasing tone he had ever heard.

Scalps Them and Runs Stooped Over had agreed that the boys might go in and each take a horse from either the Métis or the Crees. That, too, had gone smoothly; and, in addition, the boys had violated instructions by going almost into the tipis to steal a pack from the Métis—unfortunately not the pack containing tobacco, but the one containing the Jew's harps.

By daylight they were all far away, going on downriver before turning homeward by a route so devious that it tied knots in a man's mind just to think about it—yet Scalps Them tediously proceeded to untie all those knots. They had left no tracks that would mean anything to anyone, mules tracks though they were. Scalps Them declared that he himself would not have been able to find them. It was impossible to describe the route to Left Hand Bull, Scalps Them emphasized, then proceeded once more to do just that, mentioning each coulee and draw, each prairie flat and red-topped pinnacle.

Walks Far saw Runs Stooped Over's self-esteem restored. Left Hand Bull held a feast for him, at which he gave both mules to a poor family having four live grandparents and many children. The beneficiary of this generosity did not particularly care for mules, and Scalps Them secretly promised to trade horses for the mules after a decent interval.

Also, Walks Far saw practically every older boy in camp and many of the older girls wearing Jew's harps as hair ornaments. Suzy had several in her hair as she and Walks Far went for another run. She wore them again the next morning when she joined Walks Far and other women and girls going out with dog travois to pick buffalo berries. The berry pickers made a large group because of the additional old men and boys, with two mounted warriors, who came along as guards, for buffalo-berry bushes were often found widely scattered or growing in places that might offer cover to lurking enemies who viewed women's scalps as better than none.

The group picked berries well into the afternoon of that surprisingly hot and humid late fall day, then began to assemble for the march back to camp. Grandfather sat near Walks Far during the wait. He grinned at her. "You have not seen your buffalo you have been thinking about," he said teasingly, holding the grin. But as though Grandfather's words had been a cue, one of the mounted warriors rode up and told the other, "I have just seen a strange thing. Even though it is long past the mating time, there is an old bull with three cows in that little coulee over there."

"If I were an old bull, that is just what I would do," the second man said, and laughed. "I, too, would steal some wives now, so that I would not have to fight for them when the Chokecherries Moon comes again."

Walks Far tried to be calm and appear to be tightening her moccasin strings only absently. "Where are those cows?" she asked in a carefully casual voice.

The rider pointed, and said, "There by that little flat where there is an old buffalo crossing and the buckbrush makes the coulee look widest."

She noted that the wind, if there were any wind, would be to her advantage. It occurred to her that this fall day, though rather warm, was beautiful, the sky as blue as she had ever seen it above the red shale of the pinnacle tops and the sun-ripened buffalo grass. Truly, as the charging warriors often shouted to each other, this was a good day to die. Her heart was already pounding against her ribs as though she had been running, but she rose calmly and bloused her dress high within her belt until half of each thigh was bared. The people stared in astonishment at her behavior and clasped their hands over their mouths. But Grandfather only laughed in shrill glee, then yipped like a coyote. Hearing him gave Walks Far a kind of assurance that she needed.

She drew her knife, held it sharp-edge-up in her hand and called out, "No one must follow me," then set off toward the coulee at a fast trot. With good luck, before the sun had moved the width of a finger or two across the sky, she would show these people that she, a woman, could do something that a Pikuni man of her father's generation had done. With bad luck she would be dead or dying, or what was nearly as bad, left a laughing stock for life.

She entered the coulee well below the place pointed out to her, then turned up the dry, silty bed for such cover as it could provide. Going as silently as possible, she yet speeded her trot a little, despite the brushy patches that stung and bloodied her legs. She saved her full speed for the instant she would see the four buffalo, and she hoped to pick out the fattest of the three cows before they ran.

She was almost upon them before she saw them lying at the edge of the grass to her left. All four seemed to be off and running hard before entirely rising to their feet. But Walks Far was already at full stride. She avoided a vagrant patch of buckbrush and passed the angry-eyed bull to close with the speeding cows on the open prairie. She could smell them, could hear the complaining sounds from their stomachs, and saw them lift their tails to spread manure so widely that no one would ever gather it for buffalo-chip fuel. And of course she saw the shining black horns that could deftly slash her body open, hook under her ribs, and toss her higher than the animals' shaggy hump as they still ran on.

But Walks Far was seeing an exceptional buffalo! A "yellow one," so called because, rather than turning from yellow to black when a yearling, it was one of the very few that remained yellow like a calf for as long as it lived. Robes from "yellow ones" were much prized, and that cow was in such a position that Walks Far would have been forced to choose it anyhow! She did not stretch her good fortune by failing to look out for badger or prairie-dog holes, rough ground or patches of prickly pear, any of which could lame her and bring defeat.

Making a silent prayer to Sun because of a swift gathering of fear, she managed to close with the cow on its left side and drive her knife, sharp-edge-up but slanted to the rear, into its belly, cutting back toward its flank. And in withdrawing the knife, she gave a sharp, hard slash at the cow's rear leg, high up. The still-running cow swerved toward her faster than Walks Far was able to make a matching swerve and hold her pace. A shiny black horn hooked at her, tore open her dress and burned the flesh across her abruptly sucked-in belly. It had struck her knife arm too, half numbing it to the elbow. Walks Far nerved herself to keep running, to close again with the enraged but still running cow, and it took all the will power she could summon. She knew she was sobbing, as much from fear as from approaching exhaustion.

How many times she stabbed and slashed at that cow, successfully avoiding its terrible horns, she never knew, but it could hardly have been more than three. She stepped in an unseen hole and was so jarred that she bit her tongue. She faltered, unable to run on. The cow faltered too, and with its entrails bulging wetly from its bloody belly, with its left hind leg dragging, it tried to run a few paces more, then went down. Walks Far was able to reach the fallen cow, and warily cut its throat. She would have sung her triumph if she'd had breath for it. She could only sit helpless upon her buffalo, her head throbbing, her chest heaving as though from a power outside herself, and her vision curiously narrowed yet strangely clear. She had one small feeling of regret: She wished this opportunity had come to her *after* One Horn got around to changing his name to Kills Them on Foot.

The berry pickers streamed toward her, chattering their excitement. The mounted man who had reported the buffalo reached her first. He too was excited and he held out a drinking horn filled with juice from mashed berries. "I am glad I was here today to see this," he said in grinning admiration.

A crowd of skillful hands went swiftly to work skinning and butchering that cow. Only then did Walks Far discover her kill to be a double rarity—not merely a "yellow one" but also a "narrow cow," said to be the swiftest of all buffalo! Such cows were not especially noticeable, except when their peculiar narrowness at the shoulders could be seen directly from head or rear. Oddly, they often grew very fat.

The two warriors offered their horses as pack ponies with most uncommon eagerness, and walked willingly back to camp with the women and girls and travois dogs. Walks Far thought that a man returning to camp as the most honored member of a successful war party must feel a little like this. Grandfather played the part of a hopping, talkative herald, shouting out to the curious people, "Walks Far Away Woman, the Pekony woman, has run down a buffalo on foot and killed it with her knife! It was seen by all."

Walks Far decided to make no ostentatious display of her kill. From the tail she would fashion a beautiful fly whisk for Red Hoop Woman, and from the hide, though it was far short of prime, she would make a rare yellow robe for Scalps Them. Bore though he might be, he was also one of the kindliest men she had ever known. Moreover, she had only recently learned, entirely by accident, that he had actually bet Left Hand Bull one of his best horses that she would ride Crazy One. Even more surprising was the fact that he had been able to keep his mouth shut about it.

Also, consulting with Grandfather, Scalps Them secretly, swiftly, and deftly carved a magnificent redstone pipe bowl embellished with a recognizable Walks Far sitting on a downed buffalo and holding an exaggerated knife in hand. Walks Far first learned about it when old Father of a Mudfish brought it and the arm-long ancient magic stem he had fitted. He wished to add tufts from the hair of the yellow one to the adornments already on that stem.

One Horn talked no more of changing his name, and though he left the tails of his two buffalo on his mother's tipi, those tails now looked distinctly droopy.

Chapter Fourteen
LAST SAY

(October 1874 continued)

Two or three days went by, with all the people talking so much about Walks Far's feat that she hardly listened to anyone, not until a gleeful Suzy came running over to say, "One Horn is angry and being very funny. He says he is more put out with the people than with you, and he says no one bothered to speak to him about any race, much less about whether he wished to race a woman, a crazy one at that. He says he is afraid you will slice his belly open with your knife when you find him winning."

Walks Far was astonished, and as irritated as One Horn. The people were blithely matching them in a footrace, and were no doubt already betting on the outcome. "When is this race to be?" she asked.

"One Horn wants it tomorrow," Suzy said. "He wants to get it over with. I am betting on him because he is my cousin, but I am betting on you because you are a woman and my friend. I wish everybody could be friends—you and One Horn. I like everybody."

Walks Far also wanted the race over with. She felt a kind of weariness at having gotten into a situation where she could exercise no choice, if the people were to have their way. She must win, though to do so would only humiliate One Horn.

Next day, when the sun was at its highest and would not get into their eyes, Walks Far and One Horn toed a line scratched into the earth at the edge of camp. Walks Far had her skirt drawn high inside her belt. All the people were there, in the best of humor, and their bets of robes and blankets, or of fancywork, lay in parallel rows to one side. "I have never before bet on a filly," Runs Stooped Over said in a loud voice. One of his wives shouted, "I often wonder if you know the difference anyway!"

Grandfather, grinning and scratching his ear as he sat on the ground, made a sudden confession. "The only way I ever won from women was by outliving them."

Far out on the level prairie, so far away that their horses looked hardly larger than dogs, two mounted men were facing a feathered lance they had driven into the ground. Though Walks Far and One Horn could not see that lance from their starting line, they must race around it and back. They did not look at each other, and both pretended obliviousness to the camp humorists. One man, adopting the voice of an old woman, called out, "One Horn, my fine granddaughter, do not bring dishonor to our tipi out there. You must try hard to come back still a virgin. When you see Pekony Man's sacred *che* uncurled, you must squat quickly and put sand in your *shan.*"

One of the shirt wearers raised his voice in a quieting howl, tapped a drum lightly—*one, two, three*—then *BOOM!* Walks Far and One Horn were off together from a near-standing start.

For a while, both were content to run abreast, easily and steadily. Then, suddenly, One Horn tested Walks Far with a startling burst of speed, which she at once knew she could never match instantly. Yet he had barely shown her his back before she drew abreast again. "What is your hurry?" she asked, and hoped he was the one a little unnerved. They slowed a trifle, as though by spoken agreement, and again ran on steadily. Rough ground, the hills and holes of a prairie-dog village, lay in their path, forcing nimble footwork that Walks Far knew would tax One Horn no more than it taxed her. Beyond, also directly in their path, a small patch of prickly pear appeared. That might prove a greater hazard, but Walks Far saw that it could be taken in a leap. Still, she abruptly decided to swerve around it, and saw One Horn's magnificent leap in perfect stride gave him a full double arm's-length lead. She sprinted and hoped One Horn might again be feeling a little unnerved that she had drawn abreast so quickly.

Walks Far was almost enjoying the race, yet she wasted no more breath in taunting One Horn. It was proving to be a long way to that feathered lance driven into the ground. When they neared it at last, Walks Far saw too late that she and One Horn, each determined to be on the inside in rounding it, had chosen to make the turn in opposite directions. Both put on a burst of speed that brought them crashing together, tripping each other into a rolling, tangled, flailing tumble that set the two mounted men shouting with laughter.

Walks Far was up and running again, now trying to round the lance in the direction opposite her original intent. But One Horn had also changed, and, as the two of them met again, the breathless men on horseback were treated to a second tripping tangle on the dusty ground. As Walks Far came round facing the camp, the tipis looked small and far away. They did grow steadily in size, though all too slowly. She let One Horn run half a pace ahead of her. He ran faster than at any time on the way out. She saw the gleam of sweat upon his back, the shining rivulet it made draining down the crease along his spine. She felt it was still too early to pass him. She would let him lead now and hear her breathing just behind his shoulder. She was there when she leaped the prickly-pear patch with him, there when they crossed the prairie-dog village. She waited until they passed a stunted, lone rosebush she had carefully noted on the way out. She saw the people nearly full size now, though her vision was blurred and narrowed by the pounding in her temples and the torment in her lungs. But she sprinted, swiftly led One Horn by a full arm's length, and knew she had never run faster, not even on the day she fled the Pikuni camp. Behind her, One Horn's breathing wheezed and sobbed, sounding irregular and rasping, almost groaning. It was a kind of music to her ears. But she felt One Horn draw abreast! Slowly, despite all she could do, he gained enough that she saw the pounding of his heart against his ribs. One Horn crossed the finish line and went stumbling down in retching collapse.

Walks Far, in a society that had no place for failure, was deeply conscious of having failed to win that race, but she thought she knew a way to turn failure into something else. She did not break speed in the slightest, she leaped over the vomiting One Horn, and ran on down the curved line of tipis, swung out in a wide loop, and, still running hard, turned back toward the staring people. In sheerest agony, she held her pace, slowing it to a walk only as she came up to the crowd again. She wished she could manage a smile. In what she hoped was a thoroughly nonchalant walk, she passed through the crowd. It parted for her in silence. Her legs felt as though she were still running. Oddly, she felt herself to be one of the onlookers—she saw herself make it to Red Hood Woman's tipi, swing the door aside on its toggle, go in out of sight. She heard a sound from all the women's throats that rose and fell away like a huge, long sigh before it came back as a high-pitched cry of triumph. Then, and only then, did Walks Far herself collapse, and let her humiliated spirit return to her wracked body.

Late that afternoon, with sudden chill and a dull northern horizon threatening the first snow, there was a women's feast in Red Hoop Woman's snug tipi. When the time came to tell a story, Walks Far lifted a part from the Blackfoot creation myth. It seemed that after Old Man—Napi—had made the earth from a ball of mud that Muskrat, after three other creatures had failed, succeeded in bringing up between his forepaws from the deep water, Old Man looked around and decided that the land he had made needed some people as well as more animals. So, he made First Man and First Woman, and that caused him to think again, so he said, "You two are going to have to get along together. How are you going to do that? It will always be as you now decide."

First Man sat down and thought hard about it. After a long time he suddenly had a happy idea. "I will always have first say!" he told Napi triumphantly.

First Woman smiled as she readily agreed. "And I will always have last say!"

Buffalo Berry Woman laughed as appreciatively as anyone, then said in her literal-minded way, "Although that is a very good story, I cannot believe Old Man made any people without Old Woman being there. It always takes two, just as in a race."

PART TWO

Winter Travels, 1874–1875
and
Memorable Events through 1876

Chapter Fifteen

THE HONORED BROTHER

(Early Winter 1874-1875)

Cold Maker came to the Redwater country and stayed. Old Father of a Mudfish predicted an exceptionally cold winter. Walks Far heard Grandfather agree, then add, "There will be two or three of them." The people fled the windswept open prairie to set up camp in the shelter of the badlands around the head of Cedar Creek near Big Sheep Mountain. Some of the families, because the Big Muddy River had already frozen hard enough to support horses, went first to Fort Peck to trade before rejoining the band in its Cedar Creek camp. Red Hoop Woman would have none of this. She let Scalps Them's younger brother and Buffalo Berry Woman take the portion of robes and hides she and Scalps Them wished to trade.

Suzy's family was among these early traders. She came back riding half frozen into camp, but resplendent in a heavy and beautifully bright fringed plaid shawl over a new red dress that was even brighter. Of course, she had gathered all the news and gossip that circulated among the women of three tribes. Also, she had heard that Joe Culbertson had gone down the river on a fireboat and would spend the winter in Mis-soo-a.

Walks Far was reminded of her vague but enduring curiosity about Suzy's family. Obviously they were richer in fine things than any other family in camp. Their attitude of constant hard work and striving for excellence seemed compulsive, with a well-nigh frantic accumulation of pemmican and robes, of every kind of Sioux wealth, including not merely an excess of wintertime necessities, but also of greater quantities of beautiful handiwork and fine clothing than any family could have use for. Moreover, and equally odd, Suzy's parents sometimes publicly displayed a tenderness for each other that bordered on bad taste, yet there was a deep sadness in that tipi. Again, Walks Far asked Grandfather about it as they and Fire Wing lay snug in their robes in the tipi while gusts of night wind crooned in the tipi poles above the closed smoke ears.

"I have already told you two moons ago," Grandfather said. "They are sad because of their favorite son."

Yet this time Grandfather was in a mood to go on. "Early last summer, a year ago, he went to take horses and scalps from the Snakes or the Crows. It was his first war party as a man, and he did not come back. No one from that war party came back. Suzy's parents are now sad because of that son. He could have been a great chief."

"But other people's sons do not come back," Walks Far

pointed out reasonably, with no intent of sounding cool, "and besides, Suzy still has an older brother who looks like he will become a fine man. Was he not on a war party that brought back scalps and horses before I came here?"

"All that is true," Grandfather agreed, "but he was not announced as the favorite son. You should have seen *that* young man! As I said before, he was as generous and wise and brave and handsome as I used to be—as all young men were when I was young. People who did not even know him, who had never seen him before, would say, 'Who is that handsome young man? He will be a great warrior and a great chief!' There was nothing he could not do, and his parents sacrificed everything to honor him and help make him great. It is sad. You should have seen him."

"I wish I had," Walks Far said, and careful sarcasm edged her voice as she went on, "I wish someone had told the Snakes and Crows not to kill him. Though I really can't imagine there ever was such a man."

If Grandfather noted the sarcasm, he ignored it, told her thoughtfully, "Well, if you will try to think of all the best parts of One Horn and Horses Ghost, all put together into one young man, with all the virtues of Left Hand Bull, Runs Stooped Over, and old Father of a Mudfish added in, you will be thinking of someone a little like that favorite son."

"Who *is* this Horses Ghost?" Walks Far asked, as she had in early fall. "I very much wish to see this Horses Ghost! He certainly must be worth seeing, if just mixing him in could make handsome men of those other four!"

"You will see him," Grandfather promised. "He is One Horn's *kola*—and just as crazy. I had forgotten that he is now with some Miniconjous. But he will be back."

"I can't wait," Walks Far said. But she was soon thinking of something else, for Red Hoop Woman had got her way about going to the Black Hills to winter. They would leave in a day or two. Several families were going along, at least as far as friendly winter camps south of the Yellowstone or Elk River. Some would go even farther, all the way to the agency, or almost to the Platte River, as Walks Far understood it. There they would allow themselves to be counted and their names to be written down in exchange for rations and canvas for a fine lightweight tipi to bring along when they fled north in the spring to become "wild Sioux" again.

Two mornings later, the morning before they would start southward, Grandfather had no more than left the tipi in all his winter clothing when his hooded head was back inside the door, urging her to come see. She found Suzy's parents honoring their lost favorite son, and without a feast. They had chosen a swifter, more dramatic way. They stood before their tipi in the cold wind and the light snow, with the tipi cover rolled high as in the heat of summertime. They wore their finest clothes, and the father beat a drum while they sang honoring songs to and about the favorite son. They ended a song abruptly, and abruptly sawed off each other's long hair and let it blow away in that cold wind. They then gave away everything they owned—horses, the tipi and its furnishings, the winter's food supply, and all the wealth of fine things they had made or collected. Most of the things went to the poor, the old, or the unfortunate, but even the rich took a little something to help these parents honor their favorite son.

Soon, when the parents had nothing except the clothing they wore left to give, they stripped in the bitter wind and gave the clothing away too. Then, with a cry from Suzy—she and her less honored brother had swiftly done the same—all four stood completely naked and barefoot in the snow, owning nothing at all with which to face the northern winter as they again sang joyful honoring songs.

The people did not, of course, let them freeze or starve. They let them get only shiveringly chilled before politely inviting them in to a fire, then gave them old clothing, carefully selected so as not to offend the spirit of their honoring. Walks Far, feeling proud of Suzy but heartsick too, gave the oldest thing she had that would get her dressed again.

For the next day and more, as the small southward-bound party of people rode toward the Yellowstone in the wintry cold, with Grandfather wearing all his winter clothing and lying completely hidden beneath a robe on a travois behind one of the mules, Walks Far's heart ached even more for Suzy. All the members of each family looked much the same, hardly distinguishable in robes or blankets, their backs hunched against the north wind and swirls of drifting snow as they rode—all except Suzy, her mother, and her notably silent older brother. All three trotted behind, on foot. All wore their hand-me-down clothing and carried packs while leading burdened half-wild travois dogs that tried to chase even the suspicion of a jackrabbit. The father, armed with a bow he had been given, helped the other men ride outguard on the horse they offered him. He may have been coldest of all, but Suzy's light skin made her lips look bluer than anyone else's. Walks Far did honor Suzy and that brother—the whole family.

Exactly as Red Hoop Woman predicted, the north wind felt far less bitter when they got beneath the bluff along the Yellowstone. The horses also suffered less, for here the light snow lay undisturbed and protected their unshod feet from the frozen ground.

At midafternoon, before crossing the frozen Yellowstone, almost opposite the northward-flowing Tongue River, the women huddled out of the wind while Scalps Them and One Horn scouted the south bank. Red Hoop Woman, who had been silent all day, suddenly began telling Walks Far of a big fight with Longhair Custer and the trail finders for firewagons near this place in the summer of the previous year. "The men set a trap, a *wikmunke*, for Custer, but he wouldn't let himself get caught," Red Hoop Woman said. "Then, farther upriver, a few days later, another *wikmunke* worked. There was a hard fight, and Longhair's horse was shot from under him.

"All the women and children—there were some Cheyennes who had joined us—could watch that fighting going on across the river from a bluff on our side. The fighting was on a big flat over there. While we were watching, some of the soldiers, instead of fighting, were also on a kind of bluff, just playing that strange, loud music of the whites by blowing through big shiny things, bigger than any flute.

"Sitting Bull was at this fighting and, though I can never quite decide whether I really like that man, he certainly showed up a crazy medicine man and did a very brave thing that day. The medicine man had told the young warriors that his charms would protect them from the soldier's bullets, but many were quickly wounded. Yet, because none were actually killed, the medicine man kept telling them to press closer to the soldiers.

"Sitting Bull got mad about it. He said this was foolishness. He told the medicine man that he had stronger medicine of his own. The medicine man said he had heard some very strange stories about Sitting Bull's medicine, that it often made him behave like a frightened old woman, and this must be one of those times.

"Sitting Bull just looked at him hard, then walked out onto

the open ground carrying only his pipe and tobacco pouch. Bullets began to kick up dust all around; but he sat down, filled his pipe, lit up with his strike-a-light, and called for others to come smoke with him. Four important men went, taking Sitting Bull's pipe and smoking as though they were in council, but they kept begging him not to expose himself like that; and they wanted to leave, but not until Sitting Bull got that pipe smoked all the way down and the bowl scraped out did he get up and walk back out of the soldiers' sight."

Red Hoop Woman admitted that the Sioux and Cheyennes had not hurt the soldiers much, but a whole year had gone by and they had not dared to return! [All activity in connection with advancing the Northern Pacific Railroad came to a standstill following failure of its financiers in the Panic of 1873.] "Also," Red Hoop Woman declared, "the people will see about those soldiers said to be in our Black Hills. Left Hand Bull and Scalps Them are not quite sure that the treaty forbids a road for firewagons, but everyone knows and agrees that it forbids the whites even to enter our Black Hills!"

The signal came to cross the river, and on that side Walks Far saw no hoped-for sign of human presence, neither there nor a short way up the Tongue River, where fresh snow lay deeper. Red Hoop Woman suddenly announced, "I am going to tell you something else. I am not going to ride around shivering all night while the men wander all over this country looking for a friendly camp. I am going to set up my tipi in that clump of trees over there, make a good warm fire, and boil up some meat with plenty of good hot broth." Before her declaration was quite all out, Scalps Them rode back a way to give a signal, exactly as though he had heard her and agreed. Then he and the other men rode scouting around.

While Walks Far and Red Hoop Woman unpacked the mules and set up the tipi, Grandfather came out of hibernation. He plaintively begged for something to eat NOW, without waiting for hot stew. So, Walks Far took out the largest piece of dried meat she could manage in one mouthful and, while helping Red Hoop Woman with the poles and tipi cover, chewed the meat into a juicy pulp that the toothless Grandfather could deal with. She could not help thinking what a nuisance he was while they were traveling like this; but he took the mouthful of softened meat with genuine gratitude and said, "Woman, your fine teeth and sweet mouth are enough to save an old man's life."

At that moment Suzy's brother rushed up excitedly. He had

just seen a fine elk, and he begged for Grandfather's flintlock. Walks Far had never seen Grandfather relinquish that gun and was surprised to see him quickly check the priming in the pan, then hand it over. She forgot all about the boy or Grandfather until she heard the report of the gun, happily followed by a distant call through the cold air, "Meat—come."

"We will go," Walks Far and Suzy said, and Walks Far, with the thought that it would be but a short way, decided to give Suzy one of the mules, while she herself took Crazy One. She certainly had no wish to make a pack animal of Crazy One, but she did want him to become accustomed to bringing in deer, antelope, and elk. Accordingly, they set off, leading the two animals, with Grandfather walking between and hanging onto Crazy One's mane. Red Hoop Woman had given Suzy a butcher knife. Walks Far carried an axe.

They found Suzy's brother with the fallen elk somewhat farther away than expected, near a riverbank grove much like their own. He thanked Grandfather for the gun, and on being asked if it were reloaded, he answered an indignant "Of course!"

He already had the animal partly dressed out, and the rest of the work went quickly, with Walks Far using the sharp axe deftly to sever the head, then quarter the kill. For some reason she felt hurried, oddly apprehensive, the more so when Grandfather, who held both Crazy One and the mule by their ropes in one hand and his gun in the other, suddenly said, "Let us hurry away from here."

They were starting to hang both the forequarters and hindquarters over the mule's back, and bundling the other desirable parts of the elk in its own skin for packing on Crazy One's back, when Walks Far went suddenly chilled. "Enemies!" she shouted. Charging hooves pounded loudly enough in the snow and were accompanied by high-pitched yipping. She felt a cool, whispering breath she had felt before. But the arrow had already missed her. She thought it struck her axe, that it was perhaps the same arrow that she saw suddenly materialized high in the boy's shoulder, almost in his neck. He stumbled, then seemed to dive directly under the forefeet of the horse of a rider who was almost upon him with a lowered lance. Suzy screamed and rushed to defend him with her butcher knife.

Grandfather, still holding the lead ropes to both Crazy One and the mule, raised his long old gun. He fired, but his hold on the lead ropes was broken by the second enemy charging against them, plunging his horse between Grandfather and the two animals in order to separate him from them. Grandfather's gun went flying, and Grandfather appeared to spin out from the cloud of powder smoke. He went down hard and lay still. Walks Far heard the enemy's horse scream, saw it going down, still in the momentum of its charge. The rider was already off, charging back on foot at Grandfather, a spear-tipped bow held in both his hands, ready for stabbing.

Walks Far sprang with the axe to stand over Grandfather's twisted figure, and while hearing a sickening intensity in Suzy's screaming, she swung that axe, with all her strength and at arm's length, in a wide horizontal sweep, let go the handle. The charging man appeared to dodge, but only to swerve the wrong way, so that the blade caught him squarely in the lower ribs, burying itself to the helve. Walks Far was upon him, her knife out. He was writhing upon the ground, trying to wrench at the axe with both hands. Walks Far grabbed him by the hair and swiftly cut his throat.

Suzy was still screaming. Someone else was rushing at Walks Far. She almost stabbed Suzy's brother! "Load the gun quickly," he commanded as he wrenched the axe from the dead man's ribs. Suzy's screaming stopped; she stabbed once more, very precisely, at an obviously dead man upon the ground. There was a third enemy! He sat his horse less than an arrow flight away at the edge of a small grove of trees, keeping his eyes on them as he pounded with his hand at the lever of a breech-loading gun that would not close. Walks Far snatched up Grandfather's gun; and as she ran to cut loose his powder horn and bullet pouch, she gave a sob of relief to see that he was starting shakily to rise.

Suzy's brother, with pain-grayed face and with the now-broken arrow shaft protruding from his shoulder, was in a battle rage. In a kind of ecstasy he strode seven or eight paces straight toward the mounted enemy to stand there and taunt him. He held up the bloodied axe and called out insultingly, "Here is where the fighting is going on! But maybe you are only a she dog that has tagged along with the Crow dogs! Or maybe you are a Crow *winkte!*"

Here the boy jerked his breechclout widely aside and gripped himself while shouting, "How do you want it?" He turned then and bent over, showing the Crow his bared backside. [Janet

Sinclair learned from Walks Far that Sioux, Crows, and Assiniboins, all enemies of each other, had mutually intelligible speech.]

Walks Far got a new load in the old flintlock, the priming in its pan, and she felt tempted to try a shot herself at the Crow. She, too, felt proud and raging. She had saved Grandfather's life! She, a woman, had killed an enemy in battle! a warrior of those Crows, who were a kind of special enemy of both Blackfoot and Sioux. The remaining enemy's taunting was better than the boy's, more imaginative and experienced in the verbal insults. Suddenly he kneed his horse about to ride away at a dead run, and Walks Far heard five or six voices begin yipping. Scalps Them, Suzy's father, One Horn, and two or three other men were coming fast, and all but Suzy's father and One Horn charged on past to chase the fleeing Crow. Grandfather was on his feet, tottery and apparently a little dazed, for he suddenly fled in creaky fright from One Horn and might have shot him had not Walks Far clung to the gun when he tried to grab it from her.

"There are dead enemies here," the boy said, proudly announcing the obvious to his father and One Horn. "That one over there charged me with his lance, but I was able to dive to the ground on the opposite side of his horse, just before he reached me. He caught the point of the lance in the ground in such a way that it twisted away from him, but his horse had stunned me with a hoof. I could not get the lance right away.

"Then the enemy came charging back, leaning down as he went by to count coup on me with that quirt he has on his wrist. My spirit had returned to my body by that time and I grabbed the lashes of the quirt and jerked that Crow down off his horse on top of me. My knife was ready. We killed him—Suzy and I.

"Then I ran to help Grandfather but saw that enemy there get Walks Far Woman's axe in his ribs so hard that it lifted him off the ground."

One Horn, coming as near to beaming at a woman as any Sioux man ever did in public, went on to provide her a doubled measure of astonishment by saying, in the most friendly, admiring fashion in the world, "It is too bad for that Crow that he had not learned about our Pekony Woman."

Suzy's father withdrew the broken arrow from the angle of the son's neck and shoulder and said clearly, "Your brother would honor you!"

Chapter Sixteen

GOLD AND SOME BONES

(Winter 1874–1875)

There was feasting on elk meat and a soup of dried berries that night in the tipis of Scalps Them's little band—feasting and celebration over the Crow scalps, with a careful guard kept through the night. Suzy's family was again on its way up in the world. The less than favorite son had proved himself not unworthy. He and his father had horses again, and there was much good clothing for men and women and also an almost new Crow tipi of canvas, though lacking enough poles. For, although the third Crow man had escaped, the pursuers had killed two women and a child found hiding with their horses, the packs, and the tipi. The people decided that all this captured wealth had obviously been destined for Suzy's family, not only because of the family's need, but also because of the immense store of grace they had acquired through so much giving. [This killing of the women and the child shocked Janet Sinclair. Walks Far agreed, saying that while it had not been at all shocking to her then, she now knew it to show that "those gone tams have plenty bad Indian things, too." Walks Far was also of the opinion that the Crows, whom she rather admired because they fought practically everyone except the Nez Percé and the whites, would "all be kill now, if buffalo days and war tams not gone."]

Suzy's brother considered taking a new name, and honored Walks Far by saying he wanted one that, while good Sioux, would also be like a good Pekony name. Together they settled on Kills When Wounded.

One Horn declared those Crows crazier than Pekonies to have attacked like that when they themselves were endangered by just being in Sioux country. One Horn grinned at Walks Far as he said it, but Kills When Wounded snapped. "That is not a nice thing for you to say to her."

One Horn and another man spent much of the next day in cautious scouting through heavy new snow before Scalps Them's little band found the big camp of Hunkpapa and Sans Arc Sioux, with an adjacent camp of Cheyennes, all planning to winter here between the Yellowstone and the Big Horns. One of the families from Left Hand Bull's band had planned to go no farther, and Grandfather and One Horn and his mother would remain with it. Suzy's parents, in their improved circumstances, also decided to stay; but two families from the Tongue River camp joined for the trip to the Black Hills and possibly on to the agency. Like Scalps Them, they wished to find out for themselves about the white men reported to be in the Black Hills in violation of the six-year-old treaty. [Janet Sinclair located a copy of the Treaty of 1868, as ratified by the Senate and signed by the President. In Article 2 she found a clear description of the lands ". . . set apart for the absolute and undisturbed use of the Indians herein named . . . and the United States solemnly agrees that no persons except those herein designated and authorized to do so . . . shall ever be permitted to pass over, settle upon, or reside in the territory described in this article."]

Walks Far knew that Scalps Them had a more specific but related reason for this wintry journey southward, a reason that went far beyond the convenience of letting Red Hoop Woman have her way. For Scalps Them, in addition to his mission of bringing back a personal report to Sitting Bull and Left Hand Bull on developments in the Black Hills, had been given a charge of seeking ammunition and guns. The chiefs did not wholly trust either the traders at Fort Peck or the Métis to keep their promises, even when no white chiefs or soldiers were watching.

One possible source would be the Cheyenne chief Two Moon,

something of a trader himself. Also, there were those white men, farther south toward the Platte River, who furtively traded in guns, just as some of the individual white men who worked for the agencies or for agency contractors had been known to do. Walks Far had heard about this kind of thing from her dead husband, but because of something he had once explained to her, she felt vague doubts about a belief Sitting Bull, Left Hand Bull, Scalps Them, and many others appeared to hold: They thought the whites on the Platte River might be from a different tribe, one less knowing but more reasonable than the tribe of whites spreading along the upper Missouri.

In any event, Scalps Them brought trading stock along, not only the pair of strong young mules and as many choice robes as could be managed, but also a handful of both the big round and the small round pieces of that bright yellow metal so valued by whites. For several years past, until the previous summer, there had been living in Sitting Bull's camp as his adopted brother a mysterious white-man-become-Sioux named Grouard, or Standing Bear. He, along with Two Moon, the Cheyenne, had advised the chiefs to collect all these pieces of yellow metal from any one who happened to have some, or who acquired them in raids. The young men were in the habit of punching holes in them for stringing as a neck ornament, though they thought the silver ones prettier. Standing Bear and the Cheyenne chief said, "Those big pieces of the yellow metal will buy you Winchesters and much ammunition. They will buy you more of the single-shot Remingtons and the short Sharps. The smaller pieces are worth a half or a quarter as much, according to their size. This is the metal called gold, and the whites want the Black Hills because they have heard they can find much of it there. Perhaps Scalps Them may be able, by taking along that gold, to more than double the number of repeating rifles in the bands of Left Hand Bull and Sitting Bull. We need those guns for robe hunting and for defense against the Crows, the Snakes, and Pekonies, but especially if there is war with the whites. Already they are trying to keep us from having guns."

In resuming the journey toward the Black Hills, Walks Far acquired a nickname she never wholly lived down. The start southward was made on a bright, cold morning following the first bad blizzard of the winter. She mounted Crazy One a little off guard, half forgetting his inclination to buck each morning as though asserting a matter of principle. Thus it was that she found herself sailing through the air to land completely buried in a fortunately deep snowdrift. Onlookers thought it hilarious, and forever after someone would call her Out of Sight Woman.

Walks Far enjoyed that long trip, cold as it was. They crossed southwestward from the Tongue River to the Powder River, then on to the Belle Fourche River, with the snowy Big Horn Mountains rising into the icy blue sky on the right. But the Black Hills disappointed Walks Far a little, for they were far less than the Rockies or the Big Horns. Still, as a place for wintering Red Hoop Woman had hardly done them justice—and just as she had predicted, many Teton people—Hunkpapas, Sans Arcs, and Miniconjous—were camped along the fine streams, and there was much leisurely visiting, with winter games and dances. Fuel and forage were abundant, the deer plentiful, and bears not uncommon.

And there were no white men after all. Walks Far heard how Longhair Custer and his soldiers had stayed but a short while, departing long before the summer was over. True, a large party of ordinary whites had then started for the hills to dig for the gold Custer had reported, but the army had turned those whites back, exactly as the treaty required. Still, it was said that the white men wished to make a new treaty, had even proposed at Red Cloud Agency that all Sioux be moved to Oklahoma! a place Walks Far had never heard of. Also, there were people here who had gone to Red Cloud Agency in a unusually early and large winter gathering of wild Sioux from the northwest. Many of these had come back to the Black Hills disgusted with the tame Sioux who had refused to support them and start a war, had actually opposed them after they cut up a flagpole and tried to burn the agency buildings. Those tame Sioux had even moved to the defense of a handful of frightened soldiers. But even those tame Sioux had at first resisted agency efforts to count them, then had submitted. That was when the wild Sioux had enough, and returned to the Bad Lands or back to the Black Hills, fleeing from that counting as though from a smallpox epidemic. [Walks Far was unable to make exactly clear to Janet Sinclair this resistance to a census, especially after Janet's reading about Red Cloud revealed that the counting of those Sioux who submitted produced a total substantially larger than the estimate upon which the issuance of rations and treaty goods presumably had been based.]

Walks Far met Cheyennes here, too, and if the Sioux were buzzingly disturbed, the Cheyennes were in a truly murderous mood. A large number of them, also camped near Red Cloud Agency, had been told that they would receive no more rations or other goods until they accepted removal to Oklahoma. They too wanted to fight. And as though hearing all this were not enough, Walks Far herself shared in the fear and mystification created by a white man who went with wagons into the Bad Lands for an inexplicable but highly disturbing purpose. If he was telling the truth about his plans, he was up to something worse and more frightening than tearing up Mother Earth for gold. Even the white men at the agency appeared to be either not sure about what this man was doing, or were themselves hiding something. It was noted, however, that they spoke disparagingly of the man, calling him something that in their own language meant "the bone sharp." [This man was Professor O. C. Marsh of Yale, come to check on a report of extinct animal fossils in the Bad Lands.]

White Tail, a chief, flatly accused Bone Sharp of being a gold thief trying to sneak into the Black Hills by trickery. But Bone Sharp, true to his word and accompanied by but a few soldiers, went only to the Bad Lands, found some strange and monstrous bones, loaded them into his wagons, and departed, fortunately for him, just before a large party of Miniconjous and a few Hunkpapas went to attack his camp. The whole mysterious business, Walks Far could see, was not only of itself puzzling and frightening to the people but it also made them more disturbed and suspicious about the whites.

Then, suddenly, angry riders spread fresher news to all the camps. A party of ordinary whites, about thirty men and one woman, had eluded the army in the shortest days of this cold winter and were here in the Black Hills, building a stockade and digging for gold whenever the frequent storms permitted. Many people said, "Let us go and kill them all," but to Walks Far's surprise, Scalps Them cautioned against this. "Leave them alone, for in the spring we will be able to see whether the white man keeps the treaty," he said. "Let us wait and see if the white soldiers come and throw these diggers out." The chiefs of bands wintering in the area also took that view.

Walks Far felt no special interest in all this, and hardly any in Sioux politics or in stories of dissension and disagreement among their chiefs, but she was grateful for a happy effect on Scalps Them. He became less of a talker and more of a listener. Everyone he approached about guns told him they were even harder to come by than ammunition these days, even from the most greedy white men, though they wished him good luck. So it was that Walks Far and Red Hoop Woman, leading the mules, followed Scalps Them in lengthening and seemingly useless wandering during one of the coldest of winters remembered, such cold that during two periods travel was impossible. Both horses and people would suffer frostbitten lungs at the least need for exertion.

Yet Walks Far thought it her most eventful and adventurous winter, and altogether, what with much dancing in many friendly tipis and the games in the camps, she had a wonderful time and saw some strange and ridiculous things. At Red Cloud Agency she saw Red Cloud himself, lately conceded to be chief of all the Oglalas, settled in a house the whites had built for him. Out of her Blackfoot heritage she was both shocked and amused to discover that Red Cloud raised many of those tame birds that white men called chickens—and relished their eggs!

At an army post, either near that agency or the Spotted Tail Agency three days' ride to eastward, she saw a white woman in a beautiful fur hood and slim fur-trimmed dark clothing who rode a magnificent and spirited horse, and did it with amazing skill, the more amazingly because of a saddle that had the woman sitting half turned upon the horse, both her legs on the same side! Walks Far thought it at once ridiculous and magnificent, and for some reason she often remembered that woman when somebody disparaged the whites.

In a camp near Spotted Tail Agency, Red Hoop Woman discovered that among Sioux who had taken the white man's road there lived a certain Moon Woman, who, as Red Hoop Woman established after much enjoyable tracing of family relationships with other women, could be none other than the daughter of Walks Far's Sioux mother's oldest half sister! She and her husband, Turns Red in the Sun, lived to eastward between the Pine Ridge and the Niobrara River. They raised white man's cattle! Walks Far no longer felt great interest in finding Sioux relatives, but Scalps Them's search for arms led in the general direction where they were said to live. It had been whispered that he should seek a strange, non-Sioux Indian named Fergus Bushytail. Bushytail came trading from the Oklahoma country; and he had a way of producing guns out of nowhere, though he would begin by looking surprised and asking where you could have heard such a crazy story, and if he didn't like you, the matter would end there.

Chapter Seventeen

FERGUS BUSHYTAIL

(Late Winter 1874-1875)

Walks Far felt glad that Scalps Them's persistence had brought her to these rich relatives. They lived in a pretty place, a wide, shallow valley with plenty of wood and grazing all around, and a fine, ice-covered stream.

She suffered a sudden timidity on first seeing all this, not from fear of a cool welcome, but because any people, even Indians, who stayed permanently in one location, who lived in a solid, dirt-roofed log cabin, with a wagon in the dooryard, and who, besides a corral, had a grass-roofed shelter just for horses! well, such people could hardly prove other than odd or mildly frightening! And Walks Far had never taken a meal, never spent a night, within four walls. Unknown customs surely must govern such living!

She felt confident that any Indian people who were forced to live the isolated life of this cousin, Moon Woman, and her husband, Turns Red in the Sun, would be delighted to have visitors. The welcome did indeed prove warm, even before Walks Far managed to get in the word that she was related *(hunka),* was a cousin *(tahunsa).* Turns Red then called Scalps Them friend and brother, and in the voice of a holy man, a *wicasa wakan,* he declaimed, "We are all relatives!—*Mitakuye oyasin!*"

Walks Far found herself sitting on one of the robes carpeting the cabin's earthen floor and drinking extremely strong tea already hot in a huge iron coffee pot upon a magnificent stove. There were tin cups or bowls enough for everyone, with a big tin box of brown sugar and a wide shallow basket of all the sunflower seeds a crowd might eat. Except for the stove and its almost ridiculously large brood of pots and pans on top or hanging on the wall around it, and except for a corner woodpile that Walks Far thought large enough to last two moons, the cabin was furnished very much like a tipi, and as sparsely, though behind her, half curtained by a gray army blanket was something she guessed to be a white-man-style bed. She liked the tiny window, with a fresh green branch of cedar braced on it to soften the light. The cabin felt quite roomy, except for the oppressively low ceiling of beams and small poles supporting the earthen roof. Children hid behind the stove or roosted on the woodpile.

But Walks Far kept at least one wary eye constantly on that huge stove. She didn't dare leave the thing unwatched. It seemed threateningly alive, red-eyed and panting, and ready at any moment to advance upon its four squat, bowed legs. Fortunately, however, the stove did appear to be safely tethered to the low roof by the same hollow iron thing that so ingeniously led the smoke away.

To Walks Far the cabin felt insufferably overheated. If a tipi were this hot in summer, she would have rolled up the cover and prayed earnestly for a whiff of cooling breeze. But Moon Woman got up and fed more wood to the stove, remarking that cold air had got in while the door was open! She had an unusually expressive face and an abrupt way of moving. Except for that, she was a near double for Red Hoop Woman and of about the same age. Their interests were much the same—children, complex genealogy, and other matters that did not grip Walks Far until Moon Woman said to her, "I remember my mother telling how your mother was captured by Pekonies who attacked our small hunting party. Her husband was clubbed down from his wounded horse. Your mother tried to run, but a Pekony lassooed her." Walks Far told the rest of the story briefly, including the fact that her father's first wife tried to stab her mother, just as her mother later tried to stab a Cree woman her father brought home.

"My father was keeper of a powerful medicine bundle. He had many ponies and, with three hard-working wives, was becoming a very important man by the time soldiers killed him and his wives on a freezing morning on the Marias River four winters ago. People called him a strange name, Talks With No-Goods, but that name was only because they were surprised that a Pikuni Blackfoot would bother to learn anyone else's language, especially that of the Sarsi, a very small tribe who live near the Northern Blackfoot."

Walks Far hoped she could find a new husband who would be content with but one wife, but who would combine the qualities of her father and her dead husband. She reviewed the men she had met and danced with during her travels this winter, and regretted them only for the fact that none had measured up.

Moon Woman was promising, "With supper we will have some very good roots I have raised in my own garden!" It developed that when the agent had urged gardening upon the people, Turns Red had volunteered his wife for making one. In fact, as he belligerently declared, "I too used the hoe for almost a whole day, making sure I was seen by many people. I am not a man to be scared by the wild part of the Oglalas, not by all those Miniconjous, Hunkpapas, or Sans Arcs who say they will kill any Sioux who picks up the hoe!" He went on to declare that if any of those wild Sioux from the northwest should come and try to trample "my" garden, or kill "my" white man's cattle, or burn "my" grass, then those wild Sioux would find him and his like-minded neighbors less tame than expected. "I, Turns Red, have spoken. It is well known that I do not make idle threats. I have counted coup against Pawnees and Kiowas, and not so long ago as some people might suppose."

Walks Far found the talk about "my" garden, or cattle, or grass, sounding very strange indeed; and she noted with a kind of amusement that Scalps Them, who himself had often talked bitterly and threateningly about Sioux who picked up the hoe, now sat an utterly impassive listener. Only the heat in the cabin appeared to bother him, for he untied the strings holding the sleeves of his deerskin shirt together under the length of his arms, and throwing both sleeves back over his shoulders, he said, "Friend, I am curious about how you got these white man's cattle you have."

Turns Red's answer was a little unexpected: "After the buffalo disappeared from around here, the white soldiers gave enough cattle to start a herd, not just for eating, to those of us who would go into the agency and give our names and be counted. Later, about three summers ago, the beef ration issued to a family head each moon at the agency was changed to include one cow on the hoof." A smart man like Turns Red, it appeared, could trade something for those cows to people who were going to eat them anyhow, and Turns Red ran his increasing herd of cattle with little more trouble than he ran his ponies. Of course, he dared not go south to the Republican River and hunt buffalo any longer—the Pawnees might come and steal some of his cattle. Besides, choice beef now appealed more to his taste than did buffalo meat. [Janet and Dewey were surprised that Walks Far did not disagree: "Good beef, sometams she bes'." Dewey told Janet, "These cattle-raising Sioux, like Turns Red, did pretty well for years. When beef prices went sky-high early in World War I, they got talked into selling off their herds. Then white cattlemen leased the reservation ranges and, by 1917, were really coining the money. The Indians got left and found themselves worse off than they had been since the buffalo were finished."]

Turns Red had not, of course, made his explanation so briefly, and Walks Far was thinking that Scalps Them might have met his match as a talker. Swiftly she became conscious of something else, of distant singing, but such singing as she had never heard before—never such rolling sounds, never a voice so rich, so brilliant, so tremendous. The sound of it grew as though the singer approached with his horse at a trot.

One of the wide-eyed children roosting on the woodpile said excitedly, "Singer comes!"

"He is a trader," Moon Woman explained as the children ran outside. "He is an Indian who has a store like a white man's store a little way beyond the reservation line. The people call him Four Eyes as well as Singer. But he calls himself a white man's name, Fergus Bushytail."

Walks Far could almost see Scalps Them's suppressed excitement on hearing that name, knowing that the man he sought was walking in, surrounded by expectant children.

"*Hau*, friend Singer," Turns Red said. "You have come at a good time. We have relatives here from beyond the Black Hills. Some friends from up the creeks will come tonight, and we will dance. Maybe I will kill a calf."

Singer was already at the stove with his mittens off to take a bowl from a box on the floor and hold it out to Moon Woman, who stood ready with the coffee pot of tea half tilted.

"Thank you, friend. Thank you, brother, but I can only stay to warm my feet by your fine stove and my belly by drinking some of Moon Woman's especially fine tea. I must hurry on, though I would like very much to stay."

Walks Far, while noting Singer's Sioux to be barely adequate, found his speaking voice nearly as remarkable as his singing. He spoke in an extraordinarily deep and vibrant voice, with an unfamiliar slow laziness, too, and the sound was strangely exciting. She had not seen his face clearly, could see little more than a bulky buffalo coat with a turned-up high collar, a long coat worn with huge, loose buffalo-skin riding moccasins that gave him the feet of a bear. Yet he moved like a mountain lion.

Still standing, he turned and took a great gulp of the tea, then set the bowl on the edge of the stove and gazed down accusingly at the children. Walks Far saw that he wore a fine kind of sky-blue cloth wound round his head, much as a woman might wind it. The blue was covered all over by a design that suggested tan flowers and tadpoles. A fringed end of the cloth hung down on one side. His face was stronger than it was handsome —a striking face, strong as the Hunkpapa Chief Gall's powerful face—even while he stood there smiling hopefully at the children, and she guessed his age to be about thirty-five.

Turns Red said to him, "My relative who is here from the north is named Scalps Them. He is Hunkpapa, and a friend of Sitting Bull. He says he has been looking for you all winter."

Singer, still smiling and pretending to wait patiently in front of the girl who stared up at him, answered almost rudely. "I have been here all winter, as you know." Then he added, "Scalps Them, my friend, are you the lost Hunkpapa with the two stringhalted old mules for trading?" He did not wait for an answer but spoke immediately to the little girl, and what he said was plaintive. "Have you no sweet stick for me?"

"No!" the child cried.

"Why—?" Singer said in the saddest of voices. "Why do you selfish children always try to hide it from me!" His hand shot out and groped at the child's neck under her hair, triumphantly withdrew half a stick of peppermint candy, and popped it into his mouth. But he quickly found another piece in her left ear, and let her keep it. Walks Far was as mystified as the children. He grabbed the smaller of the boys by the buttocks, and that boy seemed to make an impolite, terrifically windy noise as Singer brought forth still another half stick of peppermint for him, then went about proving that all the children had been hiding a similar stick somewhere, enough for everyone in the cabin to have a piece.

Walks Far could not keep her eyes off Singer, and she found it impossible to look away when their eyes met and held. She felt a sensation as though his palm slid over her breasts to search there for a piece of the candy, and was relieved when he turned toward the stove and downed the bowl of tea in big swallows to say, "Friend Scalps Them, I am glad you did not shout to tell me I am crazy. I now will tell you that I have heard those mules you have are pretty good mules. But it is strange that you should bring them here, where good mules are more plentiful and worth less than in the north."

"I have more than two very fine young mules," Scalps Them said. He brought forth a small bag from inside his shirt, loosened it from around his neck, and poured gold pieces out into his own hand.

Singer gave them a casual glance, said, "It is too bad that some poor, ignorant Indian did not know any better than to punch holes in them, which makes them much less valuable! Still, I may know of a crazy white man—but let us not talk about that right now. I think I can stay for a little while and have you tell me about the country to the north, where I have never been, where all the women must be so very pretty." He smiled first toward Walks Far, but carefully included Red Hoop Woman and young Fire Wing as well, then kicked off the long bear-paw moccasins, quickly shucked out of the enormous coat, then another, and throwing everything onto the woodpile, poured himself a second bowl of tea. He took a lump of brown sugar, and, sitting himself down, completed a series of motions that seemed to be but a single movement of muscular grace.

Walks Far had been absolutely stunned the instant Singer shed the coats. She could only clasp her hand over her mouth at the spectacle of those apparently everyday clothes—color and splendor beyond her imagining.

That sky-blue, patterned cloth around Singer's head was fastened above his ear and the dangling fringe by a huge silver medal. He wore a shirt of thick, rich cloth that looked soft as a mole's skin and was the brown color of a buckskin horse's brown eyes. Like a mole's skin, it changed its color a little with the light. It hung outside tight-fitting buckskin trousers of sand-yellow, leaving little of them to be seen because the yellow-

stitched black tops of Singer's soft leather boots encased his legs
to midthigh. The beautiful shirt was belted, first by a sash of the
same blue material Singer wore round his head, and on top of
that by a wide black belt gleaming with metal studs and a tiny
pistol, besides supporting a knife larger than her own, though
very plain. Walks Far saw, tucked under the belt, a superb
pipe-and-tobacco bag beaded in red, white, and blue. The pipe,
the largest and strangest she had ever seen and beautifully
carved from a kind of tobacco-stained white clay, hung against
Singer's chest from a big silver chain around his neck.

Walks Far saw Red Hoop Woman to be likewise simply overwhelmed. Moon Woman smiled at their wonderment, and
while shifting pots on the stove and adding more wood to the
fire, she whispered loudly, "Singer is a Cherokee." The explanation meant nothing to Walks Far; she had never heard of the
Cherokees, so she whispered back, "Who are they?"

Singer had not missed the whispers, and laughed, asking,
"Have you not heard it said that there are two kinds of Indians,
the Cherokees and all the others?" He laughed again and told
Scalps Them, "You are a truly rich man to have such fine-
looking wives."

Scalps Them clarified the situation twice over, explaining
Walks Far with increasing detail, then adding boastfully, "She
has been given a Sun-stone and power over wind and storms,
she now rides a big buckskin horse no man had been able to
break, she has run a buffalo on foot (it was both a yellow one and
a narrow cow), and killed it with her knife! This fine robe I now
have across my lap is from that buffalo. Also, she nearly won a
footrace with the fastest running young warrior in our band. I
saw all this with my own eyes. And, friend, you will be surprised
at this: I counted third coup on a Crow warrior she killed with
an axe, then cut his throat in the Sioux way!"

Singer listened politely and with obvious interest, and at the
end he addressed her directly, saying only, "So you are a
Pekony, a Piegan—what the whites call in their language a
Blackfoot." He smiled and added, "I have heard of them."

Red Hoop Woman had a question for Singer: "Are you married?"

"No," he said. "I am not, but there are two women in my
house in Oklahoma who would say I am their husband! Those
two are both running so hard on the Jesus Road that I think they
are going to catch up with the white preacher. I do not like

white preachers, or the Jesus Road—only the Jesus Road songs."
And with that he threw back his head and sang a part of a Jesus
Road song that seemed to leave the cabin echoing with his rich,
powerful tones.

He stood up abruptly and, in defiance of all regular convention, swiftly crossed to the women's side to crowd in beside
Walks Far. "I would like to look at that knife," he said.

She hardly watched his careful examination of it. The slight
pressure of his upper arm made her whole body feel strangely
light, and suddenly she seemed to need much more air in her
lungs. Feeling abruptly guilty, she had to look at Red Hoop
Woman. Surprisingly, Red Hoop Woman showed no disapproval at all, seemed only to share the excitement.

"This is a fine old Scotch knife," Singer said. "The blade is
different from most, but it is Scotch. My grandfather had a knife
like it. A pretty girl should not wear such a big sticker where
the young men can see it. It will scare them away."

"No young men have come around to complain," Walks Far
told him, and she heard herself giggling.

"I am sure they are going to," he said.

Turns Red interrupted by calling loudly to his older boy, "Go
unsaddle Singer's horse. He has decided to stay awhile. Then
ride and tell people that Singer and relatives are here, and we
are going to dance."

Singer laughed, then said, "Friend, I know why I am a poor
trader. People can see inside my mind."

Walks Far took the whetstone Joe Culbertson had given her
from its case and asked Singer to read the message on the paper
wrapping. He peered closely, then held it at arm's length. "I
must put on my 'spectacles'; I have eyes that the white medicine men call farseeing," he said. Suddenly he had them on and
was telling Walks Far the message on the paper, repeating in
Sioux exactly what Joe Culbertson, speaking Blackfoot, had told
her it said. Incredible! Such mysterious, awesome power!

She felt filled almost to bursting, though now with suppressed
laughter at how funny those things made Singer look. He urged
her to put them on, and she grew apprehensive, not from fear
of appearing as ridiculous as he did, but from an unexpected
reluctance to see far into the future, which she had understood
his Sioux to suggest that those spectacles enabled a person to do.
Fortunately, when she put them on, she saw precisely what she
saw without them, though fuzzily. Unlike Jack Sinclair's looks-

far thing, these spectacles made nothing seem to come closer or go farther away. Apparently they lent their mysterious power only to someone like Singer, someone who already had eyes with the power for farseeing into the future.

All three women, then Fire Wing, put on the spectacles, with the laughter growing more breathless at each change. Singer retrieved them, put them safely away, and returned to the men's side, but Walks Far's knife was not gone from his mind. He asked her a question that somehow became one of the most unbelievable but imaginative stories she had ever heard.

Singer began by explaining that neither the handle of her knife nor the grips of his tiny pistol were made of bone, but of something much rarer. "It is called 'ivory' and is from the teeth of an animal that lives in that same hot country from which the first black men came. Those animals are twice as high as a horse. They have no hair and are without hooves, and they look as though they have a tail at each end. Their ears are as large as stiff-frozen deerskins and swing back and forth on the sides of their heads. From their mouths grow two of the ivory teeth, long, up-curved teeth, and those teeth are long as a man and big around as a man's leg. Yet, the really strangest thing about these animals is that they cannot reach the ground with their mouths! For this reason they have been given a nose that hangs down between those big curved teeth and all the way to the ground, like a long, heavy tail. That nose can tear up trees, turn big rocks over, and pull up grass. These animals feed themselves by grasping something with the tip of the long nose as easily as though with a hand, after which whatever is grasped is drawn by an upward curling of the whole nose to the mouth. Just watching that animal feed himself made me feel uncomfortable. It appeared to be using its tail to stuff itself at the wrong end with all that grass!"

Walks Far thought Singer the most talented story inventor ever. For years her knife handle served to remind her of how convincingly an impossible story might be told. But for now she was getting terribly hungry. She and Red Hoop Woman nearly always served supper while sufficient daylight to eat by still lingered; but here, with darkness descending, Moon Woman made no move to start serving the men any of those fragrant things she cooked in so many pots at once. All she did was rise to strike a match and touch it to a strangely shaped bottle fastened to the wall and having bright metal behind it.

The bottle suddenly gave an impressive flood of light, but Walks Far was shocked by Moon Woman's wastefulness, just as she had already been shocked by the wastefulness of Singer and Turns Red in lighting their pipes. None of these rich people could bother to hold a twig or take a hot coal from a fire-burning stove hardly out of arm's reach. Instead, they simply wasted hard to get matches.

Moon Woman did not sit down this time. She dragged a nearly full sack of flour from behind the stove. Obviously, she intended to make bread. Walks Far liked bread very much, and she and her sister had made it in the Blackfoot country, baking it slowly in the ashes. She watched Moon Woman's procedure intently, but she also had an awareness of Singer insistently trying to convince Scalps Them about something. At the same time he admitted that he lived much like a white man, that in Oklahoma he had a father and brother who ran a big store, a blacksmith shop, and a boat that carried wagons across a river. There was a third brother who ran a store like Singer's, but far to the southwest.

Moon Woman had placed a big pan on the stove to hold melted grease about two finger joints deep. She rolled back the top of the standing flour sack, dropped in a pinch of something called soda and, with her hands, carefully mixed in enough water to make a dough sufficiently thick to be lifted out piece by piece. She patted each piece into a cake nearly the size of the pan and fried it, building a heap of the finished cakes much too slowly for Walks Far's hunger. Blue smoke from the sputtering grease smelled delicious as it floated by, layered between the lazy swirls of tobacco smoke already hanging in the air.

Abruptly a shocked Walks Far forgot her hunger. Confident words firmly spoken by Singer jarred her to consciousness. If she had heard them from anyone else, she would have regarded them as just too unbelievable, too absurd to be considered. Singer was telling Scalps Them, *"The wasichu—'the whites'—will steal your Black Hills before two more winters! Ten winters from now all the buffalo will be gone!"*

The buffalo gone! Walks Far could see them in their limitless thousands up there on the wide, high prairies between the Missouri and the Yellowstone, and ranging in thousands more, north of the Missouri, on the Milk, the Marias, the Bow and Oldman rivers, and always around the Sweet Grass hills.

But Singer went on, "You have seen here that white man's

cattle now eat all the grass that once fed the buffalo, though, fortunately, those cattle belong to Indians like Turns Red.

"Just six winters ago the whites finished the iron road they made for their firewagons to run up the Platte and on over the mountains to the everywhere-water. That road cut the buffalo into two herds. The southern herd is going fast. And you can see that the northern herd is also growing less. It is shrunken into smaller country, and now the whites are building another iron road through those smaller hunting grounds. When that road is finished, the white buffalo killers and their skinners will make the prairies white with buffalo bones. You will think the prairies are black with white men. In winter you will see buffalo hides stacked in long rows like the cordwood cut for the fireboats on the Missouri. In the spring, wagons will haul those hides to the iron road. Soon all the buffalo will be gone. I have seen this; Turns Red has seen it."

Turns Red had been nodding agreement, like any man hearing his prejudices confirmed by an expert speaker, but Walks Far saw Scalps Them give his most confident grin, heard him say, "We will stop that iron road. We will keep the whites out of the country—all except some traders."

Singer was on the point of relighting his beautiful pipe, but he held the fire and gazed sadly at Scalps Them before drawing a deep breath to go on, "You know that I also am an Indian. I will always be an Indian, and I don't like most whites any better than you do. Therefore, I will say to you that there is something wrong with all us Indians: Always we see happy. All of us, until it is too late! And I think maybe the Sioux are the worst of all.

"But, brother, because you are my good new friend, I will tell you something that saddens me to hear myself say. But I should say it, and you should hear me. Be attentive!—*Wakin ksapa yo!* —*You cannot stop the whites from coming!* It has been too late for that for a long time. There are too many of them."

Scalps Them started to speak, but Singer again demanded that he be attentive; and Walks Far saw the visible effort Singer made in groping for convincing words with which to go on, "Turns Red knows that I fought in a big war between all the North whites and the South whites. I was with the South whites, and we were beaten. That war lasted four winters long, and in each summer there were great battles in which about as many white men were killed—in just one or two days of fighting—as there are of all the Sioux people, the men, the women, and children all together!

158

"Do you know that the whites make a mark on a piece of paper for each person in their tipis—and send those marks to their Great White Father? He has many men who do nothing else all day of every moon but count those marks! It takes them ten winters! But, by then, there are already so very many more whites that they have to start the counting again. They never catch up, the whites are so many-plenty-many. Even after that big war there were more of them than when it started."

Singer wasted another match, still without lighting his pipe, for abruptly he began to speak again, "It is not the army nor even the buffalo killers who are your real enemy. It is all those too-many ordinary, hungry white people who want land, some of them to dig for gold, but most of them for farming. They cannot understand why you don't want to farm, just as you cannot understand why they want you to do so. But I sometimes think maybe we Indians understand our enemy less than they understand us. And they are coming, more and more of them are coming, faster and faster. There is no end to them. They will cover all your country like the big gray lice on a sick pony in springtime.

"Since just last summer it has been much too late. I know this because I see what is on the white man's talking papers. Long-hair Custer sent a message to all the talking papers. He said he has found gold in your Black Hills; he said he thinks the land around there will be fine for farming. Now so many whites will come that *not even the Sioux and the army together* could stop them for long—two winters, maybe.

"There was a time when something might have been done. But there is another thing wrong with many of our Indian peoples: The Sioux kill Rees and Crows, they kill Snakes, Arapaho, and others. Sometimes they kill the Cheyennes, too. And all those people kill Sioux. But instead of fighting each other, instead of counting coups, all Indian people should have been helping against the whites before it was too late.

"Although I do not like most whites, and though I have seen much of the bad things they do to Indians and to each other, I can say something good about them: Their young men win honors without scalping their neighbors and stealing their horses. They are banished and kept in a big stone house or put to death if they do that. They are also banished or put to death if they kill women and children on purpose, especially of their own people! Sometimes, they try to be very generous to those they defeat in their wars though they are often very stupid in their generosity."

Walks Far found all this terribly disturbing, even the merely puzzling parts, and frightening from a man who could put on those funny things and see into the future. But, in a way, this story was harder to believe than the one he had told about the big two-toothed animal who fed himself with his tail. Still, Singer was a disturbing man, and in more ways than one.

She knew Scalps Them well enough to see that although he had pretended to listen politely, Singer simply bored and irritated him, not only because Singer proved such a dominating talker but also because the things Singer said were either unwelcome or a kind of nonsense lacking any saving humor. But Scalps Them was holding back more fury than Walks Far had guessed. Though he did not want to offend Singer too much, he could not resist saying, "Maybe there is still another thing wrong with some Indians. They learn so much from the *wasichu* that they talk like a *wasichu*—in a loud voice. And I have heard it said that when Indians have worn the blue soldier clothes for a little while, they think no one else knows how to fight!"

Singer only laughed, much as though at a joke on himself, and he said, "Sometimes a person can see nothing to do but fight, and in his own way. If I happened to be the man with the guns in that crazy story you have heard, I think maybe I would make a trade with you, because you are my good new friend, and because you would be better off to die fighting anyhow! If you will come to my store in four days, I think maybe we can see the crazy man in your story. Now let us say no more about it. It is good, it is finished!—*Hechetu alo!* Let us all see happy, let us eat, then let us dance for a while."

Chapter Eighteen
THE KISSING DANCE
(Late Winter 1874-1875 continued)

Walks Far got to eat at last. With the men served, there was still plenty of everything—singed jerky, boiled beef and a fat broth with dried berries in it, hominy, those bitter potatoes that she did not much like, but also a new and most tasty white man's root called carrot—all with that wonderful fried bread and, of course, the tea. There was salt to be licked if a person wanted to, and Walks Far had been appalled at the amount of it Singer appeared to sprinkle into everything except his tea.

People began to come, and Walks Far was instantly relieved. She had feared that because Moon Woman and Turns Red did not live in the usual Sioux way, and because they clearly disregarded certain minor customs and etiquette, there would be no dressing up for the dance. But the people came in all their finery! She changed as quickly as she could into her *winkte* dress, and of course it was much admired, though Singer seemed not to notice. While some of the men were tightening the heads of their ordinary flat Sioux drums by heating them cautiously over the stove, Singer was making a drum of his own. He had taken an iron cooking pot about half full of water and stretched wet deerskin over it, but before he felt satisfied with the surprisingly deep tone that drum produced, he added and took away water until he must have had to remove and replace the head six times. Perhaps it took him so long because a girl of about Walks Far's age and also in a pretty dress kept laughing and talking with him in a strange language. Walks Far felt sure that that girl was showing off a knowledge of white man's talk. Also, and more happily, Walks Far was able to conclude that the girl's face was one that could change the weather! A good look at her and Sun would hide his face behind the clouds.

Turns Red and Moon Woman pushed aside the blanket curtain at the end of the cabin, lashed the bedding to the white-man-style bed, and stood the whole on end in the corner to make more room for the crowd. Drums began to throb, and children moved out of the way. Astonishingly, the first dance would be a kind of a courting dance, and among strangers! Walks Far sat with the other women intending to dance, against the cabin wall on one side, while the men dancers sat along the opposite wall. The drums at the stove end of the room stilled, but two rather elderly men advanced into the open space. They carried drums and beat accompaniment to their own singing as they began dancing, shuffling up and down the middle of the cabin four times.

Walks Far, seeing Singer apparently content to sit with the old men and beat his stupid drum, searched quickly for a second-choice partner. Ordinarily a girl or woman knew who her partner would be; it was usually understood when one received an invitation or was arranged before the dancing began. But here, the partner a girl got would depend entirely upon a combination of her will and fast footwork. Walks Far decided upon the best available, a near-double for One Horn, though he looked less lean.

The two dancing men finished their four turns and shuffled quickly out of the way. Silence descended. Along their wall, one or two of the men grinned nervously, and all kept their eyes averted from anyone's face. The girls, too, held their eyes averted. The silence grew almost palpable. PAU-OOM!—One enormous resonant beat from Singer's drum. Walks Far was up, and in a single long stride had kicked her chosen partner's moccasin sole.

Again in silence, Walks Far and the other women and girls took places to the right of their partners in a line looped round the open space; and as all the drums and the singing started again, Walks Far and her partner grasped each other's belts, caught the drumming rhythm with bent knees, and, in a kind of two-step, shuffled sideways around the open space with the other dancers, all singing to the rhythmic pulse of the drums. The swaying, rocking dance went on and on, with three pauses just long enough for the drumming and singing to cease, then start again. For every song must have its four parts, though all those parts may be identical.

When a true intermission came, Walks Far's partner did not slip outside, so she knew he was not disgruntled from being chosen by her. She talked with him and liked him. His name was Owl Head, and she felt confident that he would come for her in a dance where the men chose. Dancing under the lamplight was nearly as pleasant as dancing around a fire, and seemed to do more for the color in people's clothes and ornaments. She was having a fine time, or should have been. But Singer's overriding voice and drum, the memory of his touch—something about him—nagged at her with a throbbing insistence.

Different dances were called, but the changes in name meant little more than a minor variation from the first dance—an almost identical rhythm of drums and quality of voice, the same relentless, near-hypnotic repetition to draw dancers and onlookers alike into a kind of trance beneath the yellow lamplight. Around midnight, and before everyone ate, Walks Far danced a variation in which first the women dancers, followed later by the men, teased their partners four times with bowls of meat before surrendering them. On the Redwater last summer the meat had been stewed puppy, but here, this time of year, it was only beef.

In another variation Walks Far and her partner danced with the others in single file, the man ahead. At a swift increase in tempo the man turned and grasped the girl's right hand to shake it between their faces. In a tipi at night, with the fire low, a girl might get her hand kissed in that hitting-in-the-face dance.

As the whole crowd ate, four mature men—unfortunately not including Singer—seated themselves in the open space and ate a ceremonial dish. Again, the dish should have been stewed puppy, with the last man of the four getting only the tail. Walks Far felt hopeful, but she tried not to be too expectant when the four men rose and one by one pointed to the girl he wanted to stand opposite him. The first man chose the homely girl in the pretty dress, but the second man, who was much more hand-some as well as being younger, pointed to Walks Far. She felt much as she had when, as a sixteen-year-old virgin back in the Blackfoot country, the band chief had honored her with the privilege of lifting a coal from the fire to light his ceremonial pipe.

Now the four men and four girls danced toward each other and retreated. They alone sang to the low drumming as they advanced, but they stilled their own voices as they danced backward, and other singers came in to a louder drumming. As the four parts ended in abrupt silence, each of the four men in turn struck Singer's drum, briefly counted a coup, and made a gift to a likely child from the crowd.

For a time after that, Walks Far and the women only watched. Men came out as the spirit moved them to sing their own songs and dance their own individual dances to the drum-ming. They went quick-footed around a circle, with their knees bent, but their heads up and their chests out, and now and then they flashed into a frenzy of quick footwork or broke into wildly sinuous, whirling leaps that ended with a sharp yell.

People began calling for Singer. He finally raised an acknowl-edging hand, then briefly schooled one of the drummers in a strange, fast rhythm on the water drum. Satisfied, he drew off his high boots, stepped into the dancing space, and marked a square around himself by four sharp knives driven into the packed-earth floor, then sang to the strange rhythm.

Walks Far heard the homely girl explaining that she believed Singer's song to be taken from a white man's dreaming song for calling a certain kind of animal near for hunting. "To under-stand that song," the girl said, "you have to know that beyond the everywhere-water there is a big-humped animal that the *wasichu* call a camel. Singer's song keeps saying, 'The camels are coming, The camels are coming.' That is all."

Singer, holding his head high and with his eyes gazing off toward the distance, began to dance. Above the hips he did not move, except that his whole body shot unbelievably high as he seemed to spring on one leg and toe while his opposite knee was held uplifted for extremely fast kicking—kicking that sent his defenseless feet flashing dangerously between those sharp knives. Then, with the drum quickening at each change, Singer kicked his way around the four sides of the square. He repeated the turn three more times, and never looked once at the knives!

Walks Far saw such odd dancing to be not only dangerous but very hard work, though she found it monotonous, and *much* too long. He had borrowed her knife for the dance and on returning it he smiled openly to whisper, "I am pleased that the pretty woman has a beautiful dress!" But he went directly to a dignified matron and before the eyes of the whole delighted crowd exposed the fact that she had been hiding a trader's hank of bright beads in her sleeve. And back he turned to his stupid old drum!

As the mixed dancing began again, more of the older people joined in. They seemed a little less formal here, less custombound in their fun. Walks Far was surprised to see a new, suddenly relaxed Red Hoop Woman dancing like a girl, then chattering excitedly with a strange man during an intermission. Even Red Hoop Woman could take a holiday!

Several people were looking at Walks Far, waiting for her answer to a question she had failed to hear. The question was repeated, "Are Pekony dances different from Teton dances?"

"No—only the kissing dance," she blurted. She had never mentioned this dance for fear Red Hoop Woman would be scandalized and believe her worst suspicions about the Pekonies confirmed. Now Walks Far hurried to flatter these Sioux with what she believed to be the truth. She explained earnestly and in some detail that Pekony dances were much like Teton Sioux dances, except that she thought them simpler and fewer. But her listeners, men and women, would not be diverted from the kissing dance. They eagerly insisted on knowing all about that dance.

"It is much like any dance," Walks Far said, "It is a very simple dance for both married and unmarried people. The men bring blankets and stand in a line facing a line of women. When the drumming and singing begins, the woman on the right, at the foot of the line, dances to the left between the lines and chooses a man she thinks would like to give her a blanket. They dance together to the head of the line, and the man throws a blanket over both their heads. Then they dance back to the other end, and the woman gets to keep the blanket. That is all."

"But they kiss under that blanket?"

"Yes, and they must keep step all the time. The people keep them shoved straight along between the lines."

Someone wanted to know, "Must they keep their hands in sight, outside that blanket?"

"They hold each other's arms," Walks Far said, and she felt obliged to add, "That dance can cause much trouble. Some men can't afford to give a blanket to just any woman who chooses them. They get mad about it. Some men get mad when their wives or their girls choose another man too often. Sometimes, an important man who has brought a lot of blankets gets mad because no one chooses him. Ah, yes, that dance can cause much trouble!"

But Singer had been listening, and he was not afraid of trouble. He snatched down the old blanket that had been used for a curtain, folded it over his arm, and planted himself at the head of the open space. "I am already at the head of the line!" he challenged. "Let the woman who knows about this dance show how it is done."

Eager people joined him, and they shoved Walks Far to the foot of the line. Walks Far couldn't refrain from throwing a fearful glance toward Red Hoop Woman and Moon Woman, but she saw no disapproval. They too wore excited smiles, and actually looked as though they waited only for a push to join in. Red Hoop Woman, especially, wore an expression as though tonight she was game for anything, once!

The drumming started, and all eyes were on Walks Far. With an anticipatory thrill, she bent her knees and swayed into the dance, two-stepping sideways between the singing lines. She felt a little embarrassed, but she also felt herself and the man waiting for her to be the most splendid people in that crowded cabin.

She kicked his instep. He whirled the blanket over them with a grand flourish, and almost before that blanket had settled, was dancing with her expertly, momentarily confusing her with a quick, elaborate step designed for losing two of each three gained. And Singer certainly needed no lessons in how to kiss under a blanket at the same time. . . .

Walks Far could hardly take it, and she felt a kind of relief when the last singers in the line stopped them. Singer ducked from under the blanket and, as he and Walks Far took their places, she handed it to another of the singing girls. The girl danced down the line and abruptly thrust it at a man after she had nearly gone past him. Walks Far, in line opposite the resplendent Singer, ached to be given that blanket soon again.

After a while the people went back to the more sedate dancing and, in an intermission very late in the night, a young couple who were special friends of Turns Red and Moon Woman began to dance alone. They danced out through the door into the cold, starry night, then walked back in for their hoods and robes and mittens. The dance was over. Guests, except for Singer, departed quickly, leaving the one-room cabin feeling suddenly quiet and empty with only the six adults and four children remaining.

Walks Far spread her bed robes beside one wall and, with the lamp blown out, she heard Singer rolling himself into a robe against the opposite wall. Even that was an excitement.

Much later she was roused into that hazy-mazy borderland between waking and sleep. She felt as though she had been dreaming a wholly erotic dream, one from which she had no wish to waken, but someone was insistently whispering her name. There were big, gentle fingers at her cheek, her lips. She opened her eyes and found a man looming over her in the graying light. "I am going," he whispered. "But we will see one another in three days." He kissed her questioningly, and her kiss gave quick answer.

Chapter Nineteen

GUNS FOR HUNKPAPAS

(Late Winter 1874-1875 continued)

On the appointed day, in the late afternoon, Walks Far and the others rode up to Singer's trading store to find that it differed from her cousin's cabin only in being twice as long. On the frozen creek below, the rickety corral and shelter for horses were much the same. A rusty stovepipe and a low door revealed the added feature of a dugout cut into the snowy slope behind the store.

Singer came out and waited to greet them as they approached. He almost danced with energy and looked more colorful than ever, with the brown shirt behind the huge carved pipe hanging round his neck now replaced by an equally rich pale blue one, tighter across his shoulders and chest. "Welcome, friends," he called out. "You are going to help me feast tonight. I remembered this morning that this last day of the moon is my birthday. I now have thirty-five winters."

He went on to address only Scalps Them in adding, "Friend, I have talked to the crazy white man you thought to be me. He has most of the things you want. But I cannot get them for you until it is snowing. I do not think it will snow tonight, though we must be ready. And we must talk, while we drink Candido's excuse for tea."

Candido was at the stove, which Walks Far saw to look neither so frightening, so new, nor so hot as her cousin's stove. Candido, a wiry, middle-aged man, might have been all Indian, though he had a huge moustache. He wore the clothing of an ordinary white man, but with a thick gray coat that was sleeveless and showed a black and white woven pattern of strikingly bold design, which Walks Far liked.

Along with the tea Singer gave them some wonderfully tasty and meaty nuts he said were pecans and some choice dried berries he called raisins, but which Red Hoop Woman knew were only dried grapes. In setting them out, he spoke directly to Walks Far for the first time, and in a near-whisper. "I have been much afraid you might stay with your relatives," he said. "I must give you a present for choosing me in the Pekony dance." Then, leaving her no time for an answer, he began being playfully attentive to Red Hoop Woman and Fire Wing.

Walks Far saw that Singer obviously lived here in the smaller part of his cabin, that there was a doorway from it into the store. She counted Singer's rich shirts—four of them hanging in a row on the wall near the head of his high, homemade white-man-style bed in the corner. She saw added riches in other colorful clothing, with boots and moccasins making a row of their own on the floor beneath. At the foot of the bed stood a pair of wood-slatted small leather trunks clearly designed to be carried by a pack pony. All around the walls and from overhead hung much truly fine Indian workmanship—quilled or beaded bags, cradle boards, war clubs, lances, shield covers, and the like. Also, there were two guns. In front and to one side of the stove stood a hip-high, flat-topped thing that rested on four legs and was made entirely of wood. Only later would she hear it called a table. It held a lamp and some small things Walks Far could not see very well from the floor. Old wooden boxes were up-ended on the floor below and around it.

Singer was saying earnestly, apologetically, to Scalps Them, "Brother, it may be that we do not have much time, and you will understand that you must go away from here as soon as you have the guns, even if it is in the night. It is too bad that we must therefore trade in the way of two white men, swiftly and without seeing all that we are trading. I do not like to do this and you do not like to do this, but we must. Turns Red will have told you that I am an honest man.

"I have seen your mules and they are fine mules," Singer went on. "For them, for the gold, and for your robes, I will trade you the powder, lead, and percussion caps, which I have here in plenty. Also, I will trade you some guns and some things your women will want to have, and I will show you five very ordinary pack ponies, but any of them will get you where you are going and you can choose two for replacing the mules."

Walks Far then heard him explain that there was, however, a small catch. For, though all the guns were of the desirable short kind called carbines—the ones with a saddle ring on the left side—there were, unfortunately, only four shoots-many guns. Two of these were the Winchesters, which loaded from the side, and two were the kind of gun called Spencers, which loaded through the butt.

Scalps Them knew, Singer said, that both those guns shot only rimfire cartridges, which could hardly be reloaded and therefore forced the owner of such a gun to find a trader whenever new cartridges were needed. Singer had forty cartridges for each of those guns. However, he went on, there were more of the single-shot, altered-to-center-fire carbines called Sharps than Scalps Them would wish to carry, and for these Sharps there were plenty-many cartridges that were of the same size that part of the army still used. They might be of advantage. Moreover, Singer asserted, he could provide one proper bullet mold and one reloading tool for each four of the Sharps. If he, Singer, were going where Scalps Them was going, he might even prefer the Sharps.

"So, brother, you think about this while I look at your robes and skins, and while your women look at some things in the store. Then, while they are setting up your tipi, we can trade before we feast. We both will be happy that it is finished."

Without giving Scalps Them so much as an instant for grumbling, Singer led Walks Far, Red Hoop Woman, and Fire Wing directly into the end of the cabin that was his store, and for the first time ever Walks Far was enabled to touch the fine things in such a store. Red Hoop Woman said, "Everyone shall have a fine, soft red blanket, and enough of the calico and red flannel for two dresses each." As Singer stacked up these things and others, he made marks on a piece of paper, and Scalps Them began to get nervous. But Singer insisted that they would need a lot of the best linen thread, and he marked that down, but gave each of them a thimble and a black paper of needles without making any mark. Red Hoop Woman and Walks Far then selected several hanks of large and small beads, mostly blue or white, which Singer again marked down, and as they were leaving, he gave Fire Wing a Jew's harp. That set them all to laughing, Singer too, when they explained why. So he gave her a fine tin flute instead, then added a big gift twist of tobacco for Scalps Them.

Singer came outside with them, pointed out to Red Hoop Woman the obvious site for putting up the tipi, told them what to do with the horses and mules, and begged them to take all the wood they wanted from his woodpile. "Come back when it is dark," he said. "Candido will not cook until it is already dark and people are waiting."

As Walks Far and Red Hoop Woman worked together swiftly, setting up the tipi poles, then from the back raising the heavy lifting pole with the tipi cover attached, Red Hoop Woman sent Fire Wing off to find small wood for kindling. After a while she spoke, "You are saying nothing?"

"I am thinking," Walks Far told her as she grasped one side of the loose-hanging tipi cover while Red Hoop Woman took the other, and each walked her side around to the front. Then, as they began lacing the cover together with the wooden pins, Red Hoop Woman added, "About where you are going to sleep tonight?"

"Something like that," Walks Far admitted.

"Maybe you should not think so much," Red Hoop Woman declared, and utterly astonished Walks Far by adding, "If I had seen such a person when I had no husband . . ."

They both let the matter hang there as they worked together to weight the bottom of the tipi cover to the frozen ground with heavy stones, then went inside to hang the dew wall.

"What of Fire Wing?" Walks Far said.

"She will go to sleep early and she will wake up late. And she is at that age when all young people believe anything but that which is true," Red Hoop Woman said.

They brought in the packs of camp gear and bedding, and when Fire Wing came with kindling, they laid a small fire ready to light. After boosting Fire Wing up to insert the highest lacing pins, they worked the smoke-ear poles into the smoke ears, and then, with the tipi door hung from the second lacing pin and the fire alight, camp was made. They needed only to wash and do some primping before it grew too dark to see well.

Walks Far agreed with Red Hoop Woman that it was an odd circumstance, though a happy one, for a man to make so much of his birthday, or even to remember more than the moon in which it occurred. Yet Walks Far was not being wholly open in this. A part of her earlier silence had risen from her awareness of something that, though hardly a real coincidence, had brought her a disturbing sense of wonder tinged with fear. She remembered that she, too, had been born on the last day of a moon—the previous moon. But it surely meant something.

Long ago Walks Far's mother had pointed out to her that a buffalo has twenty-eight ribs, one for each day in a moon, and that the last day was special for all two-legged people, but much more so for those with the good fortune to be born under its favorable sign. Therefore, that both she and Singer had been born on that last day was, on the face of it, all to the good. People did what they pleased on that day. Still, a person must always be wary of even the smallest coincidence and never take one lightly, except of course in the case of words happily lending themselves to the Sioux delight in puns. She would not weaken any good power in a coincidence by talking about it, and if there were any bad power in it, she would take care of that herself. The whole matter didn't amount to much, but it was enough to make her wonder whether she was somehow getting entangled by those mysterious spider men the Sioux believed to be weavers of trickery—the *iktomi*.

The first thing Walks Far noted, as Singer welcomed them to his living space again, was the superb buffalo robe now tossed upon his bed. With it was an equally fine blanket strip, expertly and tastefully quilled. At the same time her nostrils were assailed by a strong but not unpleasant fragrance from the two pots Candido had on the stove. He was also making a kind of bread by patting the dough into very thin disks, which, instead of frying in grease, he baked carefully on a large, thin sheet of iron raised a little from the fire where a stove lid had been removed. He had made a stack of the bread. Now he started cooking meat, spreading great slabs atop the stove to sizzle and smoke.

Singer passed around a bottle and a stack of small metal cups nested together. He told them he did not drink whiskey, that this was something else, and that he saved it only for feasting with friends. The deep red drink proved pleasant, though stingy in the mouth and throat and surprisingly warming on the way down. Then there was a strange yellow something taken from a shiny metal box and freshly cut into little square chunks.

At first taste it proved curiously flavorless, then overwhelmingly strong. Singer explained this dish to be a white man's something called cheese, which, as Walks Far understood from his Sioux speech, was made by a tedious process from the milk of white man's cows after the milk had been permitted to rot. Walks Far was simply revolted. The mere thought of eating another piece put her close to gagging. Hastily, she ate some raisins and a couple of pecans. She could think of only one or two things that could possibly be worse than rotten milk. The ways of the whites were indeed strange, sometimes disgusting.

But the meat Candido prepared could hardly have been better, and with it came a huge mountain of rice nearly covered with fragrant black beans and bean sauce dark and thick. It smelled delicious, but at the first mouthful Walks Far gasped from the burning, eye-watering shock and exclaimed in Blackfoot *"Apstahkaipoko!"* [Janet, who had asked Dewey to teach her some simple Blackfoot one evening while they were parked on a hilltop eating hamburgers bought at a drive-in, was pleased to recognize the term *apstahkaipoko*. It meant "pepper," or more literally, "it tastes like tobacco."] Walks Far had been able to go on eating, but thereafter carefully mined the plain rice from beneath the beans and sauce, using a disk of Candido's very thin bread folded into a scoop, just as she observed him to do when everyone, men and women, had begun eating together.

And a man doing the cooking! Practically *serving* the food to women, too! Walks Far had eaten food prepared by males only once before. That was when she had gone with her husband's war party against the Snakes, with two boys then doing the crude cooking, as was traditional.

Walks Far suddenly felt a blast of cold air. She had heard no sound, but a youngish man with a Winchester cradled in his left arm and with his right thumb on the hammer stood backed against the wall inside the closed door. Except for his long hair the color of grass killed by early snow, and except for shocking, palest blue eyes in his unusually dusky face, he could have been any Indian who looked thoroughly dangerous.

He and Singer said *hau* together, and Singer went on speaking to him in an unfamiliar language, while he stared rudely at each strange face as though to fix it forever in his memory. Then, without a word, he dragged a box up to the empty table to sit with the Winchester across his lap. Candido served him, and he began a solitary meal, using the first knife and fork Walks Far had ever seen anyone eat with.

Singer offered something of an explanation. "His name is Duck, and he lives with us. Because of the color of his eyes, the whites were sure he was one of them and they took him away to school when he was about ten. But after four years, he escaped. He is a Comanche and he speaks only enough Sioux to buy or sell something. I have told him many times that to bring a gun in from the cold to where it is warm will make the gun sweat, then rust."

"No care. I keep," Duck said in Sioux, and those were the only words he spoke throughout.

The meal ended with a wonderfully sugary and light kind of bread served with a bowl of peaches, not a stew of dried peaches, but seemingly fresh yellow ones cut into halves and beautifully preserved in sweet syrup. They came from a shiny metal bucket, and Walks Far ate more than her share to compensate for those impossible beans, and wondered why Candido had not served them with the meat. Altogether it was a fine feast. Singer filled his big pipe with some superior kind of tobacco, and everyone, including Duck before he slipped out, smoked it with him.

At a word from Singer, Candido too went out, then he came back with an odd thing somewhat resembling a violin, which Walks Far had once seen played by the Métis. But Candido only used his fingers on the strings. He sang as he played. All of his songs seemed to suggest sadness and to be much the same except for their tempo. Walks Far got a little tired of them, though she thought it interesting and curious when Singer explained to her that each song openly conveyed, in words intelligible to anyone who knew the language, a story about a boy and girl in love. Walks Far's songs, as well as those of her people, were often made up only out of a careful arrangement of sounds that the composer liked but that, except for a brief refrain, might carry no meaning in words clear to anyone else, even when the sounds might cast a powerful spell.

After a while Singer rose and lifted the fine buffalo robe from his bed to hold it outspread between his wide-flung hands. "This is the finest robe I have ever taken in trade," he said. "It has been made soft without damage to the hair." After everyone had admired it, he came to the point. "I have long wanted very much to have some woman finish this robe, and now that I have seen that fine yellow robe you have, friend Scalps Them, I wish to ask the woman who took it and finished it to stay awhile and dress this one up. I have everything here, and there is good light —if you are not too tired from much long riding in the cold?"

Walks Far heard herself saying lightly, graciously, "I will stay for a while and fix that robe, if you wish."

With Red Hoop Woman, Fire Wing, and Scalps Them gone, and with Candido washing dishes, Singer led Walks Far at once into the cold store. He did not offer to kiss her, but immediately lit a candle lamp and carried it about with them. He urged her to gather up all she would need to embellish the robe by using large beads and cone-shaped dangles made of tin in lieu of the deer's hooves on Scalps Them's robe.

Back by the stove Singer arranged the lamp for her, and she sat on the floor, neatly trimming the hair away from beneath the bright and tasteful blanket strip. She stitched it down to cover the seam where the two halves of the buffalo's skin were sewn together, along the line of the animal's backbone. Singer sat and watched her work. It was a rather slow and tedious task, and she had no expectation that it would get finished.

Candido stacked up the clean dishes and said something to which Singer responded in exactly the same words. Then just as he went out, presumably to the dugout, he smiled as he said something more. Singer translated it: "Candido says you are very beautiful, that you are also very much woman."

Singer sat and watched her, and she kept on stitching in the silence. She wished that, if nothing else, he would sing one of his rolling-thunder songs. After a time, after she had stitched down about one third the length of the blanket strip, he spoke at last: "Candido did not say that your hands are beautiful, but they are beautiful too. You do everything fast and well."

"Always I try to do so," she said, now certain that he actually wanted the robe finished. The fact irritated but relaxed her. "Do you really think the *wasichu* will steal our hunting lands, that the buffalo will all be gone?"

"I am as sure of that as I am sure spring will come. But let us not speak of that, tonight."

Walks Far had another question. "Do you believe that any two-legged person can live to be one hundred and twenty-eight winters?"

Singer got up to put wood in the stove before answering. "I have talked to a relative whom I knew to be one hundred and twelve winters," he said. "Anyone who lives that long might possibly live sixteen winters more, though I would not like to bet very much on it. But my relative got his power from a bear."

And shortly, Singer was telling her a marvelous story about a bear and a fox. The story had everything—adventure, humor that was both subtle and broad, plenty of trickery, some sadness, and a good spicing of the risqué. Singer knew any number of such stories. He told her that they belonged to his people, and she recognized them as stories of a superior quality. She had the blanket strip sewn securely into place, and the tin-cones-and-blue-bead dangles, alternating with dangles of black beads and small yellow shells, decorating one side and the lower edge of the robe. It would be very handsome, but she was suddenly determined not to finish his tiresome old robe tonight. "It is late," she said. "I will finish this tomorrow."

Singer took out a fine watch, one that would speak to him with small bells when he wished. "It is but little more than halfway to the middle of the night," he said seriously. Suddenly his eyes were smiling as he added teasingly. "But that is very late, and I am sure that my birthday is now past. Last night, I dreamed that on my birthday I was dancing under a blanket with a beautiful woman, but she stabbed me with a long knife—"

Walks Far had already snatched her knife from her lap and had reached across Singer's lap so swiftly that he winced toward her as she drove the blade hard into the floor close beside his hip. "You have now been stabbed," she said, and left the knife standing there.

Singer's strong face lighted like an eager child's face. He carefully removed the precious pipe from around his neck to hang its chain over the guards of her knife. Then, and not until then, did he take her in his arms.

He kissed her exactly as she wanted to be kissed. Still holding the kiss, he stood up, lifting her easily and carrying her to the high, white-man-style bed to drop her sprawling upon its covering buffalo robe. Smiling down at her, he began to undress.

For one of the few times in her life Walks Far felt awkward. Her husband had always come to her bed or called her to his in darkness. Now, though the strong light added a kind of excitement, undressing in it under Singer's eyes made her feel strangely ungraceful, and when she was able to slip naked between the blankets under the robe, she wished she had known some attractive way of going about it. But Singer, too, she saw, was looking a bit ridiculous. Only his handsome shirt remained, but in his all-too-obvious impatience he was having trouble twisting it off his powerful shoulders and over his head.

He only dimmed the light before he slipped between the blankets with her, his arm encircling her hips. "I saw you were even more beautiful than I hoped," he whispered, his lips nuzzling at her ear. "Long legs without being a bony woman."

Walks Far wound herself close, pressed quiveringly against him, and in the stillness she breathed raggedly amid their fierce kisses. Singer bit her neck, her belly, and she groaned with pleasure. Her thighs would be marked with purpling welts. Singer had teeth like a wolf.

He did not try to enter her until she urged her body beneath his. He was a heavy man, but that was a part of what she wanted, and she could feel him in there, thick, warm, solid. And they did do a kind of blanket dance, moving beneath it to the rhythm of abandon. She began to cry out to him in a language he did not need to understand.

Walks Far had wanted it so much that it had been almost painful. She felt faint, but roused to gladness that Singer had not yet parted from her body. He raised his head to look down at her lazily and happily to ask in wonder, "Are you always such a wildcat?"

She smiled but did not answer. Her eyelids felt ready to close with a will of their own and let her down into stuporous sleep. She could not keep them open.

"Not so soon!" Singer told her in sudden alarm. "Come!" He dragged her roughly from the bed, and with his big hand tightly gripping her arm, drew her out the door to the woodpile in the stinging cold of such a clear, freezing night that the stars were like crystals of ice. "We will rub each other with snow," Singer said.

Walks Far tripped him and ran away over the snow's frozen crust. He chased after her for a way, and she could hear the crust breaking under his greater weight. He stopped and shouted, "Woman, are you crazy! We will get bloody ankles."

She ran back, dodging around him, and was in bed, looking demure with the covers up to her chin when he came in again. She eyed him closely, then pretended dismay, saying, "Little boys should not run around naked in the cold. I can see now that there is nothing for us to do but go to sleep."

Singer also pretended dismay and spoke sadly, "Yes, I should have known this would happen to me." Then he brightened hopefully, "Maybe you can think of some women's cures . . ."

Much later, in the quietest part of the night and with the lamp long out, Walks Far found herself helpless in a dream such as she had never dreamed before. She was falling, falling endlessly and forever into terror, dark emptiness, and cold. She tried to scream, but no scream would come—not until she landed hard.

Singer's shadowy head and a shoulder appeared over the edge of the bed above her, and he reached down an arm to help her up. She still felt frightened and confused. "The cabin is turning over!" she cried.

Singer exploded with laughter, and managed to say, "You must remember that a person can fall from a white-man-style bed." He broke again into laughter, then kept giggling like some simpleton. "The cabin is turning over!" he mimicked her in his strongly accented Sioux. Walks Far flung herself upon him, wrestling to stop his stupid giggling, make him pay for it as well. Swiftly, deftly, her hand silenced him, held him readied as she straddled him. He tried to turn her under, but she stayed on top and rode him until she sensed he was close to breaking, then collapsed upon him in her shuddering triumph.

Next day, after Walks Far finished the robe and Singer asked what she would like for a present, she wished only for enough calico to make Grandfather a shirt. Singer appeared to be amused as he gave it to her, and even more amused as she immediately began work on it. He watched her silently, then said abruptly, "I wish very much for two things, but neither is possible. I wish you were staying here with me, and I wish I were going to the northern country with you. I shall think about you often, and I shall worry." And then, pointing up to the wall, he added, "I am going to give you that gun."

It was obviously an almost new single-shot carbine, a very short and simple one. It hung from a peg on the wall by a wide black leather strap having a big brass buckle and a shiny snap for the sliding ring on the left side of the gun. A black leather belt with leather cap box and cartridge box hung with it. Walks Far felt dazed by good fortune and by her impatience as Singer took down that gun and handed it to her. She immediately pushed down on the lever and opened the breech.

"I took that gun from the enemy in the last days of the white man's big war," Singer said. There is not much that can go wrong with it. Also, it is possible to reload the cartridges without tools, and the gun can even be used as a muzzle-loader if a fired cartridge is left in it. It will be a good gun to have, where you are going."

Singer loaded it with one of the very thick brass cartridge cases that had an extraordinarily wide-rimmed base. The base had no primer, only a tiny hole to admit the flash from an ordinary percussion cap. A fired cartridge could be easily removed by a person's fingers.

There were fourteen cartridges in the leather box on the belt, and Singer found a bag of fifty balls for reloading them. Walks Far put on the belt, slung the wide black strap over her left shoulder, and with the big brass buckle at her breast, let the carbine hang muzzle-down at her right hip like a cavalry trooper. When Singer shortened the strap, the muzzle hung just above her ankle. Of course, she would ride with the gun across her thighs, with the shoulder sling preventing any chance of dropping it from her horse.

Walks Far slid her palm over the smooth wood and metal of that gun as though she found it such a treasure as she had never actually hoped to possess. No other woman in the band owned a gun, nor did about half the men. No other woman, and not too many men, owned such a fine horse as Crazy One was, and no other woman would be so finely dressed as she. What more could she want? She wanted what she had shared so surely out of the confusions of elbows and knees in the darkness last night, but she wanted much else that went with it. . . .

Singer was teasing her again. "If you will give me your gun for just a little while," he said, "I will decorate it for you." He found some large, round-headed brass tacks and set about driving them into the dark stock, forming a double row all around close to the butt, then a neat cross on one side, a circle on the other, all of which made her gun more handsome than ever.

Candido came from the store, where he had been trading with a young man and two elderly women, and watched with approval as she hung the sling across her breast again. He surprised her by saying in the first Sioux words she had heard from him, "I will teach you how to throw that knife, if you wish."

Singer told her that throwing knives was better than throwing axes, and the three of them went down by the corral. After Singer stood a board against the haystack, Candido demonstrated with his own knife while giving instructions to Walks Far. Such murderous skill appeared possible only by magic, and after her first trials she began to be sure of it. Yet she improved steadily, suddenly began to get the hang of it, and soon did well enough that Candido exclaimed over and over in musical sounds that Walks Far never forgot, *"Yo no lo creo!"* But Walks Far knew she would have to practice a great deal.

Singer drilled her on sight settings for her gun. He would point to distant objects while she made the appropriate choice of either the rear notch or of one of the two lifting leaves. He said he had fired the gun, that it hit close enough to where it was aimed.

Late the next afternoon it began to snow, not heavily, but steadily enough that Singer spoke unhappily. "Duck must now go get the guns. We must tell Scalps Them, and you must help his wife pack for being ready to leave while it will still be dark for a time. We will tell them to sleep well, that we will wake them up."

That night was the last one Walks Far would spend in a cabin for a long while, or in which she would see a room full of yellow lamplight made into swift-enfolding blackness by a single breath. She sank with Singer from a moment of timeless peace into deepest sleep.

Duck came only a little late with the guns, all carbines as promised. Scalps Them insisted they be brought into the light for him to see that each was complete and functioning. Oddly, a coffee mill was built into the stock of one Sharps, but Singer said it would not work for that purpose, though it would work well for grinding clay or ochre for paint. All the guns and ammunition were then padded with hay and made up into four equal packs for loading on the two indifferent pack ponies included in the trade. Together, those packs hardly equaled the weight of two men, but they would nearly double the firepower of Sitting Bull's and Left Hand Bull's bands. Reluctantly Walks Far packed her own gun, but where she could get to it easily. Scalps Them, of course, carried his battered Winchester openly.

Candido surprised Walks Far with a gift, a long, handsome quirt he had himself made by plaiting strips of whitened rawhide alternating with blackened strips in an intricate arrangement over a heavy handle of lead. At almost the last moment Singer walked down with a parting gift to be shared with Red Hoop Woman, a deep wooden box having a sliding lid. It contained layers of good-quality candles, with the top layer entirely replaced by blocks of matches packed in tightly.

Walks Far stood aside in the darkness with him for a moment before she warily mounted Crazy One and rode away without a backward look. She knew that their meeting had been one of those rewards that persons may feel they deserve but do not much expect to receive. Nor should they tempt the spirits by asking for more than is given, and by dwelling upon the matter.

Shortly after full daylight they struck a well-traveled road from a point that would hardly suggest their departure from Singer's store. Nothing happened until the cold second day. At midafternoon, with snow falling again, they followed the road up and out of a coulee. Just at the crest they heard the creaking of much leather and the jangling of metal, but only an instant before about twenty-five soldiers with two Sioux scouts materialized from the falling snow.

"Keep going," Scalps Them said in an intense, low voice. He turned out to the left, giving the road to the soldiers and holding up his hand to say *hau* in passing. A thoroughly frightened Walks Far had not seen soldiers since that unforgettable early morning of a much colder day on the Marias four winters ago. Those soldiers had fired into the Pikuni Blackfoot lodges a little after first light, killing her father and mother along with more than 160 other people, and including old Heavy Breast, the band chief, who advanced waving the certificate of friendliness given him by the agent. Heavy Breast knew the soldiers had made a mistake, that they were looking for Mountain Chief's band. Many of the people had been too sick from smallpox for running, but the fourteen-year-old Walks Far had run, and she had seen the soldiers burning the lodges and rounding up the horses.

Most of these soldiers here appeared to be much younger, only boys, and they looked as cold as anyone would in this long, cold winter. All had ridden past now, and Walks Far saw Scalps Them loosen a little inside his robe. But the soldiers halted! One of the Sioux came galloping back, calling out that all must wait! Red Hoop Woman gave one moan in resignation and fright, and Walks Far knew they were sharing a kind of terror. Scalps Them waited calmly, too calmly and without a complaining word.

Scalps Them showed no strain as he and the scout greeted each other, *"Hau!"* They looked enough alike to have passed for brothers. "The young soldier chief wishes me to ask you a question," the scout said solemnly. "He wishes to know why you are riding around freezing your ass off in a country that the Great Spirit has forsaken. Also, where do you think you are going?" Walks Far was praying silently, her hand inside her blanket clutching the Sun-stone in its bag under her dress.

Scalps Them's voice came wearily. "Because I must, brother. I must have peace. You know women! The younger brother of my wife and of my wife's younger sister ran away to some wild Miniconjous. Now, it is said that he lies among them with a broken leg. I will have no peace unless he is found before those Miniconjous break up their winter camp. So, now I am going over there." Scalps Them waved his arm through a wide northward arc. "*Over there* can be a very big country in winter. Now, once when I was a young man . . ."

"Yes, brother," the scout interrupted. "Yes. But if you have come from the east or the south, maybe you have heard of an Indian named Drake, or Duck, who has strange eyes that are almost white? or of a white man called Hixon who is said to be broad as a toad?"

"No, I do not think so," Scalps Them said, "but your strange Indian with the white eyes makes me think of my older brother-in-law. He has a white thing grown over his eye—it is his right eye if I remember correctly—so that he can no longer—"

"Brother," the scout said, "you have very fine horses except for those two with the heaviest packs."

"Friend, I must tell you about the trade I made for them. I got not only those two horses but also that fine—"

"Brother, I must go back to the young soldier chief. He has little patience when his ass is cold."

That night, snug in the tipi, Scalps Them's ceaseless talk turned toward that scout, and he observed, "Maybe I did not fool him so much as he let me think. But I must have fooled him more than Singer fooled me. Singer thinks he is very clever, but he told me too many times the first night that the guns had not yet come. . . . Do you remember that steep little gully—just west of the corral—with the brush growing in it? That is where he had those guns, and others, all the time! I found early on the first morning where he was hiding them—in a deep hole dug in that brush, under a dead horse, and only a good arrowshot across the creek from his door."

Chapter Twenty
EVERYTHING BUT
THE PINTO PONY

(Spring 1875)

In the Moon of the Birth of Calves, or Moon of Frogs as some would say [April], Walks Far neared the winter camps on the Tongue River after delay in the Black Hills. Now the advance guards of spring outraced her everywhere. She was eager to see old friends, to hear the women's news that Suzy seemed somehow always the first to know, yet most of all she was anxious to see whether Grandfather was still there to count one winter more. She would like to see old Father of a Mudfish too, but no longer for any worrisome reason. Walks Far needed to give none of her wealth for that outrageously expensive medicine that made a girl abort, but might also prevent her from ever having babies again—unless, that is, the girl was able to counter that unfortunate effect by buying another of his medicines, which was said to be even more expensive but less sure.

Scalps Them was bringing back not only ammunition and a few very good guns, but also one bit of good news: Soldiers from Fort Robinson to the south, after being stopped on the first attempt by frostbitten men and animals in the exceptional cold, had come to the Black Hills and had taken away the white miners and the one woman. The *wasichu* was still keeping that much of the treaty. The bad part was that the *wasichu* still talked of changing the treaty, of having all Sioux come to the agencies, be counted, and start farming!

Suddenly, while still on the trail, Walks Far became Grandfather's captive again. He emerged grinning, not looking one day older, from a hidden, sunny nest on the approach to the camp, and playfully stopped the whole party with his ancient flintlock. Scalps Them helped him up behind for the ride on in. Walks Far gave him the shirt she had made, as soon as the packs were unloaded. Of course Suzy and others came to help with the tipi, and just as expected, Suzy was full of news: Did Walks Far remember the funny little man, Feather Earrings, who had made the first buffalo kill in the big hunt last fall? the same man whose wife had been stolen by a Yankton man at Frenchman's Creek two winters ago, when Feather Earrings had only laughed, had even sent the Yankton the stolen wife's horse to show there were no hard feelings? Well, would Walks Far believe it, Feather Earrings had been sent by Left Hand Bull to meet the Métis at Frenchman's Creek again this winter and, on the way back, he had stopped at Fort Peck to visit that Yankton. Now it was the Yankton who was missing a wife, not the one stolen from Feather Earrings in the first place but a much younger and prettier one!

By the time the tipi stood ready, Suzy had brought Walks Far pretty well up-to-date on camp events, though none of her other revelations quite matched the first for neatness of turn. Walks Far cut in two a fist-sized ball of pressed sunflower-seed meats received as a parting gift from Moon Woman, and as Suzy nibbled with pleasure at the half given her, she thought of something else, "One Horn has come back!" She said this as though announcing the greatest of happy news.

Walks Far took all the horses to throw them into the camp herd, hobbling some, simply loosing the others, and keeping Crazy One to the last. As she worked with the hobbles, she saw a stranger watching her. He looked like the same rather dandified young man she had barely glimpsed in camp a little while ago, and she now had a feeling that he had followed her. Unexpectedly, he was on One Horn's favorite horse.

Though the afternoon sun shone brightly, a very chill wind blew, yet this young man, like all the others, had rushed the season by going shirtless and without a robe since the first day of this moon. The white man's vest, beautifully embroidered and flowered, that he wore open left his chest and arms bared, and was purely for show. He swung his horse close, and Walks Far mounted Crazy One quickly.

"Wait," he said, and began speaking without apology. "You are Walks Far Away Woman, the Pekony woman? I know who you are because I know that fine horse, and because people have said that you are very pretty."

"That is my name," Walks Far said. "What is the name of a stranger who seems to have followed me because he thinks he knew my horse before I did?"

"I am One Horn," he told her, quite as though surprised that she would not have known.

He was One Horn's age, mounted on One Horn's horse, and like One Horn he wore a coil of tiny rope and a miniature moccasin at his belt to show that he had stolen ten or more horses. Also at his belt was an identical wide-bladed, double-edged knife with a handle fashioned from the jawbone of a bear and ending at the top in one of the bear's fangs. This showed that he too was a member of the bear society. Also, as with One Horn, ceremonial torture at the time of his first sun dance had left eight puckered little scars in a double row neatly pitting the skin on each of his biceps. Except for a double cross painted on this man's leggins to show that he had ridden a dismounted friend to safety in a fight with the enemy, the leggins might have been One Horn's. But with this much, which Walks Far took in at a glance, she saw the resemblance ending.

For Walks Far was also seeing that this man, though lean, was not stringy and wiry like One Horn, but was trimly and neatly muscled like Singer, that he even had plates of muscle on his belly, and was very much like the remarkably handsome Pikuni she'd had to shoot. The line of his nose was un-Sioux, nearly straight from his high forehead. He wore his long, heavy hair loose. It was freshly washed and oiled, flowing splendidly in the wind, and he disdained a single eagle feather. The sunlight shining on that blue-black waving hair made a kind of halo around his head. [Janet Sinclair was impelled to wonder in her notes, "Is she the clever old Indian—or am I so far gone? Every-time she describes one of her handsome men and I look at Dewey, there is a definite resemblance."]

To Walks Far the man she saw was so much like the one in the daydreams she had been having both before and since meeting Singer that she was now feeling a kind of assault, and was momentarily so peculiarly defenseless that she could not move, could not even avert her eyes. He had kneed his horse close, his arm was sliding around her, and the big, self-confident fool was saying in a low, coaxing voice, "I think I am going to win a kiss from you in a horse race. Why don't we have that kiss now?"

Walks Far, feeling somewhat like a helpless dreamer who tries desperately to wake up, was suddenly able to move. Twisting her body away, she swung her new quirt high, to lay its long, greased lashes stingingly across that handsome nose. Then she headed Crazy One back toward camp on a dead run. But almost at once she heard shouted laughter. There, half hidden in a tiny coulee, was the One Horn she knew, and he was nearly falling off his horse.

She suddenly felt ridiculous, galloping headlong into camp, fleeing blindly as though a Crow war party pursued her. She abruptly slowed to a sedate pace, but for a reason she did not quite understand, she had never felt so furious. She went into the tipi and got her gun, refusing to speak to anyone. She then found Suzy and asked, "What is now the name of your cousin who used to be called One Horn?"

"Did I not tell you? His name is now Horses Ghost. He and his *kola* traded horses, and then they decided to trade names as well. The herald announced it. One Horn is so handsome you will surely know him when you see him."

Walks Far rode directly back to the herd, and on the way she passed very close to Horses Ghost and One Horn. They had found a small depression in which to have a smoke out of the wind and now sat on the ground facing each other before their horses. The old One Horn could not resist a long-toothed grin at her, which she pretended not to see. She went on and loosed Crazy One, then trotted back exactly as she had come. But when she got abreast of the two young warriors, she stopped abruptly and called out their names. The new One Horn grinned a little sheepishly, and the old One Horn leaned back on one elbow to laugh, but their expressions chilled to a kind of horror. Walks Far was swinging up her carbine and she willfully expended one of the precious cartridges in a quick shot aimed between their moccasins.

Those two, both of whom had dreamed of the bear and had taken the bear's medicine, who therefore must unfailingly and unflinchingly charge every enemy while at the same time being careful to make "huff-huff" sounds like a bear, now simply let out a single surprised yell and were up and running in opposite directions, as though entirely forgetful that they were sworn to stay and defend each other to the death. It was so funny that Walks Far happily inspired them with another wasted shot. She regretted that no one had been there to see them. Still, it occurred to her that she might later regret having humiliated such a handsome young man before witnesses. She couldn't shake him from her mind—Whirling Medicine Cloud Sacred Horses Ghost, now One Horn, almost as splendid as his former name, was as wonderfully attractive as everyone had said. Walks Far began to regret that, in addition, he was obviously rather stupid—about some things at least.

Early next day Walks Far became conscious that the tipi was being watched. She went outside for neither wood nor water, nor even to adjust the tipi smoke ears to the wind. Instead, she spent the whole time mending and sewing. Red Hoop gave her a knowing, excited smile but made no comments. Grandfather came back inside and watched her for a time with an especially wide grin. At last he said, "I think there is a starving dog out there watching this tipi. Maybe you should throw him a little piece of meat."

"I have seen starving dogs all this cold winter," Walks Far said, "and we have no meat to throw away."

"That may be true," Grandfather said, "but this is a very fine dog. I think maybe he is worth taming and keeping around. He reminds me of the fine dogs we used to have when I was young, before the first smallpox of about ninety winters ago. Since then, even the dogs seem to be less handsome. You seldom see one like him these days."

"I have heard people call that dog One Horn," Walks Far told him lightly. "I have dreamed that I shall never have a dog with that name, not even such a very handsome dog."

She gave the remark no further thought until near evening, not until Suzy came in and chanced to reveal that Horses Ghost and One Horn had decided to trade names again. They had already petitioned the councillors, insisting that the change be announced this very night. The councillors had showed some impatience, but after Horses Ghost and One Horn each agreed to give a good horse to a poor man, their request was approved. Accordingly, Walks Far felt little surprise on hearing the camp herald riding close and crying out that Horses Ghost was again

One Horn, and One Horn was again Horses Ghost. But she
found it embarrassing when the herald came to a dead stop
before her tipi to shout his announcement twice over, and in an
especially loud voice.

Therefore, Walks Far felt a trifle disconcerted next day when
a chill, cloudy morning was followed by a beautiful sunny afternoon but, still, no one watched the tipi! Suzy was not sure what
had become of One Horn and Horses Ghost, but she thought
they had said something about going hunting. Then, well after
supper and in the full darkness, Red Hoop Woman slipped into
the smaller tipi almost whispering her excited message. Horses
Ghost and One Horn had come to call on Scalps Them. They
wished to welcome him back from what they had heard to be
a most successful journey. They would be flattered to hear all
about it from Scalps Them himself, and they brought him a
present of fresh meat taken only today. Both of them, Red Hoop
Woman said significantly, were wearing all their coup feathers
and dressed in their finest.

Walks Far slipped outside with her, and together they huddled under the same blanket, their ears close to the cover of the
larger tipi as they eavesdropped shamelessly on the conversation within. For a long time they heard nothing but Scalps
Them giving chapter and verse on the long trip south, and how
skillfully he had first searched out a source of illegal guns and
ammunition, and had then hoodwinked army patrols for half
the long way back. The two young men spoke in dignified
admiration. They declared Left Hand Bull to be a lucky chief
indeed in having the inestimable advantage of a trusted brother-in-law like Scalps Them, one so deservedly renowned, and
not merely for his bravery, resourcefulness, and wisdom, but
also for his helpfulness and generosity.

But One Horn was curious about the Pekony woman and the
fine new gun that appeared to belong to her. How did it happen
that even such a woman as she should have acquired that gun?
Had she axed or knifed a soldier?

Scalps Them chuckled and agreed that she was more than
capable of it. But the truth was simply that the too clever trader
who had the guns, besides being an Indian-turned-white-man,
was surely a "coffee-cooler," a peacemaker or a real coward,
and an unbearable know-it-all besides. At the same time, he was
so exceedingly envious and vain that he just had to have his robe
decorated like Scalps Them's robe before he would complete

the trade. So, Scalps Them had demanded one more gun, which the trader had refused. But then, after Walks Far had quickly decorated the robe, that sneaky trader, laughing inside himself at Scalps Them, had grandly presented Walks Far with that strange little gun.

One Horn had another question, one that Walks Far and Red Hoop Woman recognized as leading to the real point of the visit. They knew that Horses Ghost, who said nothing now, would be listening the hardest. One Horn was curious, he said, as to just how Scalps Them regarded the Pekony woman—did he look on her as a sister, a daughter, or perhaps some other kind of relative? In fact, suggested One Horn, the Pekony woman's place in the tipi and in the family might be said to be downright puzzling. He had never heard of a situation quite like it, certainly not one so prolonged.

Scalps Them was not much help. "I think of that woman as all of those," he said. "I have become so glad of having her in this tipi, she is so valuable just for herself, that I do not worry too much about how she fits into our Sioux way."

One Horn seemed at a loss as to how to press on, and out of the silence Horses Ghost laughed to say, "But if some person wished to have that woman, he would not know how he ought to go about it."

"A worthy person will find the way," Scalps Them intoned. "But I think usual ways are usually the best, especially with respectable and strong-minded women."

Again there was an appreciable silence, in which Horses Ghost drew a deep breath, then said, "You would not care if somebody courted that woman?"

"It would depend upon who that somebody happened to be," Scalps Them said. "I would surely want to know who I might be getting for a kind of son-in-law."

Horses Ghost spoke slowly and distinctly. "Is it all right for me to court that woman?"

"I would be very glad to have you for a son-in-law," Scalps Them said, "but there is one more question you must ask. No, do not ask it of me! You have to ask the only person who knows the answer."

Next morning, when Walks Far went for water, an expected encounter on the way took place as though entirely by accident. Horses Ghost greeted her by name and hastened to say, "Sometimes I am very foolish; I let my *kola* load me up with a story I should have known was not true."

Walks Far, with her eyes downcast but carefully showing no anger, silently stepped around him and went on. He was still standing there when she came back, so she granted him the slightest of smiles.

"Wait!" he said. "Did you speak to me? Let us talk a little. I think about you so much that I feel as though you are talking to me. Now that we are so near each other, I seem to hear your pretty voice more than ever."

Walks Far flung a swift, apprehensive glance all around and pretended to hesitate, but she hurried silently, demurely past. Then, just at the point where she would go out of his sight, she looked back and let him see another hint of a smile. She couldn't help feeling more or less ridiculous playing the virgin daughter of the tipi.

But Horses Ghost played the game in earnest. He came to stand outside that evening, and Walks Far peeked through the door to see him in all his colorful finest. At the back of his head fresh eagle feathers denoted four first coups. A necklace of polished bear claws made his chest look all the more magnificent, and he held a bright new trade blanket neatly folded over one strong arm.

After a while he put the blanket on the ground and solemnly began playing a flute. He played well, and Walks Far liked that, but she could see his flute to be but a superior one of the common kind. It held no special power!

Red Hoop Woman and Left Hand Bull's wife came around to give Horses Ghost a smile of approval in passing, but Walks Far would not show herself so soon. Not until the last of clear light did she go outside and around to adjust the smoke-ear poles from the rear of the tipi. But just before again disappearing inside, she looked back lingeringly and this time with an unmistakable and excited smile. After he had gone, she and Red Hoop Woman had a long, serious conversation.

For two more days Walks Far refused to talk with Horses Ghost when she went for wood or water or out to care for the horses, but she managed to show increasingly that she might like to do so.

Suzy came guiltily but happily to divulge a secret she said she should neither know nor tell!—but Horses Ghost had promised his second-best horse to old Father of a Mudfish if he would make him a "twisted flute" and dream for him the powerful tune to go with it! Walks Far knew about those large cedar flutes. They were sacred, mysterious—*wakan*—holding a dangerous power. By their shape, and in the way red paint was applied, they suggested the phallus of a stallion, unquestionably the most virile of all creatures. Still, such flutes were made truly irresistible only with the magic of a specially dreamed love-medicine tune lilting from them. She thought old Father of a Mudfish, that old dreamer, would need a couple of days at least to shape the two pieces of cedar wood for the flute, no matter how swiftly he might dream of the magic tune, which Horses Ghost would then still have to memorize. Walks Far decided to enjoy the courting more, before it was brought too swiftly to its end.

There was another open secret that she pretended not to know about. Red Hoop Woman had enlisted some of her matron friends to make a new tipi, a fine light one of canvas that must have come from the neighboring Cheyenne camp.

In the second evening Walks Far added much warmth to her smile, and on the third she made herself look her best, short of dressing up, and when Horses Ghost played his ordinary flute, she went out to stand somewhat aside from the tipi door. She smiled her natural smile at him, making it a welcoming, expectant smile.

Horses Ghost snatched up his blanket while the last note of his flute still hung in the quiet evening air. He hardly could have been more direct in the way he rushed up and said, "I am glad you have decided to talk to me. Does that mean you have also decided to like me? I like you very much, and think of you all the time. I think you are very pretty and I hope you will be my woman."

"Do not talk so loud," Walks Far cautioned before answering, "I do not know what to think, because I do not know anything much about you. If a person were to ask me, 'Who is Horses Ghost, what is he like?' I could say only that he is very handsome, that he is a very attractive-looking man who, when frightened, can run nearly as fast as One Horn can! and that he thinks he can get away with doing whatever he wants to with strange girls. I am not sure that I would like to be the wife of such a man."

A disconcerted Horses Ghost forgot about his blanket. He gaped at her in utter astonishment, as though finding it incredible that any girl, especially a girl wearing such a flattered, eager smile, would speak to him like that, at a time like this.

He stammered, half shouting, "I have tried to tell you that that was a mistake! and how it happened!"

Walks Far saw she had so confused him that he was close to sullen anger. "It is getting chilly," she said. "Let us wrap into your fine blanket while you tell me about the Horses Ghost I do not know. You too have a nice voice that I like to hear."

They stood together in that blanket until darkness and convention made them part, and when Walks Far went in, she knew two things: Horses Ghost was actually less stupid than most men; she would have eloped with him tonight, if he had asked her to. But he only said in a quite dignified way, "Can you not tell me what you think your answer will be?"

Walks Far longed to slide her hands over those shoulders, to lock her arms around that strong, unscarred neck as she fit herself to him profoundly. Instead, she told him, "I think maybe the answer will be yes, though I still wish to know more about what you are like."

In the chill dawn, with only a few people stirring, Walks Far was warmed to see five horses tied in front of Scalps Them's tipi. She called inside to tell him, "Somebody has given you a present of some horses."

"I heard them," Scalps Them called back, "and I have been thinking about getting up to look at them."

"Stay in bed," she told him lightly, and added in words she would regret. "There are only five. Also, they are horses that you must have seen before. I would think somebody would have tried to give you some new horses."

Horses Ghost and One Horn, with two boys, disappeared for exactly nineteen days, perhaps the longest, slowest days Walks Far ever had to endure. She spent her spare time practicing throwing her knife, viciously. To her it seemed incredible that the other people in camp could go so unconcernedly about their affairs, laughing and joking while she felt so utterly miserable. She dwelt with a terrible fear that the man she suddenly loved beyond enduring had already become food for ants and coyotes and magpies, was already making a patch of taller, greener grass somewhere in enemy country.

Grandfather watched her knife throwing with a special grin, and at last he said, "I am going to tell you a story of something

192

told to me by a good white man who lived with us for a long time, about eighty winters ago. He had had many wives before that—white wives, black wives, and Indian wives. He said Indian wives were much the better in every way but one. He said it was sometimes possible for a white woman or a black woman to get tired of hearing her own voice, but he believed that no Indian woman ever did!"

And Grandfather added, "I think maybe you should make a little change in your good story about women always having last say. Make it a story that will help them remember they should never say too much."

On the twentieth morning four strange horses were picketed in front of Scalps Them's tipi, and Walks Far sang ecstatic gratitude to Sun, then and there, before she so much as took a good look at the horses. They proved to be a beautiful pinto, two fine bays, and a magnificent roan bearing an army brand, though this horse had not been shod for a long time.

Suzy reported that One Horn and Horses Ghost had returned only shortly before, and they had eaten a whole buffalo hump! Horses Ghost had then washed his hair and begun singing a song, over and over, until One Horn told him that friendship had some limits. Now, they were asleep. Yes, both of them were all right, they just looked a little thin.

To Walks Far that day seemed longest of all, so long that as early evening neared, she was already caught in the narrow world of her endless waiting. At last, after washing her hair and bathing, she put on her *winkte* dress and finest moccasins, then waited some more. She was scented with broad-leaved sage, with sweet grass and mint. A streak of vermilion emphasized the parting in her hair, a dot of it turned the frostbite dimple in her cheek into a beauty mark. She had a few small things in a beaded bag at her belt. She was self-hypnotized, already under a spell. Horses Ghost came early, and again the low sun made a nimbus around his handsome head.

She was not at all surprised to see a scabby old coyote, obviously invisible to Horses Ghost and the camp dogs, come out of nowhere and sit watching expectantly. Horses Ghost started to play a big new flute painted red at the ends! It had five finger holes and a sliding stop called a saddle, but shaped in this case like a bear for adjusting the pitch, and the plaintive whistling tune it played in that spring evening air was too insistent to be denied.

Slowly Walks Far gave herself to its powerful enchantment. She stepped outside the tipi, not to linger there but to be drawn onward toward Horses Ghost. The movement itself seemed to make her less and less an actor who performed a calculated part. Her spirit or essence—her *Nagila*—seemed in some curious way to be either so expanded or detached that she was made spectator to her own entrancement. She saw herself follow onward as Horses Ghost, still playing the tune, backed off a way, then stopped to wait. When she came up to him, he touched her with the flute, doing it hesitantly, fearfully, as though knowing his act held great and frightening power.

Her spirit felt frightened, deeply concerned about the Walks Far who would now follow wherever he might choose to lead her, even to immediate disgrace and utter ruin. But her spirit breathed in relief to see Horses Ghost trying to rouse her, as he should do. He called her by name over and over, in growing alarm, and he tried desperately to shake her from her trance. Abruptly, he rushed her to the tipi of old Father of a Mudfish, and he, too, was alarmed. He cried out, "I have dreamed a too powerful love-medicine tune! even for such a strong-minded woman!" He lay her down, he sang over her in a shrill, wailing chant, and he blew into her nostrils what seemed to be tobacco pounded fine as dust. Walks Far sneezed violently, her eyes watered, and her spirit and her body joined comfortably together again. She now felt different in one way only. That difference was revealed in the surprised question she asked of Horses Ghost: "Husband, what are we doing here?"

For Walks Far and Horses Ghost regarded themselves as now married, and the people viewed their marriage as one kind of elopement, even though they had not run away together. Walks Far, by publicly following Horses Ghost in a state of helpless entrancement, had made a form of surrender to his powerful medicine. People rushed to greet them as they came from the tipi of Old Father of a Mudfish. It was as though, long gone, they were now welcomed home from a true elopement by approving relatives and friends.

They were escorted to the new tipi, which had been set up a little apart. A fire had been laid ready for lighting. Walks Far lit the fire and purified her tipi with sweet-grass smoke aided by prayer. Food already prepared for the feast was brought in, but Walks Far broiled a tiny piece of meat herself and served it to Horses Ghost before he ate anything else. Then there was drumming and dancing and singing, with some of the songs having ordinary words that were perfectly intelligible to anyone, for the aim was innuendo, risqué humor, and shocking puns, especially for the time when the bedding and other things were carried in. Of course there were many, many presents. Scalps Them returned more horses than he had received from Horses Ghost, including all the same ones, save the beautiful pinto. Quite in contrast to Walks Far's expectation and hope, he had kept that pinto rather than the big roan!

People left them alone in their tipi at last and, after a while, as Horses Ghost waited in bed in the darkness, Walks Far skewered a small piece of suet on a splinter, held it among the coals of the low fire until it burst into flame, then carried it like a tiny torch to the bed and carefully inspected her husband's face.

"Woman! What are you doing?"

"I am making certain I do not get into bed with One Horn."

He laughed, said softly, "Now, I think you are my crazy Pekony woman."

Shortly he called to her from the darkness, a trifle impatiently, "Woman, what are you doing now?"

"I am rubbing myself with mint for you. Here, I will rub you also."

"Woman, I am very glad you know about these things. Put some more of that suet on the fire, for I wish to see my pretty wife."

Within a little while, Horses Ghost loomed above her, one side of his face and one shoulder lighted by a final flicker from the suet on the fire, and as he pressed upon her, she rose to welcome him. But at that moment an urgent scratching at the tipi door and an apologetic voice from one of the older boys in the band arrested them. "Horses Ghost, I am Falls Down Laughing. One Horn says he supposes you will not get up very early in the morning and that he wishes me to go hunting with him. He asks that you lend him your spotted gray for me to ride."

Horses Ghost shouted from his awkward position, "Tell One Horn he can take all my horses—if he wishes to risk what is going to happen to him. And you, Falls Down Laughing, are going to lie down crying when I catch you!"

The boy's suppressed excitement burst into laughter as he ran.

So, the spell had been broken, but not for long. Walks Far's nipples again gleamed from the intensity of Horses Ghost's caresses as she stopped breathing and once again held ready to receive him. But with almost uncanny timing, a second scratching at the tipi door was followed by the voice of another older boy. His message came with a rush, "Horses Ghost, I am Rabbit Leggins. One Horn wishes me to say he is very sorry that he may have interrupted you at the wrong time. He is so sorry that he has sent me to give you a present of two cartridges for your gun. He fears you have but one, and will need these two before morning."

Walks Far heard the cartridges dropped inside the tipi and Horses Ghost's strained shouting, "Rabbit Leggins, I am going to hang One Horn and you to a tree by your heels. I am going to geld you both with a very dull knife before I skin you alive so slowly that you will not die for two days!"

As Rabbit Leggins hooted and ran, Horses Ghost said plaintively, "Woman, you know that this could go on all night! It is One Horn who should be making sure no one bothers us." Abruptly then, and without pausing to twist on his breechclout, he reached for his gun, rushed to untie the door, and run a little way out into the chill moonlight before turning to peer up at the crossing of the tipi poles and assure Walks Far, "I didn't think he could have got up there."

Then, unexpectedly, Horses Ghost raised his voice into a tremendous call that the whole camp could hear, "I am Horses Ghost. Queer Person, I wish you to come here!" Walks Far was puzzled. Everyone knew Queer Person as a plump, overgrown, egg-shaped fifteen-year-old boy with the mind and grin of a happy seven-year-old. Yet he could cock his head as though listening to spirit voices and in monotonous tones repeat word for word any story he had ever heard, or every sound spoken by each orator in the biggest and longest of councils. Oddly too, if it were humanly possible, he could do almost anything he was told to do, no matter how ridiculous, though old Father of a Mudfish protected him from most of that.

Queer Person came up breathless and Horses Ghost said to him, still in a very loud voice, "Queer Person, we have always been friends, is that not true?"

"Yes, friend Horses Ghost."

"Good, friend Queer Person. I am very sad to have to tell you that tonight all my other friends have forsaken me and are trying to slash my new tipi. But I know you are loyal, and that you would like to ride one of my horses for a couple of days . . . ?"

"I am a true Lakota, I am therefore loyal, friend Horses Ghost, and I would very much like to ride with you."

"Have you ever shot a gun?"

"No, friend Horses Ghost, but I know how to cock and aim, then squeeze the trigger off slowly."

Horses Ghost's voice rose louder still. "Take my gun, friend Queer Person. I have loaded it for you. I wish you to walk around out here until sunup and shoot anyone who comes near my tipi or near you."

"I will do it," Queer Person said, then added happily, "I will shoot them in the belly."

Horses Ghost came inside to close the door and hurry back to bed. As he took her in his arms, Walks Far asked in a whisper, "Did you really leave that crazy boy with a cartridge in the gun?"

Horses Ghost whispered back, "Woman, I will tell you this much, not even the bravest will want to leave their tipis to find out. Every old man in camp is going to have to hold his water all night. We will not be bothered anymore about whatever it was we had started to do."

"Have I found a husband who is so absent-minded!"

He laughed and answered by moving himself against her. Walks Far moved with him for a moment, then led him on until they were at last wound together into the warmth, the closeness, and all her less than maidenly dreams of him were fulfilled. And as she calmed, she was conscious of a camp held so silent that people must surely have heard the lovers' cry, the breaths that came like sobbing.

Walks Far wakened from deep sleep just before dawn to that sweep of memory that is like no other. She found Horses Ghost ready as he still slept and she wanted to press herself against him, to feel the warmth and tenderness, his closeness and power once more. But she released him to rise quickly and blow a coal to life from a piece of punkwood left in the ashes. Then she called, "Husband, I will see to the horses. You must go get your gun from Queer Person and go hunting. We need fresh meat of our own in this tipi."

Chapter Twenty-one
A SUN DANCE
(Toward a Day in July 1875)

Never was there such a glorious spring, such faultless weather, in the valley of the Yellowstone. Grandfather declared it exceptional and insisted he had not felt so young in years. He waited four full days after the wedding before moving in at breakfast time. When Walks Far and Horses Ghost looked up to see him there with all he owned, they laughed together, and Horses Ghost said teasingly, "Woman, you did not say you already had a husband. Maybe you should tell me more about the Walks Far Away I do not know."

Along all the creeks that spring, heavy fragrance from blossoming thickets of chokecherries and wild plum so scented the days and nights that it was hard to smell out a camp, even from close by. Also, as Grandfather pointed out, the bothersome flies were few, for the cold winter must have done them in. Horses grew sleek on new grass that had never smelled so rich from their cropping. The sparse junipers on the hills were never so pungent under a midday sun.

Walks Far had her own fine new canvas tipi, which let in much more light than one of buffalo hide. Also, when packed on a horse, its bulk and weight were less. [Janet noted, "She says she'll make a fine tipi for Dewey and me, if we'll 'jus' cut and peel 'all them goddam poles,' and drag them around wherever we go. Also, she would like to see how we stop water from running down inside the poles in a long, hard rain or melting sleet, and how we keep the fire from smoking badly sometimes, no matter how the smoke ears are adjusted!"]

Walks Far's new young husband was a proven hunter and warrior, as handsome as any on the prairies. No man in two bands of Sioux and one of Cheyennes was his equal in wrestling contests, whether on the ground or from a horse. He was so great that the older and heavier Runs Stooped Over seemed to derive an odd kind of pride from being defeated by him. And his appearance and voice, his intensity, caused him to shine among older men in their complicated and prolonged religious rituals. He could instantly repeat Walks Far's most complicated cat's cradles.

That spring, that whole year, was much as Walks Far felt a happy life should be. Naturally she was prepared for a lifetime of gathering wood or buffalo chips, of carrying water, of digging roots and picking berries, of cutting the meat for drying, then pounding great quantities of it into pemmican by swinging a heavy stone-headed maul. Always there would be the hides to be dressed, the sewing to be done, the endless housekeeping chores demanded in a growing family. For, of course, there would be babies now and then. How could her life be otherwise? This was the way of all the prairie people.

And when her man came in at anytime from hunting, she must take care of his horse, change his moccasins, quickly serve him food, fill and light his pipe. All this, too, Walks Far was more than glad to do, for it often ended with the tipi door closed. Both she and Horses Ghost lingered in that stage of being in love when no discovery about each other was too trivial, when nothing that either one ever had to say could be dull, when just being with each other made for adventure. Never, of course, did he lash her with his quirt, as most husbands did when impatient.

Still, Walks Far quickly broke Horses Ghost of two things. First, though he was an accomplished whistler and she liked to hear him when he did not let it fall into a kind of nervous tunelessness, he whistled after dark! She knew this to be a way of inviting bad spirits who would make him go crazy. He scoffed, but she demanded that he break himself of the habit, and slowly he did.

Secondly, though he was tender with her and more thoughtful about some things than most men were, he could be blindly demanding and childishly sensitive, and he had a habit of ordering her to do something she clearly was already doing, or that it was impossible for her to do at that instant. Walks Far didn't like this at all. One day, about midafternoon, she decided to make her point. Horses Ghost came in from no particular place and instantly demanded, "Woman, give me some food—hot food. A chilly wind has come from the north."

"You can see that I am busy just now," Walks Far said, "There is warm food in the pot, if you are in such a hurry."

Horses Ghost showed a look of astonishment, of hurt shock, then turned without a word to duck out through the door again. Walks Far gave the incident little thought. He would drop in elsewhere, be offered food and conversation, and would soon be back filled with meat and good humor, and no doubt eager to relate some stale camp news she'd heard yesterday from other women. But after a short while Walks Far heard people snickering, and she peeked from the tipi to see Horses Ghost sitting on the ground out there, facing the door from three or four tipi-pole lengths away. From the waist up he was bared to the chill wind, and though stoic he might be, his magnificent sulk was apparent.

Walks Far decided to stay in and stitch ahead on extra moccasins. People passed before the tipi with uncommon frequency, but no one shook the deer-hoof rattle or scratched at the door to be invited inside, and no one taunted or even spoke to Horses Ghost. They only kept on snickering as they went by. After a time One Horn crept secretly up behind the tipi to say in low-voiced concern, "Walks Far Away Woman, I wish I knew what is happening."

"Nothing is happening—nothing you can do anything about."

Horses Ghost sat there in the chill wind all afternoon and throughout the evening. Finally, just before it grew too dark for people to see, Walks Far filled a big bowl of hot meat and broth. Then, not because the situation had grown too embarrassing, and not because she worried about his starving, but only because she feared the chill wind might turn him into a dried-up old man before his time, she carried that food out to him. And he took it.

They both pretended nothing had occurred, and neither of them ever mentioned it, but Horses Ghost always looked to see what she might be doing before he gave orders, and sometimes he did things for himself. Walks Far could certainly say this for him, he seemed to have learned something else from that unseasonably chill wind, something more than most men ever would. For next winter, when drifted snow lay deep in the coulees and the buffalo chips on the wind-bared ridges were about the only source of fuel, he said, "Wait, I am going with you. Too much of that cold wind is not good for my pretty wife. Besides, I have heard of a woman who got lost in a sudden blizzard and froze to death while picking up buffalo chips."

Meanwhile Walks Far could never let a chance pass by to tease Horses Ghost. From the first he seemed unreasonably disturbed by the fact that she was not tattooed—had no blue dot on forehead, chin, or wrist. Consequently, if she should die and take the spirit trail up the Milky Way to the Sioux Place of Many Tipis, she would fail to pass an inspection by Owl Maker, a witch, who would surely throw her back to earth to become a ghost. Horses Ghost insisted that a single awl prick, with blue clay rubbed in by a proper person in proper ceremony would save Walks Far.

She teased him by declaring that when she died she was going only to the Blackfoot-country Sand Hills anyhow, there to live a shadow life, forever dressing the shadow hides of the shadow buffalo he would kill. Moreover, being a Sioux ghost for a while might be great fun. If she got tired of it, she could then get her ghostly self tattooed. Horses Ghost was shocked, and he would never let the matter rest. He appealed to Grandfather, but Grandfather said that the wife he had liked best of all had missed getting tattooed, and if she haunted him, it was only pleasantly.

Walks Far could always say that although that too perfect spring and the rest of the year would be the very last in which the wild bands would live in their old ways, her own daily life was not actually typical of the life of other women. Horses Ghost's pride in her skill with horse and gun matched his other delight in her, and they left Grandfather to his own resources and rode off for days at a time like a pair of young warriors gone hunting or just prowling around. The country they covered was relatively safe, though they were indeed a little reckless, even with One Horn along, as he often was. For shelter on these trips they fashioned a wikiup cover shaped like a bowl. It could be inverted over a flexible framework of willow wands cut on the site and thrust into the ground at both their ends. Three people might curl inside if necessary, but One Horn slept outdoors whenever the weather was tolerable.

On one fine night he begged them to let him in, and complained of something that reminded Walks Far of a story she'd heard in the Blackfoot country, a story told by a very stocky woman who claimed to have been born far away to the west, on the edge of the everywhere-water. It seemed that a cannibal giant once lived by the everywhere-water—not just a small giant, not like the one who listens around camp at night carrying a bag made from two buffalo hides for collecting his breakfast of those children who keep on talking instead of going to sleep—no, this was a truly big giant. He ate grown people, all he could catch, and their horses too! Although he did this for only a part of the year, the people got tired of it. So they all joined and killed him, then decided to gather a lot of wood and burn him up. But all the rising sparks turned into mosquitoes, which some people said were much worse than just one cannibal giant!

And Walks Far added, "That's what the old white man says."

"Why do you often say that about the old white man when you finish a story?" Horses Ghost wanted to know.

"It is a Pekony way of saying there is nothing more to be told, or, sometimes, of saying that you yourself are not responsible for such a story," Walks Far explained. "I will tell you what my father told me about it:

"When his father was young, when hardly any of the people had seen a white man yet, one with a white beard and a bald head came to live in the camp. He was crazy. He ate only berries and roots. If anyone tried to talk to him, he would just grin. He talked to dogs and he talked to the spirits he seemed to have all around him, but he would not speak to any person.

"One day some of the men were sitting around talking, and a woman who had just got married happened to go by. One of the men said, 'That woman is lucky anyone would have her. She is so ugly she makes Sun hide his face, though maybe she is good for scaring owls away at night.'

"Everyone suddenly got so quiet that the man quickly looked around and saw the woman's husband sitting there, so he added in a hurry, 'That's what the old white man says.' "

On one of their trips the three of them found two horses. They didn't steal them; they actually found and caught them without much trouble—white man's big horses, broken and shod, but pretty old. Those horses had got away, no doubt, from one of the parties of miners who went through to the Black Hills from the mountains in the west. Such miners, who looked like men who knew what they were doing, acted as if the country belonged to them. They made the people angry, but the chiefs said not to kill them.

Also, four young soldiers who seemed to have run away from the army in the west came through. They camped right among the scattered bones left from the fight where Walks Far and Suzy almost got killed by the Crows. Somebody stole all their horses that night. Next morning early, who should come riding along on some poor horses but Feather Earrings, with his wife and nephews? Feather Earrings, who could speak a little white-man talk, was so sorry for the young soldiers that he traded them four horses on the spot, taking half their guns and cartridges in exchange. He got two of the long single-shot rifles carried by walking soldiers and two of the fine revolvers that held six shots each.

Walks Far learned on one of their early trips just how crazy Horses Ghost and One Horn could be. The three of them had stopped to eat something in shade and cover above a well-traveled trail between two camps. After a little two riders appeared on the trail below them, a boy and a middle-aged man.

Horses Ghost shaded his eyes to look, then said, "I know him. He is an Oglala named Spirit Buffalo. He is a great talker about the things that are always happening to him."

"Maybe we ought to give him something more to talk about," One Horn suggested.

"Yes, let us do that," Horses Ghost agreed. "You do the counting. I will shoot in front of him, and you shoot behind him."

At the sound of the two shots the boy galloped for cover, but a surprisingly agile Spirit Buffalo instantly was off and behind his horse, blazing away with a Winchester that seemed to hold no end of shots. All those shots came well directed at the powder smoke from Horses Ghost's and One Horn's carbines. Spirit Buffalo had them, and Walks Far too, trying their best to squeeze down into Mother Earth. One bullet struck so close to Walks Far that it stung her face with the dirt kicked up.

"Spirit Buffalo," Horses Ghost called out a trifle plaintively, "you know me; we are friends. We only wanted to give somebody a little scare." Horses Ghost stood up.

Spirit Buffalo lowered his Winchester and shouted back, "I do not know for sure who is now most scared, though I do know somebody who is going to be worse scared if he does not bring me eight new cartridges pretty soon." He mounted his horse, called to the boy, and rode off.

Walks Far tried to tell Horses Ghost and One Horn exactly what she thought of them, throwing food and anything in reach at them. She had not been both so frightened nor so angry since the time she believed she had caught the *winkte* casting a spell on her footprints, but before she finished, she realized she had been using some especially expressive Blackfoot words they wouldn't understand. So, she started over again, more carefully, and before she got through with them, they were looking at each other for sympathy. She told them to grow up, that they shouldn't be out of their mothers' sight. She told them they were crazy; she told them they were stupid; she told them to go ahead and get themselves killed for nothing for all she cared. By the time she ran out of breath she had used so many words that she couldn't find another one for either of them until after they had all eaten a supper that she made them serve themselves that evening.

More than the foolishness and fright of the incident had disturbed Walks Far, and though she said nothing about it at the time, both her husband and One Horn had overshot badly in their downhill shooting. As she continued to watch them, she observed that they had only an elementary notion of the proper way to shoot. Both her first husband and Singer would have laughed at them. So, next day she said, "I think something is the matter with both your guns. They do not appear to shoot as well as mine. Let me show you." When she had proved that she could beat them easily—with either her own gun or theirs—at shooting at a cross marked with charcoal on a dead tree, they both submitted to her unobtrusive coaching, though they pretended they were only humoring her. Their marksmanship soon equaled her own, and Walks Far regarded the expended cartridges as a good investment.

The Moon When Chokecherries Are Ripe [July] seemed to arrive suddenly. It was the moon when the various bands on the Yellowstone gathered and placed their tipis in a huge circle for the sun dance, the greatest of all religious ceremonies among the Sioux.

And with the beginning of that moon Walks Far knew herself to be pregnant. She prayed to be a good wife now, a good mother and housekeeper. Henceforth she would mark the elk-antler handle of her scraping tool with dots to record the number of hides she had dressed. She would enter into the contests at which women displayed their fine handiwork. Also, in due course, she would go to the ceremonial quilling parties and, if she were judged to be among the first four, a tally of her work would be marked upon the dew wall of the council lodge, with a line running up from the marks to a sign for her name. Thus her quilling count would share a place with the count of her husband's war honors in the council lodge. Lastly, though she felt the prayer to be totally unnecessary, she prayed as a matter of form to be ever faithful to her husband and to become honored as a woman of great virtue. She might then play a significant part in the sun-dance ceremonies, though she noted that among the Sioux no woman filled the leading role, as a notably virtuous one always did in the Blackfoot version.

In camp one evening, shortly before the sun dance, something happened to Blue Blanket, the much younger of Runs Stooped Over's three wives. He was the only man in the band who had more than two. He and his brother-in-law had ridden off upstream, declaring they would bring back a couple of white-tailed deer, but it wasn't long before both men appeared from the brush downstream! and each had at the end of his lariat a person who needed to run hard to keep from falling. Runs Stooped Over had either grown suspicious on his own, or someone had tattled. The two young people were lucky on two scores: Runs Stooped Over had not killed them outright, as he might have done, nor was he dragging them cruelly over the ground as he brought them to face the people. Now nothing much was likely to happen to the boy, Holy Drum.

But Walks Far shivered from the horror of what could happen to Blue Blanket. Runs Stooped Over might turn her over to the members of his secret society for a kind of mass rape, after which she would be driven from the camp. He might also brand her for life as an adulteress by himself cutting off the end of her nose, or by demanding that her shamed brothers do it. Walks Far had seen such punishment, and she saw no difference between Sioux and Blackfoot in this.

When the two young people were brought to a stop, Runs Stooped Over glared at them while they fought for breath. As though trying not to let his anger show, he said, "Holy Drum, I have loaned you horses to ride since you were very young!"

"I love Blue Blanket. I cannot help it. I will fight you for her."

Runs Stooped Over nearly failed to hide his astonishment. He stared at Holy Drum, then said, "I do not know whether you are very brave or very foolish." And he spoke to Blue Blanket. "I have never beat you," he said. "I have been good to you."

"What you say is true, and I am very sorry, but I cannot help loving Holy Drum. I have loved him for a long time. I am sorry, but we were going to run away together."

Runs Stooped Over seemed to search for something all around the horizon, first over one shoulder, then over the other, and at last he said, "If you two love each other, let us say no more about it." He slid from his horse and loosed the lariats from the pair. Old Father of a Mudfish handed him a drum. He struck it and called out clearly, "You can have that woman. I do not want her anymore."

He looked like a man who didn't know what to do next, but suddenly he mounted his horse again and said to his brother-in-law, "We will have to hurry up if we are going to find any white-tailed deer."

Walks Far was relieved and delighted to see the matter ended without tragedy. She couldn't help admiring a side of Runs Stooped Over she had never suspected, but it occurred to her that a part of her reason for thinking him so generous and noble rested upon everyone's notion that it was a man's world.

Walks Far found the Sioux sun dance to extend not for just five but through twelve whole days! though the first four were largely social. People who hadn't seen each other for a year renewed old friendships and exchanged the news. The entire period of the sun dance became a time for the young to seek mates outside a band largely composed of their own relatives. Boys and girls searched for a stem of grass having four heads. To present one of these to a member of the opposite sex thought attractive constituted a waiver of the rules about accosting strangers and engaging them in conversation. And, of course, boy met girl in other ways.

Even a boy-crazy adolescent like Fire Wing might try a traditional way of arresting the attention, however briefly, of a young man she found attractive. She confronted him in what was called the remembering-to-be-polite game, though her action was always quite the opposite of politeness. In fact, a girl playing the game expected anything she said or did to be taken in its exactly contrary meaning. For moral support she needed another girl to come along and hold her hand. No girl dared behave so shockingly all by herself.

She would arrange to encounter the exciting and handsome young man as though by accident, but instead of hurrying past him with downcast eyes, she would stop dead still, staring at him boldly, rudely. As though shocked by what she saw, she would find voice to scream, for example, "Oh, you horrible face! —*Ita kin sil yela!*" She and her companion would then turn and run, throwing terrified looks back over their shoulders and genuinely screaming. Walks Far once saw a girl who found this adolescent game so exciting that she made herself truly hysterical. One young girl did play this game without a helper and so persistently confronted a married man old enough to be her father that she had to be sent away with relatives in a different band. Walks Far couldn't remember girls in a Blackfoot camp being quite *that* silly.

The second four days of the sun dance saw the medicine men —not the ones who cured, but the *wicasa wakan,* who performed as priests—preparing those who would dance. Some, Walks Far knew, would undertake the ordeal to become medicine men themselves, and some simply to gain honor. Others danced in fulfillment of a vow made when self or wife or child was sick, or during some harrowing experience while on a war party. Sometimes a man vowed to dance or undergo other torture in exchange for success in stealing a good horse. Suzy's brother, Kills When Wounded, had vowed not only to dance but also to first undergo a separate torture, one that was not exactly a part of the sun dance ceremony, though it was almost invariably performed at the same time.

The last four days were occupied by the sun dance itself. A most honored warrior—Walks Far was a little surprised to find that Feather Earrings from her own band had been chosen— rode off symbolically to war. He found the "enemy," a forked cottonwood tree, and marked it with red. After further ceremony honored women and the mothers of children who were soon to have their ears pierced, went out next day in procession and chopped down the tree, then peeled it to the fork. Young men bore it to camp on carrying sticks and painted it red, blue, green, and yellow for the four directions. Ceremonial objects, along with two rather large cutouts of blackened rawhide, were attached at the fork of the pole. Those cutouts represented

Cyclone, the chief of all evil, and Crazy Buffalo, the tempter of women. Both were shown equipped with exaggerated sexual organs.

Walks Far heard the people taunting and whistling at those two figures as the pole was raised, but the power of the two spirits soon so dominated the camp that she saw men and women talking, joking, and otherwise behaving with each other in a sexual way that would not only have been scandalous but thoroughly indecent at any other time. Walks Far told herself she would never get used to the contradictions among these Sioux. The Blackfoot didn't do anything *just* like that! It was hard for her to refrain from swinging her quirt at some leering man's face, and to try rather to suggest in witty though plain terms to its owner that, even if she were not already well cared for in such matters, she would feel very strong doubts about his adequacy. If some man stupidly persisted, she would say, "Oh, go away, you old limber lance." The warriors, Horses Ghost and One Horn among them, of course, put the traditional, definite end to this license. They shot the two figures down with arrows and trampled them into the dust in a war dance.

Walks Far saw that Horses Ghost was truly the handsomest warrior there and that when the spirit seized him, he could dance all others to shame. She heard many people say so, even when they had no idea she might be listening. Also, she overheard in darkness, and not exactly with displeasure, that it had been outrageous the way she had somehow managed to snare Horses Ghost. And for that matter it was equally outrageous that Scalps Them and Red Hoop Woman, as soon as they saw Horses Ghost coming, made such a great show in sudden pretense that Walks Far was their daughter, when they hadn't even bothered to adopt the bare-legged, brazen young Pekony hussy.

With the twelfth day came the actual sun dancing. The participants chose one of several forms, some of which were more tormenting than others, but all were highly praiseworthy. After the sun-dance leader and sacred medicine men returned from greeting Sun on a hilltop at dawn, they painted the dancers in red and blue stripes to indicate the form of dance elected. Kills When Wounded had chosen the most demanding form, and he would first submit to special torture in accordance with his vow made last winter as he fought the Crows. He honored Walks Far and Suzy by inviting them to be there with him, to wipe the blood away as old Father of a Mudfish performed the torture. He also asked four mature and highly respected warriors to hold him motionless upon the bed of sage, but he was, of course, determined to render them unnecessary. When he healed, his arms would show a pattern of puckered scars like those that Horses Ghost already wore.

Old Father of a Mudfish knelt over him with needle and knife. The needle lifted a peak of skin from Kills When Wounded's biceps, and the knife sliced the peak away, eight times for each arm. Walks Far and Suzy, using wisps of sweet grass, wiped away the blood and the sudden sweat as the torture progressed. Kills When Wounded made no sound, nor did he faint. The ordeal may have been made the worse for him by the fact that Walks Far and Suzy wailed, exactly as they were expected to do. They saved each wisp of the bloodied sweet grass, for it would make powerful incense for holding the fidelity of a loved one, or help bring just about anything else a person might pray for while it burned.

Walks Far saw another young man, one who already wore the scars on his arms, singing nearby. He endured the slow burning on each wrist of a small piece of punk made from the pith of cottonwood. Both he and Kills When Wounded then danced in the long buffalo dance that followed. They rested while Walks Far saw and heard screaming children, held down upon beds of sage, confirmed in the ways of the Sioux by having their earlobes pierced against chips of wood with a needle-pointed awl.

For the culminating ceremony Kills When Wounded now joined the other painted dancers who were having their breast muscles, or the skin under their shoulder blades, or both, skewered and attached either to one of four poles by ropes, or to a suspended buffalo skull by thongs. Symbolically, Kills When Wounded was a "captive" who must free himself. He hoped his suffering would induce visions. He chose to be pierced through the breast, for this meant that during each of the three major pauses between the four principal parts of the dance the two ropes from his chest to the pole would be tightened, until he was forced to stand tiptoe. His "captor" took a good pinch on one side of his chest and held a honed iron arrow point ready while asking, "Shall the cuts be deep or shallow?" Kills When Wounded said, "Shallow," for that meant that the cuts should be deep. Walks Far saw an incision made on each side of the pinch, a skewer thrust through and, when the same was done on the other side of his chest, the ropes were attached. He sang while Walks Far and Suzy wiped blood from his chest and ribs, the sweat from his eyes. They adorned him with a crown of sage from which he might break a twig to chew. From his neck Suzy hung a quill-wrapped and breath-feathered whistle of eagle bone. He blew that whistle as he danced with the others in moccasins and breechclout, tethered to a tall pole and looking at Sun, while twenty wounds in his flesh already swelled in the summer heat.

Ceremonial singers started with a slow dance song, and the spectators joined in. Kills When Wounded danced through four long periods of gradually increasing tempo, each period with four songs of four parts each. During the first three periods Kills When Wounded only pretended to try to free himself, but during the fourth and final period, as evening and sunset approached, he struggled in a kind of frenzy. While friends and spectators sang and called encouragement, Walks Far watched him now doing his utmost to free himself, straining hard against the ropes in order to tear the skewers from his flesh.

Some dancers succeeded with seeming ease, one man fainting as he did so, but because his skewers were already out, he lost no merit. Kills When Wounded danced on in writhing, twisting effort, settling his weight against the ropes until Walks Far found it unbelievable that the skewered flesh did not tear away. Most of the dancers finally freed themselves, some deciding to earn a little less merit by permitting a friend to jerk their bodies free. Kills When Wounded would accept no help. He was not alone in this, but only he remained of those who had submitted to special torture. Walks Far saw that his sacrifice and his fervor began to grip the crowd, to make him the center of its sympathy, admiration and pride. People said he was skewered so deeply that he could never free himself by his own efforts.

Among the important men, and as usual accompanied by the five or six warriors of his close personal following, sat a certain chief and visionary who could count nearly seventy battle honors. His influence was growing much wider than his own Hunkpapa band. He had begun life with the name of Slow, but now he was called Sitting Bull. Walks Far thought him quite unprepossessing, except for the odd forcefulness and intensity that often clothed him.

She saw Sitting Bull consulting with his cronies as they

watched Kills When Wounded. Shortly, Sitting Bull rose and, stepping forward with his marked limp from an old wound, announced that he would feel honored to be permitted to help free this admirable young warrior, Kills When Wounded.

Kills When Wounded spoke gratefully to Sitting Bull for the great honor done him, but firmly rejected the offer. Not until near dark did he manage to tear himself free—the last to do so. He was then in ecstasy from a vision that came at last. His "captor" trimmed away the torn flesh where the skewers had jerked from his chest. He walked to his tipi almost unaided by the proud family escort, and only then did he faint. Walks Far herself helped purify that tipi, but bad spirits got in. They built their invisible fires around Kills When Wounded until he was burning up. Good spirits came and fought with the bad spirits, so that part of the time he spoke of wonderful visions and part of the time he said terrible things. His arms and his chest swelled unbelievably. For a long while before he suddenly began to mend he could not endure the touch of softest robe or blanket on even the chilliest night. Horses Ghost said it made his own arms hurt all over again merely to look at Kills When Wounded.

Chapter Twenty-two
SKY EYES
(Summer 1875 through Late Spring 1876)

With their sun dance over, the people soon broke up into their separate hunting bands. But they felt renewed, together as one in spirit. Everyone had shared, either by devout supplication to Sun or by sacrifice in the torture that brought release. This, with visions and dreams, had helped resolve the conflict between the demands of self and society and of the earth on which they dwelt. It had been cruel, but so was much of their life on the prairies. Walks Far understood all this only vaguely, but she knew that even the spectators and the most minor participants had given something of themselves in their fervor while seeking the true way of life. And they were now all the more Lakota! —"The Men"!

The band already looked forward to the fall hunting. They crossed to the north side of the Yellowstone, went up Big Porcupine Creek and over to the Big Dry in leisurely stages, then moved eastward to the Redwater. Nothing of great moment happened to the band that summer. A small girl named Much Giving was struck just below the ear by a rattlesnake one morning while helping her mother root up vining cedar. She died despite anything old Father of a Mudfish could do. A middle-aged man named Long Dog abruptly climbed to the top of his tipi at sundown one very hot day and tried to fly away. The fall killed him. Pekonies stole some of the horses, but Feather Earrings went after them taking Horses Ghost, One Horn, and three other men. Each one rode off weeping openly from his loss and rage. They got most of the horses back. They also brought home two Pekony scalps. Walks Far danced with those scalps. She was Lakota now.

When the band swung east to the Redwater, Assiniboins, who viewed the Teton Sioux as invaders of their hunting grounds, tried to drive them away by setting a prairie fire. But by the power of Walks Far's Sun-stone the wind suddenly changed, and it was the Assiniboins who had to flee for their lives. In places, particularly at steep coulee crossings, the accumulation of old buffalo manure was so deep that it smoldered for days.

Word came that the army had stopped more whites from going to the Black Hills and had even burned some of their wagons, but so many whites had kept right on coming that the army had given up its efforts to throw them out. Now it was trying only to keep the miners from fighting each other over the best places to dig for gold. It was said that some of the whites now wanted to take the Bighorn Mountains hunting lands as well as the Black Hills!

But that fall, in the first big organized hunt, a pregnant Walks Far, a woman "growing strong," as the Sioux put it, watched her own man race in with his bow among the fleeing fat cows and, shortly after, he was at work beside her in the butchering. They made plenty of meat, the two of them, that last good summer.

Walks Far's baby was born an outlaw. She entered a wintry world within a robe-hunting camp sheltered in badlands near the head of the Little Dry on the last day of the moon, the one called by the Blackfoot, Moon When the Jackrabbit Whistles at Night [the last day of the February moon, 1876]. Thus it was the day special for two-legged persons, and it was also Walks Far's twentieth birthday.

The baby could hardly have been more innocent about its outlaw status than were Walks Far and Horses Ghost, or any of the rest of the band. All were now outlawed because they had failed to come in to an agency by the end of the previous moon, as ordered by the Great White Father. The time that was allowed for delivering the message and for the wild bands to comply if they had chosen to do so would have been short enough in summer. Now, in a winter more exceptionally cold than the last, with the forelegs of horses raw and bloodied from pawing for grass through the hard-crusted snow that lay everywhere, not even the message had yet reached many of the bands.

The people in the north knew only that at a big council called by the whites which had met far to the south in the early fall just past [1875], the chiefs had angrily refused even to consider selling either the Black Hills or the Powder River and Big Horn lands. Many had seen the white travelers following on the thieves' road of Longhair Custer. Red Cloud himself had seen some of the soldiers digging for gold exactly like the miners they had gone to drive away. What was the use, the chiefs asked, of dealing anew with the Great White Father when he appeared to be either quite willing to let white men violate the treaty or else lacking in power to enforce it? The warriors at the council had grown so angry that some yelled for the charge!— *"Hoka hey!"* And the whites showed obvious fright. Little Big Man of Crazy Horse's band had galloped straight at the whites, with a loaded Winchester in one hand and extra cartridges between the fingers of the other, yelling that he was going to kill them. He had been stopped, because such behavior at a council was wrong, and Young Man Afraid of His Horse, the Oglala soldier chief, had established good order. But all of that had happened while Walks Far and Horses Ghost made meat on the Redwater.

Walks Far made simple advance preparations for the birth of her baby: a deerskin tanned very soft for catching the baby on, two bladders ending in nipples, and a kind of tiny buckskin sleeping bag that laced up in front. Red Hoop Woman made and gave her a highly decorated one, and a married sister of Horses Ghost made another, as she was expected to do. To stuff these and serve as both diapers and warm blanket Walks Far collected many ripe, dry cattails, which she fluffed into soft down and put away in a large bag. Also, before it snowed, she had collected a bag of dry powder from a rotten log and had filled another with dry buffalo chips pounded into powder. These were to be used for the same purpose as the cattail down, which was generally regarded as superior. However, if the baby developed a rash, a change to one of the other materials often appeared to help. Women argued about the matter.

Walks Far also fashioned two very small beaded bags in the form of a turtle, a creature so notoriously hard to kill that its protective power should be made available to guard the baby. A piece of the umbilical cord packed in tobacco would go in one bag to be worn by the baby to prevent it from becoming a thief or developing other bad traits. The second bag was only a decoy for confusing the bad spirits.

When the time drew near, Red Hoop Woman suspended a stout pole horizontally from the lodgepoles at the rear of the tipi. This horizontal pole or bar was at a height to allow Walks Far to kneel with it across her breast and under her armpits. Thus, she could plant her knees firmly on the ground or hold them raised a little above it. Two old women with reputations as midwives, and who had been given presents in advance, came in. They brought deerskin bands for the bellies of baby and mother, put big swabs of sweet grass to soak in water boiled with sage, laid out a puffball with a hole punched in it, added a bowl of buffalo grease and their knives, and were ready. One of them told Red Hoop Woman pointedly, "We are in charge here; if we need your help or advice, we will ask you for it."

The other old woman added, "If things do not go well and we need any help, it has been arranged for old Father of a Mudfish to come and give Walks Far Woman a magic dust to make her sneeze. He will then sing his magic song that puts a turtle in to chase the baby out."

Walks Far felt no reason to be apprehensive. She had prayed every morning for an easy delivery and a healthy baby. She had eaten nothing from the insides of any creature and, of course, she had eaten nothing from a bird! particularly those birds that dust their feathers, for that might have made delivery "dry" and difficult. Not even Horses Ghost's eagle feathers, nor so much as a goose wing for fanning the fire, had been allowed within the tipi. Also, she had been careful, both day and night, never to turn her body abruptly and risk twisting the cord around her baby's neck. Fortunately, winter had made it easy to avoid so much as the sight of a badger or any other of the animals that sometimes back from their burrows. Seeing one do that might have caused a breech birth.

At the onset of her final pains Walks Far knelt with her elbows hooked over the bar. One of the old women, facing Walks Far and gripping the bar with her own hands, knelt solidly on the ground, with her knees keeping Walks Far's knees spread wide apart. At the end Walks Far held the bar squeezed hard beneath her armpits. It seemed to her that the baby took forever, but the old women said it came very fast. They caught it in the soft deerskin, cut and twisted the umbilical cord and dusted it thoroughly with the powdered fungus from inside the puffball. They then wrapped the deerskin band around the baby at the navel.

One of the old women next turned to banding Walks Far's belly and making her comfortable in bed, while the other swabbed off the baby with the soaked, warmed sweet grass, though she did not clean its mouth. This was one act reserved for Red Hoop Woman, who stood as a kind of godmother. The child would be sure to grow up showing the qualities and traits of the person who performed the act, and Red Hoop Woman suddenly felt herself unworthy. She said she would run and bring Suzy's mother. But Walks Far would have none of that. She demanded that Red Hoop Woman do it. Suzy's mother was a woman of such enormous virtue, character, and ability, and with such an exaggerated mysticism, too, that Walks Far could not believe her entirely human. Red Hoop Woman was persuaded to go ahead. The old woman greased the baby all over, laced it into the down-filled bag, and gave it to Walks Far. It was a perfect little girl, with big dark eyes and more hair than most babies are born with.

Grandfather said that his first child had likewise been a little girl, one simply called Baby until she was old enough to walk and have her ears pierced, even though on her fourth day she had been named Sky Eyes for a reason he had now forgotten. Horses Ghost appeared instantly forgetful that he had been planning on a son. He rarely called his daughter anything but Little Girl, though Walks Far liked the name Sky Eyes very much, and that was the one given at the formal naming feast held before the new moon had passed. Oddly, Grandfather never used anything but Good Girl.

For the first four days, until Sky Eyes could be breast fed, Walks Far nourished her from one of the nippled bladders. They were filled with warm soup made either from dried berries or meat, or both. Shortly, Sky Eyes was also taking the tender meat Walks Far first chewed to a paste, but she would be nursed until she was about four, and Walks Far would try to avoid getting pregnant again, lest the milk stop. No one ever let that baby cry much and, if petting and cuddling weren't effective, Grandfather would act like its grandmother and help out by crying with it. Walks Far was expected to spend about ten days resting in bed, but after five or six days she could no longer endure the inactivity, so she resumed all but the heavier part of her work. [She told Janet Sinclair that while Indian women might, when necessary, bear a child alone and resume their work or travel, this was unusual. She said birth was regarded as a very powerful and mysterious event, and that a new mother was usually treated with all the tenderness and care a family gave a wounded warrior.]

There were many presents. Walks Far ultimately received nine cradle boards, traditional gifts from relatives who vied in thus showing off their handiwork. Some of these cradle boards were so heavily ornamented as to be almost too cumbersome for general use, and were, therefore, a nuisance.

Around this time, well before the ice broke up on the Big Muddy River, about half the people took all the band's winter-hunt robes to the traders at Fort Peck. They made a good trade for everything except guns, which the traders said were still forbidden, though they did let a few cartridges go. Some of the robes were then taken up Frenchman's Creek to the Métis, but the Métis had no guns, and but a few cartridges, to fit the Spencers only. They had taken nearly all their limited stock to trade with the Sioux bands in the big winter camps south of the Yellowstone.

In the Birth of Calves Moon [April] the whole band also went south of the Yellowstone and joined Sitting Bull near the mouth of the Powder River. They were just in time to move on to Tongue River for a council of all the northern bands, called by Sitting Bull. Walks Far heard how, in the moon before this council, soldiers from the south had surprised a combined camp of Sioux and Cheyennes to eastward on the Powder River. The people fled their tipis with a loss of only one woman and two children, and then, as the soldiers burned the lodges, the warriors counterattacked and killed three or four of them. The rest of the soldiers quickly retreated, but a part had already driven about seven hundred horses away. The warriors got most of these back in the night, but the retreating soldiers captured a hundred of them once more, and this time cut their throats. Some people said that these Sioux, under He Dog, and especially the trading Cheyenne chief Two Moon, had not been sure they liked Sitting Bull's talk of war—not until now.

Walks Far learned what most of the people already knew: Other soldiers, around seven hundred of them under General Gibbon, had assembled from the Blackfoot country and the Crow country to march eastward along the north bank of the Yellowstone. They were now opposite the mouth of the Big-horn, camping at a stockade built by some white traders and wolfers the past fall. The presence of these soldiers made the people far more angry than fearful. [Walks Far still felt delight now after seventy years recalling how Two Moon and his Cheyennes had seen this camp as an opportunity for recouping some of their recent loss in horses. Walks Far said, "When sun-down and cold, Two Moon put on blanket lak Crow scout for soldiers. He go walk 'round in that camp. Those soldiers wake up in new sun and find bes' horse and mule gone! Crow scouts got thirty-two horse they keep safe on island in river. Those horse, she's gone too! Nobodies steal horse better than Crow—nobodies but Two Moon and Cheyennes, that tam!"]

At Sitting Bull's Tongue River council he spoke a simple message: *The whites want war; let us give it to them!* The wild bands, all those wintering on tributaries of the Yellowstone, readily agreed, as did those of the people who had gone south to the agencies for wintering, and now came back.

Meanwhile, Suzy fell in love with a young Oglala who re-turned with He Dog's angry people. He was a nice-looking boy with famous relatives, but although he had been on two war parties and had just participated in fighting with the soldiers, he had never done anything to distinguish himself very much. He did have a truly good horse—but just that one. Though he was older than Suzy, they were both a bit too young for marriage. His name was Stands Alone.

He and Suzy went through the identical water-path ritual by which Horses Ghost had courted Walks Far. When he came to wait outside her tipi in the evening, Suzy never even had a chance to pretend the smoke ears needed adjustment. Her father went out and gently but firmly told the boy to come back and start courting next year, or maybe the year after that. Nevertheless, Suzy and the boy were able to arrange to meet next evening at a point where the Miniconjou and Sans Arc camps nearly merged, where the people of one camp would assume that the young couple belonged to the other camp. But strangers always looked twice at Suzy on account of her white blood. Anyhow, someone must have recognized her and tattled.

Now she had gotten to be so strictly watched that she was inadequate as a source of news.

The growing camp shifted to the Rosebud at the beginning of the Thunderstorm Moon [May], and still it grew. Anyone who would fight the whites was welcome. Some people talked of exploiting general hatred of the whites by uniting all the tribes to drive them from the prairies. Sitting Bull sent out messages accordingly, one of them calling for a council of the tribes living north of the Missouri River to meet on Beaver Creek at the beginning of the next moon. Yanktons, Santees, Assiniboins, Plains Cree, Plains Chippewa, Mandans, and the three divisions of the Blackfoot tribe were invited. Most of these were traditional enemies of the Teton Sioux, and the invitation was delivered to them along with a gift of tobacco and a cartridge, offering a choice of either peace or war.

Walks Far went to this council. One of Sitting Bull's cronies was the chief envoy, but Feather Earrings was also included because his reputation as a warrior extended north of the Missouri. Moreover, he could be a persuasive orator, and because of his obvious general cleverness, along with an ability to understand a few words from both languages spoken by whites, he was regarded as something of a man of the world. He was known as a good listener, too, and would take along his latest pretty, young wife, who had many Yankton and Assiniboin relatives. It was thought desirable that one of the envoys be a persuasive young warrior, and Feather Earrings suggested Horses Ghost because he had been especially impressed with him during the pursuit of the Pekony war party during the past summer.

Horses Ghost felt no enthusiasm about going. He and One Horn, with two others, had been planning a little raid on those thieves' roads running into the Black Hills. Young warriors newly arrived from that direction exhibited scalps, horses, revolvers, watches, and other trophies, which they said were so easily taken as to result in more fun than real honor. Walks Far had to remind Horses Ghost that parents who allow themselves to be separated while they have a new baby run a serious risk of causing the spirits to think the baby is unwanted. But Walks Far wished very much to go to the council on Beaver Creek, and was able to have her way. She looked forward eagerly to a possibility of seeing old friends, of hearing Pikuni Blackfoot speech again, of showing off her handsome husband and baby, and she took along all her finery. They traveled without a tipi, taking on a packhorse only such hunting wikiups as Walks Far and Horses Ghost had used on their honeymoon trips. Walks Far hung Sky Eyes in a fine cradle board from the saddle at her left knee instead of on her back. That was *not* the way to carry a baby, Horses Ghost complained. He seemed to let it bother and worry him almost as much as did the fact that Walks Far had never been tattooed.

The first leg of their route from the Rosebud to Fort Peck on the Missouri ran nearly due north. The spring that year seemed at least as beautiful as the one preceding. Grass on the hills and flats grew especially green and lush. Antelope, deer, and buffalo all seemed to have wintered well, though Walks Far saw more eagles than usual, and the wolves and coyotes looked well fed. There would soon be plenty of berries along the coulees. The whole party, except Sky Eyes, got more or less sunburned.

They reached the Missouri, the Big River, on the third evening. Walks Far would not have to swim it alone, this time, and it happened that she did not have to swim at all! A young white man was on the other bank. Feather Earrings called to him, identifying himself. The white man ran upstream a little way, jumped in a big wooden boat, and came over to them in no time. Walks Far felt surprised that he arrived precisely where they waited, even though he had his back to them all the while he worked hard at making the boat go.

She got a different kind of surprise when he turned around and smiled, for she was seeing not exactly a young white man, but Joe Culbertson. He recognized her, too. He already knew everyone except Horses Ghost, and he told Horses Ghost he was a lucky man to have a half-Pekony wife who could stop cloudbursts. The way he said it—well, it was hardly the proper thing to say. Even more impolitely, he spoke directly to her, and in Blackfoot, "I see you still have that fine knife."

"The stone you gave me keeps it very sharp," she said. "It has easily cut the throat of a Crow."

Joe rowed them and all their things across while they held the ropes of their swimming horses. Walks Far, feeling safe from the under-water people, found this way of crossing the Big River on a spring evening truly pleasant. Everyone chattered about it—all except Horses Ghost. He sulked, and Walks Far knew she would have to explain Joe Culbertson.

Joe showed a careful curiosity about what their rather odd

group could be up to, and their explanation that they came to visit some of Feather Earrings's Yankton friends and relatives did not appear to satisfy him, but he was able to tell exactly where those friends and relatives were camped. They stayed the night in Yankton tipis, and in the morning slipped away northward toward Beaver Creek with their hosts and two important Assiniboins.

The council proved a big disappointment. As Feather Earrings said, "We have ridden hard for nothing." Also, they would probably miss the sun dance, which this summer was to be held earlier than usual. Walks Far heard very little of her Blackfoot speech. A very important Pikuni or Piegan Blackfoot chief named Little Plume came, all right, and brought two others, but all three had the air of men who were interested merely in learning what was going on. Little Plume had thoughtfully left his people camped a day's ride to the west, where they could be in no way excited by the council. He could, if he wished, lead more warriors to join Sitting Bull than any other chief at the council, but Blackfoot and Teton Sioux were long-time enemies.

Walks Far and Feather Earrings agreed that Sitting Bull's close friend made a poor chief envoy. He could hardly have been more arrogant and less clever. He, with two or three of the more bitter Yanktons and Santees, declared, "All whites are dogs and cowards who must be swept from the prairies—all except a few traders we will allow at certain places. The Tetons are going to do this, but help is needed. There will be plenty of horses and mules, plenty of white women for the victors after all the white men and those Crow dogs who help them are swept away. Sitting Bull will sweep them away. The Tetons will do this by themselves. Then, those who were remembered as not coming to help will suffer!"

Little Plume spoke through an Assiniboin woman interpreter. Even so, his sarcasm came through. He said, "You must already know that I have little liking for the white man's world, the white man's road, or most white men. Yet I will say that I like some white men as much as I dislike most of the others. Also, I will tell you this: An Indian who thinks all white men are dogs and cowards, whether or not they are the kind of white men an Indian would want to have around, is an Indian who is badly fooling himself!

"I have already heard some strange things about this Sitting Bull who has such a strange way of asking for my help. But perhaps I am getting old and my mind is easily mixed up. Or perhaps I don't hear very well anymore. But I am clear about what I will say now: I too am a great dreamer of fine dreams, but too often, after I wake up, I see that my dream has no meaning for a person who must use his eyes to get around in daylight. I am sorry I cannot stay here longer, but I have to go get my people and take them hunting."

In departing, he told some of the Plains Crees and Chippewas that if the Sioux came to his country, they would not find him an old man who had grown too tired for fighting.

Soon after the council broke up, two Santees or Yanktons chanced to meet a fifteen-year-old boy of Little Plume's band out looking for his father's strayed horses. They shot the boy, who lived long enough to get home and tell the story. The result was a threat of all-Indian war north of the Missouri. Many Yankton warriors decided they had better not go help Sitting Bull, not just now. Some did, and a few, by near individual choice, came from the other tribes at the council. Walks Far missed much excitement at home from having gone. There had been a big battle with soldiers, and Suzy had a husband after all.

Walks Far, Sky Eyes, and the others got back south of the Yellowstone to find Grandfather well as usual and to learn that the still growing camp had not only held the sun dance but had moved a day's march westward onto the Greasy Grass—the Little Bighorn. Separate camp circles of Teton subtribes, and another of Cheyennes, crowded the flats within a long loop on the west side of the north-flowing river. Walks Far had never seen so many tipis and people—so many horses! Just to ride [the approximately four miles] straight from the Hunkpapa circle at the southern or upstream end of that camp to the Cheyenne circle farthest downstream took longer than would be needed to skin and heavy-butcher a buffalo. There were hundreds of tipis. Many of them, in addition to sheltering the warrior father and son, sheltered other warriors who had come without families and tipis of their own. Some warriors were living in wikiups, and doing their own cooking. Individuals came riding in from distant places and tribes, a few in white man's clothing. Several Arapahoes who arrived in a group were only saved from death as bitter enemies when the chiefs declared that anyone was welcome who would fight. Still, most of the agency Sioux had failed to answer Sitting Bull's call. Though Red Cloud's son, Jack, was in camp, Walks Far heard that he had come entirely on his own, and had, in fact, started before Sitting Bull's council sent out its call for a general war.

That whole camp throbbed with excitement, was pulsing to the drums of scalp dancing over a victory on the Rosebud only four days past. [This fixes the date of Walks Far's return as June 21, 1876. The Rosebud battle of June 17 preceded the battle on the Little Bighorn by more than a week, and was fought by some one thousand Sioux and Cheyennes against a northward-advancing force of about the same size under General Crook. It was a long, hard day of stubborn fighting by both sides. The army called it a "drawn" battle, but although most of the Indians departed at nightfall, Crook buried his dead in the darkness, rode his force over the graves to hide them, and also departed, turning back southward from where he had come.] Some of the people mourned dead warriors now dressed for their last journey and lying in laced-up tipis set apart. But scouts reported that the soldiers from the south were still riding back upon the road made by their coming.

Thus, Sun had already given substance to Sitting Bull's vision at the sun dance a few days earlier. For Walks Far heard how Sitting Bull, a man she knew to be about forty-five, had sat upon the sage for torture. Fifty of those small pieces of flesh were cut one by one from his arms before he submitted himself to Sun in dancing. His skewers tore out about dark. He fainted then, and was granted a vision—*soldiers falling upside down from the sky!*

Both One Horn and Suzy's brother, Kills When Wounded, had been in that big fight on the Rosebud because, as One Horn explained to Horses Ghost and Walks Far, "We just never got around to going for a raid on those thieves' roads to the Black Hills," and he went on to say, "A party of Cheyennes discovered those soldiers while out hunting, and about a thousand of us, Sioux and Cheyenne, rode out in the night to get there. It was said that Crazy Horse and Two Moon had a plan for some kind of trap to work on the soldiers. The police societies rode to the front and on the flanks to stop any warriors from rushing on ahead, but when we got close to the enemy and saw some of his Snake scouts, nearly everyone yelled and charged. A Sioux boy about twelve years old that I did not know was in that charge was the first one of us to be killed.

"We and the soldiers kept charging each other back and forth. Between times, we pulled our breechclouts aside and taunted those soldiers with signs that even those *wasichu* could not help but understand. One bunch of soldiers yelled and taunted us back with the same signs until a young soldier chief got very angry and made them stop. Many plum trees grow in some places there, and the petals were falling all around us and those soldiers as though it snowed. The whole country seemed to smell of plum blossoms and powder smoke.

"Neither I nor Kills When Wounded was able to count a first coup. It was the longest, hardest day of fighting most of us had ever seen." And One Horn added wryly, "I noticed a few of both Sioux and Cheyennes who decided very early in that fighting that they were already tired, and ought to go home and get something to eat!"

One Horn had succeeded in taking a soldier's revolver with lots of cartridges, and in the grass had found a truly beautiful, very long breech-loading gun with two barrels. But it was only a shotgun without any ammunition and such a nuisance to carry along that he threw it away again. Kills When Wounded had taken a rather poor Snake horse and a lot of carbine cartridges.

"But you should have seen that Oglala boy, Stands Alone! He was everywhere. He counted first coup on a Snake scout he killed in the first charge. The Snake scout fired when Stands Alone was so close that it set his hair on fire! But Stands Alone killed the Snake with an even closer shot, taking horse, weapons, and scalp, all while beating the fire from his hair! He loaned the horse to a dismounted Oglala and then killed a soldier, getting carbine and revolver, with plenty of cartridges for both, as well as grabbing the soldier's fine big gray horse. Old warriors who had been in many fights were soon asking, 'Does anyone know that boy's name?' . . . No, Sitting Bull was not at that fighting; he is still too sick from his sacrifice at the sun dance."

Walks Far heard One Horn relate the advice he gave to Stands Alone while they rode back together that night. One Horn had said, "Suzy's father is my uncle, and I know a lot about him and his wife. Be in no hurry to do anything—not for two or three days. You should wait a while so that they will have plenty of time to hear all about you."

So it was that on the second morning after the Rosebud fight Suzy's father found a Snake horse and a fine army horse, complete with all its military equipment, picketed before his tipi. Within a little while he was saying to Stands Alone, "Maybe you are older than I thought, for I have been hearing some pretty good things about you. I was only afraid that you would not amount to much. I did not want Suzy to have to live in a six-hide tipi at the poor end of camp. But I do not believe that will happen now. If you and Suzy want to get married, you can have her."

"Like some other people I know," One Horn said, "they could not wait awhile for everything to be done in the way it should be. They were married last night in my mother's tipi, and now, for a while, my mother and I do not have even a six-hide tipi of our own."

"Both of you are welcome here with us," Walks Far said.

"You should have been at that fighting on the Rosebud," One Horn told her. "A Cheyenne woman was there with her brother. The soldiers shot the brother's horse from under him, and the sister rode straight out into the shooting so that he could jump up behind her. The Cheyennes are speaking of that fighting as 'where the young girl saved her brother.' They say her name is Buffalo Calf Road."

Though the story impressed Walks Far and she envied the Cheyenne girl, she thought no more about it. Yet on the second morning following, just before she wakened, that Cheyenne girl, whom she had never seen, came to her in a dream and stood outside the tipi, pointing far down the river toward its junction with the larger Bighorn. The girl repeatedly cried out in terrible urgency some message that Walks Far could not understand. That was all, but its power lingered in such a peculiarly worrisome and frightening way that in preparing breakfast Walks Far felt like a person who had slept cold all night. She wished she had talked to Grandfather about it before he slipped away without breakfast. Horses Ghost and One Horn listened, then said that the dream surely had no meaning; it was only a sleeping dream, only a woman's waking-up dream. They too had heard someone cry out—Sky Eyes crying to be nursed!

They began to talk about going hunting. They needed to get some meat, yet the hunting around this camp was the poorest of the spring. The camp would have to move from the Little Bighorn very soon because so many people had already killed nearly all the game, and also because so many-plenty-many horses were swiftly eating all the good grass. It was getting dusty too, which made man and horse want to drink more water than was good for them.

The talk of hunting suggested to Walks Far that she might

conveniently remember more of her dream. Thus, she was suddenly enabled to recall seeing herself helping to butcher elk that Horses Ghost and One Horn had shot downstream where the two Bighorn rivers join. Both men declared that place to be both distant and already much overhunted, and also a most unlikely place for seeing elk this time of year anyhow. Besides, Horses Ghost insisted, she ought to stay home and catch up on her work. Nevertheless, Walks Far got her way, and with Sky Eyes at her back, they all rode off together with their guns.

Shortly before they reached the junction of the two streams, a party of five or six young Sans Arc warriors showing obvious excitement suddenly signaled them to cover. The Sans Arc were glad to see them and their guns. They wanted added strength for a *wikmunke*—a trap already set up. For just a short while earlier they had happened to see a white man—from Gibbon's western soldiers no doubt—cautiously examining the country to the south from a hilltop some distance farther on. The white man had four or five Crows with him.

The trap was nothing more than the common decoy-and-ambush tactic used on large or small scale by all the people of the prairies, but the lay of the land just here was especially well suited, and it offered the white man only one possible route of approach. The two smallest and most boyish-looking of the Sans Arcs would ride unguardedly toward the white man and the Crows, discover their danger only at the last minute, then turn and flee for their lives. The pursuers should then come dashing headlong behind, to be led directly under the guns of ambushers waiting where it looked as though no enemy horseman could possibly find cover.

Everything began as expected. The two decoys soon came racing back over a low ridge, riding low and fast. Two of the Crows came after them, but not quite in all-out chase. They held up and waited on the face of the ridge, circling impatiently as the white man and four more Crows appeared. The decoys slowed, also circling, but as though undecided about where to run.

Walks Far saw the white man, a rather trim one in an exceptionally big hat, stop a little below the ridge top and raise one of those looks-far things to his eyes. She had seen that man doing exactly the same thing from a ridge near the Marias River two summers ago on a day she would never forget. For a moment she felt unable to move, and then, with Sky Eyes on her back, she quirted Crazy One into the open, dashed between the two surprised decoys, and galloped some distance toward the ridge. When close enough, she called out his Blackfoot name, Siksikak-wan, then added a warning, "Go away! Go away! Hurry! *Mistaput! Mistaput! Neotukit!* You will be killed! There are many enemies here. I am Walks Far Away Woman. You gave me your knife."

She pointed upstream, "Over there is the biggest camp and more warriors than you have ever seen!"

Jack Sinclair raised his hand high. "Come away with me," he called back. "Ride hard. I will wait for you."

"I do not wish to do that now," she told him. "Go away, hurry! *Mistaput, neotukit!*"

Jack Sinclair signaled to the two Crows in his front, and his whole party disappeared back over the crest, though one Crow lingered there to exchange insults with the taunting Sioux now galloping angrily up around Walks Far.

She did not apologize, but only explained with a partial lie, saying clearly and carefully, "He is a good man and an old friend in my father's lodge. If he had not given me this knife when I had to run away from the Pekonies, I might now be dead. *I now know that my dream was to tell me to warn him.*"

It was an explanation she knew her listeners would understand and accept, disappointed and angry as they might be. She saw Horses Ghost to be sullen and jealous, but he added for her, "My wife is a medicine woman who has a powerful Sun-stone. She has also dreamed that we will shoot some elk."

A loyal One Horn had to speak up. "She will surely find enough elk for all," he assured the Sans Arcs.

Walks Far began to pray hard as they turned back along the stream, all hunting expectantly where she knew no right-minded elk could possibly be. Therefore, she was the most surprised of the hunters when they blundered onto a herd of eleven and killed six, one of them falling to a shot from her own gun. She felt awed by her own power. Not only had the actual dream clearly meant something that had now been explained, but she had prayed the promise in the added little lie into fulfillment. She felt humbled by her obvious attunement with mysterious forces, and was herself the person most impressed. But she wished she had thought to dream those elk fatter than they were. Also, before another day was done it would occur to her that in dreaming those elk she had possibly saved a life in addition to Jack Sinclair's life.

For One Horn had failed to kill an elk. He had missed his shot and was then unable to extract the fired cartridge from his Sharps until it could be forced out by a rod pushed down from the muzzle. That cartridge was one of those he had taken in the recent fight with the soldiers on the Rosebud, and when he tried another of them, the same thing happened. Those cartridges were all apparently a trifle too small. On firing, the soft metal cases swelled tight in the breech. That evening, back in camp, he found that they would work properly only in the guns also taken in that day's fighting!

It was lucky for One Horn that the difficulty had been discovered in time, while he was shooting at something no more dangerous than a four-legged person.

Chapter Twenty-three
HAND TALK FOR SCALPS THEM

(Sunday, June 25, 1876)

Walks Far saw the next morning dawn with a war-bonnet sunrise above the hundreds of tipis spread over the wide, grassy flat beside the Little Bighorn. The ground mist appeared to burn away from no more than rays of rose and copper light fanning up behind the ridge across the river. Horses Ghost and One Horn remarked on that sunrise, declaring it to be a good omen for a war party. Walks Far thought it heralded a very hot day, but one without any wind to help dry the elk meat.

Red Hoop Woman came by for a moment and said, "Scalps Them and Left Hand Bull have heard of more soldiers, moving around and coming from the north this time. They were seen late yesterday riding up the Rosebud valley over there to eastward." Red Hoop Woman wasn't excited about it, and apparently, neither were the chiefs. The only excitement in camp stemmed from a brawl among some of the Oglalas the night before. Red Hoop Woman said, "Buffalo Berry Woman was over there and saw a man hit the drum and throw his wife away. The wife tried to stab him, as was expected, and she gave him a bad cut. Lots of the Oglalas took sides, and people got hurt or had their tipis slashed before the police society got them quieted down."

Walks Far knew that Suzy and her husband would probably go away with the Oglalas soon, and she hoped Suzy would not get caught up in what appeared to be an almost continual squabbling among them.

Again, shortly after midmorning, Red Hoop Woman reported more news of soldiers. "Gall's wife says they have been seen to the southeast, on the high ground between this place and the Rosebud."

"Is no one going to go fight them?" Walks Far wanted to know.

"Scalps Them and Left Hand Bull say they have heard these soldiers to be much fewer than those driven back the other day. They would be crazy to attack a camp as large as this one. But someone will keep an eye on them. You know we are going to have to move in a day or two. The men say they are going after those soldiers then."

Walks Far gave the matter no more thought; if the chiefs saw nothing to get excited about, neither did she. Besides, it was going to be the first truly hot day thus far. Grandfather did not wander away that morning, but was content to sit in the shade and watch over Sky Eyes. He kept the too playful puppies away and switched the flies from her face as she lay naked on a robe, waving her fat little limbs and gurgling while Walks Far cut meat into long, thin strips for drying. A pair of old men and several young boys came by and invited Grandfather to go fishing up the river with them, but he lazily declined. If he felt any premonitions that this would be a memorable day, one that would witness the wild Sioux's finest hour, yet lead inevitably to utter destruction of their world, he gave no sign of it, but appeared as surprised as anyone else when, in the early afternoon, it all began to happen.

A distant cloud of dust suddenly appeared well upstream to southward. People rose to their feet, talking in swift low voices as they shaded their eyes and gazed intently. From an overlooking hill to the southwest, came two boys lashing their ponies into a dead run. "Soldiers are coming!" they cried. "Plenty-many soldiers! We saw them chasing maybe ten warriors back to camp. Some Indians are with those soldiers. Shoot some guns to wake people up. We will ride to the Oglalas and Miniconjous." [The soldiers reported by these riders comprised Major Reno's portion of Custer's divided regiment of cavalry. Reno advanced over rather flat ground on the west side of the river toward the upper or south end of the huge Sioux camp. Custer himself, presumably bent on attacking the lower end of the camp, led a larger portion of the regiment. It also advanced northward, but beyond the river to eastward. There, a ridge screened it from eyes in the camp for a considerable time.]

There was near panic. More men were shouting and more women were screaming than Walks Far had ever heard. Horses Ghost and One Horn found their guns and war bags, and Walks Far snatched up Sky Eyes, laced her frantically into a cradle board, and slung it on her back. Grabbing her own carbine and a rope, she ran with a speed that soon had her leading all the other women and most of the men toward their horses on the hill to westward. She saw Suzy and her husband coming, too, as she caught Crazy One, then held the horses of Horses Ghost and One Horn while they quickly prepared themselves for war. From his war bag Horses Ghost put on a fringed buckskin shirt painted yellow and perforated all over with holes a little larger than an eye. He added a bear-claw necklace, quickly painted his face red, made vertical scratches in the paint with his finger-nails to represent the claw marks of a bear, and added black circles around his eyes and mouth. He lacked time to prepare in detail and with proper songs, or to blow yellow powder all over his horses. Instead he merely blew a little of the powder into his horse's nostrils and under the horse's tail to help strengthen its wind. One Horn had just finished identical preparations.

"Go to the other end of the camp, to the circle of the Sans Arcs," Horses Ghost told Walks Far, and started with One Horn for the advancing dust cloud in a hard lope, joining a streaming swarm of warriors. *"Hoka hey!"* Horses Ghost shouted "Let's go! brothers. There is the enemy! It is a good day to die!" Walks Far would have ridden with them had it not been for Sky Eyes on her back. Nearly all boys of fourteen years or more rode with their fathers or brothers. Most of the men and boys were armed only with bow and arrows, and if they failed to take a soldier's carbine, they might be made ecstatic by suddenly falling heir to a battered muzzle-loader abandoned by a warrior who had taken a better gun.

Suzy was mounted, screaming that they should flee together now, but Walks Far estimated the time still allowed her by the advancing dust cloud. In doing so she saw enemy Indians swinging out toward the Sioux horse herd, but they suddenly lost their nerve and veered away from the swarming Sioux warriors. Guns began to pop distantly under the hot afternoon sun.

"I am going back and get some things for the baby," Walks Far said, "I am going to see about Grandfather and get my *winkte* dress."

"Then I too will get some things," Suzy said. "But we ought to hurry. As you can see, the fighting has begun out there."

Walks Far felt no real expectation that Grandfather would be at the tipi, yet there he was, and with most of the things she had come back for gathered and ready. Many women and children were still gathering things for flight. Also, there was much calling and screaming. But it abruptly silenced, then grew wilder than ever, with people running frantically as a sparse scattering of bullets began striking among the tipis. Walks Far mounted Crazy One, and as she desperately hauled Grandfather up behind, the sound of firing increased, and Grandfather said, "I think the soldiers are surprised and have now got down from their horses to shoot carefully at the warriors. They are not yet *trying* to shoot into the camp."

Walks Far was not reassured by Grandfather's guesswork, particularly when, as she rejoined the waiting Suzy, she saw a running woman spin around and go down, blood frothing from her mouth. Afterward, Red Hoop Woman told her that two of Chief Gall's children had also been killed there, while he rode out with the warriors. Moreover, as she and Suzy threaded their way northward among the tipis and through all the confusion of the thoroughly aroused camp, Walks Far could not still a nagging worry about the safety of Horses Ghost and One Horn. For, though she certainly never said so aloud, she did not believe their bear medicine to be the luckiest a warrior might possess. She herself, out of the Blackfoot portion of her heritage, felt especially inclined to view the bear with near reverence— was he not of all animals most like a two-legged person? Yet bears often were slow and clumsy, so that they got shot. True, they were creatures hard to kill, but much of their reputation came from the fierce way they continued fighting after being wounded, and they rarely got away safely after that!

Walks Far was thinking of this as she and Suzy rode downstream through the dusty uproar and commotion of the huge camp, and not until she had nearly reached the Miniconjous where Horses Ghost had told her to go was she conscious of having fled one fight toward another about to begin. For warriors abruptly began rushing off downstream ahead of Walks Far and Suzy, while some of those who had started upstream to the fighting there came galloping back. A chief shouted, "More of the soldiers are riding north behind that ridge over there across the river! They are going to strike this end of camp. The lay of the land, with the ridge dwindling away, makes it almost certain, unless they decide to run away from us."

One chief after another led the warriors to meet the threat, and the soldiers rode into a perfect trap that could hardly have been more successful had it been carefully planned. It worked in such a way that all the shooting hit hardly anything in the camp.

Walks Far sat before a friendly Miniconjou tipi and nursed Sky Eyes while that fighting went on. It lasted not a whole lot longer than the hungry Sky Eyes needed to get her fill, only about as long as it would have taken to boil a big pot of water over a hot fire. Walks Far could hear shooting and see the clouds of dust, but she saw almost none of the actual fighting.

A young son of the tipi where Walks Far waited came dashing home. His sweat-soaked horse was doubly wet from splashing across the ford in the river. He too was sweating, and in an ecstasy of battle and victory. A watch on its chain and a fresh scalp showing short brown hair hung from his fingers. He held both up proudly for his mother and all others to see, then said to Grandfather, "This was a brave *wasichu*. All of them are now dead, I think. But all those dogs of Crows and Rees got away. When they saw so many of us, they held back on the high ground, then rode away very fast.

"That shooting you now hear is from the warriors walking around to finish off soldiers who are only wounded and pretending they are dead."

Walks Far and Suzy were among the very first of the women to go looking for all the wealth in useful and valuable things that must be strewn around on that hill across the river. Walks Far had two things in mind. One was a soldier's hat for Grandfather, whom she left behind. Lately, he had been complaining that the sun hurt his eyes. She hoped also to get for Horses Ghost one of those rubber ground sheets such as One Horn had taken from the soldiers on the Rosebud. Almost immediately after splashing across the river, she and Suzy came upon three dead soldiers already stripped of everything. Somewhat unexpectedly, they had also been beheaded. A little farther on she saw a carbine on the ground, but it was badly broken. Suzy found a fine army bridle lying in the grass.

More than two hundred dead soldiers and about seventy dead horses lay scattered, both separately and in bunches, along that hill, and a thinning haze of dust and black powder smoke still lingered over them in the hot afternoon air, yet already the flies and the ants were at their work. And the smell! a battlefield smell such as Walks Far had never smelled before, and which she would never forget, a smell of dust and burnt black powder blending uneasily with blood and vomit and urine, with sour leather, human excrement, and horse manure, not to forget the odor of stale clothing sharpened by fresh sweat, nor the strong ammonia smell of horses killed while they too were sweating and in fear. All this unsteady stew mingled in the heavy heat with something else, perhaps the smell of death itself.

A fire had been lit, and warriors in their victory frenzy danced and howled as they burned some of the soldiers' useful things, things for which the women screamed. And all around was a more terrible screaming, with wailing, keening notes, for women found dead warrior fathers and husbands, brothers and sons scattered over that battlefield. Walks Far saw a thin woman abruptly cry out and run to collapse over the body of a rather elderly warrior, moaning his name. But soon she sat up and drawing her shawl over her head and face, she began a mourning wail that could last through the night and into a new sunrise unless relatives came to take her and the body away.

Walks Far heard the total of dead warriors given as about forty, and again she heard it to be more like ninety. Whether either of these figures included both Sioux and Cheyennes she did not know. Among the dead warriors, and the many wounded, were some struck by their battle-raging fellows amidst the cloud of smoke and dust in a final fury of charging the last few soldiers from all sides at once.

Walks Far and Suzy hurried about the business that brought them. Warriors had already taken the soldiers' weapons and unfired cartridges, also their watches and knives, but by no means everything. Clothing at least remained to be stripped from the dead. Again women screamed. Walks Far saw two of them fighting each other in an argument over who had reached a soldier's corpse first. The loser went away screaming to vent her fury by stabbing the next dead soldier, as some women were already doing. That soldier's cheek whiskers had been so impressive that a warrior had scalped them from one side. Some of the dead soldiers had been wearing stiff straw hats rather than the common floppy black felt. Also, many had on coarse brown work shirts instead of the shoddy army blue.

Walks Far hurried to a dead gray horse that looked as though it had been a particularly fine animal. She took the bridle, and from behind the saddle she unlashed exactly the rolled-up rubber ground sheet she sought. A tin plate and cup was neatly strapped at the end of the roll. The cracker-and-bacon-filled saddlebags were useful too, as was the extra-high-quality sleeping blanket the soldier had between saddle blanket and saddle. He lay twisted there, so close to his horse that Walks Far needed to step over him to get at the saddle's cinch.

A very tall, high-waisted woman of near middle age busily stripped a soldier a little way off beyond Suzy. Suddenly that woman called a loud invitation to everyone: "Sisters, come here! Come look at the big *che* on this *wasichu!*"

Walks Far did not abandon her own soldier. She noted his very fine hat, with a gold cord around it, lying crushed beneath his shoulder. That shoulder, or the arm, appeared to be broken, for the arm was folded beneath him in a very odd way. He had been shot through the chest, and the side of his head was crushed in as though by a war club. He looked to have been about Singer's age, and was darker than most white men. Like Singer, he wore those rich boots with soft leather uppers that reached well above the knees and were ornamented at the tops with yellow stitching in a kind of floral design. All the other dead soldiers in sight appeared to be wearing much shorter boots.

It occurred to Walks Far that those high boot tops could be converted easily into fine carbine cases for Horses Ghost and One Horn, but she couldn't get the boots off, even with Suzy's help. So, because the tops were all she wanted anyway, she drew her knife and made a cut all the way round at each ankle, then cut away the parts over the feet, and drew the long tops off easily. The light blue trousers, with the wide bright yellow stripe down the outer side of each leg, would make handsome leggins for Horses Ghost when she got time to cut the front and the seat out. She cut the soldier's suspenders and began stripping off every stitch of his clothing, and it appeared to her that he must have been richer and handsomer than most of the others, many of whom were clearly hardly more than boys.

Walks Far could feel no pity for any of them. They should

have stayed out of this country, and left peaceful people alone. And in being soldiers, they were, by and large, the worst kind of white men. The Blackfoot often called all white men "stone hearts" because they left their parents and families for years to come and live among strangers, yet keep themselves apart. Clearly, most of them lacked the feelings of any normal person and, just as clearly, soldiers were the worst of all. Walks Far thrilled to the triumph of their destruction. Yet she felt a vague regret that this white man had been unlucky enough to die. He looked as though he might have been nearly as handsome as Horses Ghost, and possibly as fine a person. But such soldiers had killed her father and her mother that freezing morning on the Marias River not six winters ago.

She found that the bullet through the soldier's chest had left his exceptionally fine blue shirt and buckskin jacket practically undamaged and unbloodied. In the shirt pocket she found one of those little sticks Singer used to write with, some small, folded white papers sewn between squares of leather, and also a small leather case filled with that kind of green paper that she now very well knew to be used by white men in their own trading. Around the soldier's neck she found a silver chain and a curious medal showing an old man wading a creek with a child on his shoulder. She took that from him too, and only at the last moment did she see his ring. How could she have missed it! there on the hand she had been forced to drag from beneath him to take off his upper clothing! It was a heavy gold ring, and from it flashed a large stone transparent as ice. Six smaller green stones were arranged in the form of a three-leafed plant on each side of the flashing stone.

Walks Far could not get that ring off until she used her knife to deftly amputate the finger, then trim it down. Suzy brought her spoils over, and they examined the ring together, marveling at the clear stone's fiery flashes in the late sun. A big, pock-marked warrior leading an army horse loaded with loot stopped to look. "That is very pretty," he said. "Have either of you found any of that green paper the soldiers carry? I will trade you something for enough of it—maybe a blanket. I am a Brulé, and I do much trading in the south."

Suzy had thrown all the green paper she found to the rising evening breeze, but Walks Far showed him some. The man looked like a mixed-blood, and he made faces the way a white man would as he took the papers and counted them before giving her a pleased smile showing his wide-spaced teeth, teeth like large yellow kernels of corn.

"You are very lucky," he told her, and holding the papers separated into a thick packet and a thinner one, he said of the greater, "For this much I will trade you a blanket, and for what is left, and the ring, I will trade you another blanket."

Something about him made Walks Far wary. "Give me the first blanket," she said. "I will keep the other papers and I also wish to keep the ring."

The man handed over a blanket and gave back the smaller packet of papers, then grew conversational: Did the two young women know that these were the soldiers of Longhair Custer? "Yes, it is certainly true," the warrior told Walks Far. "Those marks on the saddle blankets and other things mean 'seven' to the *wasichu,* and 'seven' is the sign of Longhair Custer's horse soldiers. They have come from the east, from their fort on the Big Muddy River, where the iron road the *wasichu* wanted to make has stopped. Some of the warriors here saw this 'seven' sign at that place earlier this spring. Also, one of the dead men is a black man from there. His name is Tit. It is now known that Longhair is among the dead." [The aged Walks Far told Janet Sinclair, "Somebodies say two Lakota, one Cheyenne kill Custer; somebodies say two Cheyenne, one Lakota. But Hi'm hear that tam how one Santee man from Canada shot 'im. If he don' do it, he got anyhow Custer's horse."] "Plainly it is Longhair, though with his long yellow hair cut short. It is said that many of the soldiers who attacked the north end of the camp still live, for they soon ran away to a hilltop where it is hard to get at them. The real fighting has been here. . . ."

The man paused, eyed Walks Far's knife, and decided to say, "For your knife and the ring, and the rest of the paper, I will trade you the other blanket and a rubber one, a soldier's strong knife, and a soldier's revolver with fourteen cartridges."

Walks Far was astonished. She had no idea the ring could be so valuable. "No," she said. "I wish to keep the knife and the ring."

"I will also give you this new army carbine with some cartridges if you will give me your old carbine and cartridges, along with the other things."

"No," Walks Far said again. "I think my husband will like that ring." She set about packing her loot on Crazy One, and as she and Suzy prepared to ride off, the man said abruptly, "Maybe your husband would also like this very fine big army horse. I will trade him for the paper and the ring."

"I have told you no."

"Woman, I think you are crazy."

"I think one of us must be," Walks Far told him as she turned away downhill toward the river and the camp.

Unexpectedly, she found Grandfather just where she had left him. Obviously, he had been telling a pair of warriors of old battles, and Walks Far heard him add, "I agree that you have won the Lakota's greatest victory, though when I was not too much older than you, when all the Lakota were men before the first smallpox winter, I do not believe it would have taken us so long. Not with such an opportunity."

Grandfather was delighted with the hat, and though it actually proved to be too large for him, no one realized that fact. When someone quickly gave him a fine eagle feather to stream from the gold cord, that hat was truly impressive, though it did give Grandfather a rather top-heavy look. All the long way north through the near riot of the celebrating and mourning camp, painted warriors shouted, "Where is that hat going with that boy?"

Walks Far was deeply relieved to find Horses Ghost and One Horn resting in the tipi, neither of them showing a wound. They had been eating cold elk meat and some very hard army crackers taken from a soldier, but were waiting for Walks Far to come home and cook them a hot supper. "I was beginning to get worried about you," Horses Ghost said. "It will be dark pretty soon." She saw with a kind of disappointment that he had taken a rubber ground sheet and other things along with the hard crackers, but she showed him the ring. It fit only his first finger, and he held his hand away appraisingly. "It is very pretty," he agreed, "but it is too bad that it was made of the yellow rather than of the white metal, and that those smaller stones are only green instead of blue."

He casually handed the ring back to her, and she saw him to be interested only in hearing about the fighting at the lower end of camp, and more especially in telling her all that had happened to him and One Horn since they had painted themselves to ride out and fight the soldiers at this end. Walks Far talked and listened as she cooked, but first she strung the ring on the chain with the medal and put the whole around her neck under her dress. If Horses Ghost didn't care to have a ring worth at least as much as a good horse, she would keep it herself. And neither Horses Ghost nor One Horn appeared to notice Grandfather's new hat.

Walks Far gave the barest outline, as she understood it, of the fighting across the river from where she waited in the Miniconjou camp with women returned from their panicky flight in fear that the soldiers would try to cross a good ford just there.

"As the soldiers rode down along the ridge," she said, "Two Moon and the Cheyennes, who as you know are camped farthest downstream, were first across the river. They hit the head of the soldier column hard. Very soon many Sioux got there too, and most of them, with some of the Cheyennes, slipped around to the east so fast with Crazy Horse that the soldiers had to get down from their horses and fight hard where they were, all strung out in little bunches and getting cut off from the trail they had come over.

"And Grandfather and I saw this: A lot of the soldiers suddenly tried to fight their way downhill toward the camp! They were brave but crazy. Maybe they thought all the warriors were already fighting, for they surely did not know that plenty-many warriors were with Runs the Enemy and waiting for them under what can be seen only from below and looks a little like the riverbank, though it is quite a way up from the real one. We saw Sitting Bull, with his arms still looking sore from the sacrifice, go over there on his white horse. He crossed the river singing about his visions and rode around talking to the warriors and waving a very crooked lance.

"When the soldiers found out what they were running into by coming downhill, those who could make it fought their way back up again and rejoined what was left of the others. In a little while the warriors rushed the last of them. Then Suzy and I went up on that hill with a lot of other women and got some fine things. On the way back here I heard how a three-stripe soldier had got off by himself in a pretty good place and kept shooting. He hit several warriors who tried to get at him, but he too is now dead.

"That is all I wish to tell you now—except that I saw a crazy thing just before I got here. Some warriors had put on soldiers' clothing and were having fun riding in rows as the soldiers ride. I thought we women had got all the clothing! But now I wish to hear all about what you have been doing."

Horses Ghost began a brief account of their day: "After you

saw us ride toward the enemy, we joined Scalps Them, Runs Stooped Over, Kills When Wounded, young Stands Alone, and Feather Earrings to form our own small fighting party. We were with Left Hand Bull and the rest of our band's warriors, and Left Hand Bull was clearly working with Gall." [Walks Far explained to Janet that there was nothing like a central command or overall direction among the Sioux, though renowned fighting chiefs might exercise more or less leadership over a varying number of warriors willing to follow them at a given time. Janet Sinclair quotes Walks Far as follows: "Anybodies ask name of chief 'command' ever' bodies, they don' know ol' tam Indians people."]

"When the soldiers saw so many of us coming," Horses Ghost went on, "they decided not to charge into camp. Three out of four got down from their horses and began to shoot at us from the open ground. Each fourth soldier rode away quickly, leading all the horses into that little patch of woods you have seen there near the river, opposite the high, steep hill the other side—"

One Horn interrupted with a detail: "A soldier could not stop his big horse to get down with the others. That horse bolted right in among us so fast that some of the warriors tried only to get out of the way, but Feather Earrings and Runs Stooped Over crowded in on either side. They blamed each other for killing the horse as well as the soldier, but Scalps Them said, "Brothers, accidents always happen in war.""

Horses Ghost spoke again: "Pretty soon, all those soldiers shooting at us from the ground saw there were so plenty-many of us that we would soon be all around them. They too then hurried into the patch of woods where their horses had been taken. But they covered each other by fire as they went, and nearly all of them got there safely—"

"But those woods were no safer for them," One Horn told Walks Far and Grandfather. "The soldiers were too few for defending those woods all around, and warriors began to get in there too. Feather Earrings saw the soldier chief and the Ree chief of the enemy Indian scouts talking very fast about what they should do. Feather Earrings took a shot at them that almost blew the Ree's head away and spattered his brains against the soldier chief's face. Instantly, the soldier chief began to yell at the soldiers and race his horse at a dead run toward the river and the steep hill beyond it. The soldiers followed him, each one riding as fast as he could make his horse go."

"Chasing those fleeing soldiers made the most exciting part of the day," Horses Ghost said. It was just like running buffalo! And we killed at least thirty of them as they raced to the river and were crossing it. Scalps Them and Feather Earrings, with their Winchesters, got in some very good shooting at the river! Though luckily for those soldiers they just happened to strike the river at a shallow place. Still, they had to jump their horses down one steep bank, plunge across, and jump their horses up another one. All of us counted many coups and took guns."

Grandfather spoke for the first time. "But you let most of the soldiers get away onto that hill over there."

"It is true that we did not at once follow those who got across the river," Horses Ghost explained, "though after a little while, after some other soldiers came from the south and joined them, as did their packtrain, we went up and attacked them again. They were very lucky to have found a hill with a small hollow place at the top. It is just big enough for them. They shoot from behind dead horses and their packs and boxes. They have dug holes with their plates and knives and they are fighting bravely. The packtrain brought them plenty of ammunition. They even surprised us once by charging out and making us draw back a way."

"A person you know well had got closest to the enemy when they made their charge," One Horn added, laughing at the memory. "I have seen how Runs Stooped Over truly runs stooped over, and very fast!"

Horses Ghost continued, "Nevertheless, we kept at them. Those soldiers are in bad shape. They have no water, and many of them are wounded. A few warriors will watch them and keep them bothered through the night. A hard attack tomorrow will wipe them out. All the chiefs agree. . . .

"No," he assured Walks Far, "no one you know has been killed. Some were hit, including Scalps Them, but he will soon be all right. Old Father of a Mudfish took care of him right away. There is no chance that he will die. Red Hoop Woman came home early and is also taking care of him. But a very funny thing happened!—to Runs Stooped Over, of course. While we chased the soldiers to the river, Runs Stooped Over caught one of them and fought him hand to hand. That soldier threw up all over Runs Stooped Over while getting a knife thrust up under his ribs. It even got in Runs Stooped Over's eyes! All day we called him Bad-Smelling Animal, and he—"

"I want to know about Scalps Them," Walks Far said, and

even then she was only slowly able to learn that Scalps Them's wound was not exactly such a minor one after all. "But he is in good hands," One Horn told her cheerfully.

Walks Far dropped everything she was doing, abandoning Sky Eyes, supper, and all. Without stopping to tell Horses Ghost and One Horn what she thought of them—and that was plenty —she ran to Red Hoop Woman.

When she returned, she could agree that Horses Ghost and One Horn very likely had been right in accepting old Father of a Mudfish's prediction that Scalps Them would live. But it was absolutely certain that Scalps Them could never talk again. His mouth must have been open at the moment, perhaps in a warrior's whooping, when a soldier's bullet passed through both his cheeks so neatly as to knock out only a single tooth. But in its passage that bullet had also very nearly severed Scalps Them's tongue.

Old Father of a Mudfish had carefully honed a small knife, then quickly completed the bullet's work and applied sage to stop the bleeding. He sang a song and dusted one of his puffball powders over Scalps Them's cheeks. He ordered Scalps Them to take nothing but water for four days, and no more of that than he had to. The tipi had been purified to keep the bad spirits from building their invisible fires around Scalps Them. Old Father of a Mudfish had wrapped the severed end of the tongue carefully to take it away for drying and return to Scalps Them. Scalps Them was now resting as comfortably as could be expected. Nothing more could be done. He was not suffering too much from the spirit fires, at least. Walks Far saw a smiling expression in his eyes, as though he had just thought of a good pun he wanted to make for her, but she had seen no dead soldier's face that looked so horrible.

She returned to her own tipi to find One Horn gone, as well as Grandfather, and Horses Ghost playing with Sky Eyes. He told her accusingly, "You left her alone with me," and he added, "Be attentive, woman. You must *never, never* leave my little girl alone with somebody who is not her mother. Hurry and take care of her now, for I have told One Horn to tell the warriors who are far from home at those fires out there that we will bring them some meat."

Soon, in the darkness, Walks Far and Horses Ghost carried out the food, then stayed rather late at one of the fires near the woods into which the soldiers now on the bluff had first fled. As

Walks Far and Horses Ghost rose to leave, two blanketed warriors walked past a little way off. Horses Ghost looked at them curiously, and asked, "Where are you going, brothers?"

"We are hungry," one of them said. "We are going over there to eat," and he gestured toward another fire. This answer sounded wholly reasonable, though a trifle odd because of the fact that there was plenty of meat obviously broiling at the fire being passed. Also, though the answer had come in Sioux as good as anyone's, something about the voice had sounded not quite right. Moreover, that pair of warriors seemed to be walking much too deliberately for hungry men. Walks Far and Horses Ghost talked about it all the way back to the tipi.

Some years later Walks Far met one of those men and compared notes with him. He proved to be a Blackfoot half-breed and cousin of Joe Culbertson's named Billy Jackson. He had been serving as a scout. The other was an interpreter. Both, along with some soldiers, had failed to get the word about fleeing from the woods to the bluff. Billy and the interpreter had stayed hidden in the woods until well after darkness, then put on the clothing of dead Sioux to walk away just as Walks Far saw.

[Janet Sinclair was astonished and delighted when Walks Far revealed that she had chanced to hear a radio reenactment of this battle on its fiftieth anniversary date, June 25, 1926. A young clerk in the general store in town had smiled to say, "Too bad you ain't a Sioux, but maybe you'd wanta hear this anyhow." Walks Far told Janet, "That radio, she's pretty good, all right. But she's got two-three somethings mix' up: Gall already fightin' Custer soldier down-a-crick same tam Hi'm know he still chase Reno soldier outa woods up-a-crick. Gall ver' mad at soldier and got ver' good horse. But nobodies she's ride four mile that country and fight two places almos' same tam! And Sitting Bull not stay up coulee and make medicine. He gone with warriors and Runs the Enemy. Hi'm seen!"]

Chapter Twenty-four

A COYOTE BARKS
AT THE TIPI DOOR

(June–December 1876)

In the late afternoon next day Walks Far mounted Crazy One with Sky Eyes slung at her left knee. She was lost in a vast crowd of moving people and their thousands of horses, all riding upstream toward the Big Horn Mountains, where the people usually went this time of year. It was a fine place, there, the best for cutting new tipi poles, for making repairs, or for fashioning new things in leisurely summer days while waiting for the buffalo to fatten again. Now, as she rode, Walks Far and her baby were enveloped not only in dust raised by the countless number of dragging travois and lodgepoles but also in the black smoke billowing from fires set by the warriors to burn the grass all around the abandoned camp. The forever-silenced Scalps Them, his back straight as any man's, rode on a flank, out of the dust at least.

Horses Ghost and One Horn had spent the whole morning shooting with arrows and bullets at the soldiers on the bluff. Those soldiers were in a good position and fought well, even coming out twice to charge the warriors, and they had a whole packtrain load of cartridges. Walks Far had worried again about Horses Ghost and One Horn, with their bear medicine, but neither had been hurt. However, it was sad enough that Runs Stooped Over had died up there this morning, closest of all to the soldiers. Because he had found death facing the enemy, it was honorable to leave his body where it fell.

In the early afternoon word had come to break off the attack. Sitting Bull believed enough soldiers had been killed. And anyhow, it was already past time for the camp to move and for the people to go about their summer affairs. Even with the best of hunting, such a huge assemblage of Indians could never manage for long without some outside source of supply. Living off the country demanded smaller bands. Moreover, another force of soldiers had been discovered marching southward toward them. Fighting would be unwise, just now, for although more than two hundred carbines and revolvers each had been taken, this was only after the soldiers had fired a good portion of their cartridges and after the warriors had also used up most of theirs. So, as everyone agreed, another day of such fighting was no longer possible, certainly not for the present.

Walks Far knew that the people—the women especially— were saying there had already been enough of fighting for one summer. Had not the soldiers been defeated twice, first on the Rosebud, then here on the Little Bighorn? This was surely enough to make the *wasichu* leave them alone. Now, it was time to take their loot into the Big Horn Mountains, to dance and to feast, and to go back and forth to the prairies while thinking about hunting in earnest in the fall.

Walks Far saw bands and families as well as visiting warriors go their own way from the beginning, though the final breakup for the fall did not occur till about the middle of the Ripe Plums Moon [August], on the Powder River at Bluestone Creek. It was there that a tearful Walks Far and Suzy exchanged parting gifts, and Suzy rode away with her young husband's band.

[Two winters later Joe Culbertson told Walks Far and his Yankton wife (who also had been present on the Little Bighorn) how he had learned at Fort Peck of Custer's defeat at the end of the third day following the June 25 event. A party of Yankton warriors crossing the Missouri frankly explained that their cavalry horses and arms were trophies from the battle. Word reached the head of the telegraph line at Bismarck, North Dakota, on July 5. The operator sat at his key for twenty-two hours to send the dismaying news and list of dead to a people just then celebrating their centennial as a nation.]

Following that breakup into bands on the Powder River, life for the people—their old ways—began hastening to an end they still could not foresee. Meanwhile, this was the best of summers. They felt they had won victories and that the *wasichu* had surely learned something from defeat. This lay already in time past. Though some of the young men enjoyed themselves harassing the army's camps, running off the horses, shooting at outposts, and burning the grass in the encircling country, fall and winter would come round again—seasons for hunting, not for war. Walks Far saw some people move off from the Powder River breakup in a leisurely southeastward journey in the general direction of the agencies, feeling secure in the faith that they would once again be fed there through the winter, then be re-outfitted in the spring for another happy season of early hunting and fighting in the north.

Still, though Walks Far was no more farseeing than others concerning the people's hastening evil fate, she did receive warnings of misfortune for those in her tipi. Four times during the band's easy days moving from Tongue River to the Big Dry she dreamed in the night that the base poles of her tipi had cracked in a country where they could not well be replaced. Four times she carefully examined those poles and found them perfectly sound, yet she was not reassured. Also, she was given a more immediately frightening sign. For, as the camp prepared to move on, one sunny morning, and with Horses Ghost there to see the accident he had so often predicted, Walks Far mounted Crazy One and slung Sky Eyes's cradle board at her left knee from the elk-antler saddle horn. Incredibly, that strong, sound antler snapped off as it took the insignificant weight! Sky Eyes tumbled into the dirt. Though she was not in the least hurt as Crazy One snorted and danced away, Horses Ghost spoke in a flush-faced fury to say, "I told you that would happen." Walks Far knew he would never wholly forgive her, and she also knew that for such an antler to break as it had done could be nothing less than a powerful sign. That antler should have supported her own weight!

But the clearest sign of all—one with a meaning anyone would understand—was given Walks Far in the first camp on the Big Dry. With Sky Eyes on her back, she returned along the water path to her empty tipi and was suddenly chilled by terror. A young coyote, hardly more than a pup, came trotting up through the grass and stopped to bark three times at her door.

A familiar, scabby old coyote appeared from nowhere and, nipping viciously at the young one's flanks, chased it away. But it *had* barked at her tipi. Someone from the tipi would surely die! No one else saw it, and Walks Far did her best to pretend she had not seen it either.

During the last few moons since Sky Eyes had been born Grandfather had stayed increasingly at home, especially now that the baby was developing a personality and becoming fun for him to be with. But one morning, as he had so often done in the past, he slipped away before breakfast with his old flintlock. Walks Far thought little of it until the sun had gone down and he still had not returned. Suddenly she dropped what she was doing, and feeling guilty about leaving Sky Eyes swinging in her cradle board from a tipi pole, she ran straight to the western ridge, chanting a prayer on the way.

She found him in a little thicket of the prairie rose bushes, still propped up in a sitting position by the stems and thorns she already knew his skinny old back no longer felt. Grandfather had finished his winter count, whatever its actual sum. In any case, it totaled enough that he had seen all the greatest days of the Lakota, or Tetons, that is, of the Titonwana—"the Dwellers on the Plains." As in all his adventures, he had died with the Lakota band that hunted farthest west. Walks Far chose to believe he had been dead for but a very little while, and that because she found his eyes open, he had seen the sunset once more before he died.

As Grandfather's body was carried back to camp, the women did not yet begin to wail. As was expected, they only cried, while the men also wept unashamedly. In order to be certain, according to custom, that Grandfather was actually dead, he was not prepared for burial until a night and a day had passed. Then, by common assumption, and quite as though nothing different had even occurred to the people—including all those who were in the habit of treating him with polite derision—Grandfather was given a funeral as though he had been no less a personage than Left Hand Bull, or even a fighting chief like Gall.

No mere exposed burial scaffold on a hilltop for him! Grandfather's scaffold would be out on the open, level prairie. A new tipi, a spirit tipi, would be erected over it. His relatives would do this for him, and nearly everyone was his relative.

So, after the night and day had passed, women dressed

247

Grandfather in the finest the camp could provide. Men painted his face red, striped it with blue according to his secret societies and ceremonial honors, adorned his thin hair with all the surprising number of eagle feathers to which the old men remembered he was entitled, and fitted him with spirit moccasins beautifully quilled on the soles. His old drinking horn, some paint, and other personal property, including the flintlock and all that went with it, was placed beside him as he was wrapped into the robe.

Then began the worshipful mourning by the women, the wailing and the weeping by all, four days of it. Men and women cut their hair short. Those men whose grief was greatest went about with small wooden skewers thrust through the skin of arms and legs. Walks Far and Red Hoop Woman, as well as many other women, made slashes in their legs, three above and three below each knee. Walks Far laid the second finger of her left hand upon a solid piece of wood, and holding a knife blade to a joint, had Red Hoop Woman sever the finger by striking the back of the knife sharply with a heavy stick. Then Walks Far struck the back of the knife that Red Hoop held on the joint of one of the fingers of her own left hand. [Janet Sinclair exclaimed to Dewey, "All the first joints of the last three fingers on her left hand are missing! I never noticed it before, though the bone seems to show on one, and it looks horrible."]

For a brief while each morning of those four days the men and women formed separate groups to walk all around the camp in a kind of loose procession, silently weeping, wailing, and singing their mourning songs. At the first sunrise Red Hoop Woman and Walks Far, with other devoted women, were sitting below the waiting scaffold on their turned-in insteps and facing Sun, with shawls or blankets thrown over their heads. Beginning with an animal sound from deep in their throats, and apparently without any relationship to their breathing, their voices rose quaveringly into a high, singing wail that seemed sustained by some power outside themselves. Walks Far and Red Hoop Woman led off in this at the first sunrise, and were still at it at midnight when Horses Ghost and Scalps Them brought old Father of a Mudfish to help persuade them to rest awhile. Old Father of a Mudfish reminded the whole band that the Sioux way required them to honor Grandfather with more than mere outpourings of grief. During these four days the people must work especially hard, the women making fine or

248

useful things, the men hunting or making weapons, with all striving to do that work at their best. That too was a good way of honoring Grandfather.

With the four days past, Grandfather was wrapped in a finest buffalo robe, with a tanned skin bound over that, and his body was placed on a travois. Left Hand Bull, acting only as a close male relative, led the travois horse to the scaffold. Another particularly fine horse was led by the once poor man Takes a Cheyenne Lance, the same who two summers ago had been saved from the necessity of abandoning his aged and crippled mother when Grandfather ordered Walks Far to give up her first gift horse to him. At the scaffold women hoisted the bundled Grandfather up and lashed him securely to the cross poles, which rested on four peeled forked posts ringed by a strip of black for each of his surprising number of war honors. Because Grandfather owned so little, warriors gave shields and drums and other things to hang from the poles. Takes a Cheyenne Lance led the fine horse close. It had been painted with red spots. Kills When Wounded, as Grandfather's youngest relative among the warriors, stepped forward with his new army carbine in hand and said earnestly to the animal, "You are a horse that any man would be very proud to own, and you should be happy that we have chosen you to go with our Grandfather." On saying that, he shot the horse carefully.

As the crowd cried, women swiftly erected a new, undecorated tipi over the scaffold, closed it tightly, and sewed the door shut. Feather Earrings cut off the dead horse's tail. Holding it in his teeth, he scampered like a boy up the front of the tipi, then tied it to the lifting pole while singing to Sun. With that, the funeral had come to its end. Old Father of a Mudfish stepped forward to remind the people of the fact. But he too broke down and, with a sob, he was only able to say to the men, "Come." They all rode far out together and killed a two-year-old buffalo bull. Singing, they dragged it back to Grandfather's spirit tipi at the end of their lariats, and added its tail to the lifting pole.

No one could remember such a funeral, nor so much peace and goodwill in camp. For a long while visitors, on seeing all the people with their hair hacked short, instantly assumed that Left Hand Bull's spirit had been the one to take the trail up the Milky Way, beyond the Wind.

Walks Far was proud indeed to learn that Horses Ghost had

won the race to kill the sacrificial buffalo, and that he had used but a single arrow. Still, he returned to the tipi in a bad humor. She saw him to be scratched and bruised, his shortened hair filled with dirt from a bad fall taken when his swerving horse stumbled and threw him just as he loosed the arrow. For a moment his spirit had left his body, and the men feared his skull or his neck might be broken. But his spirit returned quickly, and he had mounted his uninjured horse to sing with the other men while dragging the buffalo back. He seemed resentful of Walks Far's attentions when she sought to assure herself that his scratches and bruises were truly slight. He would not let her help wash his hair. At last he spoke of what she knew had been on his mind for the past four days. "Woman," he said. "Be attentive. I don't know what to do about you, for I have told you before this that you must *never leave my little girl alone!* You know you should not have done that, not even to go looking for our Grandfather."

Two mornings later the people moved a day's march away from Grandfather's spirit tipi to a good campsite near a truly vast herd of buffalo. There, in the first run of the organized fall hunting, Horses Ghost downed even more fat cows than Feather Earrings could claim. He rode up smiling his triumph as a smiling Walks Far stood waiting to care for his horse. But his smile faded strangely, and his handsome face abruptly paled. His spirit left him again, and he toppled slowly from the horse's back to fall crumpled into the grass at her feet. And his spirit did not return, though he kept breathing as if asleep and with his heart beating fast and strong.

People helped her with the travois, and she got him warmly to bed in the tipi. Only then did he rouse a little from his strange sleep to look up at her with a terrible helplessness in his eyes. He could not speak, nor could he move his fingers for an intelligible sign. Walks Far gave him water and found that he could swallow, so she quickly heated a big bowl of fine fat broth and held it to his lips until he had drunk it all. But he had hardly lain back when he threw it up, and his spirit appeared to fly again.

Old Father of a Mudfish came in through the crowd. He had on nothing but a strangely twisted breechclout—not even moccasins. In one hand he carried a turtle shell filled with water and in the other a bundle of eagle feathers and a folded piece of deerskin containing many tiny packets of powders. He spread these things beside him as he sat down facing Horses Ghost, and said to Walks Far, "Take his robes off, and his moccasins. And send everyone else outside." When that was done, the old man's long hands smoothed and pressed very slowly over Horses Ghost's body and head while he watched Horses Ghost's face intently. He next kneaded Horses Ghost's belly very hard and carefully, then brushed him all over with an eagle feather. While doing this, he gave abrupt voice in a chant so weird and piercingly high that the silent Walks Far was startled.

He took a big pinch of powder from one of the tiny bundles and sprinkled it on the water in the turtle shell. He then dipped the eagle feather and moistened his own lips before shaking a few drops between Horses Ghost's lips. Again he began to sing, though not such a startling song this time. While singing, he watched Horses Ghost intently, but there was no flicker of a change. Old Father of a Mudfish paused to take powder from another packet, and when he blew a very little of it into Horses Ghost's nostrils, Horses Ghost's head did twist slightly, and the muscles of his throat moved as though he tried twice to swallow with his mouth open.

Old Father of a Mudfish instantly took up that startlingly weird and piercing chant again, and along with it came a mysterious kind of whining accompaniment, exactly as though some invisible helper was singing there with him in the tipi. Walks Far saw that old Father of a Mudfish sat with his head thrown back, his eyes closed, and his lips unmoving. But those two frightening voices went on and on. The sounds ended so abruptly and with such a peculiar final note that the sudden silence was now what startled. Walks Far held suspended, waiting, but Horses Ghost remained as before. Old Father of a Mudfish also seemed to be waiting, or else in a trance.

Softly the whining sound rose again, low pitched and vibrant, seeming to fill the tipi, and though no whisper of breeze stirred outside on that hot summer afternoon, the smoke ears flapped as though to a strong wind, the tipi shook, and its poles creaked (Walks Far would swear to it). Once more there was silence, and once more old Father of a Mudfish, now agleam and dripping with sweat, watched Horses Ghost intently, and himself looked to be the sicker man. After a while he laid the eagle feather upon Horses Ghost's chest, gathered his other things together, and as he went out paused to tell Walks Far, "Cover him up. If he gets cold, put warm stones at his feet and under his arms. You must not give him any more of that fat broth. If he wakes up and wants to eat something, give him only the leanest meat, with ripe plums—no fat meat at all. And not very much water."

If he wakes up! Walks Far was terrified now, and One Horn came to say grimly, "If his spirit does not come back, I am going to put that horse's eyes out with the quill of that eagle feather. Then I am going to shoot it in a way to make it die slowly."

One Horn, Red Hoop Woman, and Walks Far sang over Horses Ghost all afternoon:

"Friend, we are waiting . . ."
"Cousin, we are waiting . . ."
"Husband, we are waiting. . . ."

And in the evening, after warning Walks Far to have a lot of berries ready, One Horn went out and came back with all the men who had dreamed of the bear. It was known that the bear men doctored sick people in secret rites. They came into the tipi with faces already painted to represent the bear and with their hair tied into knots representing the bear's ears. Of course, they wore bear-claw necklaces, their bear knives and their per-forated yellow shirts with a mysterious flap hanging open at their chest. They brought rattles and drums and branches of sage.

With the men's voices, their drums, and their rattles all blending into a slow, cadenced, lumbering kind of rhythm that did sound bearlike, one of the men painted Horses Ghost's face like the others, but instead of putting him into his shirt, he only wet his chest and arms in little spots, then dusted the spots with yellow powder and tied his bear necklace on.

One Horn said, "The bears want some berries." Walks Far quickly produced a big bowlful. All the bear men dug into them ravenously, smearing their painted faces in a shockingly glut-tonous, bearlike race to get the largest share. One Horn spoke again to say, "Woman, you must go now." A man wearing a bearskin over his shirt and making growling, whoofing sounds chased her out. He stayed on guard outside the door, again growling and whoofing threateningly if so much as a toddling child came close. But Walks Far could hear the powerful sing-ing, the drums, and the rattles inside, and the impressive si-lences during which a low growling might be barely audible.

When the bear men went away at last, Walks Far thought Horses Ghost looked even worse, though she felt a kind of relief to hear him groan faintly, then repeat the low groaning at long, almost regular intervals into the darkest part of the night. She made no effort to sleep, for she knew that she could not do so. Yet she was wakened at dawn by Horses Ghost's ordinary voice. "Woman," he said, "my little girl is crying to be nursed. You should be up by now, for you know it is the first day of big fall hunting."

Walks Far gave swift thanks to Sun, while saying to her husband, "Be quiet, your spirit left you again, and things have happened that you do not know about, for you have been very sick since yesterday morning."

Horses Ghost stayed sick for three more days, then recovered swiftly, complaining only of a declining dizziness and a slight nausea. Soon he and Walks Far were making plenty of meat for winter. She began to believe that the young coyote had possibly barked but once at her tipi door. Slowly though, she, then others, began to see a different Horses Ghost. In the beginning it was only his periodic, regular headaches. He said he could see but a little way and only straight ahead when the headaches came, that everything then wore a yellowish tint. For a day or two he would avoid the light, grow impatient with Walks Far, and seek only to be alone with his suffering. Sometimes he threw up without warning.

Neither old Father of a Mudfish nor his bear-dreamer brothers could rid him of those headaches. Walks Far tried two cures she'd learned as a child. For one, she caught horse urine before it touched the ground, and rubbed it into Horses Ghost's forehead; for the other, she rode out to a hillside and gathered what she called in Blackfoot *asapopinats* ("looks like a plume"), a spring flower growing in windy places. In summer the flower turned into cotton, which could be burned on a hot coal held under the nose for a headache cure. Both the urine and the burning cotton helped the headaches a little, though not much. Berries of the *siksinoko*, or "juniper," which Walks Far brewed into a tea to stop the vomiting, had no effect for Horses Ghost.

Most of the time, however, Horses Ghost hunted as usual and seemed perfectly well, except for increasing spells of moroseness, of violent temper fits, and of meanness. He caught one of the poorer boys of the band, a boy of about thirteen, riding a colt without his permission. Though often he had been glad to loan the same colt to the same boy, he now lashed him to purple stripes before One Horn could stay the quirt. Horses Ghost was quickly contrite. He led a truly good horse to the boy's tipi and stood there for all to see, waiting until the boy and the armed, angry father came out and were persuaded to take the horse. Walks Far felt ashamed over that incident and others. She couldn't help noticing how people showed a tendency to avoid Horses Ghost. Even One Horn seemed to be put off, and was in the tipi far less often.

Very late one evening, when she had not seen One Horn for two or three days, he ducked in through the door without so much as first scratching the tipi cover or shaking the deer-hoof rattles. Nor was there a word of greeting between him and Horses Ghost. One Horn simply demanded, "Horses Ghost, I have come to find out what you are going to do about that horse."

Horses Ghost not only pretended not to hear, he pretended complete unawareness that One Horn was even there. One Horn looked at him more in surprise and sadness than anything else. He turned swiftly to the door, then spoke to Walks Far: "Woman, I am sorry to see that your poor, old husband has grown both blind and deaf, as well as forgetful. Maybe you can make him understand that I want him to do something about that horse, before he dies."

Walks Far waited, hoping for some explanation from Horses Ghost, but at last she had to ask, "What is this about a horse?"

"Nothing you need to know anything about," he answered, and he gave his new, nervous laugh that irritated her.

Walks Far felt sad rather than angry. "You should have answered One Horn, you should have at least spoken to him," she said.

"Woman, you should at least be quiet when you don't know what you are talking about," Horses Ghost shouted at her, and again he gave that quick, too easy, too prolonged laugh. It was a little like a *winkte*'s nervous, shallow laugh, and it came most often when he was angry or morose.

In the dawn Walks Far took out her Sun-stone and prayed that Horses Ghost would again become entirely his old self. All too often it was as though a bad spirit had returned to him along with the good. Fortunately the good spirit was still the stronger most of the time, but Walks Far felt as though her husband might be two persons.

Aside from the death of Grandfather and the matter of Horses Ghost, that summer following the defeat of the soldiers on the Rosebud and the Little Bighorn was as fine as anyone in Left Hand Bull's band could remember. They had more rain than expected, but not too much. The grass was good, the berries and plums plentiful. Hunting for the buffalo and other game was all anyone might wish. Long after, Walks Far thought that she may have exaggerated and compressed the trouble with Horses Ghost out of hindsight, for most of her memories of that summer and fall were entirely pleasant.

Yet there were growing apprehensions among the people. Beginning in late summer word came that soldiers were attacking other bands and trying to herd them to the agencies. And most disturbing of all, not only the Black Hills but also the Powder River and Bighorn hunting lands were being taken away, just as Singer had foretold. All Sioux and Cheyenne who could be caught, Walks Far heard, would be taken to Oklahoma and forced to learn how to farm.

And still more news! Bearcoat Miles and walk-a-heap soldiers had come to stay. They were building a big fort on a favorite camping ground of the people, the one where that big grove of cottonwoods between the Yellowstone and the last loop of the Tongue lay sheltered from the north wind by the bluffs across the river. It was said that the *wasichu* was stringing his line of poles and talking wires to the fort. Also, it was known that the different parts of the army were now keeping in close touch with each other by using wide-ranging scouts who knew this country well. And, of course, those dogs of Crows were helping the army as usual.

In the latter part of the Falling Leaves Moon [October] word came to the Big Dry, where Walks Far was still busy making meat, that Sitting Bull, with about two thousand people from several bands, and Bearcoat Miles with his walking soldiers, had fought a battle to eastward. They met under a white flag before they fought, but Sitting Bull refused even to think about Bearcoat's demand that he surrender and go to an agency. He in turn demanded that Bearcoat and all the other whites, except a few traders, get out of the country and leave the people alone. The fighting started almost at once. A warrior, angered to see soldiers uncovering big guns on wheels, set the prairie afire and was shot for it by one of the soldiers. A running fight in flaming grass and smoke went on over the prairie and along the coulees for two days. Each time the warriors found a good position, the big guns drove them out. Those big guns were terrible things.

Finally, many of the chiefs wanted to surrender. Why not go to an agency, just for the winter? they asked. Why stay here, with the cold coming, to be harassed by soldiers? So, they raised a white flag, but Sitting Bull and many others slipped away. Bearcoat hadn't enough soldiers to keep up the chase and escort the captives too. More than half the captives soon changed their minds and also slipped away, leaving Bearcoat with about one fourth the number of people he'd hoped to get at the beginning.

For Walks Far and the rest of Left Hand Bull's band all still remained peaceful. They moved from the Big Dry to hunt for a time on the Redwater, then back to the Big Dry again. Horses Ghost's headaches and his spells of meanness seemed to grow less when Cold Maker howled down from the north and early snow made small drifts in the coulees. It was he, with One Horn, and Feather Earrings, who early in the Moon of Hairless Calves [November] discovered Bearcoat marching down the Big Dry with many soldiers, also wagons and the big guns on wheels.

Some of the foot soldiers now rode captured Indian horses, and all wore winter clothing they themselves had made from blankets and buffalo robes. The band moved out of their way by going back to the Redwater again. For safety's sake it made camp on the very edge of the badlands at Timber Creek, near the Redwater's head, and went on hunting as usual. Bearcoat turned west at the Big Muddy River [the Missouri], went on toward the mouth of the Musselshell, then back toward his fort. Nothing of note happened, except that Feather Earrings found white traders at Poplar Creek who secretly sold the band a few cartridges with a little powder and lead. Also, the band was joined by many of Sitting Bull's people after Bearcoat headed them off from going across the Line of the piles of stones into Grandmother's Land [Canada]. By the middle of the Frost in the Tipi Moon, Walks Far could count 120 tipis in the wintry camp.

There, of an entirely ordinary late afternoon, with most of the men out hunting and with a light snow falling, Walks Far, having just nursed Sky Eyes, laced her again into her cradle board and started supper. Fresh moccasins and a filled pipe were ready for Horses Ghost when he came riding in.

Shots! Walks Far heard them come, muffled through the falling snow—too many shots at once for mere hunting. And coming with those shots was a wounded elderly man who dashed a bleeding horse through the camp and yelled that the *wasichu* attacked! [This was apparently an attack made on December 18, 1876, by three companies of Miles's infantry under the aggressive and tireless veteran Lieutenant Frank Baldwin. Joe Culbertson, employed as scout, had discovered the camp.]

Walks Far frantically gathered the cradled Sky Eyes, an extra blanket, and the carbine with cartridge bag into a bundle across her arms. Suddenly the world was riven. A shatteringly loud noise and a kind of wind from just above knocked her down. Her tipi poles and the tipi cover collapsed slowly, but Walks Far was already up and out of there. She held everything still bundled in her arms, and she ran straight for a remembered thicket in the direction of the badlands. She heard a crowd of other women run screaming in the same general direction, but off to her right. Breathless, Walks Far paused there in the thicket to rearrange her bundle before running on, and when she looked at Sky Eyes, a part of her died from shock. The shot from that big gun had sent a splinter longer than Walks Far's hand and thicker than her thumb whizzing from a tipi pole to skewer Sky Eyes through her tiny body. Her baby was dead. Despite her shock, Walks Far smelled or heard a horse, and she looked up to see a soldier, with the horse's reins over his arm and his long rifle raised, gazing at her through the light snowfall from hardly a tipi-pole length away. The soldier's right mitten dangled by its string from the sleeve of his buffalo coat, and his bare finger was crooked on the trigger. Tobacco juice stained the corners of his youngish mouth. Amazingly, only one of his eyes looked blue. The other was brown. Walks Far could never imagine why she always remembered these details so clearly, when she didn't much care whether or not the soldier shot her.

She saw the soldier lower his rifle, peer quickly to either side through the lightly falling snow, and then, with an abrupt movement of his rifle barrel, signal that she should run on past him. Walks Far did so, wondering why she bothered, and almost wishing he had shot her on sight.

PART THREE

Winter 1876-1877 to Summer 1885
also
Summer 1946 and Summer 1947
and
A Few Events Down to 1958)

Chapter Twenty-five

GRANDMOTHER'S LAND

(Winter 1876–1877
to Early Spring 1878)

Walks Far and all the women and children endured a first freezing night in the badlands, then a march northward that seemed to go on forever in deepening snow. For Walks Far it was not so cold as on that first time, almost seven years earlier, at the Blackfoot camp on the Marias, when attacking soldiers had sent her fleeing through the snow. Yet it was now cold enough that many of the very old and sick soon died, and women and children froze their feet and hands. Fortunately, the soldiers did not pursue them. The suffering would have been worse without the horses, for most of them had been saved, and there were enough for the old and sick to ride most of the way and enough for everyone to ride a part of the time. They left behind a trail of many dead fires. Boys going on ahead built them at regular intervals so that the ill-clothed people could come up and warm themselves. But the people who escaped and survived—and most of them did—were met at last by friends near the Big Muddy River. Moreover, the men could hunt or scavenge a little bad meat from the frozen carcasses of long-dead buffalo out on the prairie. The soldiers had caught only about sixty horses out of the some three hundred and fifty in the people's herd, and Horses Ghost brought Crazy One in with the others. But the soldiers had burned everything after loading their wagons with all the dried meat, berries, and roots they could haul away, as well as robes or any other items striking their fancy. They made sure the tipis and everything in them went up in flames before they marched off over the divide and down Cedar Creek toward their fort on the Yellowstone. The soldiers were very tired from much winter marching, and their horses and mules were in bad shape. The warriors believed they could have followed and wiped those soldiers out, if it had been possible to leave the women and children. As it was, Horses Ghost and others did follow them a little way as they hurried on toward their fort in the Yellowstone, and Horses Ghost got two played-out but good army mules. He also missed a long shot at Joe Culbertson, who was scouting for the soldiers.

Before Horses Ghost found Walks Far—still before noon on the first numb day of that freezing march northward—and while she was warming herself at one of the fires, Red Hoop Woman and Suzy's mother gently and wordlessly eased Sky Eyes from Walks Far's arms. Singing, they went a short way aside to a juniper tree growing within a cleft on a badlands sandstone ridge. There in that tree the already freezing body of little Sky Eyes, wrapped in half of Red Hoop Woman's shawl, was lashed for as long as the thongs would hold. The chanting and wailing was brief but terrible, and as the three women turned to follow the column of shivering people, Red Hoop Woman paused to shake Walks Far and say clearly, *"It is finished.* Perhaps she is fortunate, for her spirit—her *nagi*—has already traveled the spirit trail to the Land of Many Tipis, where there are no *wasichu.* She will be happy with friends and relatives. Grandfather and all the ancestors will look after her."

Walks Far, in her numbness, feared to face Horses Ghost. He would never believe she had not left Sky Eyes alone for the fatal moment, and he would worry because his little girl had not yet been tattooed, had not had her ears pierced.

Yet when Horses Ghost came riding up, he could not have been more tender with her when she told him. They stood together beside the trail, letting other people go on while they both cried a little. That was not exactly the last real tenderness between them, although Horses Ghost did grow harder to live with, slowly but increasingly more resentful in his silences or in the impatient and hurtful things he said. Still, there was something he never tried: He never lashed her with his quirt, whatever his impatience. Walks Far would not have stood for that, as so many women thought they had to do.

For the immediate days after the people were met by friends summoned from different directions by Scalps Them, Feather Earrings, and One Horn, among others, all were temporarily safe in the shelter of cottonwood groves in the bottomlands along the Big Muddy River. Walks Far and Horses Ghost needed less help than most. They traded the two army mules and Horses Ghost's cavalry saddle, which he only rode as a showy trophy anyhow, to an Assiniboin half-breed on Poplar Creek for a very good tipi and all its furnishings, though with the poorest of poles. It was no problem at all for them to live entirely on fresh meat, though some of the animals were already leaner from winter than a person would like, and lean antelope meat is the leanest, driest fresh meat there is.

Black Horn, the agency Indian and Yankton chief who had come with the traders to Left Hand Bull's band two summers ago—the day of the cloudburst and the day Joe Culbertson had given Walks Far the whetstone—that same Black Horn who was to become Joe Culbertson's father-in-law, now sent much help and encouragement. He seconded the plan of Sitting Bull and Gall to move their people into Grandmother's Land, where Bearcoat could not follow.

News by the moccasin telegraph showed that Bearcoat gave his soldiers no rest this winter. He had them marching off both to the southeast of his fort and westward below the Yellowstone. They would soon be crisscrossing this country to the north again. As for the party of people who again talked of surrender, the moccasin telegraph brought word that gave them pause. For about the same time that soldiers attacked the camp on the Redwater, a large party of Sioux south of the Yellowstone went toward Bearcoat's fort to surrender, with five chiefs going ahead of the main party under a white flag to talk about the terms. One of those chiefs also bore the name Sitting Bull, but he was Oglala, not Hunkpapa, and he owned the finest Winchester known among the Sioux. Much of it was covered with gold, and beautifully chiseled to show hunters and animals, trees and flowers.

As the five chiefs entered Bearcoat's camp, and after passing the Crow scouts, the Crows ran out and shot them all from behind, then began cutting their bodies up. Soldiers came running to shoot at the Crows, who then fled to the hills. They feared Bearcoat would hang them for breaking the common rule forbidding an attack on anyone who got safely into camp, even though some of the surrendering Sioux had killed two Crow women on their way in.

Now, as Walks Far heard, Bearcoat had neither Crow scouts nor any of the Sioux who had started to surrender. But some Crow dog would be boasting about the fine Winchester he had taken, and many of those Sioux were already on the way to join Sitting Bull and Gall in going to Grandmother's Land.

After nearly two moons Walks Far and Horses Ghost, with many people, crossed the ice on the Big Muddy River at the mouth of Redwater Creek. Nearly opposite was the mouth of the Poplar Creek. They followed that stream northward toward its head at Wood Mountain, a short way into Grandmother's Land beyond the Line of the piles of stones. [The Canadian Northwest Mounted Police reported that 109 tipis crossed the international boundary on February 11, 1877. About an equal number came a few days later, with many more straggling in at intervals, to make a total of about 4,000 people camped around Wood Mountain and westward toward the Cypress

Hills. Some would remain for years.] Walks Far felt somehow disappointed to find those piles of stones so far apart that it was hard to see from one to another, and that most of them were only rounded heaps of prairie sod to boot.

Walks Far found Wood Mountain another misnamed feature, for it was actually but a collection of treeless clay hills, now covered with snow. Though wood was indeed plentiful, it was all in the valleys and coulees. She judged that grazing would be good, and found the stream to be a fine one. She saw a typical settlement of the western Métis already there, a straggling, incomplete circle of small, low cabins, which seemed to hold a larger dancing and community hall at bay. Among the cabins was a trader's store, and the Mounted Police soon occupied a couple of others. As a place for a hunting band to camp for a while, it might have been among the best, but as a place for so many people to remain for years, it soon lost its attractiveness. And in season, mosquitoes and horseflies were as bad as any Walks Far could remember.

A red-coated Northwest Mounted Policeman talked to the chiefs. He spoke for the White Mother, the queen. His words sounded straight, politely plain, and the gist of what he had to say was this: "You may stay here in the queen's country where no one will bother you, but you will get no reservation and no rations. You must find your own meat and you must obey the queen's law. That law forbids all killing and all stealing, including the taking of horses, and it applies equally to all Indians and all whites." The redcoat also made it clear that he hoped the chiefs and the others would find it in their hearts to leave the country, to go back across the Line into the Territory of Montana, surrender to Bearcoat, and be taken to the reservations awaiting them in the United States. But, he emphasized, so long as they obeyed the queen's law, no one was going to make them go—no one here, and certainly no soldiers from south of the Line!

Shortly, another redcoat chief came to take charge at Wood Mountain for a long while. The people were suspicious of him at first, but they learned to like and trust him. His name was Major Walsh—"Meejoor," as the people made it.

Late that spring Walks Far heard Blackfoot speech in a Blackfoot camp again. Feather Earrings and Left Hand Bull came to her tipi to say that Crowfoot, the most influential of Northern Blackfoot chiefs, had camped in the Sand Hills no great distance to westward, and that Sitting Bull was going to visit him. She might be needed as interpreter. So, Walks Far and Horses Ghost rode out with the small visiting party. On the way they learned that Sitting Bull was worried. Surrounding tribes were angry with the Sioux for coming here in such numbers, particularly when the buffalo already grew somewhat scarce in this part of the country. Moreover, Blackfoot and Sioux were traditional enemies, and Crowfoot had angrily scorned Sitting Bull's tobacco and cartridge sent him with the appeal for help against the whites last spring. If war should now break out between them, the Sioux might be forced to leave. Therefore, Sitting Bull hoped to talk with Crowfoot, and his message now was peace. A few days earlier Sitting Bull had sent tobacco that Crowfoot accepted but said he would not smoke—not until he'd had time to see how the Sioux behaved themselves.

Walks Far had been awed four or five years earlier by a mere sight of the famous Crowfoot, for he had become something of a legend in his own time. She knew the complicated story behind his rather odd name, and that although now a head chief of the Northern Blackfoot, he had been born into the Blood division of the tribe. He was perhaps ten years older than Sitting Bull, and though both of them were a bit taller than most men, neither one was especially impressive on first sight. Where Sitting Bull limped from an old wound in one of his slightly bowed legs, Crowfoot often hunched a little from the pain of a Snake warrior's bullet that had been in his back for years. Crowfoot invariably wore an owl's skull in his hair as his personal medicine, but quite unlike Sitting Bull—and this was odd indeed for a chief—he was said to be generally indifferent to religious or spiritual matters. It was also said that he rarely dreamed yet was a farseeing person who showed special skill in making for his people the best deals possible with the whites. His rages were as great as were Sitting Bull's, but they did not last so long. He could ignore the taunting of rivals when it suited him to do so.

Walks Far's father had found one of Crowfoot's feats so incredible as to suggest that he had acquired just about the strongest protection supernatural forces could provide. For Crowfoot, on horseback and armed only with a lance, had not only attacked a grizzly bear that was mauling a boy in a patch of saskatoon berries. When his horse refused to press close, Crowfoot dismounted with the lance and finished the grizzly on foot.

Walks Far was also impressed by the fact that Crowfoot's

home lodge was one of those double-size, thirty-buffalo-skin Blackfoot lodges. It required the cover to be unlaced into parts for making into loads sufficiently light for travois horses to drag. Such lodges had two doors and two fires, and were owned by only the richest of men. Crowfoot personally had more than four hundred horses, and this was more than were owned by some whole bands of people (including Walks Far's Sioux band in its best days), but Crowfoot was very generous about giving some of those horses away. In order to care for them all, he had to do the unheard of, at least for an Indian living in the old ways: he kept five or six *hired men,* for whom he provided still another lodge. And usually he had about four wives to care for his lodges.

Walks Far thought Crowfoot showed surprise to find Sitting Bull himself among the Sioux visitors, but the two chiefs smoked together and had a long, friendly chiefs' talk. Among their peaceful arrangements was an agreement to restrain the young men of the two tribes from stealing each other's horses, and all was then confirmed in a friendship dance between the Blackfoot and the Sioux. Walks Far heard plenty of Blackfoot speech, but she could learn of no people she knew among the nearly one hundred Blackfoot lodges. This was the northernmost of the three divisions of the Blackfoot tribe, and she had belonged to the southernmost. Later, Sitting Bull and Crowfoot were to meet again in friendship, and though Sitting Bull was to name a favorite young son after Crowfoot, Crowfoot was to declare that Sitting Bull spoke with a forked tongue in his promises to restrain young Sioux from stealing Blackfoot horses.

Buffalo hunting, especially for the Sioux, was not too bad that first spring and summer north of the Line. For, to the disturbance of northern tribes, the herds abandoned old ranges to concentrate in the area of Wood Mountain. Walks Far found nothing at all strange in this. Old Father of a Mudfish had merely dreamed the buffalo close by, as he always did. Ammunition for the guns was no great problem either. Meejoor permitted the Métis traders to sell enough for hunting, and at different places only a short way south of the Line, both Métis and white traders secretly sold any amount of ammunition an Indian could pay for.

Unexpectedly, Joe Culbertson stopped scouting for the army and went to work for the largest and most important of those traders. Before too long that trader had to skip the country. People noted that Joe didn't appear upset about losing his job. Then, shortly before Walks Far went with Sitting Bull to visit Crowfoot, she saw Joe brought disarmed and under escort by three redcoats to Meejoor's cabin where the queen's flag flew. Sitting Bull rushed into Meejoor's cabin, saying that Joe was a spy, was actually a scout for the army south of the Line, and that Meejoor must have him shot. But Joe easily convinced Meejoor that he and his wife had merely come to Grandmother's Land to visit her father, Black Horn, who had led his Yankton here where the buffalo happened to be. Joe was surprised at the attention he received—redcoats coming to Black Horn's camp to arrest him, to hold him under guard all night before bringing him here. By the time Joe finished talking, Meejoor willingly turned him loose, and even Sitting Bull shook his hand.

Joe went back to his father-in-law's camp, completed his visit, and returned south across the Line to Fort Peck. Very soon, however, Walks Far saw him again come riding into Wood Mountain with a redcoat escort. They had sought him out at Fort Peck to hire him as the new interpreter for the redcoats here. He was now given a cabin, with rations for himself and his wife. He always interpreted accurately and honestly, as two Oglalas who well understood white man's talk reluctantly conceded. For some reason, he did not like interpreting well enough to stay for very long.

Walks Far could not help feeling sorry to see him go. She liked his wife, a strong-minded but fun-loving girl, who, if a story told much later was true, took a shot at Joe one day, then left him. Walks Far liked to talk in Blackfoot with Joe, and even to hear him play his violin, not a crude Métis-made, two-string violin, but a beautifully shiny one he kept in a fine leather case having a nearly identical shape. Horses Ghost didn't like that violin music at all, but he did enjoy trading horses with Joe, getting flour and sugar to boot. Joe said the whites had stopped settling anywhere near the Line on either side, for fear of the Sioux here at Wood Mountain. Also, he once told how the Americans had begged the queen to move the Sioux on northward, well away from the Line. But the queen said she believed that would be cruel. She didn't think the Sioux were used to cold winters!

Much later it seemed to Walks Far that Joe's loss of interest in the interpreting job and his return to Fort Peck that fall had followed too swiftly upon the defeat in Montana of Indians from west of the Rockies. The Slit Nose, or Nez Perce, chiefs Joseph and Lookingglass had fled from the goading white settlers in their country. Though they repeatedly outfought pursuing soldiers over a very long and crooked trail on their way toward Sitting Bull in Canada, and even got across the Big River safely at Cow Island, Bearcoat brought his soldiers from the fort on the Yellowstone and caught them resting in the Bearpaw Mountains, which many of them believed to be in Grandmother's Land. The Slit Noses sent desperate pleas for help to Sitting Bull, but Assiniboins killed the messengers, and there was nothing to do but surrender [on October 5, 1877]. A few, a very few, tipis of the Slit Noses did escape during a snowstorm and made it to Wood Mountain, but any possibility of hostile Nez Perce joining hostile Sioux in any number had passed and Indians grown restive at many agencies quieted for the winter.

Although winters are always more than cold enough on the northern plains, Walks Far remembered this one to be surprisingly moderate. In Blackfoot winter counts, at least, it is known as the year of the mild winter, *itsa-estoyi*. But the mildness brought disadvantage. So little snow fell that roaring prairie fires blackened much of the country and drove the buffalo away. A few people said the Blackfoot had started the fires, but most said that the Blackfoot were not that crazy, and felt sure the fires were started by men Bearcoat had hired to slip across the Line and do it.

Because nothing prevented small parties of the people from slipping south of the Line on wary hunts, Walks Far and Horses Ghost went back late that winter for a while to old grounds on the Redwater. The party included Feather Earrings and his wife, another couple, and Kills When Wounded. Also, a strange Santee named Pipe came from nowhere just before they left, and he was accepted. He appeared to be noticeably relieved when he was sure that the Line lay well behind. His horse, his clothing, and his gun were of the best, and he proved a good enough traveling companion, except that he carried a white man's small black book from which he chanted loudly and interminably in the evenings. Walks Far thought many of his mannerisms odd as a white man's mannerisms were.

On East Redwater Creek they found signs that the white buffalo hunters were already getting into the country. Walks Far saw a neat stack of more than six hundred hides, and farther on, another. The prairie was littered with skinned carcasses, and the coyotes and wolves ran fat while winter still lingered. Singer had been all too right in his predictions about those white buffalo-hide hunters. Though the head of the iron road was still far away, the hides could be hauled to the fireboats on the Big River or the Yellowstone. Singer, for all his knowledge and foresight, had failed to take into account the larger rivers of the North.

As they stopped to look at the second huge stack of hides, then helped themselves to a couple of particularly choice ones, somebody shot at them. It came from a long way off, but they got away from there fast. That night Feather Earrings said, "Friends, if this keeps up, pretty soon we are not going to have any buffalo left."

Walks Far saw how those white buffalo-hide hunters went about it. They worked in teams of about three to five men, one doing the shooting and the others the skinning. The hunter needed to be a very good shot, because he usually lay flat on the prairie at fairly long range in order that the noise of his heavy rifle would not stampede the buffalo herd. Often he was able to kill great numbers without moving from one stand. [A count of 30 to 50 was not especially notable. The record is said to be 204, very likely taken in less than forty minutes. Often the animals appeared to be no more than puzzled to see their fellows suddenly brought down from no apparent cause. Sometimes the tongues were taken in addition to the hides. Though the prices varied, average hides brought from $1.50 to $3.00, with the very choicest bringing as much as $15.00 or $20.00.] The skinners then went swiftly to work. In winter they raced against the freezing of the carcasses and in summer against the growing stench. They used the teams from their wagons to turn the dead animals over during skinning, and they then hauled the accumulated hides away.

On the second day, around noon, and with the first hint of spring in the air, Walks Far and her party came upon a bearded white hunter who appeared to be moving to a new camp. He was in a dry coulee out of the wind and had built a small fire for boiling coffee. Perhaps he had selected this as his new campsite and only awaited his skinners and wagon. In addition to his riding horse, he had a fine young pack mule, from which the packs had been unloaded. He was a very big man, with an even bigger stomach, held in by the widest brass-studded belt Walks Far had ever seen.

He showed no concern whatever as his visitors rode up, but

went on drinking his coffee and eating his singed bread, with his rifle beside his foot. When Feather Earrings said *hau*, he answered, "How-how," but he offered none of the coffee and bread. Pipe, the Santee, said to Feather Earrings, "Let us trade him one of the fine robes we took from the pile for some of his coffee or tea, some flour and sugar."

The white man was agreeable, and he finally offered them all of what little of those things he claimed to have with him. Feather Earrings did the trading. Pipe never let on that he knew white man's talk, but he said to Kills When Wounded, "Let us see what else is in those packs."

When Kills When Wounded went over to the packs and began to stir through them, the white man jumped up in a rage of shouting. Carrying his heavy rifle in one hand, he ran to Kills When Wounded, grabbed him by the shoulder, jerked him around, and gave him a hard shove back toward the fire. At the same time he aimed a big kick, which missed. The white man was very angry, and he kept right on with his shouting. Kills When Wounded was very angry too, but he did not show it.

"He says," Pipe told Kills When Wounded, "that you are a Great-Spirit-forsaken thief whose mother was a she-dog without a husband. He says that he will kick your thieving ass up between your spirit-forsaken shoulder blades, and your spirit-forsaken balls up under your chin."

Kills When Wounded grinned and said, "I can see that he is very angry."

"I think maybe we ought to shoot him," Horses Ghost said.

The white man was still raging. He was closing his packs and making signs for everyone to get out of his camp. Pipe translated again. "He also says that this spirit-forsaken country will be no good for anyone until the thieving Sioux and all the other spirit-forsaken Indians in it are wiped out, and that if the spirit-forsaken soldiers can do nothing but sit on their spirit-forsaken asses in their spirit-forsaken forts, he himself will wipe out a few thieving—"

Kills When Wounded suddenly raised his army carbine for a point-blank shot that sent the white man spinning. Horses Ghost fired another that knocked the man dead onto his own campfire.

Everyone left that place as fast as they could gather up what the man had, including the clothing he wore. They didn't know how many skinners might come along with the wagon at any moment. After carrying the white man's huge buffalo gun but a little while, Kills When Wounded threw it away as being much too cumbersome, too long and heavy for any man on horseback to bother with. They had found the man to be wearing a second belt inside his clothing. It was of the finest soft leather, and made with many pockets holding gold discs of the largest size. Pipe declared that gold to be enough to buy everything they would want to carry away from the trader's store at Fort Peck. Or, as he also said, there was enough of the gold for them all to ride a fireboat as far as it went down the Big River, and eat fine food all the way, if they should wish to do a crazy thing like that.

Pipe said they had better let Feather Earrings keep all that gold just now, until they went through Fort Peck on their way north. He, Pipe, who knew how to do such things, would then make himself look like a white man and exchange a part of the gold for some ordinary money. Otherwise, the whites would be very suspicious of Indians trading with so much gold. Walks Far and all the others saw the wisdom of that.

They went on and had a good hunt. Nothing more of note occurred, except for a thunderstorm that drenched all the prairie and brought early darkness. But Walks Far had seen it coming in time to pray with her Sun-stone and make the downpour move on around them as they rode. Still, a strange thing happened while they rode in that early darkness. Crazy One's ears and the ears of all the other horses glowed with the blue light of heatless spirit fires!

From a last stack of white buffalo-hunters' hides, they took all the choice ones they could carry, then set the rest afire. At Fort Peck they went directly to visit with relatives of Feather Earrings's Yankton wife. They also saw Joe Culbertson and his wife. Joe was again working for the army—if he had ever actually been doing anything else—and leading the Yankton scouts enlisted to help the soldiers.

Pipe rode away early next morning, taking the choicest hide to trade for white man's clothes, and Feather Earrings gave him the gold. Pipe said he might need all day. No one gave the matter any more thought until late afternoon when a half-breed came riding by on Pipe's horse. The half-breed joyfully told Feather Earrings all about buying that good horse for almost nothing from a strange Santee in white man's clothing. The Santee had already bought a place in a mackinaw boat full of whites from the west. They were going down the Big River to leave the country. The half-breed was still marveling at his good fortune in having been at the right place at the right time.

Feather Earrings declared that if he ever saw that Santee again, he was first going to pluck out each hair on the man's body, slowly, from his eyebrows down. Then, after cutting all his tendons at elbows and knees he would throw him alive onto a hot fire.

Yet everyone agreed that it had been a successful hunting trip. They started northward up Porcupine Creek toward the Line and Wood Mountain, well supplied with meat, not to mention flour and soda, tea and sugar, all received for the choice hides they had not even needed to skin. Of course, they had traded for some new finery, too, and people would admire the white man's big gelding and the strong young mule.

But Walks Far felt no eagerness to see those dreary clay hills north of the Line again, nor did she want the hunting trip to end. Horses Ghost had fallen into welcome spells of being his former self, down there in the Redwater country.

Chapter Twenty-six
A TALK AT THE HEAD OF THE COULEE

(Spring and Summer 1878)

Walks Far and Horses Ghost, with Feather Earrings and the others, had ridden but a little way on the trail northward toward Wood Mountain when they met a small party of their own band, coming south on a hunting trip. One Horn was with the party. First greetings among the men were hardly over, and no one had yet dismounted to smoke, when everything grew tensely silent of a sudden. All the men sat watching Horses Ghost and One Horn, who had failed to greet each other. Out of this silence One Horn said to Horses Ghost, "I see you are still riding that horse."

Horses Ghost laughed his nervous laugh, stopped it briefly, then laughed louder to say, "Of course I am riding this horse. Do you want to trade something for him? I see you have somehow got a new shoots-many gun."

One Horn flushed and instantly rode off a little way, turned, and lifting his Winchester, shot Horses Ghost's horse. The horse screamed and lunged, the other men scattering before it, but as it stumbled and went down, Horses Ghost leaped clear. He fired his single-shot Sharps carbine quickly but carefully, knocking One Horn from his horse. But before Horses Ghost could more than start reloading, One Horn got off a shot from the ground. It sent Horses Ghost backward into a folded heap.

Walks Far was transfixed in a feeling of helplessness and horror. She had never dreamed of anything quite so shatteringly terrible and it happened so fast that anyone having a little coughing spell just then would have missed it all. The scattered men held their guns raised, ready to start shooting at somebody, but Feather Earrings shouted very clearly that he himself would shoot the next man who fired—whoever that man might be—and he would go on from there! Everyone knew that no living Hunkpapa warrior was more certain and able to carry out such a threat, and they slowly lowered their guns.

"We have been losing too many warriors as it is," Feather Earrings said. "Let us see now what we can do for these two."

Walks Far was already on her knees beside Horses Ghost. His spirit was still with him. He could even speak, but she found a neat little hole in his belly, and a messy, much larger wound where the bullet had gone out his back. Dimly she heard a voice announcing that One Horn was dead.

Walks Far felt sick with shock, and she was hardly less dazed now by the cruel workings of bad spirits than she had been upon finding her baby dead in her arms. Possibly she was even more numbed.

She never knew whether the other hunting party went on southward or back across the Line with a part of her own. Not until she found herself approaching Fort Peck once more, with Feather Earrings, his Yankton wife, and Kills When Wounded, all helping her with the travois carrying Horses Ghost, could she again remember things well.

Their entry into the Yankton camp attracted much attention, and brought out a curious crowd. The hosts they had left early this morning now made them welcome again before sunset. Horses Ghost barely had been made comfortable inside when a rather tall Yankton wearing a soldier's revolver, a soldier's hat, and blue leggins made from a soldier's trousers came in and talked with Feather Earrings. When he learned all that Feather Earrings chose to tell him, he asked Horses Ghost what it felt like to be shot through the belly. He was curious, he said, because he couldn't remember anyone shot that way who was able to talk about it.

"I felt a coldness at first," Horses Ghost said. "But now, I feel sleepy and very thirsty, also very sore."

The Yankton went away, but returned after a little while with

Joe Culbertson. Joe brought along a fierce-eyed, yellowish white man in soldier's blue beneath a loose linen coat and carrying a small, black leather bag. Walks Far did not need Joe to tell her that this soldier was a white medicine man of the kind who treated wounds and made cures.

The surgeon went directly to Horses Ghost and looked at the hole in his belly. Then, pursing his lips, he shook his head as he looked at the larger wound in Horses Ghost's back. He was curious about something he saw there, and Joe relayed the question in Blackfoot.

Walks Far told Joe that she had chewed some *anawawatok-stima*—"buffalo food"—and had blown it onto the wound, as people often did.

When Joe relayed this, the surgeon gave the ghost of a smile, and the two of them had a fairly long talk. The surgeon then took a large bottle from his bag and gave a big drink to Horses Ghost. Joe and the surgeon each had a drink as well, and they gave Walks Far one.

She cried out in Blackfoot, "Whiskey!"

"No, it is not whiskey," Joe said, "The surgeon drinks only the best of brandy. I have told him we are friends." Joe paused, then spoke in a kindly voice to say, "I must tell you something: The surgeon says you could not have done anything better for Horses Ghost than to blow chewed-up *anawawatokstima* on his wounds. He says that all men die from getting shot through the belly, that he is surprised to find Horses Ghost still alive, but that Horses Ghost will surely die tonight, or before another noon-time. He says he will leave the bottle so that Horses Ghost can die happy."

Each of the statements pounded Walks Far deeper into numb hopelessness and pain. But Joe was going on, saying, "I do not always believe medicine men, whether they are the kind who work with sacred things or the kind who work with cures—and whether they are Indian or white. Besides, woman, I think maybe your husband is too mean a man to die from just one little hole through him."

Feather Earrings brought bear men to treat Horses Ghost, and afterward a sleepless Walks Far watched over him through-out the night. He appeared to be no worse by dawn, or at noon. By evening he seemed better, but in the night he relapsed, so that bad spirits had him for a couple of days. Then he appeared definitely to mend!

Feather Earrings, his wife, and Kills When Wounded returned to Grandmother's Land. Before they started, Feather Earrings promised to use his best efforts in smoothing things over with relatives who would be angry about One Horn's death. He said he did not know exactly what had caused the trouble between One Horn and Horses Ghost, but it was pretty likely that both had been at fault. Walks Far told him to use as many of their horses as necessary to help insure that no feud divided the band—that is, if Scalps Them had been able to prevent the horses from being seized already. She well knew that no matter how many years might pass, Horses Ghost would need to be always on guard against a sudden act of retaliation.

Apparently neither Feather Earrings nor his wife felt complete faith that Horses Ghost would live. Together they conveyed to Walks Far, in ways both delicate and allusive, that they would welcome a certain person permanently to their tipi should that person suddenly find herself without a husband.

Walks Far felt grateful, even flattered, but was hardly tempted to seriously consider the matter. True, no woman was neater, more hardworking, and easier to get along with than Feather Earrings's wife, even if she was a Yankton. As for that small man, Feather Earrings himself, he was among the very greatest of warriors and hunters, one who actually lived by all the Sioux virtues. His years totaled at least forty, and he would undoubtedly have become a great chief were it not that he, though soon to be an old man, still tended to look upon life with the mischievous eyes of a carefree boy.

Horses Ghost recovered swiftly. Before the end of the following moon he was wrestling and racing horses in bets with the young men—Yankton and Assiniboin. The white medicine man, the army surgeon, again came with Joe Culbertson and said he simply could not believe what his eyes were seeing. Joe also told Walks Far that the surgeon declared Horses Ghost to be no human person—only a kind of walking ghost!

This last was something Walks Far herself had begun to believe. For, though the handsome person she had married still looked the same, he was hardly her husband anymore, either by day or by night. He became a busy loafer, of whom there were already too many around Fort Peck. He went about with the hectic eyes of an excited boy roaming the camp after a dance, and he ate anywhere somebody offered him some meat. Even when he came in to rest, he ignored Walks Far. Sometimes he got screaming drunk. She tried to persuade him to rejoin their band in Grandmother's Land, despite the risks of doing it so soon, but her plea only made him angry with her. In addition to his racing and wrestling bets for big stakes Horses Ghost gambled incessantly, and with amazing luck. Though Walks Far herself loved gambling games—throwing plum-seed dice in a basket, the moccasin game, and the stick game—they certainly never became the reason for her existence.

Horses Ghost won the finest tipi Walks Far had ever lived in, but dwelling in it only made her shame the more conspicuous. For everyone could see that the man of the tipi was seldom there, and that he was rarely out hunting for meat for his wife to help him unload at the door. Walks Far lived on berries and roots, tea and bread, and knew other women mocked or pitied her. Horses Ghost always took the tipi door away while he gambled, for he was convinced that sitting on it enhanced his luck. When Walks Far made another, he suffered a losing streak and blamed her bitterly for it. She filled in her time by tediously putting together a fine robe of gopher skins, first staining them red by pounding up a plant she called in Blackfoot *esimatchsis* and working it into the skin. But this robe was only a by-product. She ate a lot of those gophers for the sake of their meat. She would not bring more shame to her tipi by riding out alone for game animals while she had a husband capable of hunting.

Walks Far was making that robe when she heard in early summer that all the buffalo upon which the Sioux in Canada lived had now moved south of the Line. Sitting Bull and the other chiefs were leading the people south after them. Many soldiers came through Fort Peck, until Bearcoat Miles had seven companies of infantry mounted on Indian horses, seven companies of regular cavalry, and big guns on wheels. Also there were many Cheyenne scouts now wearing blue, and some of those Cheyennes had been fighting against the soldiers on the Little Bighorn two summers ago.

Bearcoat's soldiers marched up to where the people were hunting. Two battles were fought, one on Frenchman's Creek, with another not far away, six days later [July 17 and 23, 1878], and the people had to flee back across the Line. Again the warriors had not been able to face those big guns on wheels. The people got safely away from one of the battles because of the biggest night-long thunderstorm and cloudburst in memory. Walks Far was glad she had not been there to stop it unwisely with her Sun-stone. As the people fled back across the

Line, Gall was said to have set up a huge *wikmunke* that would have caught the pursuing soldiers in a bigger trap than at the Little Bighorn. But one of the scouts detected it. Who? Joe Culbertson, of course.

Walks Far heard also that Bearcoat Miles and Meejoor Walsh had met soon afterward. Bearcoat reminded Meejoor that the queen had promised not to let any hostile Indians come south of the Line and that, moreover, Meejoor had promised to warn Bearcoat of hostile moves. Meejoor answered that the Sioux had only gone hunting, which he did not believe to be hostile. The Sioux were simply hungry, he said. Bearcoat then declared that the Sioux had many stolen horses, to which Meejoor replied that he would be glad to help find those horses if Bearcoat would send a man who could point them out. When Bearcoat insisted that some of the Sioux were more than just enemies, were wanted for murder, Meejoor said he would have to ask the queen to talk to the Great White Father in Washington about that. The people at Wood Mountain respected Bearcoat as a fighting man, but they had learned to like Meejoor.

There wasn't much more Bearcoat could do except keep his soldiers patrolling along the Big River, which he did. Still, he was so angry from his suspicion that the Métis traded ammunition to the Sioux that he rounded up into a single big camp every Métis he could find south of the Line, about eight hundred of them, counting their women and children. He held them under guard with all their horses and carts until he grew worried about having to give them rations. Then, instead of letting them go back to the places in Montana where he had found them, he put them all across the Line into Saskatchewan. [At that time the area included in the present Saskatchewan was officially a part of Canada's vast North-West Territory. In 1882 the District of Assiniboia was organized for administration of what is now the southern portion of the present province. Not until 1905 was the province we now know organized and named.]

At the end of that Ripening Chokecherries Moon [July] things quieted down again around Fort Peck. Horses Ghost became worse than ever. He almost never hunted now, and in his gambling he began to lose as often as he won. Only his skill at wrestling and an almost uncanny ability that somehow enabled him to make almost any good horse win a race kept him from becoming a very poor man. Horses Ghost, for all his weight, became a kind of jockey. Other men who owned fast horses availed themselves of his mysterious power by sharing their winnings if he would ride for them.

Walks Far dwelt now in constant fear that her gambling-crazy husband might risk Crazy One, or even—and this was not unheard of—that he would stake his wife, and lose! She told him in so many words that she would shoot him if he did either of those things. She heard one noon that he had foolishly bet his horse in a race with a stranger, a Cree, just yesterday come from across the Line on a good horse, and had lost badly. The Cree had not been especially interested in racing, pointing out that his horse was tired from a long day's ride. But Horses Ghost badgered him into a race for the next morning, and found himself behind at the finish line! So Horses Ghost and the Cree were going to wrestle this afternoon, and half the people around were betting hugely and excitedly. Many half-breeds were betting, too. Someone told Walks Far, as she came up to watch, that this Cree was rather famous. Not only was he a renowned warrior, but he had learned to fashion things from iron. He could speak all languages at least a little, including the two white man's languages. He made incredibly difficult journeys. Le Garé, the trader in Saskatchewan, often paid him to carry important messages where no one else cared to venture at the time. That was what now brought him to Fort Peck, accompanied by two Assiniboins also from Saskatchewan.

Oddly, this Cree and Horses Ghost looked rather alike, both being muscular men and both having an un-Indian nose slanting straight from the forehead, though the Cree's nose had been broken. His full name approximated Bull Elk Hollering on the Hillside in Rutting Time.

Walks Far, despite having liked her father's Cree wife very much, shared a common Blackfoot prejudice against Crees in general. They were enemies, they ate anything, including fish, badgers, and even skunks! One of the signs of Blackfoot superiority was a singular freedom from lice, whereas the Crees, of all inferior peoples, were said to be the most lousy. Walks Far's scalp and skin crawled at the thought of Horses Ghost wrestling a Cree. Still, he deserved to get himself infested.

The two men would first wrestle on horseback, each seeking to dismount the other. They would then wrestle on foot to a second fall, or to a third if necessary to break a tie. Black Horn, the Yankton chief, was there to judge the falls and see to it that the contestants didn't get too mad and kill each other. But an impromptu preliminary match developed before the main event began. Walks Far saw an incredibly tall half-breed she knew to be called Cob Piget ride up on a tiny pony. He had very short, very curly hair and legs so unbelievably long that although his stirrups reached nearly to the ground, his knees still angled up to interfere with his elbows as he rode. He looked absurd on that pony. The people taunted him humorously, and he enjoyed it, laughing and shouting back at them in horribly broken Sioux. He rode up to Joe Culbertson's brother, John, who sat a notably tall horse, and challenged him to a wrestling match from their horses. John laughed and tried to back his horse clear, but Cob Piget shot up a long arm, grabbed John, and then, with his huge feet suddenly out of the stirrups and with one of them flat on the ground, and with the pony still between his long legs, he wrestled the laughing John off his horse. It was terribly funny at the time.

Horses Ghost and Elk Hollering were ready for the serious event. Walks Far guessed Elk Hollering to be at least four or five years the older. He wore his hair in the four-braid Assiniboin style, two shorter braids hanging from over his temples. The two men, stripped to breechclouts and moccasins, sat their mounts bareback and faced one another from a little way apart, then walked their horses toward each other, right side to right side, and with their right arms and hands sparring for a hold. Both men looked about equally able and confident, and neither could find a quick advantage. Then, almost at once, with quick snaking of arms and slashing rake of hands, each man half blinded the other, and blood trickled from either the nose or the lips of both. From the way they acted now, it was as though they held an old grudge.

Abruptly, with all of it happening much faster than it can be told, Elk Hollering found a hold that Horses Ghost had no time to break, either by his own strength or by wheeling his horse one way or the other, and Elk Hollering, with left hand both holding his horse's reins and grasping his horse's mane up close to the roots, was kneeing the animal away. It seemed that Horses Ghost would inevitably go down between the two horses, but he instantly swung his left leg over, planted it hard against his horse, and with a tremendous thrust propelled himself across Elk Hollering's horse, dragging Elk Hollering to the ground with him. The two men should have stood up and parted, then approached each other on foot for the second contest, but they went on fighting, rolling and tumbling on the dusty ground, viciously gouging and kneeing each other. Black Horn shouted at them, he fired his gun in the air, and two of his warriors pulled Horses Ghost and Elk Hollering apart and told them to start again from on their feet.

Then began about the worst and longest fight Walks Far ever saw. It went on and on until it became tiresome, perhaps because she could not much care which of those stupid men won. The end of it was that Horses Ghost lay helpless upon the ground, gray-faced under the smeared blood. One of his shoulders was strangely hunched, and the arm seemed twisted. Elk Hollering stood over him a moment, and he too was gray-faced and bloody. His chest heaved and his skinned knees quivered, but he walked over to Black Horn, made some friendly remark, and shook hands. He then walked over to the pile of goods Horses Ghost had bet, looked at it a moment, and disdainfully kicked it apart to pick up just one little thing. He kicked his own pile apart too, and called out clearly in perfect Sioux to Black Horn, "I will go away more joyfully still," he declared, "if you will give all these things to some needy, worthy person." He mounted as he was, and rode away northward with the two Assiniboins. The fine horse lost by Horses Ghost in the earlier race went along too, with a pack upon its back.

An elderly Yankton carefully and gently felt Horses Ghost's shoulder, signaled two men to hold him, then gave an abrupt, wrenching jerk that popped the joint back into place. The forearm was then bound level across Horses Ghost's body. He looked sick indeed, but he spurned any help from Walks Far so noisily and so angrily that she saw other women to be embarrassed for her. Two of his wild-eyed cronies guided him back to the tipi, and Walks Far followed.

Horses Ghost was soon quite able to go hunting, but when he gave no sign that he ever would, Walks Far decided that just about the only thing left for her to do was to swallow her pride and go herself. Perhaps the shame of it would jar Horses Ghost to sanity. She rode out before dawn one morning. It happened to be a day on which the Yanktons were holding a big dance, though that fact had no part in her thoughts.

She failed to get within range of any of the wary white-tailed deer, and she saw no faint, fresh sign of elk. The heat of the day came on, and a defeated Walks Far suddenly found herself tempted to ride away from Fort Peck forever, to swing north and go to Red Hoop Woman and Scalps Them at Wood Mountain, or simply ride westward until she came to the Blackfoot country. But a small elk that should have been resting in shade blundered lazily into her way, and she shot and butchered it.

With the quarters slung across Crazy One before and behind her saddle, and with the other choice parts bundled into the elk's skin and held on her lap, she rode back to her tipi. As she sharpened her knife and set about cutting as much of the meat as possible into long strips for drying, the sound of drums and singing came faintly from the distant dancing, which was being held on the river flat, under cottonwoods well below the camp. Walks Far, knowing Horses Ghost would be there, suddenly determined to go herself. Covering the meat so that magpies could not get at it, and hanging it beyond the reach of camp dogs, she cleaned herself and Crazy One. With the parting in her hair painted vermilion, she put on the best she had. Her *winkte* dress was gone forever, burned or looted by some soldier that morning on the Redwater a year and a half ago, but she had a beautiful dentalium-shell yoke worth four or five good horses, and it covered her dress nearly down to the waist. Horses Ghost had won it, and she had managed to keep it. With a turkey-red fringed shawl folded loosely around her hips like a kind of overskirt, then belted with her brass-studded knife belt, she needed only her fancy pair of high-topped riding moccasins and her incised antler quirt to be ready—to look better than most, if she did have to say so herself. She knew she didn't even need to dress up like this to feel the eyes of the young Yanktons or the loafing soldiers upon her.

As she neared the dancing ground, she tied Crazy One in the shade and started looking for Horses Ghost. The dance was at intermission, with a big shifting crowd and more fleet, darting children on the outskirts than was easy to believe. A half-breed or two and a pair of very young soldiers stood as onlookers. She saw Joe Culbertson and his wife, then spotted Horses Ghost. He looked as though he had been dancing, but he now squatted in the vicinity of the drummers on the hard-packed dancing place with the two of his cronies she had come to dislike most of all. She felt a swift surge of anger as she walked up to stand behind the three of them until they felt her presence. In that moment she grew more angry than she had ever been, and though she spoke without raising her voice unduly, the words were not exactly those she might have planned.

"Husband," she said, "if you feel as hungry as I know you must, you will be very glad to hear that there is at last much meat in the tipi. I have gone hunting this morning and I have killed an elk for you—!"

Horses Ghost was already upon his feet and twisted toward her, his handsome face contorted by fury and by the effort with which he swung his quirt and began lashing her. Walks Far neither cowered nor gave ground. She only stepped around quickly to his left and lashed back with her own quirt, stinging him twice across the face. Utter shock arrested him momentarily, mingling for an instant with the fury in his eyes.

He turned his back and in three long strides was at the big drum, knocking two of the elderly drummers aside in his rush. He snatched a drumstick from the hand of a third drummer and then, pointing at Walks Far, he struck the drum hard to say, "I give you that woman! Anyone who wants her can have her. I don't want her anymore."

It was the ultimate insult. Walks Far flicked her knife out, sending it swiftly on its way. The carved ivory grip suddenly protruded as though by magic from Horses Ghost's left side, with the long blade sunk in up to the guard, between his ribs. His knees buckled, and he folded into a fall that ended in the death shudder, but his hands had appeared to be groping for the knife as he went down. Walks Far followed the thrown knife so swiftly that she had it again in hand almost as soon as Horses Ghost hit the ground. She became conscious of sudden space given her and the body of Horses Ghost, conscious also of a myriad of eyes and mouths, all densely hung around her in a wide, tight circle through which she could not possibly break. Oddly, there seemed to be both an enormous silence and a tremendous shouting at the same time. A few of the men were yelling for somebody to take that knife away from that crazy woman, but some of the women were screaming that no one should touch her, and four old men around Black Horn appeared to agree.

Walks Far noted quite clearly that the two young white soldiers, their swift feet looking huge in the big shoes, were hastening away, throwing fearful backward glances over their shoulders. Joe Culbertson stood in the circle. His face showed nothing, and his eyes seemed to wander absently, but his hand was on the butt of his holstered revolver, his thumb on the hammer. Joe's wife was screaming at Black Horn, her father. Men seemed on the point of closing in on Walks Far.

Black Horn gestured for the crowd's attention and approached her, his eyes weary and impatient as he quieted the people. "Let this woman go," he said. "Let her go with my daughter and my son-in-law. Do not bother her."

Joe and his wife rushed her away, and some of Feather Earrings's Yankton relatives hurried along. Walks Far well knew that they came to help save her horses and tipi from people who, if angry, would try to steal or destroy them. Walks Far didn't feel much like worrying about that, but she and Joe brought in the three good horses that she believed to be the remainder from Horses Ghost's early gambling winnings. She never knew what became of the one Horses Ghost had been riding that morning. Shortly after the horses were driven safely into Joe's corral behind his cabin, his wife and the other women brought Walks Far's folded tipi, the elk meat, and her personal possessions. Then, with the tipi poles bound in a neat bundle to lean against the end of the cabin beside Joe's bundled tipi poles, Walks Far took off her finery and purified her knife and herself with water, with sweat bath and sweet grass, with smoke and prayer. That done, she hastened to cut up the rest of the elk meat for drying before it spoiled, even though she felt strangely close to exhaustion while doing so.

She felt no remorse, only a deep and painful sadness. True, she had killed someone, but only some crazy no-good, a man the bad spirits had made so foolish as to hit that drum in a gamble that she could not or would not try to kill him. The Horses Ghost she knew had died a slow death a long time ago. In Sioux she told herself, *It is finished.*

But it was not finished. There were thoughts she could not still. For example, what had happened to Horses Ghost's body? No doubt it would be given the burial of the worthless, laid in a shallow hole hastily scraped out on some hilltop, then left there to pollute Maka, the All Mother, the Earth.

Walks Far kept herself busy. Joe and his wife, for all Joe's army scouting, found time to hunt and make meat, quite as though they were not rich. Walks Far had plenty to do, not to mention the beading and quilling on which she felt strangely compelled to work at every odd moment. Still, her depression lingered, and she knew she embarrassed people by staring, by absently looking them squarely in the face and eyes, however unseeing and vacant her gaze.

After perhaps six or seven days she went off by herself one

morning and wandered up to the head of a coulee just at sunrise. A lone old ash tree grew there, with high prairie and silence dwelling all around. Walks Far sat a long while, rocking her body and singing a sad song that came to her. With her knife point she pried four of the brass studs from her belt, and as she completed each of the four parts to her singing prayer, she tossed a stud to one of the four winds, beginning with the north. She failed to bow her head and pull her shawl down over her face when she finished, but fell instead into her trancelike stare.

Suddenly Coyote was sitting there, his gray-muzzled face looking at her more seriously than usual. He was even a trifle apologetic when he spoke: "Walks Far Away Woman, I have been pretty busy, but I have been thinking about you. As you know, things are very bad all over the country, and for many people. But I am pretty sure that your own worst troubles are now finished. Next time none of them will be quite so bad—"

"Next time!" Walks Far said bitterly, "Who is saying there will be a next time?"

"Do not interrupt me," Coyote insisted. "I know all about what you are thinking, and I have decided to say some things to you. I know that you are bothered and confused to find out that the half-person who showed soldiers to the camp where they killed your baby is nevertheless a kind man. You should not have planned to shoot him sometime, not even before he helped you out of trouble. It would do nobody any good."

Walks Far felt herself shiver to learn how much Coyote knew. Also, she had to ask a question. "Why is it that I am so often helped out of trouble by half-persons?"

"I have not thought about that," Coyote said impatiently. He seemed to regard the question as wholly irrelevant, and again demanded that she be attentive before he went on. "There are three things you should not worry about so much. Neither One Horn, nor Horses Ghost, nor yourself are likely to dwell in that bad after-death place where murderers, *winktes*, suicides, and sometimes the ungenerous and cowardly have to go. Nor does it mean anything that your baby died without a blue dot, or having her ears pierced. As you know, some people have some funny ideas about some things that do not matter. Also, you should not worry or feel guilty about Red Hoop Woman and Scalps Them starving at Wood Mountain. They eat well, and I am pretty sure that they will die richer than most whites, and more generous too."

Walks Far felt vastly relieved by all this, and the part about Scalps Them both astonished her and gave shape to a most peculiar dream she'd had.

She saw Coyote now regarding her with his old familiar grin. "I am glad to see that you have at least not stopped eating," he said. "But I can see that you are letting yourself get thin-minded. People who get thin-minded do foolish things . . ."

Coyote let his voice trail off absently. He raised a lean, scabby hind leg to scratch a tattered ear, then looked around and added, "especially in a place such as this."

Walks Far felt embarrassed, ashamed, for she knew that Coyote was now getting around to the final thing he had come to say. She put a hand over her mouth and hung her head as he went on, "Yes, I know a place like this that used to be even nicer. The tree there is much the same. But now there is always an uncomfortable, sad breeze whispering regretfully at the head of that coulee. It is a place that even the All Mother does not seem to like much anymore. I have not stopped there very often for about a hundred winters, and all because of that young woman. She was strong and pretty like you, and it is true that she had much to be sad about. But her ancestors, going back through the old long-ago people all the way to the first-time people, had often felt just as sad. Yet they kept things going for all the people who came after them. They knew that this life is sometimes bad, but they did not know of any life that can be better than this life often is. Not one of that girl's ancestors ever tucked a halter rope under her belt to go out at sunup looking for a tree at the head of a coulee. Not while they were still young. She was the first one ever to be so disloyal to her ancestors, or to the people who should have come after her. Yes, I do not like to go to that place. I do not like to hear that girl's spirit whispering there forever about how she wishes she had not used that rope such as you are carrying."

When Walks Far was able to look up, Coyote had already gone. She saw him loping away into the sun. The talk with him, even though he'd hardly let her speak, had made her feel very much better. In fact, never again would she let herself feel quite so bad for so long.

Chapter Twenty-seven
A HALF-PERSON'S WIFE

(Late Summer 1878
through Early Summer 1879)

Cob Piget came with increasing frequency to Joe Culbertson's cabin. There was often a crowd, with half-breed dancing to the tune of Joe's or Cob's fine violins. Cob danced too, and Walks Far had never seen anyone who appeared to enjoy it so much, or who could make so much from the rhythm. He taught her to dance in the way all the breeds and their women were dancing, and she felt a little ridiculous. Though she was the tallest woman there, she stood only a little higher than Cob's armpit. Except for moccasins he wore white man's clothing. The name Cob was short for Colbert.

Joe and his wife began teasing Walks Far about Cob Piget's still unspoken but obvious interest in her. Joe said of him, "Everyone in this country likes Cob. There is nothing that man cannot do or will not try—and have fun doing it. You should see his cabin! No one in the country is much smarter at making money. He can leave you almost happy about getting skinned in a horse trade!" And Joe laughed to add, "Also, he must be the cleanest person you will ever see."

Walks Far had a serious private talk with Joe's wife, who, as it appeared, regarded all half-breeds as being hardly different from white men. Anyway, she said, having a half-breed for a husband was surely just as confusing as life would be with an all-white husband in that disordered and unpredictable world of theirs. Yet a woman could go right on being as much Indian as she liked—more so!—as far as finery and all rich things went, and there was lots of fun to be had. She had become terribly fond of Joe.

"But I do not know whether I more than like Cob Piget," Walks Far said.

Joe's wife laughed as though to say, What has that got to do with it! And when she actually spoke, it was to tell Walks Far, "If you find, after a while, that you do not like him for a husband, you can always leave him and go somewhere to an Indian husband. Meanwhile you will be very rich, and will have to work hard only when you want to.

Walks Far thought she might like Cob very much, and he plainly liked and wanted her. It was strange how they enjoyed talking with each other, even though his limited Sioux was bad and his lazy accent worse. Walks Far had somehow learned a few words of white man's speech—*eat, good, sugar, plenty*, and *come* and *go*. Also, she understood *her, him, me, you, man, woman*, and *sleep*, plus perhaps ten more words, including of course those magic ones, *goddamit, sonofabitch*, and *shit*.

Cob had a fine cabin, a kind of carpenter's shop, and a garden, with a big, strong corral behind. Among various things Cob did was the buying and selling of horses up and down the river along with a Slit Nose man who had escaped at the time of Chief Joseph's surrender. Walks Far saw that his cabin was a truly fine one. There were two small windows of glass! not of mere hides scraped and oiled to make them translucent. Those windows and the door were painted bright red, with ornate white frames like the ones on the fireboats. Cob was said to possess some magic that kept his dirt roof from leaking, even during the spring thaws and rains. The walls inside were whitewashed! And there was a wooden floor, something nearly as rare as painted window frames and doors. A fine stove made a smoky fireplace unnecessary. The whole place was almost painfully clean and neat, and much superior even to the cabin in which Meejoor Walsh lived at Wood Mountain.

Walks Far first went to the cabin with Joe and his wife, to a big feast and dance that Cob had been planning for a long time. Almost a year before, he had sent down the river for a kind of potato that was very sweet, also cans of something called shrimp, and many other strange things. Incredibly, Cob did all the cooking himself, starting the previous midnight with a buffalo calf he roasted whole over a pit of hot coals. All through that feast, Cob paid special attention to Walks Far, making sure she got some of the best of everything. But it irritated and made her feel embarrassed for him when he kept urging her to take more and more of something. If that was white people's way— the host loudly begging a guest to take much more of some dish than the guest might happen to want—well, Walks Far could only regard such urging as terribly rude. It not only suggested that the guest lacked individual personality, but it also made the host look blindly conceited. Cob's urging finally made Walks Far so mad that she said something a little rude herself. She began urging Cob to go drink four big cups of his fine river water as fast as he could down them, but he failed to understand her Sioux, even when she accompanied it with plainest sign language.

If she married him, she thought, she could quickly break him of habits like that, for he was clearly an intelligent man who would appreciate the advantages of Indian common-sense politeness. She wondered what tribe his mother had come from, anyhow. But there was the matter of his hair, those close-cropped, tight curls that made Walks Far secretly apprehensive about marrying him. She had grown up regarding long hair as somehow the mark of the human spirit, and of the fullness of any man's personality, even of his virility.

Still, when he asked Joe to translate "I'd sure be mighty happy to have you want to be my wife," then begged her to come, she thought about it for only a day or two before simply moving over and leaning her bundled tipi poles against the rear of his cabin. There was another big feast then, with presents. Cob happily declared her to be worth more horses than any man owned, but he would give a token pony and he would give it to her. He had someone slip a beautiful pinto into their corral that night!

Almost at once Walks Far found life with Cob a shocking experience. None of the many horror stories she had heard about white men had ever quite described Cob or prepared her for the reality. He insisted on doing much of the cooking, and he taught her that ordinary potatoes could be prepared in about ten different ways, some of which she had to admit resulted in a tasty dish. That was only the beginning. Ultimately, she learned to cook everything in the garden, and Cob had plants growing that not even most white men around there had heard of. White men and the soldiers would come and give Cob the price of a whole sack of flour if he would cook them just a few of those plants and his spicy meat. It was embarrassing to sell food from one's own fire to a hungry person who wanted but a helping or two.

Cob had fashioned some long wooden things that fit neatly over the shoulders and enabled two big buckets of water to be easily carried from the river, for a great deal of water had to be put on the garden. Not only did Cob insist on carrying water with her, but, more amazingly, his Slit Nose partner in selling horses also helped on many mornings. And he was all Indian! Walks Far felt constantly embarrassed by having them along doing women's work, even though she saw she could never have carried enough water for that garden by herself.

The greatest shock of all came with the meals. Cob wanted them at an absolutely regular time. He ate from a white plate, and at the table of course, with all the food already there in separate dishes before he began. The shocking part was his demand that she eat at the table, too, and at the *same time!* Other half-breeds didn't make their Indian wives do that, but he simply would not have it any other way. He told her that a pretty woman sitting opposite was the best half of a good meal. The Slit Nose—called Pogy, for Poge Hloka, or Percy, for Nez Perce, because no one could pronounce his real name—lived with them half the time, which made the meals a double trial for Walks Far.

Percy could speak little more Sioux than Cob could, but he knew Cob's language well. Walks Far also began to learn what she discovered to be called English. If she reached for anything at that dreadful table, one of those men would grab and hold onto it until she managed to say, "Please pass the biscuits," or whatever. Also, when she forgot herself, they might force her to say in penalty, "I was just thinking that we are going to have a very early fall and a very hard winter this year"—something difficult indeed for a person whose first language contained no *b,f,j,l,r,* and initial *y* sounds. Still, and not because of the penalties alone, Walks Far learned a fair amount of English swiftly.

There were so many things she wanted to learn from Cob, including an explanation of such little mysteries and rituals as the one requiring an especially fine meal to be eaten every seventh day, with a white Hudson's Bay blanket spread over the table, or why the whole cabin floor had to be washed the day before, and all his clothes the day after. But despite all his peculiarities, Cob was the most thoughtfully considerate and helpful, the most invariably kind and patient husband she had had. Also, he had a way of turning nearly everything into fun. He was a good person, and she grew very fond of him.

In due course, she showed him her ring from the Little Bighorn, and when it proved to fit him, she told him he could have it. "My, my!" he said, "Ain't that a-purty! Must be wuth fo'ty dollahs. But ah wants you to keep it." He never asked how she happened to have it. At about that time, too, she got around to asking what tribe his mother had belonged to. "She tol' me a speck of Chickasaw," he said. "None of her folks ever been slave, jus' my pappy's mother."

The term *slave* baffled Walks Far, and when he explained it, she failed to hide her astonishment. His skin was lighter than Joe Culbertson's skin.

Cob was astonished too. "Good Lord, girl, doan you know ah'm jus' a kind of half-breed niggah?" They laughed and laughed about that, and it became one of their private jokes.

Walks Far was never long without general news of the Sioux at Wood Mountain, for the Yanktons were in frequent touch with them, but all that news was dreary. Though many small hunting parties slipped south of the line and of the Big River almost routinely, they avoided Fort Peck, and Walks Far received no direct word of Red Hoop Woman and Scalps Them. Unexpectedly, their sources of information about Walks Far were a little better. She was at work in the garden one fall morning, threshing and winnowing beans in a chill wind, and with both Cob and Percy away, when a rider approached. He gave her a start even as she recognized him. He did somehow resemble Horses Ghost, this Elk Hollering, though his more mature face had never been quite as handsome, even before the broken nose.

He rode close and spoke to her in his fine Sioux, "You are Walks Far Away Woman, and this is the cabin of Cob Piget—some call you Pekony Woman?" He was appraising her as though in surprised admiration, but not too arrogantly.

"*Ah,*" she said, using the Blackfoot word for "yes."

His Blackfoot was, if possible, better than his Sioux as he told her, "Your friends in Scalps Them's lodge at Wood Mountain wish you to be happy. They have asked me to tell you that their daughter now has a fine husband of the Miniconjou, and everyone is pleased."

Fire Wing married! It seemed impossible. "Tell me about my friends; I would like to know how they are getting along," Walks Far said. "Do they have enough to eat?"

"I do not know them very well," Elk Hollering said, "though I know that they need not go hungry, for they are giving away much food to those who are hungry. Scalps Them carves little animals of wood. Also the ash bowls and the stone pipes decorated with carved animals. Le Garé and the redcoats buy all he can carve. Other men try to carve those animals, but not one of them has the true power. Le Garé has given him two new knives for the carving, also a fine saw for cutting the wood up quickly, and the burls from trees. This is all I know."

"Do you want something to eat?" Walks Far asked.

"No, I have eaten, and I must ride north, but I will stand out of the wind and drink some tea or coffee." Then, as he dismounted to back against the cabin wall, he added, "If you wish to send a small something to your friends, I will take it for you." He held his hands cupped together to suggest something small indeed.

Walks Far could think of nothing except the two thick cakes she'd pressed from the meats of sunflower seeds. She put them in a small, newly made pipe and tobacco bag she'd just finished beading, and took them out to Elk Hollering with the hot coffee. Of course, she gave him messages too.

"You must hurry with your garden work," he said. "Pretty soon the *kissineyoowai'o,* as we Crees call Northwind, will blow hard. Then the ghost dancers of the Northern Lights—the *chepuyuk*—will make us shiver with them."

"I saw those ghost dancers in the sky many nights ago, Walks Far said. "It was in the moon when many stars always fall."

"Yes," Elk Hollering agreed, "but they were then very sleepy and lazy, and they did not hiss and snicker down at people as they will when they are happy with the cold."

He seemed to be as glad as she was to talk to someone in Blackfoot, and in no hurry to start his long ride north. Later, when he was on the point of mounting, he thought of something more.

"Are not those men Feather Earrings and Kills When

Wounded of the same band as Scalps Them? Ah, then you should hear about them. They did a great thing. Even Meejoor Walsh is laughing, although he is not supposed to know about it. They went south to Miles Town [Miles City], which has grown up at that fort, Fort Keogh, built by Bearcoat's soldiers at the mouth of Tongue River. They walked around in the evening like surrendered Sioux or Cheyennes. The whites were having a big dance, and many of the soldier chiefs were there, with their best horses tied up outside. Our friends waited awhile, then took those horses, seven of the very best, with fine bridles and saddles, and they got them all safely across the Line. But it is said that no one has complained to Meejoor about those fine horses being stolen! It is also said that Meejoor has told someone he would like to be rich enough to buy those horses and make a present of them to the American soldier chiefs."

Elk Hollering related this with unmistakable glee and in the most humorous Blackfoot way of telling, but with neither a laugh nor even so much as the shadow of a smile ever crossing his strong face. He sprang onto his horse and told her. "Your coffee has a very strange taste that I like."

"It is something called chicory, which my husband got from a man on a fireboat," Walks Far said.

"You make other fine things," he told her while gazing at the garden. "The tobacco bag is very pretty. So is the way you have painted the case for that knife you are wearing"—he was look-ing now at her small pile of winnowed beans, at another of salsify roots, and he changed to a question without pausing— "How do you like living now with the half-people, having a half-person for a husband?"

It was a bold question from a stranger, but it could have come from mere honest curiosity. Yet it could also have been an insolent, leading question. Walks Far said, "I have already told you to tell my friends that I am very happy."

"I am glad to be able to do that," Elk Hollering told her, and after a distinct pause he added oddly unexpected words, "My mother was Blackfoot. But I will tell you something else that I think no one remembers. My father's grandfather was a white trader, one of the many named Mac. When I think about it, I do not know whether I like that part of me very much." He was already turning to ride away into the cold north wind.

A strange man, Walks Far thought, as she went back to her work. Obviously, he knew all about her. Like Joe Culbertson, he could sound almost irritatingly simple, yet not quite without creating some small sense of danger. And that odd, sudden confession, or whatever it was, and from a clearly confident and able man. That any Cree could be so handsome and attractive seemed somehow surprising, Walks Far thought. And Crees believed the soul resides in the back of the neck, were offended if anyone touched them there . . . so, what did a girl do with her arms? Walks Far soon forgot all about it.

Wintertimes with Cob were fun. They ate wonderfully well and lived a leisurely, almost lazy life. Walks Far had gone with Cob in his big red cart hitched to two horses and helped haul enough wood—also something out of the ground called lignite coal—to last all through the cold moons. She became a guilty spendthrift of fuel, and could never quite believe she had such an enormous pile just outside the door, that she would not need to go searching in the snow for a few poor sticks along some coulee. Cob and Percy taught her how to play cards. Percy was determined to best her at cat's cradle, and she won much small money from him. Cob taught her how to print out her name, both as Walks Far Away—which a pondering Joe Culbertson had finally decided to be the best English translation—and as Mrs. Colbert Piget. He carved each of the names carefully into the stock of her carbine, one of them to a side.

Walks Far went to endless parties, games, and dances, some at quite a distance. Most of the mixed-blood and white people owned crude sleighs they called Red River jumpers, but Cob had made a much finer sleigh, lighter, faster, and painted brightest red. The two of them, wearing their buffalo coats, could squeeze into a kind of cockpit. With lighted lanterns held between their winter moccasins, they would enjoy the ride to a distant dance in any cold safe enough for trotting a horse in. Either Cob or Joe Culbertson, or both, played their violins for the dances, which always went on all night, sometimes for two nights. Walks Far had more plain fun than ever before or since, and such funny, crazy things happened among the crazy people at those dances that she herself could not quite believe them in later years. ["Ever'bodies—Indians, white man, mix'—they's make more fun those tam," Walks Far told Janet Sinclair. "Ever'bodies, she's still laugh. Maybe they don' know 'bout Ol' Man and tricks he play on Blackfoot, but they know them trick and make happy, crazy world! When lotsa white womans come and sodbuster's farms, ever'things she's change!"]

In the next spring and summer [1879] Walks Far got away from the cabin and garden on two adventurous trips. First, she helped Cob and Percy drive horses three days downriver to Fort Buford near where the Yellowstone joins the Missouri or Big Muddy River. The two men sold even the horses they rode, but Walks Far refused to part with Crazy One. Cob laughed and paid somebody to let Crazy One ride back to Fort Peck with them on a fireboat. Walks Far found that fireboat ride half frightening and half fascinating, and nearly unbelievable. That boat seemed truly alive. It shuddered away from the riverbank with a terrible hissing and groaning, which soon settled into a kind of fluttery snoring. Still, the pulsing vibrations under her feet made Walks Far afraid to move around. Then, from just above her a tall, shiny round thing suddenly blew out white "smoke" with such a startling and unendurably prolonged blast of sound that Walks Far cried out and cowered in terror. ["Hi'm plenty scare to seen that smoke holler!" she told Janet and Dewey.] But Cob only laughed and, as usual, began carefully explaining just what had happened, and how the whole boat worked. She felt doubly reassured to see that soldiers among the suddenly rearing horses on the front part of the boat were only angry and not at all frightened as they swore at the man who pulled the little rope to make that noise.

Shortly, she found herself believing such a fireboat to be the white man's greatest marvel. ["Hi'm wish they got 'im now! They gone lak ol' tam Indian peoples. Why gone lotsa bes' thing? You know why?"]

More than once it seemed to Walks Far that the boat stood still while all the country on either side of the river sped magically to eastward. About halfway home Cob pointed out to her a place that he said he'd had his eye on for a fine bottomland farm, with plenty of good grazing on the benchland behind it. He declared that they ought to start saving money carefully.

Soon after that trip the three of them made another one, taking a few fast horses to a kind of Indian fair at the Touch-wood Hills in central Saskatchewan. Wood Mountain was somewhat out of the direct route, but they visited Scalps Them and Red Hoop Woman. Walks Far and Red Hoop Woman closed in a tearful but silent hug as the forever silenced Scalps Them formed signs of welcome with particularly expressive hands. Just as Elk Hollering had reported, Scalps Them and Red Hoop Woman were eating comparatively well from the trade in Scalps Them's carvings, though they gave most of the food they bought to relatives and other people. Walks Far could see with her own eyes much of what Red Hoop Woman told her. The country around was already stripped of game, large and small. "Women and children dig roots and pick the berries almost before they are fit to eat," Red Hoop Woman said. "There are many big bellies and much sickness. Unless the buffalo come back across the line, most everyone will starve. Le Garé, the trader, is trying to get either the Canadians or the Americans —somebody—to do something before that happens.

"Fortunately, Scalps Them cannot carve the little animals and people fast enough. The redcoats and Le Garé buy them, as do both the blackrobes who wear the crosses and also the short-coat blackrobes who wear no crosses. They are always coming to see how the people are getting along, and sometimes they send a little food and some old coats to us. A red-haired *wasichu* came to see Sitting Bull and find out about us for the talking papers. He saw the carvings and bought a great many, especially of the little people. He said that all showed the *nagila* —"the true essence of a living person"! He has sent a message to Le Garé asking for more.

"No, Fire Wing has gone from here. Some of her husband's people decided to go south and let themselves be counted for taking to their reservations. Her husband is a worthy young man who already knows a little something about walking the white man's road. Neither Scalps Them nor I did anything to talk them out of it.

"I have heard about you, that you have a fine husband who is much liked by both the people and the *wasichu,* and that you are very rich. I can see that this is all true, and that you are happy. I am joyful for you. But is it not strange and hard living with a man who does not know our Sioux ways?"

Scalps Them and Red Hoop Woman decided to go along to the Touchwood Hills, adding that Feather Earrings and Kills When Wounded had already gone, taking some fast horses. People from all tribes of the northern prairies gathered there each year near a Hudson's Bay Company post to race and to trade. They made it a time and place of truce, where the bitterest of enemies met in peace for a while. Crees and Crowfoot's Northern Blackfoot outnumbered all others, but Walks Far saw even a few Pikuni Blackfoot, though none she knew. Elk Hollering had come with a couple of extremely long-winded racers. Walks Far would always remember that he looked rather splendid, despite his ugly Cree moccasins, for he had on a white man's hat such as she had never seen. It was far higher, blacker, and shinier, and that hat rose to a perfectly flat tall top that was a little larger there than where it met the brim. It was decorated with a huge pink plume so long and sweeping, so fluffy and curled that Walks Far knew it had to come from some strange, far-away land. Of evenings Elk Hollering also wore a magnificent soft blanket barred all over with wide stripes of alternating red and white. She noted again that he rarely laughed or smiled, even when he obviously enjoyed a joke.

It soon became clear that he and Percy had brought the fastest horses. Then Elk Hollering beat Percy in an extremely close race. Walks Far, who had bet heavily, couldn't believe it. Percy, the little Nez Perce, was without doubt the finest horseman she had seen in a lifetime among horsemen. His horse even appeared to run the faster, but Elk Hollering's came in first. But this was not the only surprise. A Sarsi, just a boy on an only fair-looking horse, beat them both badly and went home rich. Both Percy and Elk Hollering were almost disbelieving. They thought they had been somehow tricked, and became friendly with each other in their indignation and mystification. They talked about their loss in Walks Far's tipi, each agreeing with the other that their horses clearly were the faster. But they finally accepted the contrary fact already proven.

Elk Hollering told Walks Far he had never eaten finer things than she prepared for a small feast. He said that until now, where flavorful food was concerned, he must have been as tongueless as Scalps Them was. Cob beamed proudly. Elk Hollering privately told Scalps Them and Red Hoop Woman that if any other women like Walks Far should suddenly turn up in their tipi, to let him know right away. He mentioned to Walks Far that he had once had a wife, but a boy had shot her by accident, and another such wife was hard to find.

Cob, Walks Far, and Percy managed to come back from the Touchwood Hills with more horses and other wealth than they took. So did Scalps Them, Feather Earrings, Kills When Wounded, and Elk Hollering. Walks Far and Cob advised them all to bet on Percy when he got into a marksmanship contest. It was at very long range against some of the Hudson's Bay Company traders and a couple of redcoats, whose shooting Percy had been watching. Those white men laughed at Percy when he asked for a turn. They said this was no game for Indians and Indian guns. Percy told them how, in the Nez Perce country, boys with old smooth bores did as well as they were doing. They all grinned, and one of them, looking at the dried rawhide that held the broken stock of Percy's battered Winchester together, agreed to a little bet. Percy barely beat him, so as not to frighten the others from betting. The end of it was that he outshot them all, making them look like boys before the big crowd, and leaving them much the poorer. Walks Far wished he had shown them what he could do at rapid fire, for in that he was almost unbelievable. She had seen him get off five aimed shots as fast as he could lever the cartridges in, three of them knocking down a small wolf running away through the buffalo grass into the sunrise. Only Finds the Enemy, her first husband, and Elk Hollering could so much as approach Percy in both accuracy and speed, but Percy modestly insisted that several Nez Perce were far better shots than he was.

When Walks Far, Cob, and Percy returned to Fort Peck, they revived their garden and went on with their usual ways. More and more of the mixed-bloods and a few whites along the Missouri were taking land for farms and ranches. Joe Culbertson told Walks Far that he had heard that Jack Sinclair had started raising white man's cattle to westward beyond Fort Benton. Many more of the whites were settling on the Yellowstone near Fort Keogh, more than here on the Missouri. There, the swiftly growing Miles Town did its best to provide the soldiers, buffalo hunters, and early cattlemen with all they might desire, and waited impatiently for the iron road to reach them. Cob drove horses there as well as to Fort Buford to sell, and he told Walks Far that a few robbing, murdering whites and mixed-bloods were beginning to make the country unsafe, more dangerous than it had ever been. He and Percy started wearing army revolvers in addition to the rifles they carried.

Walks Far saw the man who enforced the law. Joe Culbertson brought him to Cob so he could buy a good horse and go after three whites. They would be sent back upriver where they had come from, then hanged. Walks Far could have laughed at the idea of this extremely stubby little man with the big shapeless moustache, and a hat that looked as though someone else had put it on him, ever being able to catch anybody. But it happened that she remembered him from her girlhood. He, the first white man she had ever seen from close up, had been captive in one of the lodges of her Blackfoot band as it hunted buffalo north of the then unmarked Line. His captors let him grow so thirsty that he did not hesitate to drink the water in which a warrior had just washed his hair, but he defied all the warriors so bravely and fiercely that some of them said he should not be killed. So, those warriors gave him his horse and rode with him until he was safe away from the others.

Now, Joe and Cob were plainly awed by him. They said his name was X. Biedler, and that, as United States marshal for the Territory of Montana, he had more power here than Meejoor Walsh and his redcoats had at Wood Mountain. X. Biedler quickly caught the men he went after, and sent them west for hanging. But they never got very far. As Walks Far heard it, they soon tried to escape and had to be shot. Then they were hanged anyhow, to be left swinging from some cottonwoods at a sandy bend in the river as a warning to travelers. Apparently, it did no lasting good.

Chapter Twenty-eight
THE RACE TO STANDING ROCK

(Late Summer 1879 through Early Summer 1881)

In that same summer [1879] Walks Far met a white person she would never forget. Cob and Percy had been away for several days when she went to the riverbank with her water buckets one quiet evening and heard a peculiar sound. It seemed to come from just under the gliding surface and to fill the whole river. She recognized that sound, knew it to be somehow made by the blowing of many buffalo as they crossed a wide, deep stream. Walks Far suddenly felt hungry for their fresh fat meat. Tomorrow they should still be within easy ride, just north of the river. These days, with Cob as husband, it embarrassed her not at all to hunt for meat herself. So, at dawn she was out on Crazy One with her carbine, seeking those buffalo.

Though by no means the only eager hunter, she was yet among the very first, and killed a fat young cow easily. As she worked at the skinning and butchering, she saw after a while that she had strange visitors. They rode up almost impolitely close and sat watching from their army horses. One was a very young soldier, freckle-faced, yawning, and resentfully disinterested. The other was a tall, rather thin white woman sitting one of those incredible sidesaddles Walks Far had first seen during the winter of Scalps Them's search for guns. The woman watched with intense interest.

Walks Far heard her say, "Look! Look, Luther, how fast she does that. Have you ever skinned a buffalo?"

"No, ma'am, I ain't."

Obviously, the woman was one of the three or four army wives at the cantonment. Walks Far liked her voice and saw that, while she was no longer young, she was still far from being old. Also, it looked unlikely that she would get fat when she did grow old. The woman spoke to the soldier again, "Luther, have you ever shot a buffalo?"

"Oncet, ma'am."

The woman looked off across the prairie to other downed buffalo and then said, "I wonder where *her* husband is."

Walks Far straightened from her work and said carefully, "Huspan' gone Popla' Crick." She pointed her knife at the buffalo and added, "Hi'm shoot 'im."

"Oh! You speak English!" the woman said with delight. "May I step down and watch you? Luther, she speaks English!"

"Yes, ma'am."

Walks Far thought the question about stepping down a strange and unnecessary one, but she said, "Please."

The woman unhooked her leg from that ridiculous saddle and slid to the ground. Giving the reins to Luther, she walked quickly up to Walks Far, smiling and speaking as she came.

Her friendly face was pleasing, if bony and sallow, and Walks Far saw that she had very large eyes of a peculiar light brown. She wore a low, black straw hat adorned with narrow blue feathers and a lifted blue veil; a standing white collar; and a small velvet tie the color of a dark red berry was at her throat. Her tight jacket and long, full skirt were black, but set off by a seeming myriad of small round buttons like some bright blue kind of berry. These were repeated along the scalloped closure of the high black shoes. Walks Far thought the tightly fitted jacket emphasized the woman's startling bosom unnecessarily and scandalously.

"I'm Hat," the woman said. "Nickname for Harriet, short for Hatton—Oh! it *smells*, doesn't it?—but it smells *fresh!*—What's *your* name?"

"Wa'ks Pfa'," Walks Far managed to say.

"Wakspa—what a *pretty* name! Luther, her name is Wakspa—"

"Yes, ma'am."

"—and I bet you live in a tipi and go anywhere you want to in this *beautiful* country. My husband, Major Hatton, he doesn't like it—but *I* like it a *lot* better'n Texas—he says if the world had a tail, Fort Peck would be the hole underneath! But I like it, and I ask him who it was that decided to stay in his 'goddam army,' anyhow!"

Hat began to laugh hard as though at a huge joke, and Walks Far, never having heard a white woman's noisy laugh, was simply startled by it, left shocked. That laugh began with a snort, changed to the braying of a mule, and finished with a dog's barking. But Walks Far liked her.

"Mind if I just sit down and watch you?" Hat said, then went on. "I'm sure glad you speak English. I don't know a word of Indian except *tipi* and *papoose,* and *skookum* from out west. You got any children, Wakspa?"

"Had one. She's die. Long tam ago."

"That's awful," Hat said. "I had two. They both died of the bloody flux in Arkansas, both the same summer, one right after the other. I thought I wouldn't ever get over it. But the major, he took it worse than I did, in a way. Say! Wakspa, I want you to tell me the Indian name of some of these flowers and plants around here sometime, and what they're good for. Which reminds me, I didn't eat breakfast for fear of missing this buffalo hunt. You had your breakfast?"

"Tea," Walks Far said. She had also eaten a big strip of raw buffalo liver just before Hat arrived. She noted now that Hat's shoes were cracked and badly worn, the riding clothes rusty, threadbare, and old.

"For goodness sake! We'll both starve. Luther! Bring us those saddlebags."

"Jeez, ma'am! We ain't gonna eat *here!*"

"Why not? This is *real interesting.* Long as you're in the army, Luther, you ought to do something with yourself—all the country and things you get to see, boy like you. Me, I got a pressing and a watercolor of just about every flower in Arkansas and Texas—and Washington Territory too.

"Here, Wakspa, have some of these raisins and half my sandwich—salt pork and pickles—more'n I can ever eat. And we got a whole canteen of water. Oh, dear! We're gonna have to use your knife. . . .

"My! What a handsome big knife!"—Hat polished the blade with her skirt and went on—"All you Indian women wear these knives, don't you? Must be real handy—but just gives me the cold *shivers,* after what I heard. A scout named Joe Culbertson told the major all about it, how an Indian girl knifed her mean, no-good of a husband for him trying to divorce her at some pow-wow down by the river. All the *man* has to do is hit a drum and say he throws the woman away! But why am *I* telling *you?* You know a lot more about it than I ever will. But I can tell you one thing. If the major ever tried that with me, and I had a knife like this one, he prob'ly wouldn't live long enough to regret it either."

Walks Far was delighted, intrigued with Hat, and she hastened to contribute something to the meal by chopping open the buffalo's skull and dipping into the brain cavity. She saw at once that she had made a mistake; but she also saw that Hat was trying hard not to let her know it, was steeling herself and saying, "The major and I like hog brains baked with bread crumbs. They are quite good that way, but I have never tried them raw."

Hat tried them now and, as a revolted Luther softly exclaimed, "Jeez!" she tasted them, tasted them twice, slowly and thoughtfully, then said, "I believe I like them better when baked with broken hardtack. I know the major will love them. May I take some home?"

Walks Far admired Hat. She told her she should also take as much of the choicest tenderloin as she might wish.

"There's something else I'd like, when we're through eating," Hat said, then utterly puzzled Walks Far with the incomprehensible question, "May I do you with your buffalo in watercolor, Wakspa?"

"Please," Walks Far said, a little apprehensively. She felt still more apprehensive when Luther untied a big, flat, wooden case and a small box from one of the saddles, and was mystified when Hat said, "Just go on with your work."

But Walks Far was struck with astonishment at the outcome of Hat's swift effort. It was awesome—herself, her knife, the buffalo and this bit of prairie, all instantly recognizable! Walks Far knew such power existed, but to see it applied, to be a part of it!

"Oh, I'm really not much good," Hat said. "Just better than some are. I'm really best at flowers." Swiftly she made three more of those pictures and let Walks Far choose two. Walks Far treasured them for years.

That day began a strange friendship, though neither woman

ever saw the inside of the place where the other lived. Walks Far felt sorry for Hat when Joe Culbertson revealed Walks Far's own cabin to be far superior to the ramshackle structures, drafty and leaky, that the soldiers and officers lived in. Moreover, according to Joe, Hat's major was actually but a new-made captain, though a good one. He could call himself major only because of battle honors won long ago in the big war between the North whites and the South whites. Still, he was chief over both companies of soldiers here.

Walks Far and Hat spent whole days on the prairies, with either a very young or a very old soldier invariably along—always tagging *behind* the women! Walks Far's English expanded, and she learned so many things from Hat that she wished she could offer something worthwhile in return, something besides showing her certain prairie plants and giving their names in Blackfoot and Sioux, then trying to explain their uses for food or curing so Hat could write it all down. Or something more worthwhile than merely showing Hat how to lie motionless, flat on her back in the grass, and wait for the invisibly high but sweetly audible sky-singing lark to come plummeting down and reveal its tiny, hidden nest.

Late in the fall, on a day near the beginning of the Frost in the Tipi Moon, Hat asked Walks Far a confidential question: Did Walks Far believe Joe Culbertson could arrange to get five big barrels of warm clothing up to those poor Indians with Sitting Bull at Wood Mountain, and do it secretly? And another question—well, the real question was whether Joe could be trusted not to sell the things to somebody after she gave them to him. Walks Far assured Hat that she felt sure Joe would do honestly whatever he promised to do.

Hat explained that in the East there was a society of army friends that sent clothing and other things to wives and children at the posts in the West for Christmastime. Now too many barrels of those things had come here by mistake, and it was by this time too late to send them back to some big post having many women and children. So, Hat had decided to send all the barrels but one to those poor Indians. The major said it was a fine idea, though he certainly should not get mixed up in it himself. He had suggested that she talk to Joe on the quiet.

When Joe was consulted, he saw no great problem—none except about how to pay one of the Métis who owned a good sled. That would cost as much as two pretty fair horses. Hat was disappointed at that, but Joe gave one horse and Walks Far gave the other. They both sent sacks of pemmican, too. Because there was at first too little snow, then suddenly too much, the people at Wood Mountain failed to get the things until after Christmas. But, of course, Christmas meant no more to them than it had meant to Walks Far until just a year ago.

The Sioux at Wood Mountain were terribly hungry by now. Walks Far knew how former proud hunters and their wives were denying themselves so their children might have a bit more of porcupine, badger, or muskrat, or of skunk and gopher —even of the mice, which some people said were ghosts of the buffalo. Redcoats there gave every scrap from their meals. Many horses died of cold and starvation, and the people fed on their poor carcasses.

Hat gave Walks Far a Christmas present, one of two beautiful dresses she had taken from the barrels. It was a pale blue velvet trimmed in shiny black and silver braid. It fit with that strange, white-woman snugness above the waist, but it felt good, except when Walks Far grew too warm from dancing. She knew that in its own way the soft, pale blue made her as striking as the *winkte* dress had done. She wore that dress to every dance and feast she went to that winter and for a long while afterward. She could have got herself into plenty of trouble with it, if she had wanted to.

Walks Far gave Hat a hood and mittens made from wolverine furs, which she had a very hard time locating. She wanted wolverine fur for the hood because the breath does not freeze on it around the face in even the coldest weather. She also gave Hat a pair of moccasins, the first she ever beaded in floral design, rather than in the old geometric Blackfoot and Sioux designs. She made Cob a fine buckskin shirt, and again she used floral designs in beading it.

Early spring [1880] brought much excitement. Large parties of Sioux from Wood Mountain crossed the line, slipped past the soldiers on the Missouri, and headed for old hunting grounds south of the Yellowstone. Walks Far heard how one band, bound for the Tongue, had been trapped in a ravine and forced to surrender. Another party had gone to Fort Custer, built near the site of the Little Bighorn battle. There they stole from thirty to fifty horses from the Crow scouts. The army retook the horses and caught first three, then five more of the raiders.

Joe Culbertson, at Fort Peck, and his cousin, Billy Jackson, at

Fort Keogh, rode almost regularly back and forth between the two places with messages. They said Bearcoat fed the captives and treated them well, trying to convince them that surrender here was better than empty stomachs in Saskatchewan. He let some of the captives go to talk with their brothers about it. But small raids continued into the summer. Mail stages were attacked—something new, Walks Far thought—and as she heard reports of white man's cattle and horses being taken, of fighting with the Crows, and of the burning of piles of buffalo hides, she wondered how much of it was done by Feather Earrings and Kills When Wounded. She could not help feeling moments of envy.

Cob thought all Sioux had best surrender. "The soonah the bettah fo' all them po' people," he said. "They's nothin' else they can do, an' they's only makin' it wuss fo' theirselves."

To Walks Far's surprise, Percy more than half agreed, saying, "Because I had no family I did not surrender after the Bearpaw battle. When I am alone, the white man cannot stop me from doing what I want to do. But if I still had my children, I would not let them starve. Neither would I get myself killed. If I still had my children I would surrender. If I were a chief at Wood Mountain, I would surrender."

Walks Far had not known that Percy ever had children! But he continued to speak, "Bearcoat is giving land to those who go to Fort Keogh and surrender their guns. He is trading them tools for some of their horses so that they can make gardens and fields. Some of his soldiers are showing them how. What they do not eat, they can sell to the army and to people in Miles Town. Some Cheyennes are already doing that. They can get cattle, as I am going to do. That Yellowstone country is not my stolen Wallowa country beyond the mountains, but it is not a bad country. It is a country that the Sioux know, one that many of them value over all others. And there is nothing else for them to do anymore."

This argument, coming from Percy, saddened Walks Far. Though Percy dressed like a white man, spoke English better than did Cob, and had adopted some white man's ways, she knew he remained at least as deeply Indian as did she. All during that summer and fall she felt a mingled sadness and relief to hear of chiefs leading their bands down from Saskatchewan to Fort Keogh and surrendering to Bearcoat. Chiefs of great name—Rain in the Face, Yellow Twin, Black Moon, Broad Tail, Spotted Eagle—one by one, they and others led their people in, more than two thousand of them. Sitting Bull would soon be left alone in the dreariness at Wood Mountain.

In early spring of the following year [1881], Joe Culbertson was able to confirm what Feather Earrings's Yankton relatives believed: Scalps Them and Red Hoop Woman had been among those who surrendered, as had Feather Earrings and Kills When Wounded. Left Hand Bull had simply died late the past fall. So had old Father of a Mudfish. Walks Far determined to visit Red Hoop Woman soon, and, in the best part of a prairie spring, she and Cob rode south to the Yellowstone with Joe and two of his Yankton scouts. Walks Far led a packhorse loaded with presents.

The weather was beautiful, but the familiar country was not the same. Bleached buffalo bones littered a prairie that stank in many places and was often marred at coulee crossings by ugly wagon ruts. Walks Far saw only a sparse few wary buffalo, not a single elk, and but an occasional deer or antelope. The wolves alone seemed still plentiful, but they were strangely lean. The remembered sunny ash and cedar groves felt somber, the wild plums and chokecherries offered no fragrance, no promise. The eagles appeared to have sought some other country. Only the meadowlarks and curlews and the red-winged blackbirds seemed oblivious to what Walks Far felt was happening.

Joe told them that in addition to the clicking wires bringing messages from far away, Bearcoat now had at Fort Keogh itself something called a telephone. With it, soldiers or anyone else could talk to each other in an ordinary voice over much greater distances than any man could see. If Cob had not said he had already heard of such things, Walks Far wouldn't have believed a word of it!

Fort Keogh and Miles Town were also more than she was prepared to comprehend, much less absorb. She had once seen Fort Benton from a distance, seen the fireboats tied along the riverbank below the adobe and flimsy wooden structures, also the freighters' corrals beyond what she could not know were the honky-tonks and saloons. But she was not prepared for Fort Keogh and its Miles Town. It shocked, fascinated, and terrified her, though Cob said it was probably nothing now compared to Saturday nights. They were riding down a dirty street that smelled strong and sour from too much horse manure, and to Walks Far that street appeared thronged with people. Noisy freighters with their big teams and heavy wagons, lounging soldiers in blue, comparatively silent but unwashed and greasy buffalo hunters, the despised wolfers, who used poisoned carcasses to kill the wolves for their skins, and the cowpunchers with their thin, high voices all made what seemed a crowd of white men.

Indians, men and women with their children, sat in the dust between the hitching racks and buildings, raising their hands to beg. From one especially large building filled with a strange, tinkling kind of fast music, two or three rather puffy and not at all pretty, big white women came out shockingly to shout to some men just riding up. One of the women waved a bottle of whiskey by its neck. Cob explained that those women were "nothin' but white saloon and dance-hall whores," and told her exactly what they did for a living.

Cob was quiet for a moment, then said, "If'n you and me wasn't gonna have us that little ranch, I'd come here an' start me a rollah-skatin' rink. Them cowpunchahs, they shuah do like rollah skatin', all I heah." [Janet and Dewey laughed together about this, but Walks Far insisted, "Cowpuncher, he's all roll' skate, them gone tams. Hi'm seen!" Janet felt impelled to consult an elderly, white-moustached man her father referred to as "that broken-down old Texas cowpoke." The answer she got was: "Sure enough, miss. Fellers makin' these here Western movies now, they don't show you nothin' but saloons and fancied-up killers. I admit I drunk me plenty of whiskey, them days. But ever' cow town any real size—Amarillo to Miles City —they had a skatin' rink, and I cut me some figure eights in most of 'em. Talk about your pure prairie air, miss! them places smelled worse'n some ol' pool hall, a bunch of us cowpokes just in from the trail a-sweatin' in there, cuttin' capers. . . ."]

Nor, familiar as Walks Far had become with a hoe, was she quite prepared for the sight of Scalps Them working beside Red Hoop Woman, both of them with hoe in hand. Feather Earrings and his wife were doing the same just a short way farther on, as were Suzy's father and mother. Suzy's father was now chief of the band. Kills When Wounded did true white man's work, getting a dollar each day for six days, then resting one. He and other strong young Sioux were helping the *wasichu*. They used shovels to build something called a grade. The iron road, which was coming soon, would be on top of that grade. It was being built perfectly level across all the coulees, leaving a square hole framed with wood to let water go through.

Scalps Them's carved little animals could be traded here for even more than they had brought in Saskatchewan. Strangely, the admiring *wasichu* in both places unfailingly asked the same pointless question, "How long does it take you to do that?"

The people were glad to be back in this fine Yellowstone country. They could take pride in their gardens, if that was the way it had to be. Walks Far found them good Sioux still, determined as always to "see happy." Their worn tipis were pitched together in a semicircle, on a flat beside a swift, small stream to face a kind of large, round dance pavilion. The pavilion was now roofed only with poles and shading brush, but before winter they would give it walls and a dirt roof. Also, they would help one another build cabins.

Cob was caught up in the spirit of things. He knew all about cabins, how to make doors fit and roofs that would not leak. In the fall he and Walks Far would come again and bring his tools along. He would help them make a couple of strong sleighs for winter. And on the way here, only a short way out, he had seen a broken wagon abandoned by buffalo hunters. He knew he could fix it! He would have them settled and prosperous in no time, no time a-tall. But for now he would show them the proper way to use a hoe. And in the fall he would bring them seeds of some plants that white men didn't know would grow in this country, and which they would beg to buy. ["She is confident," Janet noted in her journal, "that Cob could do anything and build anything, including a *radio or an airplane,* if he had happened to think of them. But except for shortwave, she doesn't appear nearly as astonished by radio as I expected. I gather that this attitude has something to do with the spirit voices that she had always known to be all around.

"She said that Cob had a riding song that he sang joyously and that she had supposed was all his own until she heard it coming in over the radio. She told me, 'Firs' tam Hi'm hear that on radio, Hi'm plenty scare!' It was Stephen Collins Foster's 'Camptown Races.'

"Still, radio means enough to her that she has learned in her old age to keep time by the clock in order not to miss such programs as *The Whistler, Burns and Allen,* and a variety of comedians. However, she regards much of the humor as far too pallid, and wishes for 'story more funny.' By that she means stories really broad or risqué.

"Her true joy is Dewey's shortwave set. She talks with people from South Dakota to up near the Artic Circle, gossiping away in Blackfoot, Sioux, or Cree, and I'm sure Dewey would quickly lose his license if all she says were in English."]

Joe had to return to Fort Peck on the second day, but Walks Far and Cob stayed four days more with Red Hoop Woman and Scalps Them. There was dancing and a big feast, not only with the things they had brought along, but also with the meat, the flour and meal, the sugar and molasses that Cob hurried into town and bought. Walks Far went home feeling in much better spirits about the people than when she came. Surrender would always be sad, but it was better than going hungry at Wood Mountain.

She and Cob were scarcely back in their own cabin when Joe rode over with the first of three messages he was destined to bring her that summer. This one, astonishingly, came in the form of a letter. "It's from Mrs. Hatton," Joe said. "She wrote it yesterday, about noon, on the boat."

Cob told him, "You bettah read what it say, Joe. Ah'm not so good at readin', jus' writin'."

Joe had trouble with it too. It read:

To My Dearest Friend (in haste):

It is with deepest regret that I must say goodbye in only this poor, quick note. By the time you receive this, the Major and I will be far down the River on our way home for a long-delayed, three months leave and visit with relatives in Ohio where we both grew up. Afterward the Major and I will report at Fort Leavenworth, Kansas, for a wonderful new assignment which he has long sought and deserved, and which will almost certainly put him in line for another promotion soon. Mr. Culbertson brought the orders back from the telegraph head at Fort Keogh, and we were sufficiently fortunate as to be able to catch a steamer right away, although we had to rush to do it.

Though I may never see you again, I shall always treasure the memories of my dear Wakspa and of our days on her beautiful prairies, about which she patiently taught me so much, and for which I shall ever be thankful indeed. The boat is about to go.

The Major joins me in sending best wishes to you and your husband, and in hoping you both will enjoy a long, happy, prosperous life.

Love,
Harriet Hatton

When Joe finished, he reached into his pocket and added, "She took this off at the last minute and said she wanted you to have it." He handed over an elaborate and ornate necklace of dull gold set with many large and small cut stones of dull red.

"My, my!" Cob said. "Must be wuth fo'ty dollahs. Ain't that a-purty!"

Less than a whole moon after the visit to Scalps Them, Red Hoop Woman, and the others Joe came back from one of his almost regular trips to Fort Keogh and brought Walks Far his second piece of bad news. Joe was angry about it and sad, for what he had to tell was terrible. Bearcoat Miles, Joe said, was in a way more angry than anyone else, first because of the simple injustice and stupidity of the orders sent him and, secondly, because the government in Washington had made a liar out of him. That would embarrass any man, and Bearcoat liked being embarrassed even less than most men. All the Sioux now on the Yellowstone were ordered to the lower Missouri—to Standing Rock!—of all the agencies the least inviting and most thoroughly detested.

Joe had seen how they took the bad news. With tears in their eyes, they had pointed to their growing crops and pleaded with anyone who would listen that they be allowed to stay in the fine Yellowstone country and to remain under army control.

But Bearcoat Miles could do nothing for them, Joe said. His soldiers had to round them all up, more than two thousand, and march them to the riverbank for loading on the five steamboats that came. Joe's heart, too, had been on the ground. The steamers had set off in a race to Standing Rock [on or about June 9, 1881]. The Oglalas would probably get there first. They were on the *Eclipse*. It looked like the fastest boat.

Walks Far would have none of the supper Cob fixed and tried to get her to eat. She felt much too sad. Not so strangely, Sun hid himself behind clouds for many days. She hated the world —the white man's world and everything about it. Yet she had observed that the world was not entirely the white man's. There was something else, a power, which Hat and Cob called civilization. The whites were a part of it, though it could treat some of them just as badly as it did Indians. Perhaps the whites weren't really so bad after all; perhaps they had known "civilization" for so long that they had learned they must do terrible things to get along with it.

The cloudy weather came to an end, and Walks Far rode east

a way one bright morning with Cob and Percy to help them start the horses they were taking to Fort Buford. As she turned back, Cob shouted that he would see her in about eight days. Those eight days passed, and more days, until Walks Far grew worried. The only news she heard from downriver was that Sitting Bull and about 150 people—the last except a very few who would never leave Saskatchewan—had come in to Fort Buford and surrendered. Some were sick. All were so poor in horses that Le Garé, the trader for whom Elk Hollering carried messages, had needed to send them in his carts. Le Garé hoped that either the Canadians or the Americans would pay him sometime, both for the carts and for all the food he had been giving to the Sioux for some time past.

Seventeen days and no word! Then, from the garden, Walks Far saw Joe riding up followed by his wife. She knew he brought a third message, and she felt afraid of what that message would be, but she had already half prepared herself for it. Joe and his wife quietly dismounted to come up to say in Sioux, "Walks Far Away Woman, let us go inside."

There Joe changed to their old Blackfoot tongue as he said, "I am sorry to have to bring you the worst news there is: Cob and Percy are both dead. They were murdered at their campfire on the first night of their way back here, or maybe the next morning. My chief scout, Yellow Hand, found them. Even though the animals had been at them, Yellow Hand knew one of those bodies had to be Cob's because of the very long bones. Yellow Hand gathered all the bones together and piled many stones over them. He got back here early this morning to tell me this. I am very sorry and I wish I could do something about it besides having to tell you more." Joe went on to say that Cob and Percy had been killed for nothing beyond their horses and guns, and perhaps a little pocket money. A redcoat captain had also ridden in this morning, and it was now known from him that the murderers had come from the west and had known nothing about the money Cob and Percy carried home from the sale of horses at Fort Buford.

The redcoat post east of Wood Mountain caught the murderers with Cob's and Percy's horses and guns—a young white man and a half-breed. After killing Cob and Percy, they had ridden up Big Muddy Creek across the Line into Saskatchewan. There they had foolishly tried to run away from a redcoat patrol, and had shot back at it. They had killed one of the redcoats, for which they would probably be hanged in Canada, Joe said.

He went on to say that the redcoats had found the name Colbert Piget carved into the stock of one of the guns. The name meant nothing to any of the Métis the redcoats asked. But a Canadian Assiniboin, one who often rode with Elk Hollering, came in from Fort Buford, where he had just been with Le Garé's carts and Sitting Bull's people. He saw the fine horses the redcoats had captured along with the murderers and remarked that he had seen one of those horses at the Touchwood Hills the summer before, and both of them at Fort Buford only a few days ago. They had belonged to an Indian and a half-breed who lived at Fort Peck. The half-breed's name was Cob Piget. Almost anyone who had ever been to Fort Peck would know about Cob Piget.

X. Biedler also happened to be here at Fort Peck, Joe said, and he and the redcoat captain were now talking. The two of them would come to talk with Walks Far after a while, and in time she would very likely be able to claim Cob's property and money from the redcoats, perhaps Percy's share too. Joe would help her.

The redcoat captain and X. Biedler came. They asked her many questions, hardly any of which she could answer, but it seemed extremely important to those men that they know all about Cob and where he had come from.

"Where was he born?"

"Don' know that."

"Where did he live before he came here?"

"Don' know that."

"Did he ever mention living relatives?"

"He don' say 'bout that."

Walks Far began to get mad. She told those two questioners, "Cob *dead*. Nobodies can do goddam thing 'bout that now."

Joe said, "You gentlemen are wastin' your time. Leave her alone!"

But she mourned Cob. She sat on the cabin floor with her shawl drawn over her face and let that terrible wailing that seemed to need no breath begin deep in her throat, then go on and on. And a part of her grief came from guilt, from the fear that she had not loved Cob as much as he had loved her, not as much as he deserved to be loved.

On the fourth morning she fixed herself a good breakfast, then gave away horses and other things in Cob's honor. But she kept Crazy One and the pinto Cob had given her, and also his two fastest horses. There was also the money that Cob always put away in a square tea can on the shelf with his spices. That can proved to hold four big gold pieces and some paper money. When Joe counted it, he showed surprise. He said it came to $317, and told her to put it all away inside her dress and keep it for a hard winter.

Three mornings later Walks Far rode out of Fort Peck with a party of people going westward up the Milk River valley to Fort Assinniboine. From there she would have no trouble in joining others traveling on to the Blackfoot country. She would search out her old band, find relatives. They would see her coming home a rich woman, with the finest tipi and the finest of horses.

She did not even think of selling the cabin. Her last act before she left early this morning had been to open the doors and windows, stack kindling inside each corner, and set it all ablaze. She sang a song for Cob as the cabin burned, and when the people who came running saw what she was doing, they sang with her. Now Walks Far believed she was riding away from Fort Peck forever. [More than sixty years later she was to sit silent beside Janet in a car that Dewey stopped beside Montana Highway 24 while he read aloud from an historical marker reminding travelers that here was the site of "Old Fort Peck." A way beyond lay that huge, quiet lake the *napikwan*, the *wasichu*, had made by damming the Big River.

"What do you think?" Dewey asked after a while.

"She's plenty change'. Lotsa thing all change'."

"For the worse or for the better?"

"Both," Walks Far said.]

She had ridden with the other people on the trail to Fort Assinniboine that morning only long enough to get well started before she heard a hurried rider overtaking them. Walks Far did not look back, but she saw Elk Hollering go past on a horse that looked as though it had been ridden all night. Elk Hollering stopped with the men ahead. They all dismounted and exchanged tobacco, sitting on the grass for a leisurely smoke and an exchange of news.

Walks Far had a hunch. Also, though she was given plenty of time, she felt as panicky as a gambler who cannot so much as guess the odds, yet must risk all or nothing within the next instant. At last Elk Hollering rode back to her, and she didn't believe her mind was yet made up.

"Walks Far Away Woman," he said in Blackfoot, "an Assiniboin in Canada has told me that your husband has been killed." Elk Hollering's voice sounded thin with exhaustion.

Walks Far waited awhile for him to say more, and when he did not do so, she merely answered, "That is true."

"When I heard this, I started riding," Elk Hollering said. "I have been riding for several days. I had been on the way north to my people."

"I can see that your strong horse is about played out," Walks Far told him.

Elk Hollering appeared to wait, then he said, "I have had one wife. I loved her very much, but she was killed. I remember her, but my spirit is no longer sick about it. Your spirit will not stay sick either."

Again he paused, then spoke almost angrily, in a kind of switch, to say, "I have told you that the grandfather of my father was a white man. Though I like very much to eat the things white men grow in gardens, I am not a white man. I am a Cree. I no longer work for Le Garé. I am going back to my brothers and my people. They have been pushed onto a reserve on the Battle River, near where it runs into the North Saskatchewan River. Poundmaker, the chief, is my 'brother.' He has sent a message that he will need me, and I am going. I am now a man without wealth." Elk Hollering said all this carefully, the last with a kind of defiance as he looked at her horse.

Walks Far told him, "I also am going back to my people."

Elk Hollering used a single English word angrily, "Goddamnit," then went back to Blackfoot in adding, "We are both alone."

Walks Far said nothing, and he suddenly blurted, running the syllables together into a single, long word, *"Matahk-witamapinipokemiosin!"* which may be translated as, "Not found is happiness without woman!"

Walks Far forgave him for putting it that way, for making it sound so one-sided. After all, he *was* a man, with only a man's point of view. But he was a man who strongly reminded her of much of the best in each of the husbands she had had—and, for some wholly indefinable reason, even of Singer. "Take one of my fresh horses," she said. "I will go with you."

Chapter Twenty-nine

THE BATTLE OF CUT KNIFE HILL

(Summer 1881 to Spring 1885)

Four years after riding away north together, a wary Walks Far
and Elk Hollering slipped across the Line into Montana at the
end of a dangerous six-day flight from the North Saskatchewan
River. They then turned west, and after two more long days of
hard riding they saw the Backbone of the World—which here
rose from the high prairie abruptly and without foothills—come
distantly into view.

Walks Far found Pikuni relatives and friends from her old
band. They made her welcome, sharing what little they now
had. She had been away for very nearly eleven years. Though
she returned fugitive as when she had fled afoot and alone from
another band, she now had a fine husband, and like him rode
one of the finest horses to be stolen in Saskatchewan. Around
Walks Far's neck, inside her dress, hung her Sun-stone, the ring
from the Little Bighorn, the necklace Hat had given her, and
three dollars left from Cob's tea can. Neither Walks Far nor Elk
Hollering now had their guns. They had surrendered them to
Canadian soldiers at the white man's stockade overlooking the
looted and partially burned town of Battleford eight days earlier. All of Poundmaker's Crees had gone there to surrender.

Walks Far and Elk Hollering had never suffered from hunger as many of the Crees had. Elk Hollering was a superb hunter and trapper for one thing, and he and Walks Far were extremely careful never to let the dogs get any bones from the animals he killed, lest the living animals be offended and deny themselves to his traps and gun. For another thing, Elk Hollering could work for white men. For quite a while during two summers Walks Far set up her lodge on the edge of Battleford, while Elk Hollering worked for a blacksmith. The blacksmith's English was so strange that even Elk Hollering needed to listen carefully. He was a fine and friendly big white man, but it shocked and bothered him that Elk Hollering and Walks Far had never been married in church. To them the idea did have a certain appeal. Many of the people had now remarried in a church, or were planning to.

These people received something called instruction and were given a sprinkling with water, after which they were made the center of a most impressive ceremony. They dressed as whites, provided they had enough money to buy the clothes. They then went to a mysterious room, dark and empty, and sat stiffly side by side on a bench to have their pictures taken. The man who took the pictures would loan them white persons' fine clothing for the upper part of their bodies if they hadn't been able to afford new clothes of their own.

Walks Far and Elk Hollering considered the matter at length, but they had no wish to become Christian. At last they spent a lot of the money from Cob's tea can to buy fine clothes and sit for the picture, asking for the largest size. When the picture was ready and tinted, they carried it in its huge oval frame to the blacksmith. "Gott bless you, mien frents," he said and instantly gave them two dollars. Walks Far and Elk Hollering were especially sorry when he happened to be one of the first whites to be killed by the Crees when the trouble came.

Walks Far and Elk Hollering might have lived out their lives in the growing restraint and deepening misery of the Cree reserve near Battleford, but the Crees were hardly a peaceful people. Whites swore that they were downright troublesome. The restraints of the new reservation life were almost more than their tradition as a free-roaming people would let them endure. Then the treaty rations, always poor and scant enough, were withheld from those who would not begin farming, which possibly appealed to Crees even less than it did to Sioux. Those

Crees who did sullenly pick up the hoe and plant crops saw them withered by drought. They had tried the hard way of the white man, the *wapiskias,* and nothing came of it, nothing but hunger and disease. The whites would not listen to Pound-maker's pleas. The Crees were fired by their own anger and it was fanned by a common feeling among all the northern tribes. The Crees said, "Kisei men'to, our high god, will not abandon us forever! The buffalo will come back, the *wapiskias* will be swept away." Walks Far knew the part about the buffalo coming back to be only foolish talk.

In Walks Far's third summer there [1884] some of the people gave their white farm instructor a very bad beating, and when the redcoats came to arrest them, a battle nearly started. Even the wise and cautious Poundmaker was getting into a fighting mood.

It was easy to see that the many Métis here were growing equally angry. As former buffalo hunters, they were now as bad off as were the Indian people. As farmers, the first in the valleys of the Saskatchewan, they feared their land would be taken from them, for there had been no surveys before the whites came crowding in. Also, they wanted to be heard in government councils, have schools for their children. Surveyors came, but only in a few cases did they pay attention to the Métis custom of occupying the land in long narrow strips running back from the rivers. Whites pointed to stakes that now marked off the land into big squares, and in some cases took portions that the Métis had used for years. Even the whites cursed the government in the East, for they too wanted schools, and the railroad being built across Canada was passing them by for a shorter route in empty country far to the south, leaving them no way to sell their crops.

Of the three unhappy peoples in the valleys of the Saskatche-wan rivers, only the Métis had a plan, an idea, rather, for they knew where to find a leader who knew how to plan. He was one of themselves, one of their "new race," but he had been schooled for the priesthood. He could read, write and speak better than most whites and he could have passed for a white man anywhere. His name was Louis Riel. All people would remember him, for fifteen years earlier he had led the Manitoba Métis in a resistance which won them most of what they wanted. He had made the government listen. But he had spent much of the time since in bitter exile in the United States and was now teaching in a mission school no farther away then the Sun River, west of Fort Benton in Montana.

To many whites as well as Métis, Louis Riel appeared to be their man. Both peoples gave money for a Métis delegation led by Gabriel Dumont, who rode down to Montana and brought him back in mid-1884. [Perhaps no one in Saskatchewan then knew that Riel had spent nearly two years in a Quebec insane asylum and had become a religious fanatic increasingly lost to his religious fantasies.]

At first, he was welcomed nearly everywhere to make speeches and help write petitions, but by fall he had badly frightened the whites and some of the Métis, for he was forming a Métis government and also declaring that the Church must be reborn among the Métis people. A certain bishop at St. Albert here in the country was to be the new Pope. Missionary and other priests were soon saying freely that Louis Riel was a crazy man.

Also, by late fall Walks Far and Elk Hollering knew that every Indian band on the western prairies as far south as the Missouri River had been visited by Métis riders and had heard their message: This whole country is the natural home of Indians and half-breeds, who, therefore, ought to have it back. The whites should be driven out. The white man's cattle now eating the grass should belong to the Indians, for it was the whites who had killed off the buffalo, leaving the Indians hungry. Louis Riel, who once before, in Manitoba, had shown that the whites could be successfully resisted, came back again to help his Métis people. They would have a government and a country for themselves and for all the prairie Indians. If war came, that great Métis buffalo hunter and fighting chief, Gabriel Dumont, would surely wipe out the redcoats.

Elk Hollering told Walks Far, "The whites will soon know all about what the Métis are doing. Very likely they know already. Also, I do not wholly trust the Métis, for when there is trouble they too often remember the white part of themselves and do not listen to the Indian part."

With winter word came that five hundred new redcoats were on their way into the country, coming west as far as the iron road would bring them before they began a northward march. The news sent Métis horsemen riding into the empty prairies on a snowy night to cut the talking wires in many places. Louis Riel himself helped loot white men's stores of guns and take

hostages. War had begun. The thoughtful, cautious Poundmaker found that his people would not stay out of it, not when
Hudson's Bay Company posts could be taken almost at will.

Walks Far and Elk Hollering had no part in the early looting
and burning at Battleford and in the country all around. While
the whites took refuge in a stockade at Battleford and learned
what it was like to grow hungry and watch their houses go up
in smoke, Walks Far and Elk Hollering were off in the late
winter cold on a five-day ride far to the southwest into Alberta,
over the snowy and empty country to the upper Bow River.
Poundmaker had sent them with a message to Crowfoot. She
and Elk Hollering would not be complete strangers there. And
by odd circumstance Poundmaker was the adopted son of
Crowfoot.

They were to say that as Crowfoot would no doubt already
know, war on the Saskatchewan rivers had begun. Gabriel Dumont had defeated redcoats. Poundmaker could hardly avoid
being caught up in the war, which would be won more surely
and sooner if Crowfoot came to help. Poundmaker wished to
know how his father felt about it. Also, he wished his father to
know that he would not be able to come for the usual visit late
in the Green Grass Time.

Walks Far was to make an even faster ride with Elk Hollering,
but never a colder one. Frost ringed their horses' nostrils all the
way. She was surprised and saddened at the sight of Crowfoot's
camp, at the small wintry fields that revealed attempts at farming, at the poorly built log cabins that mingled either with
tattered canvas lodges or with ones of worn-out buffalo hide.
When Crowfoot greeted Elk Hollering, Walks Far could see
that he was a sick man, and she soon learned that all his remaining children were dying of the bloody cough.

Crowfoot welcomed news of his adopted son. He clearly sym-
pathized with the Crees and the Métis. Also, he spoke angrily
of the way his own Blackfoot people were treated, especially
concerning a recent substitution of detested bacon for a part of
the fresh beef rations. Crowfoot's heart yearned to help Poundmaker, but the government had taken him last summer to the
cities in the East. He had seen countless whites, their power. He
would do all he might for his people, but he was determined
that they should survive. A war with the whites would destroy
them utterly.

Walks Far and Elk Hollering were still in Crowfoot's lodge,

along with several others, when an important redcoat arrived. Crowfoot, using a white *winkte* interpreter who dressed like a blackrobe, talked politely with the redcoat about nothing much. Suddenly, the redcoat pointed rudely at Elk Hollering to say, "That man is a Cree. I have seen him before."

Crowfoot laughed as though at a good joke. "You are right about that," he said. "He is a henpecked Cree who is married to that Pikuni woman over there," and he laughed again.

Walks Far saw Elk Hollering scowl and flush darkly. She knew that he was not acting, that Crowfoot's clever answer had touched him as being a little too near the truth. The redcoat grinned and forgot the matter.

Walks Far and Elk Hollering rode back to the River People Reserve and delivered Crowfoot's regretful reply. Poundmaker's disappointment was somewhat balanced by word of Cree and Métis successes. Big Bear's Crees had risen to surprise and kill many of the whites at Frog Lake. Big Bear was now leading them toward the Mounted Police and Hudson's Bay men at Fort Pitt.

Then, along with more redcoat police, many soldiers came into the country, the first ever seen in the Canadian West. Walks Far, surprised from her bed, fired fourteen cartridges from her carbine at some of them, on a spring morning filled with the smell of poplar trees still newly leafed. She and Elk Hollering, away from their cabin on the reserve for safety's sake, had been asleep in their lodge, pitched with all the others on Cut Knife Creek behind Cut Knife Hill. They had wakened to shots, to the realization that soldiers were attacking their camp from just forward of the grassy hilltop.

Walks Far did not run for the brush with the other women and the children. She had her carbine and sixteen cartridges, and she stayed to fight. She saw the soldiers in their very strange uniforms come part way down the forward face of the hill, then appear to discover that they might be in a trap, that coulees or ravines filled with leafing poplar brush reached up and around their hilltop like the fingers of two hands held for grasping, and that the Crees would soon be around them on three sides.

Walks Far fired a shot as Elk Hollering fired his Winchester. Elk Hollering suddenly saw she was there. *"Neah!—'Go!'"* he yelled at her. She grinned at him, and he gave her a rare grin back. Walks Far felt a kind of excitement under the whistling bullets, and she found her eyes suddenly possessing an intense and peculiar clarity of sight. She lost all sense of time. Also, as she knew afterward, her memory of events came mostly in bright patches, some arranged in an order that she would later know to be impossible.

Luckily for them, the soldiers drawing back found a shallow swale atop the grassy hill. They began firing their three big guns. There was a strange new one that was terrifying at first. It sprayed thousands of bullets so fast that the individual shots could hardly be heard. But those bullets all seemed to fly high overhead, and most of the time they were aimed at the empty lodges anyhow. The two muzzle-loading big guns were far worse in their effect.

Poundmaker was a truly great chief. He had loaned his rifle to someone, yet seemed to be everywhere, carrying only a quirt, so self-possessed that he might have been calmly advising a bunch of boys how best to close round and grab the rope of a dangerously kicking wild horse. Walks Far felt proud that no one here appeared to have run from those big guns, and she was surprised to find that she, like the men, had moved closer to them in her shooting! She was brave! She had never heard of any Indians being able to face big guns before this. Elk Hollering even led a charge on one, though the charge failed.

She found herself watching the hilltop from far up one of the bushy ravines. She had no idea which one, for she could not remember having moved, yet she was very close to the soldiers and could hear their grunting curses. She seemed to have gone past the big guns, which now seemed to fire only at long intervals. One of them appeared to have blown itself off its wheels. That was what the soldiers were swearing about as they tried to get it back on. A soldier's voice called out calmly, "Steady, lads, don't let them close in on ye. And remember to aim low, downhill." Another voice, far less calm, shouted, "Alec, you stupid barstard, are you tryin' to shoot *me!*"

Elk Hollering's eyes were fixed on the crest above. A soldier's rifle muzzle appeared. An absurd little hat grew slowly behind it. Elk Hollering fired, the soldier jerked higher, screamed, and fell back out of sight. He must have turned belly up, for Walks Far saw one of his arms reach flounderingly into the air for an instant. He stopped screaming, but sobbed on and on. . . . Bullets passing through leaves overhead made an odd sound.

Abruptly the soldiers withdrew. They took the big guns with them and fought their way safely back between the warriors who by now had them almost pinched off. They took nearly all their dead with them, too. Poundmaker said, "Let them go, those soldiers now know how Crees will defend themselves."

Unbelievably, the sun stood a little past noon! Walks Far suddenly felt tired. She had not eaten a bite, and was reminded that she had never emptied her bladder that morning. She trotted off to a ravine again, and as she entered the brush, a lost young soldier, half sobbing with fright, almost bumped into her. They stared at each other for an instant before a helpful Walks Far pointed over his shoulder and said in English, "That way. Stay in coulee."

"Oh!" he said. "Thank you. Thank you very much."

[The Battle of Cut Knife Hill was fought on June 2, 1885, very much as Walks Far related it. A force of more than three hundred troops and a few Northwest Mounted Police, supported by two once condemned muzzle-loading cannon and a Gattling gun (a multibarreled, fast-firing precursor of the machine gun), were defeated by perhaps little more than two thirds their number in Crees, few of whom possessed up-to-date weapons.]

The people danced and celebrated their victory. The Métis begged for help in defending their stronghold at far away Batoche against the gathering soldiers. Though Poundmaker and the whole band set out, making a wide swing southward to avoid settled country, and lit many prairie fires to distract and impede the enemy, they went so slowly that they never got to Batoche. Perhaps the insightful Poundmaker concluded that, despite his success at Cut Knife Hill, the numberless soldiers would win the war in the end, and he saw no point in getting his people killed along with the Métis defending Batoche. Moreover, there were many distractions on their way. One day in particular was memorable to Walks Far. The warriors came upon more than twenty army wagons and captured them all, with most of the teamsters. The wagons were found to be loaded with both feed for horses and an unbelievable quantity of things for making a soldier's life pleasant. Later the same day Elk Hollering and others drove off a party of redcoat scouts, wounding one and killing another. Elk Hollering's best horse was killed under him. There was great dancing that night, with pauses to eat the good, sweet things sent the soldiers. Even the captured white teamsters enjoyed themselves. One of them played his violin while another played a melodeon and sang. Walks Far danced with the melodeon player.

Next morning Poundmaker learned that many soldiers had taken Batoche three days before. The poorly armed Métis, under Gabriel Dumont, had held them off for four hard-fought days. Soon it was known that though Louis Riel had escaped he had surrendered, though Gabriel Dumont was gone without trace. Poundmaker thought things over for only a day or two, then sent all the captives to Battleford. One of these released captives, a blackrobe, carried a letter he had written for Poundmaker to ask the general's surrender terms.

Walks Far heard the answer: There would be no terms. The general said he had enough soldiers either to destroy Poundmaker's band or drive them away to starve. Sad days followed, days of much talk, during which Poundmaker said almost nothing. He gave the people time to face up to the choice of surrendering in order to stay alive, for a while at least. Walks Far and Elk Hollering thought of slipping away and taking their chances, but they would not desert Poundmaker at such a time. They went back with the people to Battleford for the surrender, Poundmaker riding at their head. Walks Far hid her knife inside her clothing, but got into line behind Elk Hollering and handed over the carbine she'd carried for ten years, from near the North Platte River to here on the North Saskatchewan. Soldiers pointed at her, laughed, and said bad things. The soldier who took her gun read her name aloud from the side of the stock where Cob had carved it, and was then inspired to say, "Why! You ain't a half-bad looker, are you! Why don't you an' me take a little walk far enough away, all by ourselves, 'bout dark?"

"Hell, Keith," another one said, "You ain't even been in this goddam country three months yet, an' you're already thinkin' these squaws look white!"

"Shit! You throw any female woman's skirts up over their faces an' you won't see nothin' different from what you're used to."

"Shit on you too! What I heard, it's crossways on these squaws, just like on a Chinese woman!"

One of the captive wagon drivers, with whom Walks Far had danced, stood watching. He told those soldiers, "For shame. Ye should drop dead for shame," then shook his head about them.

The general, a white-moustached rounded man, came out to sit in a chair resting on the ground in front of the stockade. A bearded interpreter joined him. Behind them stood many lesser soldier chiefs, each in a different uniform. Poundmaker sat on the ground before the general, his elderly councillors sitting close, the other people sitting or standing in a semicircle. Poundmaker calmly smoked his pipe.

Walks Far sat with Elk Hollering, nearly among the councillors. She felt sad, especially humiliated for Elk Hollering at having to see him give up his Winchester. She no longer much cared what happened now; she felt little interest in listening. But almost as soon as the talking started, she began to get *really* mad. She and the other people *had not* been attacking the queen! They were only fighting the government, which let them starve. They had tried many times to let the queen know what the government was doing to them. Walks Far, in her cabin on the reserve, still had the picture Hat had done in watercolors, and it was hung directly below a picture of the queen! Walks Far admired the queen and felt sorry for her—a sad little woman who looked like she had had too many babies and no end of worries.

Walks Far heard the general insulting Poundmaker as though trying to make him mad, asking him questions in a sarcastic way. But Poundmaker only smoked his pipe and gave half-bored-sounding answers that made the general puff and almost stutter. Walks Far, from the English she knew, thought the interpreter could not have done better. It struck Walks Far that he might be enjoying the things Poundmaker said to the general.

That general tried to accuse Poundmaker of every bad thing any Indian had done in the fighting. "You are a great and powerful chief," the general said with obvious sarcasm. "Why did you not stop those things? the looting and burning, the pointless, plain murdering?"

Poundmaker shrugged and spoke mildly, "I am not a person who would want anyone to do things like that, or let such things happen. Moreover, I am very surprised to be now regarded as a chief. When I came as a chief to ask the government for food for my hungry people, no one would listen to me, not then!"

The general let some of Poundmaker's councillors and others stand and make speeches. These speeches nearly all began with the killing off of the buffalo and went on through the long tale of hunger and indignities suffered ever since. Each new speaker covered much the same ground, carefully filling in details that the previous speaker had failed to mention or dwell upon. This went on until the general clearly grew tired of it, and when a man said his mother now wanted to speak, the general held up his hand to say, "We don't listen to women."

Walks Far's voice came instantly loud and clear as she shouted at that general in her best English, "Don' you never listen to queen!"

Other women began to shout and scream, with everyone talking at once. The general was finally able to have the interpreter say that the council was over, that everyone could go back to their reserves—all except Poundmaker and four of his subchiefs, whose names were called out. They must stay to be arrested. Walks Far was chilled. She knew that even if those five were not hanged, they would still be sent to prison and inevitably die there. [Walks Far was to learn that Poundmaker did not die in prison, where the authorities made an exception in not cutting his hair and in allowing him to send a telegram to Crowfoot, his adopted father. He was released after serving but six months of a three-year sentence. Then, on a visit to Crowfoot, he was served saskatoon berry soup. Remarking that a medicine man had warned him to avoid this dish, he declared he would take a chance, but as he began to sip he choked violently, burst a blood vessel and died.

Louis Riel, the articulate and often eloquent Métis leader of the tragic rebellion, was tried for treason but destroyed his distinguished lawyer's efforts to demonstrate that he was deranged. He insisted on taking the stand himself and doing his best to show his own sanity and thus strengthen the force of his final plea for the Métis cause. Though the foreman of the jury was moved to tears, Riel was found guilty, but with a recommendation for mercy that was not accepted. He was hanged at Regina on a bright morning in November 1885.

The general at whom Walks Far had shouted was to have his career ruined by a stubborn, non-rebel Métis trapper who had been taken captive by Poundmaker along with his winter's catch of furs. These furs were confiscated at the time of the surrender and soon simply appropriated by the general and two or three other officers. In the course of five years the trapper was able to have the general branded as a thief by the Canadian House of Commons. Walks Far never knew of the ultimate irony: The queen she admired so much gave the disgraced general employment as Keeper of the Crown Jewels in the Tower of London.]

She and Elk Hollering had not yet started a long ride back to

326

the reserve when a young warrior stealthily warned Elk Hollering that soldiers were looking for him. They had his name on a paper and were stopping all people to ask where he was. It was a very long story, but Walks Far and Elk Hollering kept away from their horses and out of sight until after dark. For a time they lay hidden beneath a bridge the soldiers had built across the Battle River where it ran through the town. When the darkness came at last, but before the night got too quiet, Walks Far and Elk Hollering slipped out and had almost no trouble at all helping themselves to a fine pair of the soldiers' horses. Not until dawn did anything prove wrong; those horses were *much* too good, too perfectly matched to be ridden by an Indian couple who wished to invite no attention as they slipped out of a country crawling with redcoats and soldiers.

Early the second morning of the flight Walks Far saw Coyote waiting. "Well, Walks Far Away Woman," he said with his familiar teasing grin, "You look as though you were heading for home. I know this to be about the fourth time you have had to run and leave things you treasure behind. But I am pretty sure nothing like that is going to happen to you any more. Though things will still look bad, they will get better after a while."

Walks Far was happy to hear this, but she needed to ask, "When?"

"Perhaps not until what you call the fourth generation has come along. *They* can't kill either of us off as they did the buffalo. Pretty soon they will find there are more of both of us than ever!"

"Woman!" Elk Hollering said, "You know you should not talk to yourself aloud and in a strange voice while riding. Your horse will go deaf and cross-eyed."

Walks Far and Elk Hollering found misery among the Blackfoot such as to show them that reservation life was very much the same on either side of the Line and that the whole world in which they had both grown up was come to an end within the past ten years, or less. Two years ago, Walks Far heard, the Blackfoot had taken all of six buffalo! She heard also how a man named Almost a Dog had kept a notched-stick tally of the people starving to death the winter following. The stick showed more than 550 notches, nearly one in four of all the Pikuni Blackfoot tribe.

Now Walks Far saw the starving Pikuni building dirt-roofed log cabins and dwelling miserably apart, trying to live on the scant treaty rations while they attempted to farm. A cousin told her bitterly, "Some are so hungry that they eat their dogs and even their horses. Some eat the potatoes given them for seed, and the cattle given them to start a herd. Children have big bellies, some go blind, others die of the bloody cough."

Walks Far heard that Crees, Plains Chippewas, and Plains Ojibwas, who lacked even dwindling reservations, lived by begging in the Montana camps and towns, by scavenging from the town dumps near where their lodges had been set up, and by eating offal from the white man's slaughterhouses.

Walks Far and Elk Hollering would not do that. Also, they had had all they ever wanted of reservation life. They understood each other so well that they needed to talk very little about the matter. Elk Hollering said, "I do not much want to farm, but neither do I want to starve. The Métis in Saskatchewan had some fine farms and, except for that farming, they lived pretty much in their own way."

"You are right about that," Walks Far agreed. "I have been thinking that maybe we ought to find out how to get some land for farming and raising white man's cattle, also that we must not give away our names and let them put us on the reservation, though we should be near our Indian people."

Elk Hollering heard that a few Indians earned money in a strange way. Well to the south of the Blackfoot reservation, the iron road ran all across Montana. [The final gap in the Northern Pacific Railway had been closed near Helena, Montana, in the latter part of 1883.] The *napikwan* were thereby enabled to take away even the bones of the buffalo! The *napikwan* paid Indians to help put those bones in wagons and haul them to the iron road.

But Walks Far had heard of something else. Jack Sinclair, the people said, had somehow come to own nearly the whole country. The white man's cattle now grazing the buffalo grass in thousands were his. If some person pleaded starvation, Jack Sinclair would probably butcher a steer for him for old time's sake, but woe to any Indian who butchered one of those steers for himself. He might find himself in bad trouble with *ninana* —our "father," the agent. As for some white men who had stolen Jack Sinclair's cattle, you could see them hanging by the neck from cottonwood trees on a certain creek. Men who worked for Jack Sinclair had hung them there as a kind of offering to sun and winds.

No, Jack Sinclair's Cree wife had died. The children were grown, or else away somewhere most of the time, but he now had another wife, one who had come to teach the school on his ranch. Walks Far decided to go see Jack Sinclair, and a day later she was waiting for him well before dawn, as near his house as she dared ride without rousing the dogs. After a time she saw windows forming squares of yellow lamplight, and she waited while they paled. He came out then, and by the time he re-

329

turned from the privy, she was at the back door to meet him, wearing the knife. He was still slim and handsome.

"*Ok-yeh!*—'Welcome!'" he said, using a term that could be playfully formal, yet was also a common greeting between friends. Then he added, still in Blackfoot, "*Kai-yo?*—'What gives?' I wondered when you might show up around here again," so that Walks Far was sure now that he recognized her. And he hurried on, "That is a very good horse you are riding. I can see that he has done some hard traveling lately." Jack Sinclair sat down on the porch step and eyed the horse.

"Yes," Walks Far said, "He is a white soldier chief's horse from Saskatchewan. My husband has one exactly like him. We were with Poundmaker in the fighting. My husband was going to have to go to prison, but we got away and took horses. My husband is a half-Pikuni, half-Cree, and we have now come back here to stay. But we do not want to live on the reservation."

"I have just heard that Gabriel Dumont has also made it here to Montana," Jack Sinclair said, then added thoughtfully, "You and your husband had better not do much more riding around for a while, not on horses like those—not on the reservation or off. Maybe you ought to let me trade you out of them—or is that what you came to see me about this fine morning?"

Walks Far knew he was letting her know that he knew she had come to ask for something.

"No," she said. "I think maybe you are right about trading horses, but that is not what I have come to see you about. I have come to have you give me some land—"

Jack Sinclair was startled into English, "The hell you say!" but he returned to Blackfoot to ask, "Is that all! Just how much of it would you like to have?"

"Enough for a farm and for raising some cattle that I also want to have you give me—enough to start."

Jack Sinclair's face was swept by a swift smile, then he fixed his gaze on something far off and whistled through his teeth before speaking. "Walks Far Away Woman, there are some things you should know: I actually *own* but a very little of this land, with most of it in sight from right here. I do not *really* own the cattle, either. There is something called a bank mortgage. There is another something called a cattle company. And I could not even pay these cowpunchers from Texas and Oregon who are working for me if I did not belong to that company and have its money to use. Do you understand what I am saying?"

Walks Far understood well enough. The *napikwan* always had a way of sidestepping things, of always talking about some distant power that an ordinary person could never quite reach. Yet at the same time that power had a way of easily and quickly reaching down to a certain person, with no trouble at all! She was ready to accept that Jack Sinclair, like so many mixed-bloods, took refuge in the white side of his heritage when pressed. He was no longer Siksikakwan, or "Blackfoot Man"; he was now just a *napikwan*, ALL *napikwan*.

But she heard him speaking again, and she heard him say, "I think we can get you some land, all right." And he smiled as he added, "We will make a 'tax-paying Indian' out of your husband. What is his name? Can he speak any English?"

Walks Far demonstrated her own English, as usual having trouble with the *b*, *l*, and *r* sounds, saying, "Him name Elk Hollering. Him speak more better."

"Good!" Jack Sinclair said, still in English. "Can he grow a fair moustache? If he has braids, he'd better cut them off. And we ought to get him a suit of clothes for when we go to register the land. And I've known him all his life, haven't I? Known for a fact that he was born right here in Montana. Do you understand all that?"

Walks Far went back to Blackfoot as she said, "Yes, I understand. Elk Hollering can grow hair on his face. He already looks something like a white man. His father's grandfather was a Scotch trader. He has worked for a blacksmith. And he will cut off his braids." [Walks Far told Janet Sinclair, "When they gone, I cry, but not let Elk Hollering see."]

"He should take a white man's name," Jack Sinclair said. "We can call him Tom McKay. That is a name both the Pikuni and the Crees can say with no trouble, and it is a good name."

Walks Far saw a white woman peer impatiently from a small window beside the back door, a stern-looking, still young woman with nearly black hair and very blue eyes. Those eyes were as blue as the blue-painted window frame let into the log wall of the fine, big house. Jack Sinclair, though it was hard to believe he could have seen her even from the corner of his eye, shouted in English, "Just a minute, Jeanie."

Walks Far hurried to tell Jack Sinclair, "I want also for you to let me have a team of mules for a while when we are ready to build a log cabin on the land. Strong mules, with harness, and a wagon. And I would like two of those blue windows for the cabin, and a good stove. Also, Elk Hollering will need a gun for hunting the deer, antelope, and sheep. For all these things, I have something for mortgage, something besides the two fine horses, which you may keep while you loan me two others."

She took the ring from the bag at her neck to show him. He examined it half disbelievingly, saying, "You did not get this when you got those horses!"

"No. I have had it a long time."

"Since that day I saw you on the Little Bighorn?"

"Yes."

"Walks Far Away Woman, I must tell you that this sparkling stone is surely a very valuable diamond, and that these green stones are probably emeralds, which together may be worth about as much as the diamond, or maybe more. Anyway, that ring is probably worth *two* teams of mules, with harness, with wagons, *and* blue windows and a stove. You must keep that ring for both of us, for some winter of bad times. But you can bring Elk Hollering here, and we will see whether he thinks he is too good to do white man's work—digging postholes for a new corral."

"He will come," Walks Far said. "And he will dig those holes. He has worked for a blacksmith. And he needs a Winchester rifle."

The blue-eyed woman jerked the door open and spoke sharply, "John! Your breakfast is getting cold!" Nothing in her manner suggested any awareness that Walks Far was there.

"All right," Jack Sinclair said in English, "we were just about to come in. Jeanie, this is Walks Far Away Woman—Mrs. Elk Hollering McKay. I think I told you about her once. We're going to give her some land and a team of mules. Walks Far, this is my wife."

"How! Do! Please!" Walks Far said, and saw that Jeanie was pregnant.

"I'm pleased to meet you, Mrs. McKay Hollering Elk," Jeanie managed to say. Clearly, she was surprised to be formally introduced to an Indian woman, and much more so to be entertaining one at breakfast. She had probably been doing her best for some time to forget that Jack Sinclair had once been a "squaw man," was himself a mixed-blood.

Jack Sinclair was saying to Walks Far, in Blackfoot, "You know that it is the white man's way for the men and women to eat together, and I can promise you that fried eggs will not give you boils."

332

"John!" Jeanie exclaimed, "Don't tell me this is the one who saved your life, that time on the Little Bighorn?"

"Yup. She's the one."

"And now she's come to collect . . . land and mules! . . . for saving your life?" Jeanie seemed either unaware or indifferent that Walks Far might understand English.

"No, no," Jack Sinclair told her in the tones of a man having to explain something that anyone should easily understand. "It's because *I* probably saved *her* life, before then."

"But, John! *That* doesn't make sense."

"Well, it does to her. And I guess it does to me. Anyhow, because she did save my life once, she could be a kind of insurance for me, too, come a bad winter. But let's quit talking about that. As we Pikuni say, *ahk-so-yope*—'let's eat.' What do you say, Walks Far?"

To Walks Far her visit here this morning had brought such promise that she could not think of misfortune. She answered with a single Blackfoot exclamation—something like *"itamapi!"* It expressed her deep contentment, along with happy expectation.

Chapter Thirty-one
WHEN THE BUTTERFLY LIT

(A Sunny Day in 1946, Summer 1947,
and Eleven Years More)

On a bright Sunday morning in September, sixty-one years after
Walks Far ate that breakfast, Janet Sinclair and Dewey Elk
Hollering climbed high up Packsaddle Butte above the fallen
rocks and thinning pines. Dewey paused and pointed down to
a low shoulder of the butte where, among the thicker pines,
trees had been newly felled and sawed into short lengths. "She's
gonna be ver' bad winter we had," he said. "I seen how that ol'
white man she's chop 'im plenty wood."

Janet laughed in spite of herself, shook her head sadly, and
said, "Dewey Elk Hollering! You are absolutely hopeless." She
noted, not for the first time this morning, his curious persistence
in speaking like some unschooled young Blackfoot, and vaguely
she wondered why.

"Girl she's look at me lak you done for calling me bad name
twice a sometams she's okay." Dewey said, "Okay because I
knowed I got plenty hope." He kissed her. "Let's get going," he
said. "How's your wind and legs? How tough are you? Not just
your wind and legs, but when ol' trouble she's come for somebodies and your fist can't hardly hold 'im." And with that he
turned and struck off up the steep side of the butte toward the
eastern of its two peaks.

Minutes later, when they fell together into the tiny patch of grass within the saucer-shaped depression among the rocks at the very top, Janet's legs tingled, and she was not breathing easily. Still, she was no more winded than Dewey appeared to be. He took the army canteen from the grain sack that also contained apples and sandwiches, and when they had both drunk, he lay back on the grass and pulled his hat over his eyes. "Roll us a coupla smokes," he said.

Janet took the Bull Durham and papers from his shirt pocket and, with the deftness he had taught her, she made his cigarette. She fitted it between his lips but left it unlighted until she finished her own. "Sit up, stupid," she told him then. "You'll burn yourself."

"No, light it," he insisted, then added, "I've been looking some more at that catalogue they sent me from Washington State College. I'm sure glad I had you to tell me what a lot of it meant. I never could have figured out those 'group requirements,' or those 'term hours'—stuff like that. And I took the application to town and mailed it on the way to pick you up this morning."

"I wish we could be going to the same school," Janet said, then urged, "Come on. Sit up. You didn't bring me up here to watch you lie there with your hat over your eyes, did you? You can see our whole country from here—your place and my place and the town. I think I can just see the mountains in Glacier Park, and over there I can see two rivers running toward the Missouri. Look. We're right in the middle of the whole beautiful country, with the whole world all around us."

"I've seen it," he said. "I was sitting right here for four whole days last spring, and I watched every damned light that came on for four long nights."

"Four nights!" Janet exclaimed, "Whatever were—"

But Dewey was going on as though she had not spoken. "Lemme tell you a story," he said. "I guess that's why I brought you up here, to tell you a story before we both go away this fall."

He lay relaxed, and with the hat still over his eyes. But a kind of intensity seemed to hold him as he stubbed out his cigarette and began, "When I got out of the army and came home here, I couldn't get to feelin' right about anything. Spent half the time drinkin' beer. Between times I felt so low I even missed the army. Anyhow, I guess I began to think I wasn't Indian enough, or something, because I got the real, old-time religion. Went to all the sings and dances, went down around Heart Butte and paid for old men to open their medicine bundles. And I spent so much time crawlin' in and out of sweat lodges that I got calluses on my knees."

Janet kept quiet the way she did when she'd hear Walks Far drawing close to some dramatic memory.

"Pretty soon," Dewey continued, "I decided I'd go someplace for dreamin', like the old men did when they were young, dreamin' a spirit helper came, givin' them good medicine, a spirit helper for the rest of their lives. So, I drove out and hid the old pickup down there, and climbed up here. I built a little fire there where the rocks are black. I purified myself with smoke and fasted for four days—nothing but this canteen of water and two little boxes of those Sun Maid raisins. I offered Sun big pieces of red and blue cloth with tobacco tied on, and I prayed to Sun, Moon, Morning Star, and Earth.

"I sat here in just moccasins and breechclout, showing Sun my face for four whole days, prayin' for dreams to bring my spirit helper. But the only sign I got was sunburn. At night I shivered in the old blanket I'd brought, too cold for sleepin' and dreamin'."

Janet imagined Dewey sitting there, and her own skin seemed to feel the blistering sun and the night's chill wind.

"Anyhow," Dewey was saying, "nothing like a spirit came, not any kind of animal or bird. I gave up. Didn't even see a hawk or a meadowlark or a coyote all the way home—nothing except for runnin' into your dad just as I got back to the pickup. When I got home, I ate all the breakfasts, dinners, and suppers I'd missed, all rolled into one. I ate like a starving Cree—hotcakes and eggs, and meat and grease bread, with lots of cake and canned peaches. I couldn't hardly go in and lie down. Then did I sleep! Then did I dream! The butterfly really lit. Of course, it was only a crazy kind of sleepin' dream, but I couldn't get it out of my mind. I don't think I ever dreamed in colors before."

Janet waited for him to go on, and when he held silent, she lifted his hat away.

"It was mixed up and crazy," Dewey said. He closed his eyes in concentration. "I heard the butterfly that brings sleep and good dreams talking to me, and I seemed to be back up here. He said I must be careful and not wake up. He was a beautiful butterfly, with blue and white wings filling half the sky. I recognized his face. It was a good old man I know, one named Spitting Black Bones. He looked young, but he still talked like an old man. Suddenly he disappeared, and I could see a girl coming toward me. She came down a long hall that had green steel lockers along the walls. She was wearing a dark blue dress covered with little flecks of white. It had a bright red silk tie that came all the way down to the hem of her skirt, and she had red shoes and a shiny red billfold to match."

Janet had not forgotten that dress. She had liked it so much that she had worn it far too often.

"Then," Dewey was saying, "we were both back up here. The girl sat down on the grass right there where I'd built the little fire. She smiled at me and began to take a lot of big dead frogs out of her billfold—frogs and dissecting knives, a long enameled tray, lab manuals and notebooks. She said to me, 'If you'll cut up all these icky frogs, I'll do everything else. And we'll try to make sure they let us stay partners all year.'"

Again, Dewey fell silent, until Janet asked, "What then?"

"That was all there was to it, just a crazy, mixed-up, screwy, sleepin' dream," Dewey said, but he reached an arm up suddenly and drew her head fiercely against his chest, holding it there pressed down hard as he added swiftly, "But I can't help thinkin' maybe you'd be my spirit helper anyhow."

"Oh, yes," she said. "And not just your spirit helper. You should know by now that I'm not what you'd call all that spiritual."

Dewey hurried to say, "It's gonna be tough, the two of us bein' who we are."

"For heavensake! Don't you suppose I already decided I was that tough, weeks ago?"

The moment Dewey arrived home from his triumph, and before he had so much as spoken, the delighted Walks Far read the signs. Without a word, she immediately took the ring she had worn inside her dress strung around her neck for all those seventy years since that bloody Sunday afternoon on the Little Bighorn and handed it to him.

Later, when Janet and Dewey took the ring to have a jeweler reduce the finger size, they discovered it had little intrinsic value except for the old gold it contains. Though it is a high-quality antique, the gems are artificial. Of course Janet and Dewey did not let Walks Far know this.

During their summer vacation the next year, Janet and Dewey, with Walks Far riding between them in a nearly new pickup truck, drove generally southeast across Montana to a fair and rodeo the Crows held annually on their reservation. It was a gathering of Indian people from all the surrounding states and provinces, and from farther away.

The back of the pickup carried camping gear, most of it modern except for a well-used stove, homemade from an inverted galvanized washtub and three lengths of stovepipe. The folded canvas lodge, or tipi, was neither very old nor very new. As a common present-day solution to the problem of how to drag around "them goddam poles," Dewey had fashioned an angle-iron rack rising from front and rear bumper. Still, the poles were considerably longer than the pickup, and the solution was less than ideal.

After sunset, as they approached the campsite with its many tipis already standing on the grassy flat along a tree-bordered stream, they were signaled to a stop. A huge-chested, young crew-cut Indian with a very large old silver medal showing within the collar of his sport shirt came up with clipboard in hand. "Hi," he said. "I see you brought a tipi. I'll assign you a place, but I need your names and tribal affiliation, if any. You're gonna have to hurry to get set up before dark. And put your pickup in the parking lot, as soon as you're unloaded."

Janet wakened in a chill, bright dawn to the stir of early risers. She saw that Dewey's sleeping bag was empty and heard a fire crackling in the inverted washtub outside. She got up and dressed quickly and, as she went out, found Dewey drinking from a canvas waterbag. He smiled at her with his eyes while he drank, and suddenly she tilted the waterbag, spilling a gush of icy water down his chest and belly. Instantly he tripped her to the ground, jerked her legs high, and despite all her twisting, kicking, and screaming, poured an icy quart or more down one leg of her jeans.

Half the camp came out to laugh and applaud. Janet was furious. She grabbed a good heavy stick and chased Dewey to the creek and into the water, where they wrestled together until both were soaked. To this day many people remember that fair and summer as "when the Blackfoot boy and his girl gave each other a ducking."

But that fair is most memorable to Janet for something else. As she hung her own and Dewey's wet clothing from a rope Dewey stretched, she saw an elderly and white-haired woman, tall and gaunt, bearing down upon her. The woman's new squaw dress, though common enough, had an old-fashioned look. She was wearing new moccasins too, and they made her feet look doubly huge. The old woman's big, bony hands grasped both Janet's wrists. The blackest of eyes in the deeply wrinkled face of a white woman beamed at Janet, and a very Indian voice said, "Jan-et, Jan-et Sin-clair. Me Suzy, Suzy Stands Alone," and rushed on in an incomprehensible tongue to the stunned Janet, who could recognize only the repetition of her name.

Dewey stood off a way, grinning, and Janet found voice to appeal to him, "What is this? what is she saying?"

"Damned if I know. I can't speak any Sioux, can't understand a word old Suzy says. But she knows all about you from my shortwave set. Old gran'mother wanted to surprise you."

"She certainly did!" Janet said.

Walks Far appeared around the lodge wearing a big smile. Suzy turned quickly to her, but the two old women neither spoke nor embraced. Smiling, Suzy put out a hand and for what seemed at least half a minute held the palm reverently over the Sun-stone Walks Far wore under her dress. Only then did they hug each other and break into a rush of talk.

Amos Stands Alone, Suzy's husband, came for breakfast, a fine-looking old man wearing an enormous, undented white hat over his nearly white braids. He carried a beautifully polished diamond-willow walking stick in order to limp along with a leg left badly crooked from an old mowing-machine accident. Janet simply could not reconcile his exceptionally benign face and kindly old man's smile with mental imagery derived from Walks Far's story about him. How could he ever have been the fearsomely painted and yipping, near-naked stripling with hair on fire who won the admiration of seasoned warriors by killing first a Crow scout, then a soldier, and taking both their horses on that long ago spring day beneath falling plum blossoms on the Rosebud?

Walks Far told Janet, "Suzy gon' have big feas' for you. I think she gon' gave you somethings."

Janet also met Fire Wing's youngest daughter that day, a rather bossy woman with a short bob, a Lucky Strike hanging from her lip, and dressed like any American housewife. She looked no fresher than most women would who had just driven across two states in a station wagon loaded with a horde of dark-eyed children who begged for more soda pop all the way (and usually got it).

Of Suzy, Walks Far told Janet how white do-gooders among officials and missionaries had harassed her with offers of "rescue" for years, though they gave up when she grew old. "She's laugh," Walks Far said. "Suzy don' know white-man talk—maybe two-three word. She's know *shit.* She's laugh, say 'shit,' them tams."

"Some Sioux say Suzy keeps the old ways better than any of them," Dewey added.

But Janet discovered Suzy to be not inflexibly old-fashioned. For, at the women's feast Suzy gave, a pint flask of whiskey appeared as if by magic in her hands, and after most of it had gone quickly into the coffee and tea, that flask just as magically disappeared.

After a while Janet suddenly felt herself the focus of all those strange women's eyes. She was deeply touched, yet embarrassed and amused when Suzy presented her with a truly beautiful beaded cradle board and a pair of baby's moccasins beaded even on the soles.

Janet whispered hastily to Walks Far, "Tell her . . . how much I want to thank her . . . the nicest way you can. But doesn't she know that Dewey and I won't be married for two or three years yet? and even then we won't start having babies for quite a while."

Walks Far translated, not only Janet's thanks but, obviously, the rest of what she had said, for Walks Far relayed back, "Suzy say she know kids in now tam don' hurry got marry. Suzy say . . ." Walks Far floundered, unable to render the rest of it quickly into English. A young woman at the end of the row did it easily, "She says she knows that by the time you have a baby, she may have gone up the Milky Way, to wake up every morning in the Land of Many Tipis. She will be happier there to know you have these things, and also to have your baby know that it has, ah, a godmother there. In other words, she wants to do something for the daughter-in-law of her old friend now, before she happens to wake up and find herself dead some morning."

"Tell her," Janet said, "that I shall teach my children to remember her, as well as Walks Far Woman—and all the women and other people like them."

A day or two before Janet and Dewey were married at the end of his sophomore year (and after her graduation from Macalester College), Walks Far took her aside with a somewhat conspiratorial air and gave her four quite ordinary small glass trade beads. It became evident that Walks Far felt that the right of First Woman and all her daughters to have last say could do with some reinforcement: "You got marry, you don' speak to Dewey; you don' speak nobodies. Get out where Sun see you. Throw bead to Northwind, to Eastwind, to Southwind, and to Westwind. They's give you last say, make you boss."

On certain occasions when Janet tells this story, Dewey has been heard to remark, "She sure as hell didn't forget to throw those beads!"

As Janet had hoped, Dewey earned his degree in veterinary medicine from Washington State College, as it was then called. He was first employed in Montana's state game department, then for several years by the National Park Service in various western states before he and Janet came home to take over her father's ranch. Though that is a full-time job, he engages in limited professional practice and serves the state of Montana on appointive boards related to Indian and wildlife matters.

When Marie Nequette (now affluent, militant, and still remarkably good-looking) flies home for a visit bringing one or another of her young men, she has been known to tell Dewey he is nothing but a stand-around-the-fort, no longer an Indian, nothing but a big "radish"—all red outside but all white inside. He shifts impatiently, waves his hand with the wristwatch before her eyes and asks in Blackfoot, *"Tse tok-tok?"*—What time is it? He declares he can bleed as red as any Indian, but that the old wrongs won't be righted by dwelling in a kind of mystical dream about an idealized Indian past, or by dressing up like a white man's idea of an Indian and beating drums on courthouse steps. The two of them go on from there.

Janet had expected that she or Dewey would be presented at some time with the knife and was surprised, although not at all resentful, when Walks Far, in one of her last acts, gave it to Marie.

But Janet received another treasure early in 1958 on one of the last occasions when she saw Walks Far alive. The old woman suddenly produced Hat's heavy gold and garnet necklace as though from nowhere. "You keep," she told Janet. "Me and Hat want you keep." Janet wears the necklace whenever she can.

Walks Far fell considerably short of Grandfather's record, for one sunny spring morning, with the new grass up, she died quietly while sitting alone outdoors, at an age when she could count but 102 winters. Before that, on first hearing about flying saucers or UFOs, she had readily and confidently explained them: "Scouts come from Sun. Find bad thing white mans done Earth Mother, done four-legged people." She went on to predict that the appropriate punishment would come in due time.

In her final years she grew fond of telling people, "H'im oldes' horset'ief in Montana." On her last morning she went outdoors saying something about a coyote.